In the box was a squat metal cylinder surrounded by smaller glass jars filled with what looked like yellow sticks of wax in water. In the back of the metal cylinder was a paper-covered rectangle Reaper had seen many times before: M5A1 C4 plastic explosive surrounded by steel bolts. Reaper could see a ruddy glow and movement from an electronic device. It was a countdown booby trap timer. And it was close to reaching zero.

"Run!" Reaper yelled. "Booby trap. Out now!"

As his men went out through the door, Reaper grabbed what was left of the lock and pulled it shut behind him. Even the damaged door would help hold the contamination inside the steel-framed brick structure. Reaper followed his men for the swamp only a few dozen feet across the blacktop.

The blast thundered. A huge fireball rushed through the building, consuming everything in it.

Under the swamp water, Reaper's men were tossed by the impact. Coughing and hacking from the water that had flooded their respirator masks, the men stood up in the knee-deep water and black muck.

As he pulled off his respirator, Warrick sputtered and spat mud. "I'm starting to hate Florida," he said.

THE
HOME TEAM
WEAPONS GRADE

Command Master Chief
DENNIS CHALKER, USN (Ret.)
with KEVIN DOCKERY

AVON BOOKS

An Imprint of HarperCollinsPublishers

AVON BOOKS
An Imprint of HarperCollins*Publishers*
10 East 53rd Street
New York, New York 10022-5299

Copyright © 2006 by Bill Fawcett and Associates
ISBN-13: 978-0-06-051728-1
ISBN-10: 0-06-051728-X
www.avonbooks.com

First Avon Books paperback printing: July 2006

Avon Trademark Reg. U.S. Pat. Off. and in Other Countries, Marca Registrada, Hecho en U.S.A.
HarperCollins® is a registered trademark of HarperCollins Publishers Inc.

Printed in the U.S.A.

10 9 8 7 6 5 4 3 2 1

THE HOME TEAM
WEAPONS GRADE

PROLOGUE

PERSIAN GULF, JANUARY, 1991

"It was the best of times, it was the worst of times . . ."

"Enough with the book quotes! Make up your mind Reaper, good or bad. You going to call or fold? This bluff just ain't going to work."

John Carlson enjoyed his poker and took his card playing seriously. Navy SEAL Ted "Grim" Reaper considered messing with Carlson to be part of the fun of the game. For Eddie Schultz and Scott Miller, the other two Navy SEALs sitting around the mess-area table, just watching Carlson and Reaper was a lot more entertaining than playing the lousy cards they held.

The four SEALs were sitting on the bench seats on either side of the boothlike mess-area table. Just aft of the table area was the compact galley with its three-in-one-combination two-burner range, sink, and small refrigerator. Standing in the galley was Chief Enzo Caronti. He had just finished pouring himself a cup of hot, black Navy coffee and was watching the card game with some amusement. Long experience on board small boats allowed Chief Caronti to stand in a relaxed easy manner while his heavy, muscular legs automatically compensated for the rocking and rolling of the boat.

The calm scene did not reflect the reality of the situation. There was a war going on and it had turned into a hot one only recently. Operation Desert Shield had turned into Desert Storm in mid-January, with the beginning of the air war against Iraq. Coalition forces, led by the United States, had been conducting round-the-clock actions against Iraq and inside of occupied Kuwait. Now, nearly two weeks after the coalition strikes had begun, Iraq was striking back.

Less than twelve hours before the first cards had been dealt in the SEALs' poker game, elements of the Iraqi 3rd Armored Division and 5th Mechanized Division attacked south of the border between Kuwait and Saudi Arabia. Penetrating into Saudi territory, the Iraqi units had moved to the coastline. The advance brigades of the invaders drove into the Saudi coastal town of Khafji and quickly seized it.

The civilian population of Khafji had left their city for safer areas months earlier. All that was really left in the city were men of the U.S. Marine 1st Surveillance, Reconnaissance, and Intelligence group. Those Marines were concealing themselves from the eyes of the Iraqi forces. While the Iraqis desperately searched for them, the Marines were directing artillery and close-air support strikes against the Iraqi troops and their vehicles.

The Khafji situation had changed some coalition planning in the Persian Gulf. The land reconnaissance mission along the Kuwaiti border that the four-man SEAL element had originally been tasked with had been canceled. Now, the SEALs, a six-man boat crew, and the Mark III patrol boat they rode in, were on-station for a three-day stint of Combat Search and Rescue (CSAR) duty.

The sixty-three-foot-long Mark III patrol boat had been in the Persian Gulf since the U.S. Navy had taken action during the Iran-Iraq war in the Gulf only a few years earlier. Though an older boat, the Mark III was heavily armed for her size and was more than up to the task of escorting SEALs for their missions, or for cruising the waters of the Persian Gulf to help rescue downed Coalition pilots.

The galley and mess area were belowdecks of the Mark III. As the officer-in-charge (OIC) of the patrol boat, Chief Caronti was one of the few enlisted men in the Navy to command even a small fighting craft. It was no small compliment to Chief Caronti's skill and ability that he was now the OIC of the Mark III, a position normally held by a commissioned officer.

On the other side of the compartment, opposite the galley, was the radio space. At the rear of that space was a steeply inclined ladder leading up to the pilothouse above. Just ahead of the radio space was the officers' berthing—another compact area with little more than two bunks and a desk. That was the living area Caronti shared with Reaper for the time being. The rest of the SEALs would split up time with the crew in the four bunks in the crew's berthing area forward, a tight and spartan home that all of the Navy men were more than used to.

"I call," Reaper said as he pushed a small stack of chips to the pile in the center of the table.

"Sorry, but this corpsman is going to be the one to

nail the Reaper," Carlson said as he laid his cards on the table. "Three Jacks."

"Those certainly beat my simple pair of threes," Reaper said as he laid two cards faceup on the table. "And I guess it would beat my three sevens, too." He laid the other three cards in his hand down. "Wouldn't it?"

For a moment, Carlson just sat and looked at the cards with a stunned expression on his face. A chuckle started up from the other two SEALs at the table.

"A full house," Carlson said finally. "You drew a full house on the deal?"

"I feel that the men in this team not only deserve a competent leading petty officer who knows what he's doing at all times," Reaper said as he raked in the pile of chips, "but a lucky one as well. Oh, and thanks for the deal."

An assortment of derogatory noises sounded out from around the table. Carlson just sat and glowered at his cards as if willing them to change to a winning hand.

"I dealt him a full house," Carlson muttered.

"Hey, don't feel so bad," Ed Schultz said from his seat next to Reaper. "It's not like you gave him a royal flush or anything like that."

"Never even seen one of those during a game," Scott Miller said as he raked in the loose cards and started to shuffle them. "My deal now?"

The intent of the card game was to try and force some relaxation on the SEALs. The humor and diversion helped them forget for a moment that a shooting war was going on not very far away and they weren't in the thick of it. As highly trained warriors, each of the SEALs wanted very much to be taking part in the action over near Khafji. But their mission right now was to ride in the boat. The most action they could expect would be to swim after a downed pilot. An important job, but not what they had been training for since joining the Teams.

With the air war running twenty-four hours a day, the Iraqis were constantly being pounded from the skies. Thankfully, there had been relatively few Coalition aircraft lost. But that also meant that working on CSAR duty meant a whole lot of nothing was happening. The stress wasn't bad yet, but Reaper knew that the strain of just waiting could affect his men badly.

It didn't help that what they were waiting for was something bad to happen to someone on their side. Combat search and rescue couldn't rescue anybody unless an aircraft was shot down. It was a good thing that this CSAR tasking was only scheduled to continue for another sixty hours at most.

To keep the game from getting too serious, and because of those Navy regulations about gambling, Reaper allowed the game to only be played for small change. Pots never amounted to much. The pile of chips he had just raked in totaled only twenty-seven cents. The amount didn't matter to Carlson, of course. Having been raised in Reno, Nevada, the SEAL corpsman took his poker seriously.

Shaking his head at how the SEALs screwed around with each other, Chief Caronti turned and headed to his quarters on the other side of the compartment, opposite the mess-area table. He hadn't taken more than two steps before a bell rang. It was the call bell mounted underneath the control console in the pilothouse. That signal meant Caronti was needed in the pilothouse, and he immediately headed above deck.

The pilothouse was directly above the radio space, and just aft of the officers' berthing compartment Caronti had been heading to. It was only a few steps from Caronti's position to the ladder at the rear of the radio space. He was up the steep ladder and standing in the aft area of the pilothouse before Miller finished shuffling the cards.

The boat's navigator, Harry Katz, was sitting at the helm pulling duty as the coxswain of the craft. He had a communications headset on his head with a boom microphone extended in front of his mouth. The headset was cocked so that his left ear was exposed and he could hear Caronti coming into the pilothouse.

"What is it, Katz?" Caronti said as he leaned over the smaller man's shoulder.

"Things are heating up fast over in Khafji," Katz said. "Command out of Ras al-Mishab hooked us into communications with *High Eagle,* the joint surveillance and target attack radar system (J-STARS) aircraft overhead. They want the boat commander on line right now," Katz gestured over his right shoulder. "The other headset is over there."

Picking up the indicated headset, Caronti could see that it was plugged into the UHF remote jack box. The box completed the circuit between Caronti's headset and the AN/ARC-159 radio set belowdecks. Once hooked up, Chief Caronti nodded to Katz, who then took his own headset off.

"*High Eagle, High Eagle,* this is *Black Cat Actual,*" Caronti said into the boom mike of his headset. "Go ahead, please."

Chief Caronti concentrated on the information coming down to him from the J-STARS aircraft orbiting high above. Katz concentrated on keeping the Mark III on course as his chief listened to the information coming literally from on high. Katz knew this was a very serious situation. Major assets like the J-STARS did not spend time talking to a simple patrol boat—not unless a pilot had gone down in the Gulf somewhere nearby.

As he listened to the information coming in over his headset, Chief Caronti moved to the rear of the pilothouse. There was a chart table running along the back of the compartment with nautical charts of the patrol boat's present operational area already spread out. Above the chart table, in the starboard corner of the compartment, was the Omega satellite/navigation console. The big Navy Chief's thick fingers danced over the controls on the console as he confirmed the boat's location. In addition, he made notations on the open charts.

"Roger that, High Eagle," Caronti said, "we will respond. Notify us of any further updates. *Black Cat Actual* out."

Leaning over the charts, Caronti busied himself with dividers and other instruments for a fast few minutes.

"Helm," Caronti said at last, "come about to course one four zero, bring her up to full speed on port and starboard engines."

"Come about to one four zero, aye, Chief," Katz acknowledged. "Full speed ahead on port and starboard engines."

Pushing the two indicated throttle controls on top of the pilothouse control console forward, Katz increased the speed of the boat as well as the noise it was making as it sped across the water in a wide arc. The patrol boat had three big 650 horsepower General Motors

8V71T1 diesel engines, each one turning a thirty-two-inch-diameter three-bladed bronze propeller. Only the center engine had heavy mufflers to suppress the sound of the boat. The port and starboard engines roared with power as they blew through almost-straight exhaust systems and started driving the sixty-three-foot boat forward at nearly thirty knots.

"Katz," Caronti said as he slipped a notepad onto the control console, "keep a listening watch on the URC-94 on this frequency. Sing out if your hear anything. I'm going below."

"Aye, Chief," Katz said as he glanced at the note. Reaching past the radar display unit to his right, Katz turned the controls on the URC-94 remote control box. In the radio space below the pilothouse, the AN/URC-94 FM transmitter/receiver tuned itself to match the adjustments from the remote station. He looked up to the gyrocompass mounted above the helm position and watched the indicator settle on 140 degrees.

Heading below, Chief Caronti prepared to tell Reaper and his SEALs that their wait for action was definitely over.

———

Deep in the desert, miles away from the U.S. Navy boat, a lost pair of Marine scout-snipers tried to restore contact with the J-STARS aircraft high overhead. The J-STARS had been the only Coalition asset the Marines had been able to contact since being separated from their unit, and their situation was becoming desperate. The two men had been running from Iraqi forces since having first observed and sniped against them nearly twenty-four hours earlier. Cut off from all obvious support, the men had been fighting to stay alive and reconnect with Coalition forces—any Coalition forces. The precision fire of the scout-sniper team had been the only real weapon they had against the overwhelming firepower of the Iraqis, and even that was almost spent, as their ammunition was down to the last few rounds.

"*High Eagle*, this is Delta zero niner . . . *High Eagle*, this is Delta zero niner . . . Contact lost. Contact lost. Delta zero niner out.

"Okay, Sarge, that's it," Marine Lance Corporal Max Warrick said as he lowered his AN/PRC-68 radio. "We are out of commo. The batteries on this thing are either dead or so close to dead, it doesn't make a difference. I can't tell if anyone can hear us and I can't hear a damned thing anymore. The last word was for us to make for the coast."

"Then that's what we have to do," Marine Sergeant Pete Schaefer said. "The Iraqis have us cut off from traveling in any other direction, anyway."

Looking off to the west where he knew the highway was, Warrick could see a number of dust plumes rising from the desert sands.

"Then we better get a move on," Warrick said. "It looks like more company is coming."

The two Marines of the scout-sniper team had been watching Coalition aircraft in the distance striking against Iraqi armor all morning. The Iraqi forces that had not yet taken refuge in Khafji were being eliminated by the A-10 Thunderbolts and fighters that ripped through them. What remained of the Iraqi armored forces was scattering across the area. Those small units of vehicles and individual tanks were no threat at all to the Coalition forces in Saudi Arabia, but they could obliterate the scout-sniper team with ease.

The men had been conducting an exhausting game of hide-and-seek with the Iraqis for many hours. They were tired, thirsty, and worse.

The evening before, both men had been watching an Iraqi reconnaissance platoon. While Schaefer observed through his M49 spotting scope, Warrick had been glassing the targets through the 10X USMC model Unertyl telescopic sight on his M40A1 sniper rifle. Both men had spotted an Iraqi officer standing in the open turret hatch of his tracked BMP-1 armored infantry fighting vehicle.

The officer had just focused his binoculars in the direction of the Marines as Shaefer quietly said, "Take him."

A single shot rang out from Warrick's M40A1. The fitted Remington 700 action and match-grade barrel fired, guiding the 7.62mm M118 match round on its way. It took much less than a second for the bullet to travel the 374 meters between the scout-sniper team and the Iraqi BMP.

The Iraqi officer barely had time to see the muzzle flash before the 175-grain pointed boat-tail bullet from the M40A1 smashed into his chest, piercing his heart. Through his Unertyl scope, Warrick could see the astonished look on the officer's face as he slumped down into the BMP.

Retaliatory fire came pouring out of the two BRDM-2 wheeled amphibious scout cars that were with the BMP. The heavy KPV machine guns mounted in the turrets of the two BRDMs thundered as they put out 14.5mm armor-piercing-incendiary projectiles at a cyclic rate of

600 rounds per minute. Dozens of the B32 AP-I traveled across the Saudi Arabian desert and spent their energy into the sand and gravel hundreds of meters away from the weapons that fired them. But one projectile did not just waste itself into the desert.

Whether from intent or just luck, a single 979-grain hardened steel-cored slug passed less than half an inch over Sergeant Shaefer's left shoulder and struck the AN/PRC-77 radio on his back. The massive bullet from the KPV machine gun could penetrate nearly an inch and a half of steel armor at one hundred meters. Even though it was nearly four hundred meters from the muzzle of the KPV that fired it, the huge bullet barely slowed down as it smashed into the aluminum and plastic of the AN/PRC-77.

The radio nearly exploded as the Soviet-made slug tore it apart. The resistance of the radio was not enough to ignite the incendiary composition on the nose of the projectile, but that was the only grace it gave Sergeant Schaefer. Driven by the power of the impact, the plastic composition of the circuit boards, along with the wires, electrical components, and aluminum body of the radio, slashed across the Marine sergeant's back, tearing the skin and muscle beneath.

Any one of the wounds would have been serious enough to hospitalize even the tough Marine NCO—and there were dozens of them. The only thing that kept any of the wounds from killing Shaefer outright was the thick padding of the radio carrier, and the nearly one hundred ounces of water contained in Shaefer's Camelback hydration system. But worse than even the bleeding wounds was the almost-complete destruction of the AN/PRC-77 radio, the major means of communication between the scout-sniper team and any chance of air support or emergency extraction.

All night long, Sergeant Shaefer and Warrick had slipped along the desert, trying to evade the Iraqi units searching for them. Finally, well into the morning of the next day, they had holed up in a small depression and tried to make contact with any Coalition support through the small AN/PRC-68 emergency radio Warrick carried.

When the Marines finally made contact with a Coalition aircraft flying high overhead, they heard the bad news that no helicopter support could come in and extract them. The Iraqi forces outside of Khafji were becoming more and more scattered under the onslaught of the Coalition air strikes, but their firepower was still a major threat to any helicopter landing.

To survive their situation, the two Marines would have to make their way to the shore of the Persian Gulf. Once there, Navy forces would come in and get them out. At least that's all Warrick could positively make out from the fading voice coming over the small speaker of the emergency radio.

As he shifted his position, a grunt of pain slipped through Shaefer's gritted teeth. Warrick looked at his sergeant with concern. He had strapped a pressure bandage over the lacerations on Shaefer's back, but too much movement or strain could easily cause the sergeant to start bleeding badly again.

"Okay," Shaefer said, "we're going to have to move as fast and light as we can. So we have to destroy the extra gear. If we don't get picked up, I don't want us to be caught with anything that would give the Iraqis any intelligence. And that sure as hell includes our commo gear."

"The PRC-77's trash," Warrick said.

"Yes," Shaefer agreed, "but the crypto gear isn't. The KY-57 is pretty much intact. It has to be completely destroyed. Dig a hole and burn it."

Nodding his head, Warrick started scooping out a hole in the sand. The KY-57 was a piece of cryptographic equipment that was attached to their PRC-77 radio. The KY-57 would scramble their voice communications with their main base back in Khafji, and it would automatically unscramble incoming messages. It couldn't be allowed to fall into enemy hands, even if it was damaged.

Since the scout-sniper team was carrying that kind of sensitive equipment on their mission, they also had with them the means to destroy it completely.

On the pack harness of the shattered radio was a heavy AN/M14 TH3 canister grenade. The abbreviation INCEN in purple letters on the gray-colored cylindrical body of the grenade indicated its purpose as an incendiary device. Once fired, the TH3 thermate mixture within the grenade would burn for about forty seconds. The burning thermate would reach a temperature of 4,300 degrees Fahrenheit, more than enough to obliterate the plastic and metal components of the KY-57. The burning grenade would also pour out white-hot molten iron, welding or slagging almost anything it touched.

The smashed radio, KY-57, and other bits and pieces of equipment were placed into the bottom of the deep hole dug into the desert sand. Pulling the pin on the M14 grenade, Warrick dropped it on top of the equipment and turned away. Less than two seconds later, there was a pop and hiss as the thermate filler of the grenade ignited. A brilliant white light and smoke started to come up out of the hole as the thermate burned, igniting the aluminum case of the PRC-77.

With his face turned away, Warrick pushed sand down into the hole to cut down on the escaping light and smoke. Once ignited, the M14 incendiary grenade would continue burning, even while underwater. The little bit of sand dumped in on the grenade would hardly even slow the fire down, it would just be turned to glass by the heat. But the sand would help hide where the Marines had destroyed the gear.

"Come on," Shaefer said as he got to his feet, "time for a hike to the beach. Maybe we can hitch a ride on some swabbie's boat."

"My ass rides in Navy equipment," Warrick joked, stating a derogatory meaning for the word *Marine*. He picked up his M40A1 rifle and cradled the long weapon in his arms. His 7.62mm M118 ammunition for the long gun was almost gone, but there was no way a Marine sniper was going to be separated from his weapon.

Even wounded, Sergeant Shaefer hung on doggedly to his M16A2 rifle as he started out on their trek across the desert.

———

While the Marines struggled across the sands, support was on its way to them in the form of a small Navy boat and a handful of competent and very determined men.

"Okay, here's everything we know," Caronti said as he stood by the mess table. Only Harry Katz at the helm and Sam Johnson in the engine room remained at their duty stations. Every other member of the patrol boat's crew and all of the SEALs were seated or standing around the mess table. On the table, Caronti had spread out charts showing the waters they were passing through and the Kuwaiti shoreline they were heading for.

"A Marine scout-sniper team is about fifteen klicks north of Khafji. They're cut off from any support and the Iraqis are closing in on them. That team is in serious trouble and just about out of communications with anyone. Even the J-STARS bird, with all of its electronics, could only maintain communications with them long enough to tell them to head for the shore."

"Do we have a solid location for them?" Reaper asked.

"Not exactly what you would call solid," Caronti said. "The J-STARS was able to compute the coordinates of where the Marines were transmitting from. But since they've lost communications, where those snipers are at this moment is an educated guess at best.

"They were ordered to head for point foxtrot-echo, just north of this promontory here," Caronti said as he indicated a position on the shoreline north of Khafji. "That's where we're heading. I've set us on a course that will keep us at sea and over the horizon from land. Once past this point, we'll come about and approach foxtrot-echo from the south. We won't be within sight of the position until we come past the point, so nobody will be able to see us, either."

"Why don't they send in a rescue bird to pick them up?" said Randy Peters, one of the patrol boat's gunners.

"Without an exact location and no commo," Reaper

said, "any helicopter would need a lot of luck to spot two Marines on the ground in that desert. Being snipers, they're well cammoed-up and hiding from the Iraqis as they're moving. That's a lot of ground to cover looking for something that's already hard to see."

"Besides," Caronti added, "there are Iraqi forces scattered all over the area. Our planes are eating them up, but Intel says that there are still small units and individual vehicles capable of putting up a fight. So far, the Iraqis are on the losing end of this scrap. But a helicopter hanging around searching for a pair of men on the ground could make itself a juicy target for an Iraqi shoulder-fired missile or antiaircraft system.

"Command says that if naval assets can't locate the missing men, aircraft will sweep the beaches later today. Trouble is, those Marines may not make it to later today. And we are the closest naval asset to the area. And we can get pretty close to shore, but only pretty close."

The SEALs leaned closer to the chart to read the number that Chief Caronti was now indicating.

"This promontory in the only major feature on the shoreline between Khafji and Kuwait," Caronti said. "According to the charts, we can only expect to bring the boat to within five hundred meters of the shore. Any closer, and we run the risk of running aground and hanging up the boat. So you SEALs would have to head in to shore on your Zodiac, in broad daylight, if we can spot the Marines."

"Do we have any dedicated fire support?" Eddie Schultz, the SEAL radioman, asked.

"No dedicated air support or naval gunfire support," Caronti said. "We can call in any eagle for air support. Any aircraft around will respond to that. But as far as dedicated support, we only have what we're bringing with us, the fifty-calibers, the Mark 19, and the Mark 2."

The patrol boat wasn't large, but it carried a lot of firepower for its size. The craft had four Mark 16 machine gun stands on the upper deck, two forward and two aft. Three of the stands carried .50-caliber M2 HB machine guns. The port side aft stand carried a Mark 19 Mod 3 40mm grenade launcher in place of a machine gun. The Mark 19 could put out 40mm high-explosive grenades at a rate of 350 rounds per minute. The half-pound grenades could reach a maximum range of 2,200 meters.

There were two centerline weapons stations intended to carry an M242 25mm Bushmaster cannon, but the guns hadn't been mounted on this patrol boat and the stations were empty. But the lack of 25mm cannons didn't mean the boat didn't have a heavy punch. On the port side of the boat, across from the pilothouse, was a raised heavy weapons platform. On the platform was a weapon that had proved its worth during combat in Vietnam, a Mark 2 Mod 1 81mm direct-fire mortar with a .50-caliber machine gun mounted piggyback on top of it.

The Mark 2 81mm mortar could be pointed directly at a target and fired like a cannon, or the muzzle could be pointed up into the sky and the weapon could lob its shells in a high arc. The 81mm M362 high-explosive shell with its 2.10 pounds of Composition B explosive filler could be fired to a range of more than three thousand meters from the Mark 2. The blast from the M362 mortar round would send steel fragments screaming out in a 20-meter radius from the point of impact—and the patrol boat carried dozens of rounds of the potent HE ammunition, along with smoke and illuminating rounds. It was a very heavy punch and all of the men around the mess table knew it.

There wasn't much of a question about the importance of the mission. There were men, fellow warriors, in harm's way. Between the SEALs and the crew of the patrol boat, they had the men, mobility, firepower, and skills to pull off such a last-moment rescue.

"Okay," Reaper said as he looked at his men. The other three SEALs met his eyes without looking away. From those looks, Reaper had all of the answer he needed. "Not a problem. Chief, you get us there and we'll get them out."

The only way the rescue operation could be considered on such short notice was the fact that Reaper and his SEALs had practiced and trained for years in order to gain a variety of skills and abilities. Caronti and his men had also trained and drilled, either together or on other small-boat crews, so they all knew every aspect and ability of both their vessel and themselves.

The SEALs had been prepared to conduct combat search and rescue missions. That meant a lot more swimming than active combat. John Carlson had his full corpsman's kit, the same as he would carry on almost any kind of mission with his fellow operators. And Eddie Schultz had his radio gear. But none of the SEALs had their usual combat load of weapons and ammunition. The small-arms locker of the patrol boat, under the aft seat of the mess table, yielded up some heavier weapons for the SEALs' use.

All of the SEALs had their SIG P226 sidearms and a number of spare 15-round magazines. Reaper took one of the four M4 carbines the SEALs had brought with them. Both Carlson and Schultz also kept their M4 carbines—the short, handy weapons giving them a good effective range across the desert or beach. With Caronti's permission, Scott Miller left his M4 behind and took the boat's M60 machine gun from the small-arms locker.

A strong, powerful man, even for a SEAL, Miller could handle the twenty-four-pound machine gun with ease. The eleven-hundred-meter range of the 7.62mm ammunition it fired was something Reaper didn't mind having along with his squad when they hit the beach. The six hundred rounds of belted ammunition Miller took from the boat's stores would not be such a heavy load that it would slow the man down too much. The SEALs weren't going in equipped for heavy fighting, but they would be able to put out a storm of bullets for at least a short time if they had to.

The inflated Zodiac F-470 rubber boat was tied up to the stern of the patrol boat, lashed in place against the port-side six-man lifeboat support rack. Pulling the boat up onto the deck, Carlson, Schultz, and Miller went over each piece of it, paying particular attention to the 55hp Evinrude outboard motor that would push the rubber boat to the beach and back. If the rugged motor crapped out on them, the SEALs could have a long paddle ahead of them to get back to the patrol boat, a trip they might have to conduct while under enemy fire and transporting two, possibly wounded, Marines.

While his men went over every piece of the equipment they would use, Reaper sat at the mess-area table, pouring over the charts Caronti had left there. Once each piece of gear had been checked and double-checked, the other SEALs joined their leading petty officer at the mess table. Each man made himself familiar with the area they were heading into.

There was no way to tell exactly where the Marines would hit the shoreline. They would probably try their best to hit point foxtrot-echo dead-on. But that didn't mean they would actually reach the exact coordinates. So the SEALs all looked at the charts and familiarized themselves with every aspect of the terrain while the patrol boat came about to head north and started approaching the shoreline, only a few dozen miles away.

———

"Damn," Warrick said quietly to himself.

Looking toward the beach less than a hundred yards in front of them, a sweating and breathless sergeant Schaefer turned to his partner. Seeing that Warrick was facing back the way they had come, Schaefer tried to turn, but the pain from his wounds kept him from twisting his body around.

"What is it?" Schaefer said.

"Those Iraqi armored cars have company now," Warrick said. "There's what looks like a T-62 tank sitting back there, not more than a klick and a half behind us."

"It doesn't look like they spotted us, does it?" Schaefer said with a dry voice as he tried to focus his eyes back across the desert.

"Maybe not yet," Warrick said, "but that beach is as flat and open as a sheet of plywood. No cover, no concealment. Once we start to move across it, they'll see us for sure."

"Got any ammo left for the long gun?" Schaefer asked.

The marksmanship Warrick had demonstrated, his skill as a sniper, had kept the Iraqis off guard during the long chase across the desert. But that meant Warrick had kept expending his ammunition to keep the Iraqis buttoned up at long range, limiting their visibility.

"One round," Warrick said, turning back to face Schaefer.

"Well," Schaefer said after a long pause, "keep it for a souvenir you can tell your grandchildren about."

"Tell your own kids," Warrick said. "Look." He pointed out to sea.

Coming around the point that curved out into the gulf to the south of their position, Warrick and Schaefer could see a tan-colored patrol boat cutting across the blue water. Pulling out his AN/PRC-68 radio, Warrick extended the antenna and keyed the microphone.

"Navy vessel, this is Delta zero niner," Warrick almost shouted into the mike. "Navy vessel, this is Delta zero niner. Can you read me? Over."

Not even faint static came over the small speaker.

"It's dead," Warrick said.

"So are we, unless they see us," Schaefer said. "Pop smoke."

Reaching up onto his load-bearing harness, Warrick pulled off the gray-painted canister of an M18 smoke grenade. Pulling the pin and throwing the grenade far out onto the beach, Warrick heard the pop and hiss of the M200A2 fuze as it ignited the 11.5 ounces of filler inside the sheet-metal body of the grenade. Violet smoke, a stark purple against the dark tan of the beach, poured from the holes in the grenade. The signal was an established emergency marker. The patrol boat had to see it, and probably the Iraqis would as well.

———

"There!" Barry Dunnigan shouted from his post at the Mark 2 mortar. "Purple smoke on the beach!"

"That's them," Reaper said as he looked through a pair of M16 7×50 binoculars. "Two men on the edge of the beach. One looks like he's wearing part of a ghilley suit."

"SEALs away!" Caronti shouted from the pilothouse as he cut the speed of the patrol boat.

Not another word was spoken. None were necessary and there wasn't time to say them, anyway. Every man on the patrol boat could see the cluster of vehicles away in the desert. It would be a race to see who got to the Marines onshore first, the SEALs or the Iraqis.

The Zodiac was in the water with its outboard rumbling as the SEALs cast off from the patrol boat. Schultz was acting as the coxswain at the rear of the black rubber boat as it sped across the water. They had about six hundred meters of open water to cross before the SEALs could get to the Marines. The rest of the fire team spread out along the gunwales of the boat.

In SEAL fashion, Reaper and the rest of his men were riding the tubes that made up the gunwales of the Zodiac. They crouched low, lying across the tubes, their weapons in their hands. On the port side of the bow, Miller held his M60 machine gun loaded and ready to put out a heavy spray of covering fire. Reaper was on the starboard side of the bow, Carlson up tight behind him.

Every bump and thud of the rubber boat against the water was transmitted through the SEALs' bodies. Each man would be covered in bruises from the shocks before this mission was done. But they couldn't slacken their speed. As the bow came up and they could see across the sand, they all knew what the plume of dust rising in the distance meant. The Iraqis had seen the burning smoke grenade, and were heading toward it.

As the Zodiac came closer to the shore, Reaper, Miller, and Carlson rolled over the side and into the shallows as Schultz cut back on the outboard. The water was only hip deep, and the SEALs were running light in terms of weapons and ammunition. So moving through the shallow water was easy for them.

Running was not easy for the two Marines struggling across the sands of the beach. Almost exhausted from blood loss and dehydration, Schaefer was staggering as he leaned against Warrick. Both men reached the edge of the water as the shore erupted behind them.

A 115mm 3OF18 high explosive shell fired from the main gun of the T-62 whistled in and punched down onto the beach. The TNT filler of the round exploded, sending a huge plume of sand into the air, and steel splinters spinning across the area. The tank gunner had fired while the T-62 was running across the sand. The jarring of the tank had caused the huge shell to miss both the Marines and the SEALs. But as the big tank came closer, its gunner would be more accurate. The DShK 1938/46 12.7mm heavy machine gun on top of the turret of the T-62 began thundering.

The tank commander had opened the top hatch of the T-62 and was firing on the escaping men with the heavy machine gun. The SEALs were less than six hundred meters from the shore, and the machine gun would easily be able to take them out, or at least damage their boat so much that they couldn't escape.

The slow, knocking thunder of the DShK was drowned

out by the belching roar of the 115mm main gun of the tank as it threw another shell toward the beach. As Lieutenant Mustafa Fawzi, the commander of the T-62 watched, he saw the shell burst in the water nearly twenty yards past the black boat and the men struggling around it. He started to shout a correction into his communications headset that would put the next cannon round directly on target.

The Marines reached their rescuers as bullets started splashing down nearby like an approaching steel rain. Leaning heavily on Warrick, Schaefer stumbled through the water as his strength finally gave out completely. Grabbing the collapsing man, Reaper pulled Schaefer from Warrick and slung him over his shoulder.

"I've got him," Reaper shouted, and turned to the Zodiac.

Once Schaefer was in safe hands, Warrick startled the SEALs as he turned away from the boat and kneeled down in the water.

As he turned away, Warrick pulled his M40A1 rifle from where he had slung it across his back. Shouldering the weapon, the Marine sniper seemed to freeze into position for a moment as he knelt. The barrel of the long gun waved about, steadied, and stopped. A single shot rang out. Without even looking to see the results of his shot, Warrick stood up and turned back to the boat. The rest of the SEALs were pushing the boat around to quickly get it heading back out to sea.

Nearly seven hundred meters away, only a second from the time that Warrick pulled the trigger of his rifle, Mustafa Fawzi felt a heavy blow against his chest. At first he thought he had slammed himself against the mount of the big DShK. Then he thought of nothing at all. Fawzi's body slumped back against the turret of the tank, his blood draining out across the hot, dusty armor, staining the mustard-colored steel a bright red.

———

With his rifle in one hand, Warrick shoved the boat to help push it on its way. Then he rolled over the taut black rubber gunwales of the craft as Reaper and his men climbed back into position on the tubes.

Quickly looking over his men and making sure everyone was on board and secure, Reaper shouted to the coxswain, "Move it, Schultz. Open this bitch up and get us the hell out of their range!"

The shells from the tank were coming in more slowly now, and their accuracy hadn't improved. But the big cannon only had to get close to upset the speeding Zodiac. And the 14.5mm KPV machine guns of the two BRDMs behind the tank would soon be adding their firepower to the mix.

As Reaper and his men watched, they saw the patrol boat turn and come back along the shore. It would make a big target for the cannon on the tank. But Caronti had told Reaper about an ace he kept in reserve, a card the big Navy chief had his men put into play at that moment.

Manning the Mark 2, Dunnigan compensated for the roll and pitch of the patrol boat, paused until the boat reached the right position, and then pulled the trigger of the mortar. Immediately, Randy Peters dropped another round down the long tube of the mortar.

The fins of the M375 mortar shell made a fluttering sound as the projectile dropped down to the beach. The SEALs in the rubber boat, looking back, saw a strangely beautiful white blossom open up as the M375 White Phosphorus smoke round impacted and exploded. Particles of burning phosphorus glowed yellow as they left a trail of dense white smoke behind them. As more and more of the mortar shells impacted the beach, they created a thick cloud of dense white smoke that none of the Iraqis in the vehicles could see through.

Behind the cover of the smoke screen, the Zodiac continued to approach the patrol boat. The crewmen helped the Marines up, and the SEALs abandoned the rubber boat that had served them so well. As he saw everyone come aboard, Caronti pushed the throttles open and all three of the big engines began driving the boat through the water. It would only be a few minutes before they were out of range of even the biggest weapon the Iraqis had back on the beach.

High up in the sky, a trio of rapidly approaching dots told everyone on the patrol boat that the long-desired air support had finally arrived. The armor of that T-62 back on the shore wouldn't give any protection at all to the deactivated uranium shells fired by the 30mm GAU-8 cannons in the noses of the approaching A-10 Warthogs.

Looking back at the beach that had almost become his graveyard, Warrick watched the Warthogs make short work of the enemy forces that had dogged him and his partner for so many long hours. The stress was over and he didn't know what to say to the men who had risked everything to save two Marines they didn't know. Turning to Reaper, Warrick tried to say something, but words seemed hopelessly inadequate.

"My corpsman says that your sergeant is going to be fine," Reaper said, cutting into the awkward silence.

"Thanks. By the way, my name's Warrick, Max Warrick. I'm glad to meet you."

"Same here," Reaper said as the two men shook hands.

"If there's anything I can ever do for you, all you have to do is ask."

"Well," Reaper said with a smile, "I think my corpsman would like to know if you play poker."

Chapter One

From horizon to horizon, it was a brown world. Not a rich brown, the color of earth, or even mud. This was a bleak, pale kind of tan. The only parts of the ground that weren't tan were the washed-out areas of thick dust and the close-packed grayish gravel beds. The whole place would have to undergo heavy renovation just to be called desolate.

A rising plume of dust, thrown up by the wheels of a three-vehicle caravan, indicated the only movement across the dry plain. Leading the way was a Toyota Land Cruiser that had seen long years of hard service. The FJ62 4×4 wagon was streaked with grime and dirt that obliterated its once white paint job.

Following the Land Cruiser were a pair of large military trucks. The first vehicle was a Soviet-made ZIL-151 6×6 with a van body and towing a small tanker trailer. Bringing up the rear of the convoy was a British Bedford 4×4. The rear of the Bedford was filled with a boxy something that stuck out at odd angles against its canvas covering. On the doors of each vehicle was a magnetic sign that read TRANS-STAN OIL EXPLORATION, barely visible under layers of dirt. Though all of the vehicles looked to be well past their prime, a practiced ear would have heard nothing but the sound of engines in perfect mechanical condition under the control of skilled drivers.

One of the drivers was considerably less skillful than the others. Peering through the streaked and smeared windshield of the Toyota, Vladimir Posenovich looked up at the few clouds in the sky. There would be little comfort from that direction. Even the sky wasn't a clear blue. What could be seen of it through the grimy windshield looked dirty from the blown dust.

Posenovich should have been happy, at least reasonably so. The German geologist who hired him had paid him in hard currency—U.S. dollars—and not Russian rubles. And the cloth-upholstered interior of the Toyota was comfortable; both the heater and the air conditioner worked. But it was not his car, and Posenovich was reflecting on just how far he had fallen from being a promising young military officer, a lieutenant in the Soviet army, more than fifteen years earlier.

"So, have we reached Vozrozhdeniye Island yet?" the passenger in the front seat said.

Taking a moment away from watching the open terrain ahead of them, Posenovich looked at the man sitting next to him before he answered. He didn't like what he saw. Heinrich Stahl was supposed to be a German petrochemical geologist and was in overall charge of the expedition. But Stahl did not seem like a man who worked with his hands much, especially not in the rough world of oil exploration.

The man was too smooth, too sure of himself, for

Posenovich's taste. He reminded the Russian of one of the *zampolit*, the political officers of his military days. They would pretend to be your friend while collecting information on your reliability for their reports to Moscow.

This man just seemed too handsome to work outside, like one of those actors who played in the James Bond movies. His hands were soft and his skin only held the tan of a sportsman, not someone who worked outside under the glare of the desert sun. If he didn't watch himself carefully, Stahl would burn to a crisp in the desert air. Besides, Posenovich thought he smiled too much. He was smiling now, waiting for the Russian's answer.

"It's hard to tell anymore," Posenovich said at last. "The Aral has shrunk so much that you can't tell where the sea bottom ends and the island begins. And you should call it Rebirth Island. That's the English name for it, and your Russian pronunciation is terrible."

"Rebirth it is," Stahl said through one of his insufferable smiles.

"The waters have dropped that much?" came a voice from the seat behind Posenovich.

The woman in the backseat was pleasantly different from Stahl as far as Posenovich was concerned, and he liked her very much. She was the one bright light in the whole of the stark landscape surrounding them. Introduced as the expedition's chemist, she didn't look like any scientist Posenovich had ever known.

By any normal measurement, Veronica Haslett was a beautiful woman. Soft of voice, she tied her long blonde hair up under a blue babushka-like kerchief to protect it from the dust that covered everything, even in the closed vehicle. Only of medium height but possessing a very well-filled-out figure above and below a slim waist, Haslett was a pleasant sight in the rear-view mirror when Posenovich tilted his head.

"Oh, yes," Posenovich said, "the loss of the Aral Sea has been one of the great shames of the old Soviet Union. The plan to irrigate the desert areas surrounding here needed water, and lots of it. So the two rivers that feed the Aral, the Amu Darya, and the Syr Darya were diverted. The cotton crops grew only one year and the weak desert soil was depleted. But the old Soviet planners were stubborn. The waters were kept flowing into the fields, and the Aral Sea shrank.

"The Aral Sea was once the fourth largest inland body of water in the world. It's much less than that now. The ground we've been crossing used to be under as much as ten meters of water. Today the waters of the Aral have dropped twelve meters and they're still going down.

"That line of dunes we passed a few kilometers back was the old shoreline, I think. Or at least, they were the sands that used to surround Rebirth. That small rise we passed a few hours ago should have been Konstantin Island. It used to lie to the southwest of Rebirth. Now, it has just become another part of it."

As he looked into the rearview mirror, Posenovich felt his view drawn to the eyes of the man sitting next to Haslett and staring back at him. The gray eyes of the man never seemed to blink. They just bored into Posenovich as if the owner could look into the depths of his very soul. The look sent a shiver down the Russian's back, one he couldn't completely blame on the cool breeze coming from the air conditioner.

The man in the back of the Toyota was one of the five others who also worked for Stahl on this trip. These definitely were not soft individuals, but then men who worked in the oil fields couldn't be, Posenovich supposed. He had seen their like before in the tougher career sergeants he had served with in the Soviet military. The man in the backseat had not said six words during the long hours of the drive, and those words hadn't been German, Russian, English, or any language Posenovich understood.

Movement in the seat next to him brought Posenovich's attention back to Stahl. The man was tapping on the control panel of a tan-colored device he had placed in a bracket attached to the dashboard of the Toyota. Posenovich knew the device was some kind of global positioning system receiver that would detect their location by tracking a bunch of American satellites far overhead. It was just one more of the gadgets that Stahl always seemed to be playing with. The man had a laptop computer sitting on the seat next to a bulky cell phone handset. A wire from the phone led away to the conical black antenna Stahl had fixed to the top of the Toyota's roof.

"You may as well not bother with that thing," Posenovich said. "With the evening winds this time of year, the ground shifts so much around here that the best maps are outdated before they can even be printed. That navigation device is all well and good in its place, but we didn't have such a thing fifteen years ago. We went by the landmarks and careful navigation."

"The moving of the sands is all the more reason to know our exact position," Stahl said. "And this 'thing,' as you refer to it, is an American military AN/PSN-11 precision GPS receiver. It was not easy to come by and cost a good deal. The Americans are using them right now in Iraq and Afghanistan. If it works for them, it will do the same for me. Whatever permanent landmarks may be on this island, I haven't been able to see any. You don't seem to be lost, at least not yet, anyway."

"Oh, there are a few landmarks that don't move," Posenovich said, glad to demonstrate his knowledge and value. "As long as we keep heading north, we'll spot one soon enough. The very best of them is the system of roads built by the Soviet engineers. There are only three primary roads on the island, and we should be crossing one any time now."

"If it isn't buried in the sand," Stahl said.

The man in the backseat grunted a single word in whatever language he spoke and Stahl barked a short laugh. Whatever had been said, Posenovich was sure it was a jest at his expense. The interior of the Toyota lapsed back into silence as he drove across the landscape. The bumpy ride grew worse as the vehicle went up a gradual rocky incline. Patches of rock now stood out more often among the sand and rough scrub. Without the four-wheel drive of the Toyota, they would have bogged down long ago. As it was, the trucks behind them had fallen behind as they struggled along, while the Toyota crested the rise.

"Do not pull too far ahead of the other vehicles," Stahl said with a note of warning in his voice.

The sudden change in Stahl's voice stood out against the normally friendly tone the man used. But Posenovich had some good news to deliver.

"No problem," Posenovich said with a smile. "There's

the landmark I was looking for." He pointed toward Stahl's side of the windshield.

Cutting across the terrain a kilometer or so away was a darker line in the scrub and sand. It was a hardtop road, only sandy asphalt, but the first sign of anything man-made they had seen since the caravan left the tiny Uzbekistan village of Uchsay, 120 kilometers to the south.

"Excellent," Stahl said with a wide smile, "pull over to that rise over there and stop in the shade. Let the trucks catch up."

The chance to take a break from fighting the wheel sounded very good to Posenovich. Getting over to the road made the driving a lot easier, but pulling off into the scrub and stopping in the shade of the rocky out-crop was even better. The ex-Soviet officer sighed as he finally turned off the engine. The hot metal beneath the hood pinged and tapped as it started to cool. Regretfully, Posenovich felt the cool breeze from the air-condition-ing fade away as the engine halted. Now the only thing cooling the interior of the Toyota was the shade they had stopped in.

"Welcome to Rebirth Island," Posenovich said. "Be-hind us is the main road that runs from east to west across the island. What's left of the settlement of Kan-tubek should be about fifteen kilometers in that direc-tion." He pointed off to the east.

"You have proven the right man for the job so far," Stahl said approvingly. "Let's hope the rest of our ex-plorations go as well as the trip to this point."

As Stahl opened the door to the Toyota, a blast of hot, dry air rushed into the vehicle. The smell of dust and hot rocks permeated the air, making the air-conditioning nothing more than a memory. Picking up the pewter-colored briefcase he never seemed to be without, Stahl stepped out of the Toyota and turned back the way they had come. The two trucks were quickly approaching and Stahl stood waiting for them.

Watching the actions of the German, Posenovich thought the sight of the man standing there with a brief-case in his hand the strangest thing. He always either carried it or had it within arm's reach, but Posenovich had never seen the man open it. But the quirks of the man who had hired him didn't really matter to the Russian. He was being paid, and that was enough.

Outside of the rocks rising up to their right, there was little to look at from the interior of the Toyota. Both rear doors opened behind him and the other passengers got out. As Posenovich watched, Veronica Haslett walked back to the old ZIL-151 truck, which had come to a stop. She went around to the back of the vehicle and her legs disappeared as she climbed into it.

With a groan, Posenovich opened his door and climbed out of the Toyota. His back was stiff and his knees hurt from the long drive. And he needed to take a piss. He had always hated this damned island, and pissing on it felt like a good idea, anyway. But before he could act on his impulse, he heard Stahl call out his name.

Over by the Bedford truck, Stahl was talking to several of his men. He waved Posenovich over. Posenovich didn't like the rest of the men and he had been looking forward to a break, but Stahl was the boss. Suppressing a sigh, Posenovich walked over.

"Do remember to watch out for snakes," Posenovich said as he approached Stahl. "There are some very nasty, poisonous ones around here and the shade can attract them."

"Thank you for the warning," Stahl said politely, "but there are far worse things on this island than snakes."

"What do you mean?" Posenovich said with a puzzled look on his face.

"You don't know?" Stahl said. "I was sure you would. In fact, I insist that you know."

Two men from Stahl's crew suddenly grabbed Posenovich from both sides and slammed him up against the side of the Bedford truck. Surprised and stunned, the Russian could only struggle weakly while the two other men quickly wrapped chains around his arms and chest. Additional lengths went around his legs before he could kick them away. The ends of the chains were locked to the frame and wheels of the truck, securing Posenovich in a spread-eagle position.

As the Russian started to shout, one of the men stuffed a filthy rag into his mouth to stifle his protests.

Shock and panic caused him to struggle against his bonds. But his jerking against the chains only showed how firmly he was secured. Posenovich's struggles slowed and stopped for a moment when he noticed what the men were doing on the ground in front of him. His eyes bulged from their sockets as he watched in horrified fascination. He couldn't tear his sight away from the tools the men were laying out on the ground.

Individually, none of the items would normally get a second look. They all belonged with trucks or a convoy. There were pliers with sharply serrated jaws. Bolt cutters, wire cutters, a hammer, some large nails, a blowtorch, a knife, and a spare truck battery with jumper cables attached to the soft lead terminals. Lastly, a small green metal box was set down next to the tools.

One of the workers picked up the ends of the jumper cables and looked at Posenovich. With a vicious smile spreading across his face, he touched the ends of the cables together. The fat sparks that popped out when the two clamps touched caused Posenovich to snap his head back against the side of the truck. He started screaming hoarsely into his gag. The weak sounds only demonstrated the impossible position he was in.

Walking up to where the tools were laid out on the ground, Stahl pulled on a pair of tight black leather gloves. He watched Posenovich struggle for a moment, the screams from the struggling Russian reaching a high-pitched tone as despair started to settle in. A dark, wet stain spread across the crotch of his trousers and the smell of urine filled the air.

"All right, now," Stahl said in a soft voice, "we've barely started yet and already you act like you're going to die. That isn't necessarily the case, Vladimir. Since we are about to become so much more intimately acquainted, I can call you Vladimir, can't I?"

As the adrenaline in his system started to fade, and his shame asserted itself, Posenovich slumped back against his bonds. The screaming had stopped as the Russian stared at the man in front of him.

"The Aral Sea has come and gone in the past," Stahl said. "Someday, this area will possibly be an island again. Before that time, the Uzbekistan government does indeed want this area checked for possible oil deposits. This island should be a stable enough area if the waters come back. But you have probably figured out by now that we aren't interested in exploring for any signs of oil. No, we need some information regarding the recent past of this particular island. It's something that I'm certain you can tell us. And I assure you, you will tell me what I want to know. The only choice you have is the means by which I will convince you to give me the information I want. My men and I can persuade you with the materials here at hand—quietly or otherwise."

Reaching down, Stahl picked up a large screwdriver. Moving closer to Posenovich, he stood directly in front of the man. Rubbing his thumb across the wide, flat tip of the tool, Stahl looked into the bound man's eyes and sighed. Posenovich could only stare at the shiny tip of the screwdriver scant inches away from his face.

"There are ways to force you to tell me what I want to know," Stahl said very quietly, "and there are ways to quietly persuade you to cooperate. I'm certain your aged mother back in Russia—what was that address again? Oh yes. Flat 332, 1500 Dostoyevsky Avenue, Kiev— would like to have you back again someday. You see, we've done our homework and have chosen you very carefully. The information regarding your family does seem worthwhile now, doesn't it? Your mother would most likely recommend that you choose the quiet form of persuasion I'm offering.

"You would tell us anything we wanted to hear, given certain incentives. But I don't really have time to deal with the results of torture. It would be preferable not to have to check out lies, and then go to the trouble to convince you to speak further."

Setting down the screwdriver, Stahl turned and opened up the metal box. Inside were paper-banded bundles of currency.

"One from column A," Stahl said with a smile. Then the smile dropped away and the voice grew hard. "Or everything from column B."

Taking a bottle of water from one of the men, Stahl unscrewed the top and drank deeply. Handing the bottle back, he waved to where Posenovich was secured.

The man walked up to the bound Russian and snatched the gag from his mouth. Pushing the bottle up, the man poured water in Posenovich's mouth. Choking and gagging for a moment, Posenovich started to drink greedily. Fear, and the cloth gag, had dried his mouth out completely. Finally, the water bottle was pulled away and the Russian hung in his chains gasping.

With the panic slipping away for the moment, Posenovich could at least start to think. Just who in the hell was this man? First, he acts like the worst hard case Posenovich had ever known. Then, he talks like an American, or at least a capitalist who expects money to work for him. And he was right. Now that Posenovich had a moment, he thought he knew what Stahl was going to ask about.

"What do you want to know?" Posenovich said in a gasping voice.

"That's much better," Stahl said as he walked up to the bound man. Stuffing a bundle of money into Posenovich's shirt pocket, Stahl signaled to the men standing on either side. Without saying a word, the men unlocked and removed the shackles on Posenovich's legs. Then they stood and looked at Stahl.

"Hey," Posenovich said weakly, "what about my arms?"

"All in good time," Stahl said. "You should have learned patience during your time in the service of the greater Soviet. Especially as a young officer in Military Unit 25484. Assigned to Aralsk-7. That was the code name of the military installation at Kantubek, not too far from where we're standing right now."

Watching quietly now, Posenovich hung in his chains, breathing heavily.

"But then, you knew we had information about your military career, didn't you? That's why we hired you as a guide for our little expedition."

"You told me that the Uzbecki government wanted oil. . . ." Posenovich started to say.

"Enough," Stahl said. "The information cost a good deal, but I know that back in 1988, you were the officer in charge of the transport and disposal of biological materials here on the island. This was the largest testing area for Soviet biological weapons of all kinds. When the government decided to get rid of their stockpiles, drums were loaded aboard trains, then boats, and finally trucks. All to be disposed of here."

"If you know all of that," Posenovich said, "then you know that the United States sent a team of scientists here just a few years ago to clean up and decontaminate the dump sites."

"Yes, I know that," Stahl said. "They spent months digging up the materials that had been just dumped into pits. The bleach that had been poured onto the powder before burial did little to kill it. So the Americans paid to have all eleven dump sites dug up and decontaminated. Only there was one site they missed. A twelfth site, separate from the rest."

"So you know about that?" Posenovich said, amazed.

"What? How a young officer had a truck breakdown, so he just had his men dig a hole right at the spot and bury the drums they were transporting? Yes, I know about that. And I want to know more. Like exactly where those drums are buried."

"They had bleach dumped into them long before we even received them," Posenovich said. "The anthrax in those drums is dead—long dead."

"Let me worry about that," Stahl said. "You just decide if you're going to lead us to that burial site or not."

"Fine," Posenovich said, slumping against his chains as he came to his decision. "If you want it, it's yours."

"Release him," Stahl said. "And someone get him another pair of trousers."

Chapter Two

While standing next to the open door of the Toyota, Stahl carefully examined the display on the screen of the AN/PSN-11 GPS receiver. On the seat in front of him was his open computer. The laptop was a rugged-ized military model that seemed impervious to the dust and grit that blew all around the edge of the rock face where they had stopped. Looking down at the computer, Stahl frowned as he tapped on the keyboard. On the ground sitting next to his left leg was his ever-present briefcase.

Having changed clothes under the watchful gaze of two of Stahl's men, a subdued Posenovich walked over to the Toyota.

"Ah, my good Vladimir," Stahl said with a wide smile, "I imagine you're feeling much better now, having both changed and decided to accept my generous offer."

For a moment, Posenovich simply stood and stared at the other man. Not ten minutes earlier, Stahl had been threatening him with a gruesome death by torture. Now, he was acting like some long-lost *tovarisch*.

"It seemed like the wisest choice at the time," Posenovich said weakly.

"Indeed it was," Stahl said. He was still smiling, but his eyes had grown very cold. "And now is the time to prove that you have truly accepted the situation. Please take a look at this."

Turning the laptop so Posenovich could see the screen, Stahl continued.

"This is one of the most recent satellite maps I have available of this island. The map here"—Stahl tapped some keys and the picture on the screen changed—"shows this road that you have so conveniently located for us in relation to the whole island. Our position is marked here by the flashing red dot. What I want to know from you is the exact location of the burial site for those drums."

Nervous about what he had to try to do, Posenovich stalled for time.

"Do you know where we are in relation to the old settlement at Kantubek?" Posenovich said.

"You can see it there on the map," Stahl said sharply. "We are exactly fifteen point five kilometers from Aralsk-7."

Just saying the name of the biological weapons site would have gotten a man arrested ten years earlier. Wincing slightly at the sound of the code name, Posenovich looked away from the computer screen.

"If your figures are exact—" he started to say.

"They are precise to better than ten meters," Stahl said sharply.

"Then we are less than ten kilometers from where my men buried those cylinders," Posenovich said. "We were just over five kilometers from the laboratories when the truck broke down. We had passed a curve in the road and were out of sight of anyone who may have been watching us when the rear axle spring on the transport truck broke.

"The original plan called for us to travel to the open-air test site and dispose of the material. It was the first shipment for burial, and they sent it to us directly from the production facility at Sverdlovsk. There were three dozen one-hundred-liter cylinders of dry agent. After that first batch, all of the shipments came out of Irkutsk. Those were all two-hundred-fifty-liter drums filled with wet slurry agent mixed with bleach. They wanted us to dump that agent into pits and save the stainless-steel drums for reuse."

Posenovich stopped talking for a moment as his voice choked. His throat was still dry from the fear that had washed through his system such a short time ago. At a nod from Stahl, one of the men roughly shoved another water bottle into the Russian's hand. Unscrewing the cap, Posenovich drank with a desperate need. After a long moment, the same man who had given him the water bottle snatched it back.

"Continue," Stahl said.

"We were the only convoy to try and conduct the burial at night," Posenovich said. "Command had determined that was the easiest way to avoid detection by American spy satellites. For additional concealment, we were to drive under blackout conditions with strict light discipline. The trouble is, these roads are hard enough to drive on at night *with* headlights. A patch of sand that looked like it had just blown across the road turned out to be a soft pit. The transport truck bogged down in it and snapped a suspension spring.

"Even though we had the smaller cylinders in the truck, it was too heavy when it broke down. We couldn't repair the broken spring with all of that weight on it. So we excavated a pit and buried the cylinders just off to the side of the road, not twenty meters away from it. No one ever knew, or was ever supposed to know."

"Excellent," Stahl said, "but you probably wouldn't be amazed at just what kind of information people will sell if they think it is valuable. Too bad the old Soviet military restricted field maps to only officers. If not, we might have never met, you know."

Posenovich only nodded his head miserably.

"Brighten up, my friend," Stahl said with a laugh. "Now I have the opportunity to show you just how much faith I have in our new partnership. You may drive us to the burial site—now."

Looking over at the man who had sat so silently behind him during the trip so far, Posenovich took note of the spotless AK-74M assault rifle the man had slung from his shoulder. The weapon was of such recent issue that Posenovich had never seen that model before, with a hard stock folded over to the side of the receiver. The 5.45×39mm weapon was the tool of a professional, and that was how it was being handled. The muzzle of the deadly rifle swung over in his direction and Posenovich saw that the man's hand rested lightly on the pistol grip. The safety was switched to the central, full-automatic-fire position.

"Of course," Posenovich said as he turned back to Stahl. "But what about the Uzbekistan military? Since they took control of this island after the breakup of the Soviet Union, they have run patrols based out of the old military port support facility north of the

laboratories. They have shoot-on-sight orders for anyone who approaches that side of the island. All the
locals know that, that's why they haven't scavenged the
facility."

"A reasonable worry, my dear Vladimir," Stahl said.
"But since the Americans ran their cleanup campaign,
there is little on the island to keep anyone from. Patrols
are random at worst. And my sources have told me that
there hasn't been a military unit stationed here for over
a year. We shall not be bothered during our search.
Which I insist we start on now. Veronica!" Stahl called
out loudly. "We are leaving now, if you wish to join
us."

The sight of the lovely woman no longer held any
enjoyment for Posenovich. She had calmly watched his
interrogation in a very detached pose, standing in the
doorway to the ZIL van. It was obvious to the Russian
that she was the same kind of hard-nosed killer as any
of the men there, only in a prettier package.

Veronica had changed into some kind of blue coveralls when she had gone into the van. The snug fit
showed her figure off to the best advantage as she
climbed into her accustomed seat in the back of the
Toyota. After he returned to the driver's seat, Posenovich could feel the presence of the AK-74M just behind
him. He hoped that the man holding it had put the
safety back on, or was riding without his finger on the
trigger. One bad bump, and Posenovich could be just a
memory.

———

It was the third time the caravan had stopped. Each
time, Posenovich had thought they were at the correct

spot along the road where he had his men bury the drums so many years ago. And each time they had stopped, two of Stahl's men had broken out and assembled handheld metal detectors. The rest of the men had remained on guard at the trucks, watching both Posenovich as well as the terrain all around them. Stahl may have trusted the information he had been given about the local Uzbeki troops and their disposition, but he still felt no need to take chances. All of the men had weapons near at hand. Only Stahl, Haslett, and Posenovich himself were not obviously armed.

Despite the fact that Stahl wasn't holding a gun on him, Posenovich was more than a little nervous about not having found the drum burial site right away. As his men swept the area next to the road with the huge two-meter-square coils of the metal detectors, Stahl looked on with a calm stoicism that would have done a Russian Cossack proud.

"The drums were of stainless steel," Posenovich said. "And the sand has shifted so much over the years since I was stationed here. Are you sure those mine detectors your men are using won't miss them? They could be buried much deeper now because of the drifting."

"Those are engineer-grade Delta Pulse metal detectors," Stahl said. "The best available—not some kind of military surplus mine detectors. We're looking for steel drums, not coins on a beach somewhere. With those eighty-inch-square search coils, they'll detect metal buried more than five meters deep in much denser soil than is around here."

Turning toward Posenovich, Stahl continued coldly, "The batteries are good for ten hours of continuous use, and we have spare sets. My men have practiced with them until they can find a bottle cap under two meters of sand. The only way we could miss something the size of those buried drums is if they weren't here. And that would make me a very unhappy man."

Looking into Stahl's pale blue eyes, Posenovich was reminded of the cold, lidless stare of the sand viper his men had caught on the island once. The snake hadn't been an ugly reptile—kind of an attractive brown with light and dark stripes. But it was an absolutely deadly one. It had looked at Posenovich as if he were prey, the same look Posenovich was seeing right now.

The silence of the long moment was broken only by the sigh of the desert wind. The afternoon was going by quickly and they had yet to find anything. All Posenovich could feel just then was a rising panic at the tension in the air. Just when he thought he would scream, one of the men called out from where he had just stopped searching. Stahl barked orders and the men were suddenly scrambling to carry them out.

The verbal exchange between Stahl and his men was something Posenovich couldn't understand. What he *could* understand was the bright-eyed look Stahl gave him when he turned to face him.

"It seems they have detected a large source of metal some few meters beneath the sand," Stahl said. "The size fits the description you gave us earlier. It seems we may have found what we came here for."

As Posenovich watched, the tarps were pulled from the object on the back of the Bedford truck. In spite of his fear, Posenovich was fascinated by what was uncovered. The complicated-looking rig sat on top of the bed of the truck, taking up all of the available space in a bewildering arrangement of cables, belts, pulleys, and heavy-toothed chains. If Posenovich had been placed into the jaws of this mechanical nightmare, he would have agreed to anything Stahl wanted almost instantly.

With two men guiding the driver, the Bedford and its load was backed up to the discovery site that had been marked out on the sand. Everyone was now wearing dust masks as the sand was kicked up by the movement of the heavy truck. Once the vehicle had stopped in place, the driver remained in the cab and worked a second set of controls. Part of the assembly in the bed of the truck began to lift and extend itself out over the back bumper. Now Posenovich could see that the toothed chains were some kind of digging machine.

"It's a Mark III light mobile digger," Stahl said, obviously proud of his mechanical marvel. "It will dig a one-point-five-meter-deep trench at nine meters a minute in soil like this. That conveyor belt above the cutting chains will dump the soil to either side of the trench as it goes. In just a few minutes, it will uncover what was buried here."

"Uncover—" Posenovich said loudly as fear suddenly grabbed at his throat. "But we'll be exposed! Those chains will tear the drums open and spread the anthrax all around us."

"Not to fear, my dear Vladimir," Stahl said. "The last bits of sand will be dug out by hand. My men are very good at operating this digger. And we have all been vaccinated against anthrax. In fact, the Uzbekistan Ministry of Health insisted that all of my people receive a full series of vaccinations and boosters. We even have such a booster for yourself if needed. Additional precautions will also be taken as we approach the containers. And besides—ah, here she is, right on cue."

Approaching them from where she had come out of the back of the van, Veronica Haslett was now dressed in a shiny green plastic suit. With her head and shoulders sticking out from the front opening of the suit, the huge bubble-helmet of the garment was folded back from her head and a large glass-fronted mask hung by straps from around her neck. This was a very advanced biological protection suit with a self-contained breathing system, something Posenovich vaguely recognized from when he worked at Aralsk-7. In her hands were several very large clear plastic bags filled with something. All Posenovich could make out on the bags was the large orange sticker with a spider-like black trefoil on it—the international biohazard warning label.

"Thank you, my dear," Stahl said as he took the packages Haslett held out to him. "I hope you know how to put this on," he said as he handed one of the packages to Posenovich. "It's a military Tyvek F suit with boots, nitrile gloves, and everything you'll need to seal it. Even instructions. There's also a respirator mask in there with twin HEPA filters. Everything you'll need to protect yourself from your supposedly dead anthrax."

Taking the bag from Stahl's hand, Posenovich immediately turned to the open Toyota and started to remove the contents of the bag, laying them out on the seat in front of him. While Posenovich dressed and taped over the joints between his suit and the gloves and boots that had been in the bag, Stahl did the same thing at the back of the Toyota. While the men were now digging by hand in shifts, the others were also suiting up from the kit bags Haslett handed out. Once everyone was suited up and their respirator masks were in place, the men in the trench got down on their hands and knees, removing the last of the sand with small hand shovels.

One of the men ran a hose from the water tank hitched to the ZIL van. He dragged the nozzle of the hose up to the edge of the pit and turned the water on. The spray smelled of bleach as he sprinkled water all over the inside of the trench and the surrounding area. The dust that had been kicked up by the digger was immediately washed out of the air. In the trench, the wet-down men were now digging in soggy sand, but all of the dust was gone. With everything wet, if there was a breached cylinder, the deadly contents wouldn't be easily stirred into the air.

The odd color combination of the brown Tyvek suit, black gloves, and yellow boots comforted Posenovich as he realized just how the outlandish getup protected him. And he felt he needed that protection as he looked down into the trench and saw something he never had wished to see again in his life, There was a row of dirty-silver cylinders, drums with sealed lids, all of them together possibly holding nearly two metric tons of some of the deadliest biological weapon that had ever been made. And he had helped to expose this terror to the world at large.

While Posenovich stared, the men climbed out of the trench as Haslett approached. Her suit was now completely sealed up, the hunchbacked appearance of the getup due to the self-contained breathing system on her back. Clambering down into the trench, the suited woman approached the one drum the men had righted for her. The filler cap had been brushed off and exposed. Setting down the bag she had brought with her from the back of the van, Haslett removed an odd-looking wrench and fitted it over the cap.

In spite of the years it had been underground, the filler cap turned easily as Haslett put pressure on the wrench handle. Setting down the tool, she spread out a roll of sampling equipment and bottles. Posenovich could hear Stahl breathing heavily next to him as the woman used a very long probe to carefully take a sample from deep inside the cylinder. The noise from Stahl's breathing stopped for a moment as Haslett removed the sample probe and placed the tip into one of her sample jars. A powdery substance could now be seen filling the container. A soft tan powder that seemed to almost flow like water moved in the glass jar as Haslett placed it in a protected carrying case.

It was obvious to Posenovich that the liquid bleach he had been told was dumped into the cylinders had not reached the center of the mass that was inside them. The tan powder the woman had collected was weaponized anthrax spores. The woman carefully closed up the filler cap on the cylinder and sealed all the tools she had used inside plastic bags—double-bagging all of the contaminated equipment.

"So?" Stahl said as Haslett climbed out of the trench.

"It looks like what I expected to see," Haslett said. "Outside of that, I can't tell you anything until I've run some lab tests. I'll incinerate some and the gas chromatograph and spectrometer will tell me what I need in a few minutes. Once I have those results, the agent monitor will positively identify the material. Now let me get on with my work. This air tank is only good for an hour before I have to change it."

Stepping back, Stahl let Haslett move back to the van body on the rear bed of the ZIL. The Soviet truck had also been backed up so the rear of it faced the trench. It was obvious now to Posenovich that the van held a laboratory, and probably not one that would just test geological samples.

"Nothing to do now but wait until she tells us the results," Stahl said.

The ten minutes that passed from when Haslett had gone into the lab van didn't seem all that long to Posenovich. But Stahl was walking around the pit like an expectant father. He looked ridiculous in his protective equipment with his briefcase in his hand. The other men were all standing around their respective vehicles, just waiting. Then, the back of the van opened up and Haslett, still completely encased in her protective suit, leaned out. Her voice was muffled by the breathing mask and suit hood, but her words came across clearly enough.

"We have it," she said. "It's anthrax, that's confirmed. It will take at least several hours to confirm the strain. But the sample gives every indication that it's the big one. Anthrax 836, exactly what we had hoped for."

"Okay," Stahl said with excitement in his voice. "Time to get some of those cylinders out of there. . . ."

One of the men shouted something and pointed. As everyone turned, Posenovich felt his heart almost stop in his chest. Approaching from around a bend in the road was a pair of UAZ-469B open trucks. Each of the jeeplike vehicles held three soldiers carrying AKM-47 rifles. On the bumper of the front UAZ flew a small red, white, and green horizontally striped flag. They were Uzbeki troops. Exactly the people Stahl said they wouldn't meet on the island.

Chapter Three

On the other side of the world, concerns of people on an island were considerably different from those on the Aral Sea. Spring in Northern Michigan is sometimes only distinguishable from the winter by the lack of snow. This is something particularly noticeable on the islands of Lake Michigan. The heavy lead-gray clouds of the sky are almost a match in color for the dark surface of the roiling lake waters below. It will take weeks of energy from the sun shining down to warm those waters to a noticeable degree. In March, the cold wind blows across the waves and breaks against the evergreens growing on the relatively dry land of South Wolverine Island.

The huge rock-faced mansion on the island looked out over an open field of what was presently wet, brown grassland. It would be a field of luxuriant grass inside of a few months.

"Okay guys, looks like the horsemen are back in the saddle."

The big man rolled into the library of the house, his

deep voice booming out across the polished wood floors. Care had been taken in restoring the room to its former look. Even a close examination of the paneled walls or stone fireplace would have failed to reveal any damage. And there certainly had been damage nearly two years before when a savage fight had taken place between Ted Reaper and his friends and a group of terrorists using the mansion and the island around it as a staging area. The terrorists' plan had been for an attack on the water supply of Chicago and Lake Michigan as a whole. Reaper and his men had ended the threat within hours of the terrorists launching their attack.

"About damned time," Max Warrick said from where he had been sitting in front of the blazing fire. Setting his book down on the table next to his leather armchair, the ex-Marine scout-sniper stood and stretched.

"I mean I like a bit of relaxation as much as anyone. But this sitting around is way too much like the worst parts of being in the corps. Besides, the spring weather up here can really drag you down. I forget what the sun looks like. Time to get out and get moving."

Looking up at Warrick, Keith Deckert grinned. If he had been standing, he would have been much taller than the other man, but his legs hadn't worked since he had been paralyzed in a racing accident years earlier. His wheelchair gave him the mobility he needed, and anyone who thought they could take advantage of a cripple in a chair would have been badly surprised by the strength in the arms of the ex-Army Ranger sergeant.

"Welcome to Michigan. If you don't like the weather, hang around for five minutes and it'll change. Now, where is everybody?"

"Reaper's down in the gym working out, Mackenzie

is out in the hanger pulling some maintenance on the Skymaster. And I have no idea where Caronti is, he was with Reaper a while ago."

"He's probably down in the pool," Deckert said, "watching Reaper work out always makes him sweat. See if you can get everyone together in the office."

"What's going on?"

"Road trip," Deckert said with a wide grin. "Straker wants the Horsemen to go out and be bad guys."

———

Ted Reaper, Max Warrick, Ben Mackenzie, and Enzo Caronti were soon standing in Deckert's first floor office, surrounded by his walls of maps, computer screens, books, and files. The men made up the Four Horsemen, a team of special operations veterans from all of the services who worked as a consulting group for the United States government. The truth of the matter was that the men operated solely for an office of the Department of Homeland security. The man in charge of that office was retired Admiral Alan Straker, an ex-Navy SEAL who had known Reaper during his active service days. It was Straker who had intervened with the Federal, State, and local authorities who had wanted to prosecute Reaper when he and his friends had gone up against what had looked like a group of drug dealers looking to strong-arm Reaper into supplying guns for their operations.

When he and his friends had gone in to rescue Reaper's family, kidnapped to insure Reaper's cooperation, the real villains behind everything turned out to be a group of al-Qaeda terrorists. A massive firefight on the island had resulted in the ending of the terrorist plot and the rescue of Reaper's wife and son. The success had come at a high cost, with the death of Reaper's friend and SEAL teammate, Ted "Bear" Parnell.

Recognizing the rare mix of skills and abilities gathered in the group, Alan Straker had protected the men from the legal fallout of their actions, in exchange for them conducting special operations for him as the Four Horsemen. Less than a year earlier, Straker's foresight had proven its value when Reaper uncovered a terrorist group trying to smuggle the materials for a radiological "dirty" bomb underneath the Arizona border. For their success in that action as well as their earlier exploits, the men had been given the island and its contents to use as a base of operations. The financial rewards of capturing or eliminating a number of high-ranking terrorist operatives had also given the group a very large nest egg of operating funds. That money had gone into outfitting the men with the best equipment that could be purchased, as well as restoring the island estate to its former glory.

"Straker wants us to do what?" Reaper said as he rubbed a towel briskly over his hair. The big ex-SEAL had been showering after his workout when Deckert's summons came. The blue jumpsuit he was wearing was blotched with dark spots, showing how he had rushed to the briefing before properly drying off. It had been a long period of study and training over the winter months, and Reaper looked forward to some action to break the spell of relative inactivity just as much as the rest of his team did.

"Conduct security operations a lot like the old Red Cell team did back in the late eighties," Deckert said. "Straker wants the security checked at a half dozen nuclear sites all over the eastern half of the country, starting with the Braidwood reactor down near Joliet, Illinois, and working south. The Four Horsemen are to penetrate the reactor sites and uncover any weaknesses in their overall security. Only the head of security for each site will know just who we are and what we are trying to do. Other than that, we are to use our own resources to plan out and conduct the penetration."

"Oh, great," Caronti said. "I managed to miss out on getting exposed to all of those isotopes you guys found last year down in Arizona only to sneak in to a reactor full of the hot stuff. I hate the idea of glowing in the dark."

"Don't worry," Mackenzie said, "you didn't really want to have kids anyway, did you?"

"Besides," Reaper said. "If the sites are secure, we won't be able to get into them anyway. And it will make us operational for a few months given a couple of weeks to check out each site."

"Running up against unknown security forces," Warrick said. "It sounds like such fun."

Chapter Four

Just what in the hell have I done to deserve this? thought Lieutenant Yakubov as he was driven along the dusty road. He was more than a little pissed at his present situation. It wasn't as if he expected to be doing parade duties in the capital at Tashkent. You join the army and you pull your share of shit duties. But patrolling this island and its abandoned base was something more along the lines of punishment.

Of course, there was the question of radical Islamic terrorists to be dealt with. The Islamic Movement of Uzbekistan (IMU) had mostly been operating in the Kyrgyz Mountains and conducting raids west and north into Uzbekistan. But the Aral Sea was at the opposite end of the country from Kyrgyzstan, hundreds of kilometers from the border with Afghanistan and about the same distance from Iran. This pesthole wasn't even the armpit of Uzbekistan, it was more like a tick that had settled into the festering hole that the Aral Sea had become.

The under-strength squad Yakubov was leading had

been sent to conduct a week's field maneuvers and patrol on Rebirth Island. Captain Rostikov, the company commander, had thought such an exercise might help season the new men more quickly that training with the company. Season his men? Half the men in his squad were conscripts fresh out of training, ready to serve their sixteen months and get the hell out of the army. The only seasoning these men would get on this mission would be the break they'd have from the brutal hazing they would have otherwise received from the rest of the senior privates and sergeants at the company.

With these gloomy thoughts on his mind, the last thing Yakubov expected his two-vehicle patrol to run into was, well, anything. There were all kinds of bumps, holes, and curves on the road as it wound through an area of rocky hills. The twists and turns were due to the topography, the bumps and craters owed their existence to more than ten years of neglect. Each hill they passed look like the one before it, and the next one as well. But when they passed around one rocky rise, there was a construction project going on. This was astonishing. Surely if there were any official standing for such a project, his orders would have mentioned it.

When Lieutenant Yakubov signaled a halt, Sergeant Borutova immediately deployed the men. At his barked signal, two men jumped out of the back of each of the UAZ-469B open light trucks and covered the strangers with their weapons. Borutova's driver pulled up a belt-fed PKM light machine gun from behind the front seat and propped it across the door. With five AK-47s and a 7.62×54mm PKM loaded with a two-hundred-round belt box covering them, the unarmed strangers were helpless.

Standing up and looking grim, Lieutenant Yakubov glowered and stalled for time as he tried to think of just who these people were. They weren't dressed like any terrorist group he had ever heard of. In fact, they looked like the American technicians who had been on the island sixteen months earlier, cleaning up the Soviet's contamination.

Then Yakubov was even more astonished when one of the strangers started shouting at him—in perfect Russian. Even through the muffle of his respirator, the tone of his voice suggested anything but a man who was looking down the barrels of a half dozen automatic weapons.

"Are you our escorts?" Stahl shouted. Even as some of the men turned their weapons onto him, Stahl kept up his pretense. "If you are, you took your own bloody time about getting here. We already had to start our excavations in order to stay on schedule."

This certainly didn't sound like anyone who wasn't supposed to be on the island. But Yakubov wasn't about to be cowed by some shouting bureaucrat, no matter who he thought he was.

"Stand very still," Yakubov shouted. "My men are very well trained and will shoot at the slightest provocation." At least he hoped the weapons were loaded and that the AKs his men were holding didn't have empty magazines in them to make them lighter. "I have not been given instructions that anyone would be here. You are trespassing on restricted government soil. You could be shot where you stand."

"What?" Stahl said loudly. "You haven't been told that we would be here? This project was approved by the very highest authority. I have authorizations signed by President Karimov himself."

Stahl had made an instant decision after seeing the soldiers take up positions to cover the work site. Several of the troops were obviously young and they looked more than a little nervous. Scared would have been a better description. There was only one officer, and he had looked surprised before he forced on his grim "soldier face." It was obviously the sergeant that the men looked to for direction and leadership. He and a couple of the older-appearing soldiers looked to be the most competent, and that made them the most dangerous.

Once he had made the decision to go on the offensive, Stahl couldn't back down. When you bluff, you have to bluff big. And at that moment, Stahl was running one of the biggest bluffs of his life. With the way the officer had started at the mention of President Karimov's name, Stahl knew he was close to getting the upper hand in the situation. And the hidden cards in his hand were going to be the key to this game.

"So?" Stahl said. "What is it, Lieutenant? You wish to see my papers? That isn't a problem, I have them right here."

A distraction was what Stahl needed right now before he could take action. By the looks of the dust and dirt on these soldiers, they had probably been in the field for a while at least. If that was true, Stahl knew just which distraction might work best for his needs.

"Veronica," Stahl called out, "we have men out here. Please show yourself, dear. I wouldn't want there to be a mistake."

The use of the word "dear" was the signal to the

woman in the van that the situation was a bad one. Stahl trusted his team to react properly when he made his move. Now Haslett had to play her part.

"Just let me seal this container, dear," Haslett shouted back from inside the van. Her voice was muffled, but the sound that came through was unmistakably female. And it caused the reaction from the soldiers that Stahl had been expecting. Just about all of the soldiers turned at least part of their attention to the partially open door of the van. When Haslett came into full view at the door, she immediately had the eyes of each of the armed troops.

Analyzing the situation from what she could see through the van door, Haslett had made preparations. Unsealing the front of her suit, she had pushed the big hood back over her head and off her shoulders. She was still wearing her full-face breathing mask, but now much of her upper torso was exposed. The blue coveralls were sweat-stained and soaked. They stuck to her body and were strapped down by the carrying harness of her breathing rig. Her more than adequate feminine curves strained against the clinging fabric.

Haslett was holding a three-liter beaker half full of a clear liquid. She kept her eyes on Stahl even as the rough-looking soldier who appeared to be some sort of leader grunted out a terse command. With a dirty-toothed grin, one of the older soldiers happily followed his sergeant's order and headed to the back of the ZIL where Haslett was standing. The look in the soldier's eyes was feral. Lieutenant Yakubov was starting to seriously think he could loose control of the situation in another minute. He would have to do something quickly.

As soon as the soldiers had shown up, Posenovich

really started to panic. He was going to be caught with these terrorists, and no one was going to believe that he had been threatened with torture for his cooperation. In Posenovich's present state of mind, the fact that Stahl was in the process of facing the soldiers down didn't register. Now, he wondered just what in the hell that slut bitch was doing. Displaying her tits to the soldiers was just going to make a bad situation worse. The idea of a bunch of soldiers in the field gang-raping a female prisoner didn't even strike Posenovich as unusual. But their officer probably wouldn't want any witnesses around to make his official explanation of the incident messy.

The sweat that had been trickling down Posenovich's skin inside the Tyvek suit now became a flood. As it ran into his eyes, Posenovich didn't dare raise his hand to lift his mask and wipe them. He was frozen to the spot. His blurred vision missed the tiny nod of the head that Stahl made. With their attention elsewhere, all of the soldiers and even the officer also missed the movement. But Veronica Haslett hadn't.

In a sudden motion, Haslett threw the contents of the beaker at the soldier who was approaching her. With the liquid tossed, she ducked back into the van. As the liquid splashed across his face, the man screamed, dropping his rifle and grabbing at his eyes. As the rest of the soldiers watched for a second in morbid fascination, the man's hair frizzed up and turned red, as if it had been burned. The screams from the ruined mouth became wet-sounding and blubbery, unintelligible to anyone. His eyes ran down his face, adding their goo to the smoking red ruin that had been his flesh.

In the moment that the man screamed, Stahl acted,

pressing down on a lever underneath the grip of the briefcase in his left hand. The sides of the case popped open like a spring-loaded clamshell. As the sides fell away, the short, vicious AKS-74U "Ksyusha" compact carbine hidden inside the case was exposed. Grabbing the pistol grip of the powerful weapon with his right hand, Stahl swung the stubby gun around, holding on to the black briefcase handle solidly attached to the top of the weapon.

His targeting priorities were solidly fixed in Stahl's mind as he pulled the trigger. As the AKS-74U swung around, it started stuttering out 5.45×39mm rounds as it fired. A stream of 5.45mm steel-cored projectiles smashed into the chest of Sergeant Borutova. The 3mm air cavity in the nose of each of the dozen projectiles that struck the big sergeant caused the bullets to tumble and spin after they struck flesh. His brutal career was over, but Borutova never even felt the hammer blows of the bullets as they smashed him into oblivion.

The moment that Stahl made his move, his men went into action. The only way out of a situation like this was overwhelming violence, and that was something they knew very well. From the hidden corners of every truck, loaded AK-74M rifles were pulled out and turned on the stunned soldiers. Only one man among the soldiers got off any rounds at all, and that was almost by accident. The driver in the UAZ who was manning the PKM machine gun pulled his trigger more from reflex than intentional action. The muzzle of the machine gun flashed bright orange and white as the big 7.62×54 rounds fed through its action.

The 7.62mm cupro-nickel-jacketed bullets thundered out of the belt-fed machine gun and sped across the area. Even as one of Stahl's men swung around with his own weapon, the heavy slugs stitched across him. He stumbled and fell backward in a loose-limbed parody of a dance as his life bled away.

Stahl continued bringing his Ksyusha around, the short-barreled weapon roaring loudly as he held the trigger back. One of his own men had the same target priorities as Stahl did, only he had a much more destructive weapon at hand. As Stahl tracked his rounds toward the bullet-vomiting PKM, one of his men pulled the trigger on the 40mm GP-25 grenade launcher mounted underneath the barrel of his AK-74M.

While Stahl's rounds smashed into the hood of the UAZ, the fat 40mm VOG-25 grenade thumped out of the barrel of the grenade launcher and smashed into the side of the UZ-469B less than a second later. The roar of the grenade detonation momentarily drowned out the sound of gunfire in the area. The blast was quickly magnified by the fireball from the ignited gas tank. The PKM and the man operating it were both consumed by the blast and the flames.

Leaving the rest of the soldiers to his men, Stahl turned the hot muzzle of his weapon toward the officer standing up in the front seat of the other UAZ. As a stunned Lieutenant Yakubov stared at the sudden carnage around him, his driver shook off his own shock and stomped down on the gas just as Stahl pulled the trigger. Lieutenant Yabukov never felt himself fall from the moving vehicle as Stahl's final burst tore his chest open. Aiming the gun at the escaping driver, Stahl felt the hammer fall with a click on an empty chamber. Stahl could only watch the UAZ twist and turn madly as the driver desperately put distance and cover between himself and the weapons behind him. Bullets pinged and screamed off the surrounding rocks as the vehicle made it past the cover of the rocky hill.

Shouting at one of the men, the operator in the cab of the Bedford stood up and tossed a long, skeletal rifle through the air. Dropping his AK as he turned, the man snatched the SVD Dragunov sniper rifle out of the air as it tumbled toward him. Without pausing, the man ran for the top of the rocky rise in front of him, throwing off his respirator. Reaching the crest of the rise, the man dropped to one knee and pulled the long rifle up to his shoulder.

As Stahl and the rest of the men looked on, the man with the rifle paused and visibly forced himself still. A moment later, one loud shot rang out. Through the four-power PSO-1 telescopic sight on the SVD, the man saw a sudden splash of red spray across the windshield of the fleeing UAZ. The vehicle twisted suddenly to the side and rolled over violently. Bits and pieces of metal, cloth, and raw flesh scattered across the dusty roadbed.

The successful sniper turned and waved his rifle slowly over his head. Stahl was satisfied that the escaped vehicle was not going to help bring reinforcements to the obliterated squad. Looking across the area, Stahl could see scattered bodies lying still in death. Only one man was still moving, and that was the acid-washed soldier, who was still holding what was left of his face and moaning in a quiet gurgle.

Stepping out of the van, Haslett held an Uzi submachine gun in her hand. The sudden firefight was over well before she could arm herself and get back out of the van. She walked over to the man who had been so enthused about approaching her. Kicking his arms away, she looked down with a cold and distant expression at the destroyed face that would have given an average person nightmares for the rest of his life. But Veronica Haslett had seen much worse in her limited years. She pointed the muzzle of the submachine gun down and sent a quick burst into the red ruin in front of her.

Stahl walked up to where he had dropped the clamshell body of his briefcase. Bending down, he removed a second magazine from a clip inside the case, stood up and reloaded his weapon. Looking up at the sound of Haslett's shots, he watched the woman calmly turn from the body on the ground.

Seeing that Stahl was watching her with what looked like a puzzled expression on his face, she said simply, "The noise he was making was irritating."

Stahl just shrugged and turned to his men. The body of his man who had been ripped open by the PKM burst lay in the sand. Looking at the dead man for a long moment, Stahl showed no emotion at all.

Posenovich looked around and realized that he was still alive.

"You—you got them all," he said with a tremble of relief in his voice.

Looking up with a blank expression on his face, Stahl said, "Are you still alive?"

Without batting an eye, Stahl nonchalantly pointed his AKS-74U at Posenovich and pulled the trigger. The short burst fired in such an off-hand manner caught the Russian completely by surprise. He died with an open-eyed stare, as if he was shocked at seeing what death was really all about.

As the body crumpled to the ground next to him,

Stahl went over to the Toyota and reached into the front seat. Taking the Globalstar 1600 Satphone from its charging cradle, Stahl keyed in a long series of numbers. While he listened to the noises coming from the phone, he plugged it into the laptop computer that was still running on the front seat of the Toyota.

"Hello," Stahl said, "transportation? Yes, I would like to arrange an immediate pickup for an express package please. Yes, I said immediately. The address is as follows . . ."

Tapping a series of keys on the computer, Stahl sent an encrypted code for his exact location according to the AN/PSN-11 GPS receiver. At the other end of the conversation, the decoded numbers were being fed into an identical GPS receiver. No one who listened to the conversation would have heard anything more than a loud burst of static. By the time the static was decrypted, which was only a tiny mathematical possibility, Stahl would be long gone.

"Did you get all of that?" Stahl said. "Good. I shall await pickup."

Turning to his men, Stahl started to speak to them in the same unintelligible language Posenovich had heard.

"Will you please stop talking in that damned Gaelic?" Haslett said. "There's no one left about to hear you but me and I'm damned tired of hearing it."

"Very well, if it will please the lady," Stahl said with a bow. Straightening, he spoke sharply and with authority. "The helicopter is lifting off now. It will take it less than forty-five minutes to get here from Zhaslyk. The Mi-8 will be able to take us and the Toyota. Everything else will be abandoned according to plan.

"I want two of the cylinders taken out and moved.

Bury them both at least a full kilometer from here. Other than that, the hole is to be filled in and the demolition charges set."

"What about the bodies?" one of the men asked.

"Strip them of identification and destroy all traces," Stahl said. "Put them all in the vehicles with the demolitions. The blast will scatter their remains and no one will ever really know what happened here."

"Even Shaun?" one of the men asked.

"All of the bodies, I said. Veronica, how long will it take you to prepare the samples as I told you to?"

"I just have to heat the sealing wax," Haslett said. "That will take five minutes at most. I can prepare the samples while it is melting. But I can't confirm the strain for hours yet."

"That can't be helped at this stage," Stahl said. "We will have to accept what we have and wait for further tests later. There is no way to know how long we have right now. Those soldiers could be missed right away, or it could take days. That smoke column from their burning truck is rising enough that a search party could find it. I want Henry to stay on guard up on that hilltop with his rifle until the helicopter shows up. Then we pull out.

"Now move. We have less than forty-five minutes to say goodbye to Rebirth Island."

Chapter Five

The flight from the island had been rushed, but there were no signs of pursuit or that anyone had discovered the missing military patrol. The ride in the huge ex-Soviet helicopter had been a rough one. The pilot maintained a nap-of-the-earth posture for the trip, flying as fast and low as he could to avoid coming up on radar. Landing well outside of Zhaslyk, Stahl and his team unloaded and drove their Toyota back into the city. Along the way, they abandoned their identities as an oil exploration group. Every member of the group had several alternate sets of identity papers. The oil group had been simply a temporary cover identity for the trip to the island. It was a cutout that was eliminated with the burning of the papers that identified Stahl, Haslett, and the rest of their crew. Now, Stahl and Haslett were gone, and it was Samuel Woodrow and his wife Maxine who had come back with their crew after a several-night stay out in the desert.

Changing identities was a simple piece of tradecraft

that had well served Patrick Devlin, aka Stahl, Woodrow, and a host of past names, in his life as a career terrorist. During a mission such as this one, changing identities could become confusing, and care had to be taken to keep the names and corresponding identity papers together. But he was a master at the technique and could completely immerse himself into a new identity as easily as changing a shirt. Devlin's new partner, Christina Voorhees, aka Veronica Haslett and now Maxine Woodrow, was proving capable at maintaining the necessary deception.

It was only while in the safety of the Toyota Land Cruiser that tradecraft could be laid aside for the moment. Patrick Devlin could once again speak to the men he had been leading for years. The rest of the men in the Toyota were his most trusted teammates. They had all been conducting terrorist operations together for years. At first, they had only operated in Ireland and England against the British. But when the IRA no longer proved hard-line enough, they had become terrorists for hire. Now it was a matter of who could pay them the most, and they had just completed one of the hardest steps to the biggest payday of their careers.

Christina Voorhees had come into Devlin's crew as an expert technician. She had also proved herself more than willing and able to use violence as it suited her purpose. Long ago, Voorhees had decided that she would remain with the group to carry out their present operation. It was ambitious and well suited to her abilities as a specialized microbiologist. As far as she was concerned, any other motives she had would remain her own. For Devlin and his crew, the beautiful woman would be handled as a colorful poisonous snake might be: attractive and deadly.

In the city, the crew returned to the safe house that they had rented under their cover as a freelance film crew. All the landlord had been interested in was the hard currency they paid for the house with its secure, walled courtyard. The fact that they had paid for several months in advance made it very easy for the man to completely ignore the actions of the crazy Westerners who wanted to film the wildlife in the desert. He neither knew nor cared who the BBC were, or how they might be interested in the natural beauty of Uzbekistan.

The film-crew cover gave Devlin and his people freedom to come and go at all hours of the day or night. The loss of a man was inconvenient, but if anyone asked, one of their cameramen had remained in the field to get some additional footage and would take a train later to the airfield at Urganch. It was a loose end that concerned Devlin, but it couldn't be helped and they should be able to leave the country without any real difficulty. They only had to gather up their equipment cases and get to Urganch themselves to keep up with their deadlines. Their weapons had been left back in the desert and they were all traveling clean. It was the most vulnerable time that they would have during their travels. But each of the men and Voorhees were professionals. They had operated under stress before.

———

Nearly two days' worth of traveling put Devlin and his team in Italy, at Leonardo da Vinci airport in Rome. Devlin had taken the expression "All roads lead to Rome" to heart. It was here that the use of public roads, trains, and buses would allow his team to break up. Each person would make their own way through Europe and beyond. Not until later would they all gather in one place again. And that would be after Devlin had completed a very important and private negotiation with a very difficult and exacting customer.

For the time being, Devlin was operating as he preferred best, alone and anonymously. Throughout his career he always went to considerable lengths to maintain his low profile and protect his identity. There were no confirmed photographs of him on file anywhere, and he guarded his fingerprints even more jealously than his picture. Let Carlos the Jackal and other terrorists like him grab the headlines, splash their names all over the front pages of the world's newspapers. Those same names were also on the wanted posters of most of the world's police and intelligence agencies. Right now, Carlos was rotting in a French prison while his compatriots rotted in the ground. Devlin was still in the game and moving freely—around Antwerp, the second-largest city in Belgium and home to one of the finest harbors in Europe.

The city still held the traditional charm of Old World Europe. Yet, the fact that it was home to a major port and financial centers was not lost on Devlin. Flemish was just one of the languages he spoke well, and he could pass for a local. These were some of the reasons that Devlin had negotiated to make Antwerp the site of the final meeting with his most important clients.

Masquerading as Jan Koenraad, a dark-haired, goatee-wearing dealer in antiques, Devlin sat and drank his cup of hot chocolate with quiet pleasure at a sidewalk café. Chocolate was practically a national treasure in Belgium, and Jan Koenraad appeared to be just one of many people sitting and enjoying their hot beverage on a cool spring day. The sun was bright and the location warm and comfortable. It also had an excellent view of a nondescript building in the diamond district. The building held a number of offices, one of which was of particular interest to one chocolate connoisseur sitting in the café.

Having held his spot at varying times during the last several days, Devlin had been able to observe the comings and goings centering on the building that interested him. In particular, he hadn't noticed any pattern in the vehicles or people near the building. No repeat customer at the café stayed long enough to raise Devlin's suspicions, and the waiters only took enough notice of him to provide good service. If the office building was under observation, they were good enough that Devlin couldn't detect them.

The principle of the company that Devlin had to meet was more than simply a cautious man. But then Devlin was selling more than a normal product. Leaving sufficient cash in euros on the table to cover his bill and leave a tip, he picked up his briefcase in gloved hands, stood up, and crossed the street. In a few moments, he was inside the door of the building and heading down the first-floor hallway. The small brass plaque next to the door read IMBAH DIAMOND BROKERS. Above the plaque was a metal grill inset into the wall; below it was a small push button. Pressing the button, Devlin stepped back and waited while looking at the closed-circuit TV camera set unobtrusively above the door.

"Yes?" came an unidentifiably accented tinny voice from the speaker grill.

"I have come looking for some jewelry," Devlin said into the speaker. "Perhaps some gold work out of Saudi Arabia?"

"You are mistaken, sir," the voice said. "We are not a commercial jeweler."

"Well, then, some diamonds from the Sudan? I have come a long way."

"Such items are extremely rare and command a high price, sir. Many are searching for such."

"I would only be interested in the finest and rarest of gems available from Arabia."

"Please come in." The lock on the door buzzed electronically.

Pressing on the door, Devlin found it unlocked and was able to push the heavy steel door open easily. The office that was in front of him barely qualified as such. There was a single countertop at the back in front of a curtained doorway and a small table in the center of the room. The table had a high-intensity light sitting on the black velvet cloth that covered the top. The two chairs on either side of the table completed the furnishings. A very dark-colored black man, his skin wrinkled from a harsh sun, stepped from behind the cloth-curtained doorway behind the counter.

"I believe I am expected," Devlin said.

"You have something for me?" the black man said quietly.

"No, my delivery is for others."

"Please leave your briefcase on the table and come with me."

"I would rather not."

"It will be brought to you shortly."

There wasn't any reason to protest the minor security

matter very much. Devlin laid his case on the table.

"Could you open it, please?"

Snapping the locks, he opened the lid of the case and stepped back.

"If you would follow me, please." The man stepped back through the curtain.

Pushing past the curtain, Devlin found that it was actually a pair of curtains, one after the other, the second feeling very heavy and inflexible, as if it was made of some metal mesh covered with cloth. Beyond the curtain was another room, this one very brightly lit with just a table and chair in it. Not a single gleam of light slipped past the heavy set of curtains to the outer office. On the table was a desktop computer system, the screen showing a flowing geometric screensaver. Above the screen was the bulbous shape of a camera.

Sitting down where the man indicated, Devlin faced the screen. While he watched with one eyebrow raised just a bit in question, the man reached down and tapped a key.

"This room is shielded from all forms of electronic invasion," he said, "Conversations will be very private. The doorway holds scanner and devices that render any listening or recording device inoperable."

With that said, the man quietly stepped back out of the room into the office.

In spite of the man having apparently activated the computer, nothing had happened other than the screen turning blue. Waiting quietly, Devlin, aka Koenraad, continued playing the security game. They had every reason to be cautious. They also had more than enough reasons to want to complete their negotiations with him.

A few minutes passed and the black man walked back into the room holding the briefcase.

Setting it on the table in front of Devlin, he said, "It is clean. There are no listening, recording, or tracking devices that I can detect. No weapons either. There is only a newspaper, some writing instruments, a leather case of cigars, a small box of wooden matches, and a cigar cutter."

Then the man tapped a few more keys on the computer keyboard and once again left the room.

The monitor now lit up in split-screen mode. On the left-hand side was the bearded face of a man wearing dark glasses and the white kaffiyeh of a devout Muslim. The right side of the screen showed a thin-faced bearded man also wearing the white headdress. The brown eyes of the thin man looked steadily out of the screen, as if peering deep into Devlin's own eyes. Even if he hadn't expected to see him, Devlin would have immediately recognized the most wanted man in the world—Osama bin Laden.

"This is my paymaster, Jamal al Salim," Osama said from the screen, in Arabic. "He has been with me since the beginning and I hold him closer than a brother. It is he who will give you your instructions and forward you funds. I will not meet with you again unless you fail."

"Very well," Devlin said, responding in flawless Arabic. "But I will need no instructions. I expect payment of fifty million U.S. to be placed in the financial institution of my choosing. This is the cost of the weapon I have described to you. That is not negotiable. The funds will be used to forward the most visible and frightening attack against the United States since your organization's actions in September 2001. I can guarantee you a spectacular action that will be witnessed by the world. A greater body count and more news coverage than the downing of the World Trade towers. With the completion of that attack, an additional fifty million will be deposited in my accounts."

"Your cost is extraordinary!" Salim said, his face turning darker as his blood pressure rose.

"There is a saying," Devlin said. " 'You get what you pay for.' "

"The nonsense spouted by this infidel means less than nothing," Salim said to Osama. Then to Devlin: "Your demand is outrageous. The whole of our September eleventh plan cost but five hundred thousand. And the results of those faithful were spectacular. You are nothing but a mercenary, and a nonbeliever. A *kafir*—an infidel."

"Yes," Devlin agreed, "but a nonbeliever with something to sell. The September eleventh attacks were successful, and far more costly to you than the price I am asking. The results of those attacks against the World Trade Center and the Pentagon not only cost you all of the men involved. It also cost you your base of operations in Afghanistan and the support you received from Iraq. Your international operating network is in a shambles. You haven't been able to conduct a successful operation against the United States for years now."

"What guarantee do we have that your boasts are even true?" Salim said. "What are the details of this weapon of yours? How destructive is it? And what kind of attack are you planning?"

"I have given the details of my plans to one person," Devlin said quietly. "They are not going to be repeated here."

The soft voice of Osama came over the computer speakers.

"I know the details of this attack," bin Laden said. "And I know the weapon that is going to be used. Both are more than acceptable to me."

"But what of this *harbis*? This nonbeliever?" Salim said. "He is *kufar*, in fact, he is less than a nonbeliever—he has faith only in gold."

"Not so," Devlin said, "I also have faith in dollars, yen, Swiss francs, diamonds, and platinum."

"See how he mocks even our insults," Salim said. "His presence is an insult to all of our Shuhadan brothers."

"It is true that I have no intention of joining the ranks of your martyrs," Devlin said. "But that isn't where my value to your cause lies. I will live to perform my mission, complete my obligations, and expect the balance of my payment."

"Are you certain he can deliver what he promises, oh, Prince?" Salim said. "We are the followers of the true faith. The believers in Allah, all Praise be upon His Name. All this one believes in is base money."

"*Alaihi 's-salam*," Devlin said, echoing the same phrase Osama said. He repeated it in English: "Peace be with Him."

"So, you know how to show the proper respect," Salim said. "It proves nothing. How can you show us where your heart is?"

"You know about the sniper attack at the West Bank checkpoint in March 2002?" Devlin said.

"All know about that action," Salim said. "The brave fighters of the al-Aqsa Martyr Brigades took their revenge on the Jews who invaded and hold their land."

"Then you don't know about that attack," Devlin said. "There were seven soldiers and three civilians killed. What was never told to the public was that one of the people killed worked for the Mossad. He was identified by the al-Aqsa Brigade, but an outsider did the shooting. I know, because I was that outsider."

"That is an easy thing to say," Osama said in his soft voice. He had been impressed with Devlin's knowledge of the Islamic culture, but wasn't going to show his opinion for the moment.

"Then what isn't an easy thing to say," Devlin said, "is that the weapon left behind was the same caliber as that used to shoot the victims. But it did not match the bullets left in any of them. A bolt-action Mosin-Nagant is an easy weapon to leave behind, even a 91/30 sniper rifle. A good suppressed SVD is not. That was never made public."

Looking directly at Salim, Devlin continued, "I may be a mercenary, but that means I expect to get paid. And the only way I can insure that is to provide truly quality service. For what I ask, you will not only receive a great weapon, one that will strike fear in all of your enemies, but also the means and knowledge to produce it. This is the kind of weapon that will make anyone who tries to retaliate against you pause and rethink their plans. And then there's the bonus I've offered.

"I know how much you've offered for a nuclear device. Everyone in my business knows that. But not even the Russian mob could get you what you wanted. You have paid more than seven hundred million for twenty nuclear suitcase bombs from ex-KGB men and the Chechen Mafia. It is known among a few that those bombs were faked and that the sellers have disappeared. You spent seventy-five million for twelve kilograms of uranium from a Ukrainian arms dealer. Not enough to build a bomb, and it was low-grade material that was later captured by the Americans in Afghanistan. What I'm offering is a sure thing for the cost of three fake bombs. And that includes an attack against your most hated target."

Over the secure computer network, the thin, bearded face of Osama bin Laden looked out from the screen at the man sitting in the room. He could see and hear everything that was being said. Even though bin Laden could have understood him in any of several languages, Devlin, speaking in Arabic, had shown good manners and ability. That mark of respect carried some weight with bin Laden, but not as much weight as what Devlin was offering.

Unlike the calm, quiet demeanor he presented to the world during his carefully orchestrated interviews and videotapes, Osama bin Laden had eyes that burned in his face with the glare of a fanatic, or of a junkie seeing the drug he desperately craves. "I have heard enough," he said in a loud, strong voice. "You shall receive your pay as you have asked. A contact address will be given to you so arrangements can be made over the computer lines.

"But listen, and listen well, *kafir.*" Bin Laden's voice dropped to a hiss. "Those who thought to cheat me of the power that is rightfully that of Islam are not around to cheat anyone again. Neither are their families or anyone who mattered to them. Inside Chechnya, Russia, or the home of the Great Satan, none are safe from the rightful retribution of the Base. We reward our friends with hospitality and riches, but we are terrible to our enemies. Remember that."

Chapter Six

Identities were now the tools needed for Devlin's further travels—identities and the proper paperwork to go with them. For this operation he had to leave a cold trail behind him. Once the mission had been successfully completed, all the money in the world wouldn't save him if the leadership of the United States sniffed him out. They had invaded a country to try and capture the man Devlin had just been talking to. The fact that the conversation took place over a secure, untraceable, computer line demonstrated how much caution bin Laden was taking regarding his own health and safety. Others could be martyrs for him, but he was going to keep going even as governments fell because of him. There had been a price on bin Laden's head of $25,000,000 until the U.S. government had raised it to $50,000,000. That much money would have tempted even Devlin, if he could have pulled off the hit and gotten away.

Inside the thick leather covers of several very old books, Devlin had hidden some of his very best identity papers. The Jan Koenraad cover as a dealer in antiques was an excellent reason for him to be carrying such weighty tomes. As paper hidden inside paper, the identity documents would remain invisible to any normal search short of physically tearing the books apart.

The years Devlin had spent traveling and penetrating the borders of other countries, and breaching their security gave him another set of skills that helped him reach this point. Now it was almost relaxing to approach customs again and slip into a role he was more than comfortable with. Only the names had changed.

"And what is the purpose of your visit to Canada, Mr. Koenraad?" The Canadian customs inspector asked after examining Devlin's passport and declaration form.

"Pleasure mostly, maybe a little business," Devlin said. "I have been told for years that Toronto is one of the most beautiful cities in North America, and I wanted to finally see it for myself. That and a little antique shopping."

"And these books are part of your business?" the inspector asked, holding up one of the old tomes.

"No, just my own reading is all," Devlin said. "No real market for those, but I enjoy them. Nothing has quite the feel of an old book."

The inspector looked up at the smiling man, relaxed and appearing completely at ease. On the inspection table in front of him were the man's open briefcase and carry-on suitcase. Nothing in the way of contraband was there and the books had been mentioned on his declaration form.

"Welcome to Canada," the inspector said as he stamped Devlin's Dutch passport. Handing the documents back, he said, "Enjoy your stay."

"Thank you very much," Devlin replied, "I expect to."

But the inspector had already turned his attention to the next person in line. Devlin closed the cover of his briefcase on the two old books, his leather cigar case, and a scattering of smaller items. Picking up the case and his carry-on, Devlin walked out of the inspection area and into the maze that was Toronto's Pearson International Airport.

Stopping only long enough to exchange some euros for Canadian currency, Devlin stepped outside of the busy main terminal and hailed a taxi. The trip was much shorter than the cab driver would have liked. His customer didn't want to travel the 27 kilometers into downtown Toronto, instead asking to be dropped off at the Yorkdale subway station. But the man paid a decent tip and carried his own bags. Without a second thought, the cabdriver dropped him at his destination and drove off.

Instead of taking the cab and creating a paper trail to his final destination, Devlin chose to take the subway system into the city. The clean, efficient, and completely anonymous train took Devlin and dozens of other passengers deep into the downtown area of the sprawling city of Toronto.

The desk clerk at the Royal York Hotel was pleased to accept Mr. Koenraad as their guest for the weekend. After checking out his room and dropping off his bags, Devlin stepped out for some quick shopping. The Eaton Mall was a huge enclosed shopping area in downtown Toronto and long enough that it boasted two subway stops. One of the primary rules of tradecraft, a rule Devlin knew well, centered around knowing the area that you were going to operate in. Not only had Devlin memorized maps and major routes around Toronto and southern Ontario, he had directly familiarized himself with the areas over the last several years. Stopping at a major shopping mall and making some innocuous purchases was simple, and an easy way for an experienced operative to make certain that he hadn't been detected and followed.

He spent a long, comfortable night at the hotel following a leisurely meal a few blocks away at the Irish Embassy Pub and Grill on Yonge Street. The irony of eating at a restaurant named the Irish Embassy wasn't lost on Devlin. Neither was the good food and comfortable surroundings that reminded him of a country it was very unlikely he would ever see again. He would have to accept the simple comfort of a vast amount of money in foreign bank accounts to keep him well in his upcoming retirement.

Checking out of the Royal York the next day, Devlin prepared to move on to the next part of his infiltration into the United States. His support network was limited, but the contacts he had available were solid. The best of the local contacts was Lizabetti Cifani, an ex-member of the *Brigate Rosse,* or Red Brigades, a terrorist organization from Italy. Having grown disillusioned with the Red Brigades' failed communist ideals—and the bulk of their leadership having either been killed or arrested and in prison—Cifani had drifted through the terrorist underground of Europe and North Africa. It was after meeting Devlin that she gave her allegiance to the Provisional Irish Republican Army (PIRA), which Devlin operated with. It was through Devlin's association years later with the "Real IRA" (RIRA), a more violent splinter group broken off from the PIRA, that Cifani moved from active terrorist operations to overseas support.

It was on a weapons-purchasing trip to Libya that Devlin had first come across Cifani and developed a relationship with the beautiful woman. He had helped her relocate to Canada, where she operated underground to move funds and materials for RIRA actions in the United Kingdom. Over time, she had come to know Devlin's mercenary attitudes, and she had picked up some of his philosophy herself.

She would have the latest information for him regarding travel into the United States, as well as access to a safe vehicle and new identity papers. Lizabetti was also expecting to share in the bounty of Devlin's latest operation, something that would help her completely disappear into society.

Leaving a randomly chosen alley Dumpster near the Royal York richer by a carry-on bag, Devlin slung his new soft-sided overnight bag over his left shoulder. The contents of his briefcase had been transferred to the bag, the case left in another alley. The local street population would soon remove what little evidence remained that Jan Koenraad was in the country. The ashes of Koenraad's official documents had already joined the anonymity of the sewers in the lavatory where Devlin had applied his current disguise. The Canadian driver's license for Mike Borders, as well as an assortment of random local pocket materials, would be enough to satisfy any cursory examination of Devlin's present identity. A heavy broad mustache, matching dark eyebrows, and unkempt black hair blended with a pair of worn jeans and work shirt to give Borders the appearance of just one of a thousand other Canadian workers moving about the Greater Toronto area.

The mass transit system of Toronto worked very well to move Devlin from place to place. Reaching his destination took less than forty-five minutes, including the normal switching of trains and other tail-breaking techniques that Devlin had done so often that they were almost second nature for him. It was just another local who pushed the button on the doorway of the apartment building, the button under the name "M. Curgacio."

"Yes?" came a sultry voice after a moment's wait.

Instantly dropping the Canadian accent and mannerisms he had affected as part of his disguise, Devlin simply said, "Cifani, Naples."

A short pause followed the announcement of Lizabetti's name and her hometown. Then an almost breathless voice came back over the intercom.

"Sand," she said.

"Tripoli," Devlin returned, giving the final countersign identifying himself and the place where they had first met.

"Come up," the voice said, and the buzzer sounded as the door unlocked.

The voice sounded a little more breathless than Devlin had remembered it. He went into the lobby and to the bank of elevators. In minutes, he was standing in front of the door of apartment 608. In case there might be another person in the apartment, he slipped back into his Mike Borders persona. A physical change came over Devlin as he took on the role. His shoulders slumped, his posture slouched. Even his eyes seemed to dull and sink a bit. He was just another easygoing working schlub standing in a hallway.

The door to 608 opened almost as soon as he knocked on it. Standing in the doorway was a woman of deep Mediterranean beauty, her oval face and high cheekbones framed by a mane of long, lustrous, raven black hair. A single strand of white pearls pulled the eyes to the line of her neck, and then the look would continue down to the voluptuous figure in a simple formfitting black dress. The only thing that marred the nearly flawless classic beauty in front of him was the fleeting haunted look in the brown eyes that gazed back at Devlin, a look that vanished as curiosity swept over the face of the woman holding the door.

"Yes?" came a restrained voice.

"Lizabetti," Devlin said in his normal voice, "it's me. Let me in."

"Please," she said breathlessly, "please, come in."

As Devlin went through the doorway and into the apartment, years and pounds seemed to melt away from him as he dropped his role of the working man and went back to being himself. The changes in his stature fell away even as his bag dropped to the floor of the living room. He was still sharply alert, taking in every detail of the clean, neat apartment. It was furnished simply but with taste. And the layout of the room suggested only a single person lived in the place. Things apparently hadn't changed a great deal in Cifani's life since Devlin had last seen her several years earlier.

"Lizabetti," he said. "It has been too long to have been away from you."

"Patrick," Lizabetti said with only a hint of an Italian accent in her voice, "it is good to see you, but you have changed so much."

"A little surgery," he said, "and a little makeup. Nothing that changed me for what I am inside. You have what I need?"

"Ah," she said. "The same Devlin, always to the point. Yes, I have documents, a travel itinerary, pocket litter, funds, and transportation. Everything you should need for a successful crossing into the United States. Are you hungry? Should I fix you something to eat?"

"No," Devlin said as he took the woman into his arms. "I'm not hungry for food."

They embraced passionately, melting into each other's arms. After a long, lingering kiss, Lizabetti pulled back and turned. Stepping to the door of the bedroom nearby, she glanced over her shoulder and entered the room. She did not close the door.

Devlin followed and shut the door behind them.

———

Hours later, Devlin was in the bathroom, shaving after having taken a hot shower. The water, in combination with a special shampoo, had removed the last traces of dye from his hair. A little work with a comb, brush, and additional treatments had changed his hair to chestnut brown with silver highlights at the temples and sides. It made him look older and distinguished. The color and style was also a good match for several of his identity sets. Only the addition of facial hair, glasses, and padding in his cheeks and nostrils was necessary to complete his transformation.

Standing at the doorway of the bathroom, wearing only his Mike Borders shirt and nothing else, was Lizabetti. She was holding two steaming cups of coffee in her hands. She held one out to Devlin when she caught his eyes looking at her in the mirror in front of him.

"You are in danger, you know," she said as he took the offered cup.

"This has never been an easy business," he said warily and took a sip. All of his personal warnings were going off now, as he watched the woman's body language and listened to her talk.

"No, I mean something worse than normal," she said. "Billy Connolly knows you took the money from the bank robbery to finance your own unauthorized mission."

Billy Connolly was second in the command cell for the splinter group. The commander, Shaun Connolly, had been captured by the British and charged in connection with the August 2, 1998, bombing at Omagh in Ireland. He was serving a long prison term and his brother Billy had taken over command for the time being. Financing for the group had come from the proceeds of extortion against businesses, as well as other straightforward criminal enterprises such as bank robbery. The last robbery in December had netted the group nearly $50,000,000 in cash, a seemingly tremendous windfall for the terrorists and their cause.

The money taken in the robbery was mostly in currency printed and issued by the bank itself. Deciding to absorb the cost in order to thwart the terrorists' plan, the bank ordered the return of all of its currency then in circulation. Exchanging all old bills for newly minted currency of a different design, the bank had suddenly made most of the stolen cash little more than expensive waste paper. The only stolen money that hadn't been affected by the currency exchange was the few million dollars in foreign bills that had been taken. That cash had been barely enough to finance Devlin's planned operation. Turning to bin Laden was the only other way he had of obtaining all of the needed cash to complete the mission, as well as finance his upcoming retirement.

Now Billy Connolly had found him out.

"Why are you telling me this?" Devlin asked as he quickly weighed his options.

"If you give the money back," Lizabetti said, "maybe he will call off his dogs. All he wants to do is buy the release of his brother, either legally or by breaking him out. Surely, you can understand that? He knew you would be coming to me, so he asked me to tell him when you arrived."

"And did you?" Devlin asked as he picked up a small spray can from his toilet kit. The palms of his hands were now covered with a clear, flexible plastic, much like an instant bandage that dried almost immediately. The spray had been developed by the Soviet KGB. It was waterproof, ordorless, and resistant to most solvents. Besides protecting the hands, the spray prevented the user from leaving any fingerprints behind.

He looked at Lizabetti standing in the doorway. She had set her coffee cup down on a counter and had tears streaming down her face.

"Of course not," she said. "But he will find out. He always does. Billy knows you took your own crew with you. He isn't stupid—he knows they are absolutely loyal to you. But he also knows about some South African woman who's working with you. Does this woman mean something to you? Is she someone special in your life?"

"Only in that she can help me complete the greatest

operation of my life," Devlin said. He talked while once more reaching into his toilet kit. There was a small flexible envelope of heavy aluminized plastic material. The body of the envelope said DIOR, and there was the symbol of a spray container. Carefully tearing open the bag, difficult even with his strong hands, Devlin took out a slim aerosol container about half the size of a fountain pen. The tube said DIOR and EAU DE TOILETTE on its side. Turning back to the mirror, Devlin spoke to Lizabetti while looking at her past his own reflection.

"So, he doesn't know about me being here right now?" Devlin said.

"No, I said I didn't tell him," Lizabetti said. "But he has everyone in the network looking for you. It's only because you used your own means of getting here that you haven't been spotted yet."

Devlin turned to face Lizabetti.

"So I can't use any of the identity materials you have for me to get into the United States? Passport, driver's license, credit cards, pocket litter, all of it is useless."

"Of course it isn't," Lizabetti said. "The documents are good, and there is a car downstairs in the parking garage. You will have no trouble driving into the States. Or we can go over together, darling. All you have to do is give him the money back. I'm sure that will make everything work out all right."

"No," Devlin said. "It won't. You see, I don't have the money anymore to give back to him. And I have to go on alone."

As he spoke to the woman, Devlin took a step closer to her. She was within arm's reach, but he wasn't making any threatening moves, only toying with the aerosol can in his hand. Then he popped the cap off and suddenly stuck it in the woman's face. As he did so, Devlin held his breath.

Lizabetti gasped as the spray went off. The hydrocyanic acid was colorless, highly volatile, and extremely poisonous. Her gasp of surprise pulled the mist deep into her lungs. She fell to the floor, her eyes wide with shock, and was unconscious in seconds.

Darting to the light switch next to the door, Devlin flipped on the overhead exhaust fan. Still holding his breath, he grabbed his toilet kit and ran from the room. Even in the safe air of the living room, Devlin felt a momentary dizziness. He pulled a small, cloth-covered ampoule from his toilet kit and snapped it between his fingers. Breathing deeply, he drew the amyl nitrite fumes in. His heart was racing, but the dizziness had passed. Going back into the bedroom, Devlin dressed while waiting for the fumes in the bathroom to fully clear.

He pulled on a pair of thin calfskin gloves and began sterilizing the apartment of any trace of his having been there. The package of documents and keys Lizabetti had waiting for him on the kitchen table went into his bag. He couldn't trust anything or anyone in his old network, and that included all of the papers he had in the envelope. But leaving the package would have been a giveaway that someone unusual had been at the apartment. He would dispose of the materials later.

As he worked, Devlin considered his options. He'd had a backup plan in place well before he came to the apartment. It was riskier and would take longer than the original plan would have, but that couldn't be helped. With his old contact network compromised, it was his safest option.

Over a very short while, Devlin cleaned the apartment

completely. He emptied and washed his coffee cup, putting it away after he had dried it. He even pulled the intimate wastes from their lovemaking from the wastebaskets, bundling it up along with the other materials he was going to destroy. In the bathroom, he pulled the shirt off Lizabetti's body, wiping her down with a washcloth to remove most of any remaining cloth fibers. Then he put out a clean washcloth he found in a cupboard and placed the used one in his bag. He poured bleach down the sink and tub drains, following it with a deluge of water. There would be no traces of his DNA in those sources or anyplace else. As a last touch, Devlin dropped Lizabetti's coffee cup onto the tile floor of the bathroom. As the cup shattered and splashed its cold contents onto the floor and the woman's cooling body, he turned and walked away without a second look. With all evidence of his being there removed, Devlin carefully left the apartment building, making sure he had locked the apartment door. Heading back up the street the way he had come, he returned to the subway station.

Chapter Seven

Following his backup plan, Devlin returned to downtown Toronto, almost all the way back to the Royal York Hotel. Across the street from the hotel was Union Station. There, Devlin would be able to take the VIA Rail into the United States by way of the Sarnia/Port Huron railway tunnel. For this border crossing, he was going to use his best documents, the absolutely authentic papers for Peter Gregg, a U.S. citizen who lived in a suburb of Chicago. He had a passport that was several years old, an Illinois driver's license, credit cards, a social security card—all the trappings of a real person that Devlin had been carefully saving for several years. Bills had been paid on time from a post office box at a forwarding service, license renewals were conducted the same way. He even had a good credit history. It was a classic case of stolen identity, from a person who would never be expected to complain about it. And the changes to his appearance to match that of the passport and driver's license photos were minimal but satisfactory. In fact, changing his appearance to look a little older or heavier than the photos and documents suggested was a good idea. It was a natural part of everyday life that the pictures in such documents didn't always look like you.

The identity had been expensive and difficult to maintain over the years, but it was going to prove worth it now. Devlin, aka Gregg, was going to join the throng of people heading back to the States after spending the weekend in Toronto. There was even a special theater train that ran between Chicago and Toronto, catering to just such a crowd. And Devlin was now part of that crowd as the train left Union Station.

One of the drawbacks to the plan was that the trip would take at least eleven hours. It would be safe travel. It was unlikely that anyone would miss Lizabetti until Monday at the earliest, possibly not for several days after that. Having bought his train ticket with cash, there was no paper trail connecting Devlin with Lizabetti. The long trip on the train would give him a chance to catch up on sleep.

It was hours later that the conductor came down the aisle of the train. His call woke Devlin, who was instantly alert.

"Sarnia," the conductor called, "Sarnia, last stop."

"Sir," Devlin said as the conductor came by. "I thought this train went all the way to Chicago. That's what I bought my ticket for."

"It does, sir," the conductor said. "The Americans have closed the train tunnel to passenger traffic again, that's all. With the terrorist alerts, they do that more often than not these days. We have a bus here that will take you across the Blue Water Bridge into the States. You'll go through customs as normal and then be taken to the train station. You can board the Blue Water Limited right there in Port Huron and it will take you on to Chicago."

Devlin knew not to press for any more information and make himself stand out. Enough of the other passengers were listening to the conductor's explanation that his question seemed to have been on a lot of people's mind.

"Pain in the ass, I say," a young kid with a backpack said. A sticker on the pack stated, DON'T BLAME ME—I VOTED FOR KERRY, along with another extolling the virtues of Ann Arbor and the University of Michigan.

Devlin didn't find the comments of the young man of any interest whatsoever. But the youngster demonstrated an amazing naiveté of the world beyond his little cloister as he continued his tirade.

"All Bush ever does is bring up his supposed war on terrorism any time he wants to clamp down on our freedoms. This thing at the border is just another example. Like someone is going to try and smuggle a WMD into Michigan from Canada. They haven't stopped one terrorist attack that they've been able to prove. It's just a smokescreen for his fascist Republican cronies, is all."

In spite of the seriousness of his situation, Devlin smiled at the words of the idiot behind him. Perhaps the young man would like to discuss his ideas with Devlin's Muslim friends on the Internet. Devlin imagined that that would be fun to watch, until bin Laden had the young idiot killed.

———

The bus ride hadn't gone on very long before they crossed the Blue Water Bridge into Michigan. Looking out over the vast expanse of Lake Huron to the north, Devlin couldn't help but compare it to the disaster that the Aral Sea had become. Sometimes, the Americans were too ignorant of their own riches to realize just how good they had it, and how so many others in the world hated them for it.

The customs building was at the foot of the bridge, and the handful of passengers on the bus who were going on into the United States were asked to get their bags and come into the building.

It was a short line and Devlin was soon in front of a customs official.

"Citizenship?" was the first question.

"U.S.," Devlin answered, passing over his blue-covered passport booklet.

"Where are you from?" the official asked as he thumbed through the booklet. Travel between Canada and the States didn't require a stamp, so there wasn't anything in the passport to give Devlin away.

"Lake Zurich," Devlin said, "North of Chicago."

"Anything to declare?"

"No."

Clean shaven and well dressed, Devlin looked to be just an average person who had spent some time sightseeing in Canada. Being relaxed and open helped the ruse. He was not the kind of person normally targeted by customs, and didn't expect any problems. Then the customs agent pulled over Devlin's bag.

"Open the bag please."

Pulling the zipper back, Devlin pulled open the case. All of the papers and materials he had taken from Lizabetti's were long since turned to ash and gone forever. Even the sheets he had taken when he stripped and made the bed had been stuffed into paper bags and placed in several Dumpsters around Toronto. One of the books was gone, the cover having given up the Gregg documents.

The inspector picked up Devlin's cigar case and pulled the end off it. Three glass tubes, each nearly an inch in diameter and almost eight inches long. The tubes had a heavy gold-colored hard wax seal over the corks closing the mouths.

"No cutter?" the man asked.

"Lost it in Toronto," Devlin said. "It was just a cheap plastic one. I can get another easily enough." He wasn't about to tell the man that he left it in Europe before boarding a flight as Koenraad.

For some reason, the man just wouldn't let go of the situation.

"These aren't Cuban, are they? Those are banned in the United States."

"No," Devlin said easily. "These are Gurkha Grand Reserve Churchills. They're available right here in the States."

The customs inspector looked at Devlin, then pulled out one of the tubes.

"Open it, please," he said.

"They're soaked in Cognac before they're closed," Devlin said easily. "So the seal is a good one. I don't have my cutter."

The inspector reached into his pocket and pulled out a pocketknife. Unfolding one of the blades, he cut away the thick seal and opened the tube. Pulling out the cigar, he rolled it between his fingers. Feeling nothing unusual, he held the cigar up to his nose and sniffed it. All he could smell was the odor of good tobacco and a slight scent of cognac. There was nothing else he could see about the cigar, and it wasn't marked as being a

Havana or anything that was banned. Slipping the cigar back into the tube, he closed the case and handed it back to Devlin.

"You can return to the bus," the inspector said. "They will be leaving shortly."

Not as shortly as you will be leaving this veil of tears, Devlin thought. "Thanks," he said, "have a good day."

You won't have many more, Devlin once more thought as he headed to the bus. In a short while, he was at the train station and was able to spend some time scrubbing his hands in the lavatory. In his bag, he also had a bottle of very strong hand sanitizer, nothing unusual for someone traveling a lot.

The only thing that was keeping Devlin from worrying about himself much was that he knew he was fully immunized against anthrax. He doubted that the inspector was. A few days on the antibiotic Ciprofloxacin would help insure against a slight exposure if he started taking it right away. There was a small bottle of the antibiotic pills in his bag. The anthrax samples that had been carefully sealed inside of the cigars would be a seed culture for producing the Soviet bioweapon strain. The fragrant sniff the inspector had given the cigar had probably sealed his death warrant.

Once on board the Blue Water Limited, Devlin had little to do until the end of the line in Chicago. He reclined his seat and promptly went back to sleep.

———

Boom, boom, boom.

The pounding on the doorway echoed through the building. From far in the back, a voice called out, "We're not open yet. Go away."

The pounding continued until, finally, a large man came out of the gloom in the back and stepped to the partially glass-fronted door.

"I said we were closed, mate," He growled in an angry voice. "So quit your blasted knocking, or . . ."

The man known as William Shaughnessy swallowed his threat as he recognized who was standing on the other side of the door. He couldn't twist the locks fast enough to make up for his embarrassment and fear.

"Sorry, sir," Shaughnessy said, "I didn't know it was . . ."

"Richard. Richard Kennedy," Devlin said as he stuck out his hand. "Shake it, in case someone can see us," he whispered.

"Glad to meet you, Mr. Kennedy," Shaughnessy said as he shook the offered hand enthusiastically. "I'm afraid the Freedom Pub and Brewery isn't open right now."

"Well, I'm new in the area," Devlin said. "And I thought I would like to find out the kind of places that are around. This pub is a little off the beaten track, but it looks good. Can I get a tour of the place?"

"Sure," Shaughnessy said as he stepped back and held the door open.

As soon as Devlin had stepped through the door, Shaughnessy twisted the lock, throwing the deadbolt.

"Why have you been closed?" Devlin asked as he looked into the bar. The room was long but not very wide. On the right-hand side, the dark wood bar extended half its length. Beyond it was a group of tables in front of a set of swinging doors leading to a kitchen beyond the far wall. The corridor on the right side of the kitchen led into the back of the establishment, where

Shaughnessy had been working. Along the right-hand wall and extending to the back wall was a row of enclosed booths. In all, it was a nice looking place, in spite of being dark and empty and having the smell of bleach in the air.

"When you missed making contact and we didn't hear from you," Shaughnessy said, "Lee suggested we close the place just for a couple of days and tell people we were sterilizing and cleaning out the systems in the back. That also let us tell the waitstaff and cook to come in later in the week."

"So where is Mary Lee now?" Devlin said referring to one of Christina Voorhees' cover identities. She would be in charge of the operation at the brewery until Devlin himself showed up. Obviously, she had exercised that authority.

"She's running the secured fermenter in the back room." Shaughnessy said.

"Show me."

As they walked the length of the business, Devlin was looking at the decorations on the wall, mostly posters of different brands of beer. There was a single television hanging from a bracket on the ceiling at one end of the bar. As far as Devlin could see, the TV was the only form of entertainment for the bar.

"The place looks good," Devlin said, "but how is it working as a business?"

"That's the funny thing," Shaughnessy said. "We're quiet and out of the way, a plain menu from the kitchen and nothing fancy. And the place is turning popular. This brew pub could turn a profit without much trying."

"This isn't your father's place back in Dublin," Devlin said as he stopped and faced Shaughnessy. "It's a business cover, nothing more. Don't get carried away about making it popular. That could prove difficult."

"No, sir," Shaughnessy said quickly. He knew that crossing Devlin could prove to have sudden consequences. "No, if it was like that, we could just start watering down the beer or whatever it took. It just seems that a lot of people from the city were looking for a very quiet place they could have a brew and a chat. There has proven to be an advantage to our success, so far. We've had no trouble at all with the licensing inspectors. They want new businesses around here. And the customer flow allows us to move materials in and out more easily without drawing any real attention. That worked out well, since Lee wanted to move the processing facility off site."

Devlin had turned away and continued to move to the back of the building as Shaughnessy talked. They were passing the back of the kitchen on their left and went by two push-open doors marked MEN and WOMEN.

"She moved the processing site?" Devlin said. "Without my express permission?"

"She told me it was necessary for the processing equipment to be installed away from here," Shaughnessy said to Devlin's back. He was relieved that anger on the part of the terrorist boss for any plan change wouldn't be directed at him, at least.

They had reached the back of the building, where the space opened up to its full width. Devlin was looking at the machinery and equipment spread out in the area. There were stainless-steel pipes and wiring conduit along the walls and ceiling, connecting control boxes and power supplies to large, domed stainless steel tanks on short pipe legs, and to the other machinery. On a short raised platform were two lines of copper fermenters with their own controls, as well as insulated steam and cold-water lines leading into them. The center of the room was taken up by several long, shining steel tables with a variety of bottling equipment on them. On the back wall was a roll-up steel fire door. Opposite the roll-up door, on the area that was the back of the kitchen and lavatory facilities, was a large, insulated walk-in freezer door. Next to the door was a control box with a temperature gauge and several colored lights, one of which was glowing green.

"That rolling door leads to the garage," Shaughnessy said as he went to the opposite wall. "There's a loading dock on the other side of it, completely enclosed for a van or small truck. It makes for good security when we load or unload.

"We were able to upgrade your idea about where to hide the secure fermenter room," Shaughnessy continued. "The signal to anyone in the room that someone wants to come in is right here." He reached out and pushed down on the glowing green light. The light moved slightly with no other sign that anything was happening.

"Now, we have to go in," Shaughnessy said as he pulled open the heavy freezer door. Inside the room, it was dark, the floor covered with boxes of bottles and pallets of aluminum casks. The single small bulb in a protective cage on the ceiling cast a dim light in the room. There were other sockets inside the light fixture, but the bulbs in them were dark.

"Why haven't those bulbs been replaced?" Devlin said as they stepped into the chill room. The walls were of textured stainless-steel sheets. The far wall had a rack with several beer kegs lying flat on its shelves.

"The idea was to make the place darker than it has to be," Shaughnessy said. "If anyone asks, we just haven't bothered replacing the bulbs yet. But it does make it harder to see in here."

The door swung shut and latched with a solid *click*. The light in the ceiling went out, casting the room into pitch darkness. Flipping a switch on the wall, Shaughnessy turned the overhead light back on.

"Kind of answers the age-old question if the refrigerator light goes out when the door closes, doesn't it?" he said.

The blank expression Devlin turned to the man caused him to go visibly pale, even in the dim light.

"You have to shut the outer door first," Shaughnessy said quickly. "Otherwise you can't open the inner door."

"What inner door?" Devlin said.

"Right here," Shaughnessy said as he walked over to where the keg rack was against the far wall. Pushing on the end of the rack, he rolled it farther along the wall.

"I put it back to cover the door when Voorhees went into the lab," Shaughnessy said.

"You mean Lee, don't you?" Devlin said, pointing out the security slip in not using Voorhees' cover name.

"Yes, sir," Shaughnessy said. "Lee, of course—that's who I meant."

To quickly cover up his slip, Shaughnessy pushed in on the wall behind where the rack had stood. There was a sharp sound, then one of the steel panels in the wall popped out. Putting his fingers around the edge of the panel, Shaughnessy pulled open the hidden door. Beyond the panel was a blank wall with a scattering of old bolt heads sticking out of it in places. Shaughnessy pushed on one of the bolt heads on the left side of the opening. Then, grabbing two of the bolt heads at the same time, he pulled open an inner door.

On the other side of the hidden door was an alcove the size of a small walk-in closet. On either side of the alcove were the familiar shapes of bulky yellow Tychem Level A suits, much like the one Voorhees had worn on Rebirth Island. In the ceiling and along the walls were showerheads, all pointing to the center of the room where there was a drain in the floor. The air in the small room was thick with the choking smell of bleach.

Bright light streamed into the room from a window on the far wall. Stepping forward and looking through the window, Devlin could see a figure inside the brilliantly lit room on the other side. The room was the size of an average house kitchen, with every exposed surface—walls, floor, and ceiling—painted white. Standing in front of a stainless-steel tank at the far end of the room, surrounded by other machinery and piping, was a figure in a Tychem suit, a flexible hose leading from the suit to one of a series of sockets on the wall next to the door.

"Leave us for the time being," Devlin said as he pulled a suit off the wall. "Shut the panel but don't bother putting the rack back into place. See to it that a new car is brought here and get rid of the one I came in." Reaching into his pocket, he retrieved a set of keys and handed them to Shaughnessy. "I have been driving that pedestrian piece of Japanese engineering for over two days coming down from Chicago. I expect something a little more sophisticated now."

Accepting his dismissal with some relief, Shaughnessy went back into the cold room, shutting the wall panel behind him. He hated being near the room that stank of bleach. It never seemed to cover the imagined smell of death he connected with what was growing inside it.

Before he pulled on a Tychem suit, Devlin removed a plastic bag from his shirt pocket. Inside the bag was the leather cigar case he had carried across several continents. He placed the bag on the floor and climbed into the suit. An air mask inside the hood of the suit was attached to a long corrugated hose that was coiled below where the suit had been hanging. Putting all of the protective gear on, Devlin picked up the bag, opened the door to the hidden laboratory, and went inside.

He plugged the end of his air hose into a covered socket on the wall. Immediately, he felt a rush of cool, rubber-scented air come into the mask. The pressure of the air inflated his suit and opened the small exhaust valve behind his head. On the wall next to the door, opposite from the air system, Devlin saw a Remington 870 12-gauge pump shotgun in a set of holders, the stock on the gun folded over the barrel with a filled carrier of spare ammunition attached to it.

"Lee!" he said loudly over the rush of air through his suit.

The other suited figure stood and turned at the sound of her cover name. Voorhees was recognizable through the big clear front of her hood, in spite of the mask covering her face. The way her eyes opened told Devlin that she also recognized him.

"I wondered what kept you," she said as she came over to Devlin.

"Here," he said, handing her the cigar case.

Without another word, Voorhees went over to the wide shelf attached to one wall.

"That's the first batch of agent in the fermenter," she said as she bent over the table. "I went ahead and started the seed culture as soon as I could after my arrival. My samples came through easily enough. It's not the average customs agent at any border who wants to open a sealed package of tampons."

"I had slightly more trouble with my package," Devlin said as Voorhees opened the cigar case.

"The seal on this tube has been broken," Voorhees said as she held up the cigar tube. "It's been closed again with tape and sealing wax."

"That was the problem I ran into," Devlin said. Then he related to her the story about the customs inspector with a nose for cigars. "I wiped down the outside of the tubes and the case with bleach, then stuck it in that plastic bag. I've been doing little more than traveling and listening to the news for the last several days. There has been nothing about the death of anyone due to anthrax, let alone a customs agent at the border. Are you absolutely certain we have the proper strain of anthrax? And that it's as lethal as I've been led to understand? It would not be a good thing for us to cross our customers at this point."

"Absolutely," Voorhees said as she opened the taped tube inside a sealed glove box. "I checked it carefully while developing the seed cultures from my own specimens." She pointed to the laboratory setup next to her. Among the glassware and reagent bottles were a glass-fronted incubator, several different microscopes, a centrifuge, and other, less identifiable, hardware.

"The process has already been started with the specimens I brought in myself. Yours is simply a backup sample now. There is no question that this is the most lethal strain of anthrax the laboratories at Biopreparat ever produced," she said as she cut the cigar open with a scalpel. As she continued to work, she moved one of the microscopes into the glove box through a small airlock. After dripping some liquid on fragments from the inside of the cigar, she placed the bits on a microscope slide. Leaning forward, she adjusted the focus of the microscope and peered through the lens.

"There it is," she said. "That stain colors the spores of the anthrax green. If someone sniffed at this cigar, they are either very sick by now, or most probably dead."

"From that small sample?" Devlin said. "Just how much of the material must you breathe to catch the disease?"

"From new data," Voorhees said, "maybe fifteen spores, each of which would grow into an organism."

"Fifteen spores?" Devlin said. "And how much do we have now?"

"From my original inoculation of the bioreactor," Voorhees said as she pointed to a piece of the equipment on the table, "in ten hours a single organism would have multiplied into 1.1 billion of its fellows."

"That many in that small device?" Devlin said.

"Oh, no," Voorhees said. "I started with a sample of several hundred viable spores at least. They were cultured and then the results of that placed in the bioreactor. That laboratory-scale bioreactor, what you would call a fermenter, only holds two liters of nutrient broth."

The piece of equipment she was indicating looked like a glass cylinder with clamps, rods, and electrodes leading from it to a small stack of control boxes. Inside the cylinder was a moving mass of liquid the color of coffee and cream. A long electric motor on top of the cylinder was maintaining the agitation of the contents.

"The ten-barrel fermenter there—" Voorhees pointed to the big stainless steel tank at the back of the lab. It was exactly like several of the other systems on the raised platform in the brewery. "That holds a bit more nutrient. Nearly twelve hundred liters, and it has been processing for a day now. When the initial cultivation is done, that centrifugal filter next to the fermenter will remove the nutrient solution and concentrate the culture in just a few minutes. The filter will remove materials as small as point three five microns and put the concentrate in that solids-recovery vessel next to it. Then we take the solids to the processing plant in a sealed drum Shaughnessy had made from some beer barrels."

Amazed at the amount of incredibly lethal material that could be made in the small facility, Devlin shook his head at the apparent efficiency of the operation.

"Now just why did you move the processing facility to another location rather than setting it up here?" he asked.

"I thought it would be safer to separate the facilities," Voorhees said. "Some of the machinery I required is large and has heavy power demands. We could hide it better someplace else, like a machine shop. We needed the tools for Pressler to do his engineering work, so we set up a sealed processing facility there. It looks like it is a very workable solution and makes the filling of the warheads easier."

"We shall see," Devlin said. "We shall all see soon enough."

Chapter Eight

Low on the horizon, a quarter-moon shone down from a cloudless sky. The stars were partially obscured by the sky shine from the lights of Miami, only twenty-five miles to the north. The open water of the over two-hundred-foot-wide canal was blanketed with the heavy plant life of a southern Florida mangrove swamp. The dark waters of the canal threw back the moonlight in shimmering ripples. Even in the relative darkness, the water and the plant life could be seen. And if anyone was looking at that moment, they would have sworn a piece of the mangrove swamp had broken off and was floating up the canal, moving against the lazy current.

Inside the eight-by-eighteen-foot brown-painted aluminum hull of the airboat, Enzo Caronti carefully conned the clumsy craft across the water. Airboats were built for speed, especially the particular Air Ranger model he was sitting in. The 502-cubic-inch Chevrolet V8 engine on the stand behind him would spin the aircraft propeller in the cage behind it at over 2,400 revolutions per minute. That spin would generate more than 1,100 pounds of thrust, making the airboat skim across the water at speeds faster than fifty miles per hour. Fast enough to pull away from any boat he knew might be in the canal.

With their propellers running, airboats are very noisy. So this one wasn't running its big Chevy engine or propeller. Instead, the rectangular boat with the huge engine in the back moved along slowly and silently, pushed by a 12-volt electric trolling motor.

Acting as coxswain of the slow airboat was even harder because of the AN/PVS-5B night-vision goggles Caronti wore. Further reducing his field of vision, already limited to 20 degrees because of the goggles, was the fact that he was peering through the open mesh of a camouflage net draped over the boat. The AN/PVS-5Bs were an older model goggle, but they were the kind that Caronti had been wearing for years, so he was used to them. And the net did seem to be keeping the bugs away. Things could have been worse.

Crouching down in the forward hull of the airboat were the other three men who made up the Four Horsemen, an off-the-books action unit of the Department of Homeland Security. The leader of the Horsemen, Reaper, had the call sign "Death." Next to him in the boat was the ex-Air Force pararescue man Ben Mackenzie. Call signed "Famine," Mackenzie was a slight-looking man, but anyone judging his ability by his size was in for a serious surprise if they tangled with him. The little man had a wiry strength and a tough attitude that belied his appearance. The third member of the Horsemen was "War," specifically Warrick, ex-scout-sniper and now precision marksman of the Four Horsemen. Caronti had the call sign "Leviathan."

The assault plan for the Horsemen was relatively simple and flexible. The security force for the nuclear plant patrolled the nearly seven thousand acres of cooling canals in their own airboats. The propellers driving the airboats were so loud that they could be heard in the parking lot of the plant. Because of all of the endangered and threatened birds and critters living in the surrounding wildlife refuge, the airboat patrols were suspended at night. That was the weak point that the Horsemen were going to exploit as their means of getting into the facility.

The men had all spent weeks casing the area around the nuclear plant. Computer downloads had given them satellite photos, aerial views, detailed maps, even tourist information on the reactor site and the swamps and parks that surrounded it. Part of the security exercise was to see just how much information could be gathered from open sources to plan an attack against the plant, and the Horsemen had found a lot.

Anhinga Point Units 3 and 4 were the actual reactor buildings. Those parts of the facility, along with their control and support buildings, were off-limits for the exercise. The security force inside the fence in those areas would be fully armed with live ammunition. They would not be taking part in any exercise. The rest of the facility was considered open and fair game for Reaper and his team—as were all of the other on-duty security forces at the plant. The guards had been expecting some kind of action for over a week. They would be tired of the constant alert by this evening and expecting just another week of the same. That made them more vulnerable to the actions of Reaper and his men.

Keeping low in the bow of the airboat, Warrick had an olive-drab Spec-Ops Recon Wrap pulled down over his white hair. With the dark cloth headgear worn in "Sahara" mode, it covered his head and draped down the back of his neck, blocking his hair from view. As a sniper, Warrick was concerned with camouflage and blending into his surroundings. In a USIA waterproof swimmer's pack next to him was a Custom-Concealment ghillie suit, a collection of rags and burlap attached to a two-piece uniform that would make him absolutely invisible in the surrounding bush. It was great camouflage, but the ghillie suit was almost impossible to swim in, so it was rolled up inside the waterproof pack.

The long gun in the USIA waterproof sniper bag was Warrick's primary tool. The weapon was a McMillan M88 PIP .50-caliber bolt-action sniper rifle with a four to sixteen-power Horus Falcon steel tactical scope mounted on it. It was the same sniper weapon as that used by the Navy SEALs, and Warrick liked it. Assembled, the M88 was over four and a half feet long and weighed more than twenty-seven pounds. To transport the huge weapon on land, Warrick had detached the removable buttstock and strapped the shortened gun securely inside a BlackHawk long gun pack mat to act as a drag bag. The set of equipment stuffed inside the waterproof sniper bag gave the ex-Marine scout-sniper an effective range of 2,000 yards.

Normally, Warrick would only have loaded the M88 rifle with single rounds instead of filling the magazine. The muzzle blast of the big .50-caliber rifle would knock up dust and debris from the ground with every shot. Multiple rounds fired from the same location would put a big marker up in the air, a plume of dust that would say "here he is" to any competent observer.

On this operation though, Warrick had already filled the magazine of his M88 with five rounds. A sixth round could have been carried in the chamber but that would have been dangerous and unnecessary for the mission. On this op, there wouldn't be any plume of dust going into the air no matter how many rounds Warrick fired. And it wasn't because the mangrove swamp all around the canal system smelled of wet ground and rotten plant life, either. No dust rises up from mud, but that didn't matter. And neither did his accuracy with the weapon. The rounds were all military M1A1 blanks. Loud as hell but not a bullet in any of them, and he had an extra plastic ammunition box holding ten more rounds taped to the buttstock of the rifle if he wanted them.

The closest thing to a live weapon that Warrick had on his person or in his gear was the SOG Government Model sheath knife at his right hip and the SOG Trident folder hanging inside his right front pocket. All of the men in the airboat were armed, and none of them had a live round anywhere on their person.

The lack of live ammunition among the men didn't mean that any of the Four Horsemen were unarmed. They all carried a serious load of hardware, but most of it wasn't lethal. Both Reaper and Mackenzie had M4A1 carbines hanging from Chalker slings around their chests. Both weapons had M203A1 40mm grenade launchers secured to the rail system underneath the barrels. Reaper, Mackenzie, and Caronti had SIG P226 9mm pistols locked into BlackHawk Serpa tactical holsters strapped to their right thighs. On the front and back of each hard-shell carbon fiber holster were spare magazine pouches for the P226. Instead of using a sling while conning the airboat, Caronti had his M4A1 carbine secured into a quick-release rack on the front of his elevated seat.

All of the firearms except for Warrick's M88 .50 caliber had been converted to use either the 5.56mm or 9mm UTM Man Marker Round (MMR) ammunition. When fired, the weapons would feed and function normally, but the only thing coming out of the muzzle would be a very light composite projectile filled with colored marking compound. Effectively, all of the men would be firing relatively safe projectiles loaded with red lipstick.

The reason for all of the exotic ammunition and extensive safety precautions was a simple one. The Four Horsemen had changed sides for the moment and were acting as the "bad guys." In cooperation with the Nuclear Regulatory Agency, their boss—Admiral Alan Straker at the Department of Homeland Security—and the local head of security for the Anhinga nuclear plant, the Four Horsemen were staging an attack on the facility. Only Andrew Darrow, the security director at Anhinga Point, knew exactly what was going on and when things would be happening, as far as the attack went.

———

Earlier that morning, in a rented house in Homestead, a small city not far from the nuclear plant, Reaper and the others had gone over their plan for the last time. One bedroom of the house had been turned into a war room. Maps, photographs, and charts covered the walls.

Mounds of equipment, web gear, and supplies filled much of the remaining space. Inside the closet they had secured enough weapons and ammunition to conduct a heavy combat operation.

If a police officer had searched the house, he would have been convinced that he had either stumbled onto an active terrorist cell or a really dangerous drug gang. The airboat on the trailer in the two-car garage might have been interpreted as the final piece of evidence identifying Reaper and his men as drug smugglers. So all of the men kept a low profile just to avoid such misunderstandings as they continued the operation.

"Okay," Reaper said as they all sat around the war room, "let's go over everything one more time. Late this afternoon, we launch from the public ramp at the Homestead Bayfront Park."

"No problem I can see there," Caronti said. "The ramp will take our trailer easily enough, but in case it doesn't fit, I've checked out the Mowry and North Canals to make sure they were open enough for our needs. Launching the boat at the ramp should be a piece of cake, though. Long-term parking is nearby, so the truck and trailer won't look out of place no matter how long we're gone. Enough people use it to head out for overnight fishing trips that we should blend right in."

"As long as we pay the parking fee," Mackenzie said.

A chuckle went around the room, but Reaper still made a note to be certain they had enough cash to cover parking. More than one op had gone down badly because someone had missed a small detail. On their first operation together, they had damned near been caught going to rescue Reaper's family because they had forgotten to bring fishing licenses as part of their cover.

"So, then we head out to sea and down the coast," Reaper said.

"Roger that," Caronti said. "It's only a few miles down the coast from the launch site to the insertion point for the airboat. We can stay in the area of Biscayne Bay National park until zero hour. There's more than enough marshy areas that an airboat doing some fishing would just melt into the landscape."

"At the insertion point," Reaper said, "the gate is set?"

"Set and locked," Warrick replied. "I slipped in last night while Caronti was checking out the area with the airboat. Cut off the lock and replaced it with our own, same model as on all of the other security gates. Here're the keys," Warrick placed four keys on the table. Each of the men picked up a key and pocketed it.

"Once we get south of Turtle Point, a mile or so past the plant itself," Warrick continued, "we can cut in to shore and cross less than fifty yards of swamp and be inside the security fence in under two minutes if one of us heads in and opens the gate first. Patrols will have stopped by then and anyone who hears us will figure we're just another airboat down in Arsenicker Park. We can cut the engine and secure the camo net once we're in the canal proper. Then we should be good to go."

"Alarms?" Reaper asked.

"They look the same as all the others we saw along the fence line," Warrick said. "Pretty much standard ground sensors and anti-intrusion lines. They probably have the sensors set pretty high, otherwise they would be going off constantly from just the swamp critters. I set out the shunts Mackenzie gave me and one of those induction bypass boxes we used last year down in Arizona. I left one box at the site hidden with the shunts and we have another set ready in the airboat.

"Once we're inside the perimeter and on the cooling canals, noise discipline goes one hundred percent," Reaper said. "Hand signals only, unless it's an emergency. How long do you figure it will take us to get to the northern end of the canals, Caronti?"

"With the motor I'll be using," Caronti said, "an hour and a half, hour forty-five tops. I have two fully charged spare batteries on board besides the one already hooked to the motor. One battery alone will give us enough power to make the trip."

"Silence and surprise are going to be the keys to this op," Reaper said. "Security is pretty good at the plant and this looks to be the only real weak spot."

"That's because there's almost seven thousand acres of cooling canals," Warrick said. "The environmentalists helped us on this one."

"That's why we're using it, Warrick," Reaper said. "But once we reach the end of those canals, we'll only be about three hundred meters from a gate-security post. Those guards are going to be your responsibility Caronti. Warrick, you take point on this op. Once you open fire, that's going to be the signal for the party to begin. Mackenzie and I will be inserting the same time as you do. We'll signal over the comm set when we're in place. Then you open fire. Once we commit, it's all going to start happening fast. So what's your priority target again?"

"First round," Warrick said, "eleven hundred seventy-five meters. The gas bottle storage area just outside of the main gate."

"The flash-charge and smoke bombs are already in place," Reaper said. "I confirmed that with the security director this morning. He knows it's going down tonight, but he doesn't know how or where we're coming in. It's in his best interests to follow our directions, but I didn't think he needed to know everything."

"My second round is seven hundred eighty meters," Warrick said. "The transfer switch for the security system inside the facility perimeter fence."

"Your demonstration at the range sure made a believer out of that security director," Caronti said. "I thought he was going to have a baby right there when that propane tank went up."

"The day I can't hit a target the size of a small garbage can at eight hundred meters is the day I stop shooting and take up knitting," Warrick said.

"Still, the explosion from that gas container was impressive," Caronti said.

"That's the explosive charge in the Mark 211 armor piercing incendiary ammo I was using," Warrick said. "It was designed for this kind of work. Those rounds would make a complete hash of any of these targets, including the last two. Shots three and four are at six hundred thirty meters. The power transformers inside the western switchyard."

"That's the target list," Reaper said. "After that, it's targets of opportunity as you decide. The blanks you're using should force the security staff to keep their heads down for a while. You're sure that there won't be a problem with putting the rounds out fast on multiple targets from a bolt-gun? You may have to demonstrate the technique to the staff after the debriefing."

"Good to go on that," Warrick said. "The reticle grid

on that Horus scope makes changing targets and ranges just a matter of swinging the gun around. I can shoot that way all day long. As long as those satellite photos are on, I will be, too."

"That leaves it up to you and me," Reaper said as he looked at Mackenzie. "We get to the fence after insertion and wait for the fireworks to start. Then we penetrate and head for the administration building."

"Right," Mackenzie said, "taking a bunch of office workers and bureaucrats hostage. Just the way I wanted to spend my evening."

"Could be worse," Reaper said with a grin. "We could be out in the swamp with Warrick and Caronti getting eaten alive by bugs."

"That's if we don't end up taking the guards for a ride," Caronti said.

"You sure that our airboat can outrun theirs?" Reaper said.

"No question," Caronti said. "She's going to be the fastest thing on the water. If the guards decide to break out their boats for a chase, they're going to find out that bigger is better. That Chevy engine we have has been tuned and matched to the prop for maximum speed. Mileage sucks, but we'll get there fast. I will leave them in my figurative dust."

"If there's no questions," Reaper said as he looked from man to man, "that's it, then. Security Director Darrow is going to be our inside man on this. He's off duty and his second is in charge of the night staff. But he's remaining on-site, just like he has all week. It's going to be the night security supervisor who'll have to deal with us."

"Lucky him," Caronti said.

"Darrow has our timetable and will shut off the power at the sound of the shots. From then on, it's going to be our party. He officially can't get involved again until enough time has passed that he could have gotten here from home. We'll see just how well this security group deals with their whole night admin staff being held hostage."

"And any other little tricks we can think of along the way," Mackenzie added.

"The on-duty security forces outside of the reactor areas will be wearing goggles and protective masks and clothing. All of their weapons have been double-checked and everything is converted to fire only the UTM marking ammunition. Darrow and I both went over every piece of hardware ourselves. All live weapons are secured.

"Those guards will be gunning for us, but I think we can make it expensive for them before they get anywhere close to us. The briefing told Darrow a lot, but not everything. Safety is paramount, but Mackenzie and I have more than enough paint-ball booby traps and improvised devices to keep things from being easy for these guys. I know we'll give them a run for their money."

"Then it's away from here and some time in South Beach," Warrick said.

"Sounds damned good to me," said Reaper with a smile." That's it then, the rest of tonight depends on how the security force reacts. Caronti and Warrick, you're free agents. Keep them running around the canals as long as you can. Then try to extract. If Mackenzie and I secure hostages, we won't be coming back out. For now, it's final gear check, get something to eat and some sleep. It's going to be a long night."

"There any of that pizza left in the kitchen?" Warrick asked.

"You have been eating that same shit for nearly a week," Mackenzie said. "A dog would be sick of it by now."

"Hey," Warrick said, "it's good pizza."

Chapter Nine

The insertion into the canal area had gone off without a problem. Even launching the airboat at a public facility hadn't drawn a second glance. In South Florida, such craft were common enough that they didn't stand out. The only tight moment that had taken place during the beginning of the operation was when Caronti had to gun the motor to drive the boat up onto the land and across the hardtop construction road bordering the canal. Warrick and Mackenzie had to quickly shut and relock the gate before they could clamber back onto the boat. The momentary roar of the engine made each of them feel as exposed as an ant on a plate until everyone was back on board the boat and the camouflage netting went up.

Finally, after a long, slow trip up the canals, the target area for the insertions had come up. Once Warrick was in the water and moving toward his hide, Reaper and Mackenzie would cross onto the canal bank and start making their way to the perimeter fence of the nuclear plant itself. The dark waters slapped quietly

against the aluminum sides of the airboat. Plopping
sounds were all that could be heard as the men went
over the sides.

Each man on the team was heavily laden for the operation. Only Warrick wasn't wearing an assault vest,
but he still had a SIG P226 in a Serpa holster on his
right thigh. Caronti, Mackenzie, and Reaper were all
wearing BlackHawk Omega Elite tactical assault vests
with a dozen thirty-round magazines in the six double-
mag pouches. A Motorola Walkabout radio was in the
upper left-side pocket of each vest along with an extra
set of batteries as well as a Stinger throat microphone
system and earphone. Warrick had the same rig in the
waterproof bag with his ghillie suit.

In the thigh pockets of their 5.11 tactical trousers,
Reaper and Mackenzie had a dozen pairs of plastic riot-
control cuffs. Both men would be able to quickly secure their hostages with such rigs, which could only be
removed by cutting through the tough plastic. Strapped
to their left thighs on a drop-leg platform were Strike
three-round 40mm grenade pouches. The three rounds
of Engel Ballistic Research's 40mm CQB training
rounds could be a real surprise to the security force.
Each of the white nylon rounds launched a swarm of
6mm paint pellets when fired. The pellets would cover
a wide area, bursting when they hit a target and leaving
a splash of bright paint.

Everyone was wearing a Brownie personal flotation
device attached to his rig. The water in the canals was
close to twenty feet deep when they had been dredged,
according to the plans on file at the public records
office. Though every man on the operation was a more
than accomplished swimmer, having all of their gear

on a flotation device was just the smart thing to do, and the Brownie design stayed out of the way unless fully inflated.

There was only the noise of the swamp life all around them when Caronti cut the power to the trolling motor. The boat slipped against the plants along the side of the canal and nudged into the sloping bank. Splashes sounded up and down the bank as the frogs and other wildlife were disturbed by the arrival of the airboat. Lifting up the edge of the camouflage net and passing his gear bags over the canal side of the boat, Warrick rolled over and into the dark water. The black and green paint that covered his face made him almost invisible against the water as he surfaced. It was only through his AN/PVS-5B night-vision goggles that Caronti could clearly see Warrick as he struck out from the side of the boat. From the other side of the canal, Warrick had planned to locate his hide, where he had a clear line of sight to his targets. As Reaper and Mackenzie prepared to insert on the canal bank, they were astonished to hear Caronti's hissed curse.

"Shit!" the man said from his elevated position.

While swimming across the canal, Warrick wasn't wearing his own pair of night-vision goggles. The Simrad KN250 night-vision sight attachment he could clip onto his Horus scope was packed in the drag bag along with his primary weapon. The scout-sniper had no way of seeing the large V-shaped wakes in the water that Caronti saw from his raised position, wakes that were heading directly for him.

For one of their own to break noise discipline startled Reaper for a moment. While watching to see if there were any signs of the insertion having been discovered by the security forces, the last thing he had expected was a curse from one of his men. Crawling over to the port side of the boat, Reaper peered out into the gloom. The moon had long since set and only the stars and the sky shine from Miami and the nearby nuclear plant supplied any real light. Looking out over the water, Reaper stared in the direction that Caronti was pointing toward with his outstretched arm. Whatever it was out there, Reaper couldn't see it from his low vantage point, less than a few feet above the surface of the canal.

In the water, Warrick was slowly kicking his way to the opposite bank. The SWAT classic-style boots he was wearing didn't make his kick stroke very efficient. But the buoyancy of the waterproof bags under his arms and angled in front of him, was making the swim an easy one. The very strong paracord lines he had tied between the bags and himself made losing either one in the water something that wasn't going to happen. He could see the far bank between the bags and this looked to be one of the easiest insertions he had ever done.

In the airboat, Caronti had made an immediate decision to act. From the sheath strapped in front of his thigh holster, he pulled out his Neil Roberts Warrior Knife. The sawlike serrated section of the cutting edge made quick work of slashing through the lashings for the camouflage net. As intended, elastic bungee cords and small weights pulled the separated multiple sections of the net apart and dropped it away. Standing and with a loud groan, Caronti heaved the ends of the rear sections of the net back and over the big protective cage around the propeller at the stern of the boat.

Still unable to see what had triggered the other man's actions, Reaper went along with whatever Caronti was doing. He pushed at the ends of the net, forcing it away from the boat as it quickly sank out of sight. The men had all been through heavy combat actions together and Reaper trusted his teammates' judgments as well as he did his own. All he could see to do right then was clear the airboat for immediate action.

As the net dropped free, Caronti pulled his SureFire M3T flashlight from a holster attached to his vest. The normally brilliant light was muted by the addition of a flip-up infrared filter over its lens. The dim light that would come out of the M3T would be invisible to the naked eye, but through the night-vision devices everyone was wearing, it would faintly illuminate even the far bank of the canal two hundred feet away.

When Caronti lifted his light and pressed the button on the back, the infrared beam flashed out. Suddenly, reflecting from the far bank were more than a dozen pairs of gleaming brilliant dots. A yard behind the leading point of the ripples, which moved faster as they drew closer to Warrick, were a larger pair of dots, so big they looked like glowing golf balls. And they were spaced nearly a foot apart. Whatever it was that was moving through the water was big—really big! If the length of the disturbance in the water was any indication, this thing could be longer than the airboat, and the hull of the boat was eighteen feet long. That couldn't be a gator in the water—it had to be the Son of Godzilla come to life. And it was going to reach Warrick long before anyone in the boat could get to him.

Alligators in southern Florida were a common sight. Every water trap in the golf courses seemed to have their share of them. Everyone with Reaper had seen small ones all over the swamps. They had even spotted some big ones, from ten to fourteen feet long. But gators are normally shy creatures that don't really want anything to do with man, given the choice. During their scouting drives past the canal area, none of the men had heard any of the loud bellows—like the roar of a lion—that meant that some of the really big reptiles were announcing their territory.

Just in case they did run into a big gator that refused to leave on its own, Reaper had added a pair of cattle prods to the boat's equipment loadout. The Hot Shot SS36 cattle prods in the boat were 36 inches long and put 8,000 volts across the copper terminals at the ends of the poles when their triggers were pulled. They were all the men had with them to deal with what looked like a dinosaur moving across the canal.

Grabbing up the prod that had been secured to the port side of the boat, Reaper stood and looked at his teammate in the water. Shouting probably wouldn't do anything now except make Warrick panic. The giant reptile would be on him before he could get back to the boat or reach either canal bank. Reaper felt like he was facing a charging rhino with a golf club.

Seeing what was going on, Mackenzie snapped up his M4A1/M203A1 combination and aimed it. Then he let the weapon droop in his hands. It was only loaded with marker ammunition. Even if he had a magazine of live ammunition, the converted weapon wouldn't fire it. Every gun in the boat was the same way. That marker ammunition wouldn't even be noticed by the approaching monster.

Screw the noise discipline and trust your teammate, thought Reaper. This was just a damned exercise and a man's life was in danger.

"Warrick!" Reaper shouted, "Warrick! Get back to the boat."

A very startled ex-Marine lifted his head from the water as he heard the words. He had a moment to register a shape coming at him in the water before he was hit. The men in the boat only saw a sudden thrashing in the water as, with a startled yelp, Warrick was pulled under the surface.

The monster reptile hadn't struck Warrick directly. Instead, the mouth of the beast had closed on the soft waterproof bag holding the man's ghillie suit. As the monster felt the bag in its jaws, it jerked its head down and back, curling its tail and thrusting down into the water. Against the unbelievable strength of the reptile in its natural environment, Warrick was helpless. Still trying to maintain discipline, the ex-Marine growled his fear and rage as the water closed over his head.

Under water, the reptile twisted its head to stun and drown its prey. The bag holding the ghillie suit was strong, but that didn't matter to the tooth-lined jaws. It shredded and tore, reduced to floating scraps in an instant. Even though Warrick hadn't been seized by the merciless teeth in those jaws, he was jerked around under the water by the line that connected him to the bag.

The men in the boat watched the massive tail and body of the reptile break the surface of the water as it dove for the bottom of the canal. The water was thrashed into dark foam as Warrick disappeared. Immediate action was the only thing that could save their teammate now. Reaper knew that and responded. Pulling off his night-vision goggles, he dropped them to the deck. A yank on the red release strap of his Chalker sling, and his useless weapon fell away.

Almost without conscious thought, Reaper bent and his hands flashed to the side-release buckles that secured the thigh rigs to his legs. Long practice allowed him to quickly twist and release his equipment belt from around his waist. Finally, popping the two side-release buckles at his chest and pulling down on the long zipper freed his tactical vest. With a shrug of his shoulders and twist of his arms, Reaper's equipment fell away to lie in a heap at the bottom of the boat.

Within twenty seconds of Warrick being hit, Reaper was moving to get into the water. Snatching up the cattle prod from where he had dropped it, he jumped over the side of the boat and into the black waters of the canal.

As quickly as he had been pulled down, Warrick felt himself going up, his head breaking the surface as his ghillie-suit bag was torn away. Thrashing and kicking, the disoriented scout-sniper tried to push away from the area, to put some distance between himself and whatever it was that had grabbed his equipment. His back hit the waterproof bag holding his sniper drag bag, the same bag that had pulled him to the surface. Instinctively, Warrick grabbed onto the floating black container. Looking around, he saw the bubbling water behind him, then a sight straight out of a nightmare broke the surface and rushed in his direction.

It was a monstrous crocodile, its huge jaws open in anticipation. The gleaming teeth seemed to be lining a pale white pit leading down into hell. Pulling the weapon container around, Warrick shoved the floating bag at the oncoming maw.

"Eat this, you fucking lizard!" Warrick shouted in defiance.

The powerful jaws clamped down on the first thing

they found and, once again, the reptile dove toward the bottom of the canal. Having forgotten about the attached line, Warrick had only a moment to suck down a breath of air before he was jerked under the surface.

As the water closed over his head, Warrick felt the croc go into the death roll so characteristic of the species. Intent on disorienting and drowning its prey, the spinning crocodile tangled Warrick up in the lines hanging from his body. Both the line from the bag in the croc's jaws and the dangling line from the destroyed ghillie bag were wrapped around Warrick's torso, pinning his upper arms against his chest.

With his arms pinned, Warrick couldn't reach the sheath knife at the back of his belt. He spun and tumbled in the water completely at the mercy of the raging fury of the creature that held him at the end of a line. He bumped against the monster reptile and felt the rough skin tear at his clothes and flesh.

He was helpless, thrown about like a leaf in a hurricane. But the ex-Marine was not going to die without some kind of fight. In a sudden moment of calm clarity brought on by the incredible stress, Warrick remembered the SOG folding Trident knife in his front pants pocket. As he was being slammed around by the giant reptile, Warrick strained to reach his pocket against the force of the water. With every bit of his will, Warrick reached the rough-checked handle of the knife and pulled it out. He could never have opened the blade of the Trident without loosing it, but he didn't have to. As his mind started to blank out from the lack of oxygen and the beating he was taking, Warrick dragged the back of the folded knife across his chest.

A groove in the back of the Trident's handle caught

the strong line and pulled in it to the knife. At the bottom of the groove, exposed, was a section of the folded blade's edge. The sharp steel sliced through the tough nylon paracord and the line parted with a *snap*. He was free as the tangled lines pulled away. With the little bit of strength he had left, Warrick struck out weakly for the surface.

Even as his strength failed, Warrick felt a steel-hard grip on the back of his collar. He had nothing left to fight with and the ex-Marine's heart turned black with despair. The end of his life was going to come as he became a big lizard's midnight snack. His teeth were clenched in a silent scream of rage—then his head broke the surface.

Gulping in huge lungfuls of wet, stinking swamp air, Warrick thought he had never tasted anything so good. He was pulled over on his back and felt himself being towed through the water. Around his chest, Warrick could feel Reaper's arm as he pulled him, kicking and stroking back toward the airboat. Gripped in the same hand, Reaper had the cattle prod pointing back to where the crocodile still thrashed in the water. He never had to pull the trigger to activate the prod, and wasn't sure the tiny thing would have had much of an effect against the huge reptile. The croc was occupied twisting about with the weapon bag locked in its jaws, the bag now bent almost double.

Grabbing at Warrick as he came up to the side of the boat, Mackenzie pulled the limp ex-Marine up over the gunwale. Pulling himself up, Reaper rolled over the gunwale as well and into the hull. In the distance, lights were coming on at the security gate and a siren started to wail at the nuclear plant. It didn't matter now. The operation was a complete bust, but at least they hadn't lost a man.

"Caronti," Reaper yelled, "get us the hell out of here!"

The pampered Chevy engine roared to life at Caronti's first touch of the starter switch. Engaging the prop and risking a stall from the cold engine, Caronti spun the big airboat around almost inside of its own length and headed away from the shore. Pouring on the fuel, Caronti drove the airboat back along the canal, quickly passing fifty miles an hour and going faster.

Casting a professional eye over his two teammates, Mackenzie could see that neither man was hurt. Warrick was coughing rather weakly after having been thumped around under water, but he was breathing well enough and only a little bit shocky. Reaper was breathing hard and his eyes were huge and staring. Even the tough ex-SEAL had trouble coming to grips with what he had just faced. Looking over at Reaper, Mackenzie put on a horrible parody of an Australian accent.

"Crikey," he shouted over the roar of the prop, "that was a feisty one!"

For a moment, Reaper just stared at his friend. Then he started to laugh loudly. From where he lay on the bottom of the boat, Warrick chuckled weakly at the bad impression Mackenzie had just done.

"Are we dead yet?" Warrick asked with a lopsided grin.

———

"Well, if you had told me that's how you were going to be coming in, I would have warned you about the crocodiles," Security Director Andrew Darrow said at the meeting in his office the next afternoon.

"We were prepared to deal with gators," Reaper said, "even some big ones. But we never saw any real sign of them."

"They don't like sharing the same nesting areas with the crocs," Darrow said. "Especially now at the end of the breeding season. Most of the nests have females nearby guarding them."

"Crocs!" Warrick almost shouted. "Who in the hell ever expects to run into a crocodile in this country? Especially not one the size of a pickup truck! The god-damned things are supposed to be rare as hell."

"We have the largest single breeding population of crocodiles in the United States right here in the cooling canals," Darrow said. "No one bothers them, because of the security precautions. Even professionals, the conservationists and naturalists trying to study them, run into trouble now and then. One of those people gets trapped up a tree and we have to get them out nearly once a month. The population is rarely really aggressive except for now, right after breeding season and all. You must have gotten too close to Matilda's nest."

"Matilda?" Warrick said. "You named that god-damned dinosaur Matilda?"

"She is the largest known croc in the United States today," Darrow said calmly. "Nineteen feet long at her last estimate."

"Well, I think the old girl has been putting on weight to help take care of her babies," Warrick said. "She tried to eat me."

"Oh, if her eggs had hatched, we wouldn't be having this conversation. She wouldn't have stopped defending her nest until she had driven the boat away, or killed all of you."

"She ate my best rifle! I'm going to go out there with a cannon and turn her into luggage."

"No," Darrow said very seriously, "no, you're not. American crocodiles are an endangered and protected species. You do anything to her, and the Feds will be after you in a heartbeat. And if they aren't enough, the animal rights people will sue you for the rest of your life if you hurt her."

"Hurt her? Hurt HER? She damned near ate me!"

"Yes, that would have been tragic. But you are supposed to be able to take care of yourself and not wander around in her territory. Truthfully, the paperwork to cover your death would be something I can deal with. The reams of paperwork and investigations if we lose a croc are a nightmare."

"So's looking down the pointy end of a giant lizard," Warrick said as he sat back in his seat.

"Just how many of those things are out there?" Reaper asked.

"The population count is somewhere between three fifty and five hundred," Darrow said.

"I think we can agree that your security against intrusions here at the plant is just fine," Reaper said.

Chapter Ten

Before the men could leave Darrow's office after the debriefing, the security director received an urgent message for Reaper. The message, from the Department of Homeland Security, directed Reaper and his men to report to Admiral Straker's office in Washington, D.C., as soon as possible. To help speed the men on their way, Darrow suggested that he have his people secure their weapons and equipment, as well as clean the rental house, removing all of their materials before returning it to the owners.

Their immediate responsibilities taken care of, Reaper and his men quickly arrived at the Miami International Airport. Within two hours of receiving the message, the men were on board a flight for Dulles, just outside of Washington.

Mass transit worked well in the metropolitan Washington area. It wasn't a problem for the men to take a train to within blocks of their meeting with Admiral Straker, so they didn't bother with renting a car for the time being. The only real stalling point in the trip was having to wait for their checked baggage. Even though they had the credentials to carry weapons anywhere in the United States, it was still a lot more low key for Reaper and his men to check their carry guns along with their light luggage. Once they had their bags in hand, a quick stop in the men's room made all of the men feel considerably more dressed, with their favorite chunks of machined steel safely in their holsters.

The small suite of offices used by Admiral Straker and his staff was in one of the tall, glass-surfaced office buildings in Crystal City, part of Arlington, Virginia. However, the pair of sharp-eyed uniformed guards in the lobby looked like anything but average rent-a-cops. It wasn't until Reaper and his partners had identified themselves to the man sitting at the desk and he had waved them past the metal detectors that the guards returned their attention to the heavy front doors. The building was a secure one, for all of its plain exterior. On one of the upper floors, Straker's offices themselves had no other identification besides his name on the door.

Once inside the outer office, the secretary had Reaper and the rest of the men leave their bags there while she buzzed them into Straker's inner office. Reaper had the impression that this woman had a weapon within reach at all times. She was cordial enough, but her attitude did not invite casual conversation.

Once inside the wood-paneled office, Reaper could see that Straker still carried himself as you would expect a SEAL admiral to, even a retired one. The big man gave an impression of controlled strength and power as he rose from behind his huge wooden desk to greet the four men. The wide smile was framed by a tanned, lined face, white-streaked dark hair, and a bushy mustache. Even the backdrop of the man's office gave the impression of power, and was particularly fitting for a retired admiral. Through the wall of glass behind Straker could be seen the flowing traffic along I-395, one of the main arteries feeding downtown Washington. Beyond the ribbons of concrete rose the massive granite structure of the Pentagon as it dominated the skyline.

Straker shook Reaper's hand warmly. It was the kind of greeting that was common among men who had served in the Teams together, where rank didn't mean nearly as much as did ability.

"You've grown a 'stach since I last saw you, sir," Reaper said.

"Anything that helps disguise you among the inner beltway commandos here," Straker said with a smile as he pushed at the edges of his mustache with the back of his hand. "So, these men are the rest of your team?"

"All except Keith Deckert," Reaper said. "He's back in Michigan running our headquarters. This is Max Warrick, ex-Marine scout-sniper. He's our precision marksman."

"Pleased to meet you, sir," Warrick said shaking hands with the admiral.

"You have been a credit to your unit," Straker said. "I understand on your last mission you had a bit of a problem with the local wildlife, though."

"Not exactly a problem, sir," Warrick said. "More like nobody told me I'd be meeting Godzilla's mother-in-law with a rifle full of blanks."

"Make do and strive ahead," Straker replied. "Right, Marine?"

"Oohrah, sir," Warrick said with a grin.

Straker turned to the next man in line.

"Ben Mackenzie, sir," Mackenzie introduced himself.

"Ben is our corpsman," Reaper said, "an Air Force PJ. Tends to have to put us back together on occasion."

"Not to worry, Admiral," Ben said, "They make me positively rusty, they all duck so fast."

"A pleasure to meet you, Ben," Straker said as he shook his hand.

"And this is Chief Enzo Caronti," Reaper said, making the last introduction. "He was with the Boat Units back in your day, sir, and he still manages to get us from here to there when he has to."

"Caronti?" Straker said. "I remember you. Enough of a pirate to keep the traditions going, as I remember. You could scrounge a beer in the middle of the desert."

"Glad to meet you, sir," Caronti said, "and a man needs a good libation now and then, that's all."

For all of their grins, Reaper could see the muscles move in Caronti's and Straker's wrists as the two very big men shook hands. It wasn't a challenge—more the greeting of two warriors—though the handclasp could probably have crushed walnuts to dust.

"Take a seat, gentlemen," Straker said as he headed back to his desk. "This is going to take a few minutes."

As the men settled in the padded leather seats and couch around the room, Straker went back to sitting behind his desk.

"You men have dealt with some serious incursions into the United States," Straker said. "Most of the time working somewhat 'under the radar,' when you weren't ignoring the law of the land entirely. Now, I've got a mission for you that's just about as nasty as it comes. And possibly more important than anything you've done during your military careers or since."

The men were all sitting up and paying attention to every word the admiral said. This wasn't the kind of man given to idle exaggerations, and they all recognized the seriousness in his voice.

"The United States faces a threat right now that may be as serious as any in her history," Straker said. "There is a strong possibility of there being a viable threat of a biological weapon attack within the United States. Everything I am about to tell you is to be considered classified. You are not to repeat it to anyone outside of this room who has not been cleared by this office.

"Right after the 9-11 attacks, there were a series of anthrax attacks using the U.S. mail. Five people were killed after they contracted the disease, and hundreds were exposed. More than ten thousand were treated for possible exposure. That was from exposure to less than ten grams of anthrax. It was a wakeup call to the government and caused a major disruption to this country. There have been a number of exercises since then to test the methods we have in place to respond to a major biological attack. We've gotten better at dealing with the concept, but we still have a long way to go to improve our defenses, especially for the public sector."

"So whoever did the attacks back in September and October 2001 has come back to continue their operations?" Mackenzie asked.

"The instigators of those attacks were never found," Straker said. "I've been told there are significant technical differences in what we suspect may be coming.

The 2001 attacks were conducted with an anthrax agent known as the Ames strain. That was simply a known strain of anthrax, something that had been isolated from nature at a Western university years ago. It wasn't one of the special weaponized strains. The anthrax found showed no evidence of bioengineering. But it still killed a number of people who came into contact with it. We now have evidence of something new, and of its penetration into the United States.

"About two months ago, a customs official in Michigan died suddenly after a short period in the hospital. Publicly, his death has been reported as being due to a severe pneumonia infection. That was enough to explain his being kept in very secure isolation. And it helped us keep a tight hold on information regarding the incident, as well as giving us an excuse to treat everyone involved with preventive measures."

"You wouldn't pull us in on just a cold," Mackenzie said, "even an amazingly bad one."

"True enough," Straker said. "It wasn't pneumonia. It was pulmonary anthrax. The most lethal strain the doctors have ever seen. The lid was clamped down on information regarding the infection to prevent a public panic. If more cases show up, we won't be able to control the information flow, but for the time being, only the one case has been found.

"The doctor who treated the customs inspector is a Reserve Army Special Forces officer. He recognized the situation, put the man in isolation, and notified us immediately. Our offices have dealt with the Centers for Disease Control in Atlanta, as well as the Port Huron and Michigan health officials."

"Port Huron?" Reaper said.

"Yes," Straker said, "that's near your old neighborhood, isn't it? The customs official was working at the Blue Water Bridge at the base of Lake Huron. He was infected at his post; his inspection disk had spore traces. But whatever the direct cause, he was the only one. I've been told that this infection is so lethal that he had to have been exposed to it within days of his death. His work schedule put him at the receiving line at the bridge. That had to be where he was exposed, he didn't have time to be anywhere else. He had no immediate family and lived close by in Marysville. His apartment and vehicle have been thoroughly checked and no contamination has been found except for one of his uniform shirts, and that was a just few spores on his right sleeve."

"No time to have been anywhere else?" Mackenzie said. "It sounds like he was barely exposed if all they found were a few spores on a shirtsleeve. Pulmonary anthrax means he had to have breathed it in. If there was a cloud of the material around, there would be a hell of a lot more than just one case. Anthrax is bad, but just how virulent is this strain, anyway?"

"The CDC has confirmed the identity of the strain," Straker said. "They had such a small sample to work from, it took some time for them to grow enough to make their tests. The man died of Anthrax 836."

"Okay, besides being bad, just what is Anthrax 836?" Reaper said. "It sounds like the title from a science-fiction movie."

"More like a horror film," Mackenzie said. "Anthrax 836 was a Soviet biological weapons strain. A very nasty one. They said they destroyed all of their stocks of it back in the mid-1990s."

"From what I've been told," Straker said, "it is just about the most lethal strain of anthrax ever known. This stuff could cause a biblical-scale plague. It was developed from a mutant strain found among some sewer rats living below an old bio lab. The Soviets took that as a starting point and made 836 from it."

"Okay," Reaper said, "this is bad stuff. But the government has lots of agencies who are better equipped for combating this sort of thing than we are. My men and I are a direct-action unit. It doesn't sound like you have a target for us, or am I missing something?"

"No," Straker said, "you have come to the point of things. There are other agencies already investigating this threat. The trouble is, the CIA can't effectively, or legally, operate inside of the United States. That's still the purview of the FBI. They handle counterintelligence and are the primary investigators for counterterrorism within our borders. The trouble is, terrorists aren't criminals. What they do is a criminal act, but they have to be dealt with using intelligence actions, which FBI doesn't do very well. The intelligence reform law the Congress has passed isn't going to change that, certainly not soon enough to do this situation any good."

"But we aren't intelligence spooks either," Reaper said. "We can develop what we need to hit a target, but finding the target sounds like it's the problem here."

"There are ways of getting you the intelligence skills you need," Straker said as he leaned across his desk. Pressing a button on the large phone that sat on the side of his desk, he called out to his secretary. "Mrs. Beacon?"

"Yes, sir?" came the response over the speaker.

"Could you please go into the other office and ask Ms. Deveraux to come in here?"

"Yes, sir."

"And just who is Deveraux?" Reaper said, suspicion in his voice.

"She is going to be the newest member of your team," Straker said. "Consider her an intelligence specialist, and an extremely accomplished one. She was an operative with the Czechoslovakian *Statni Bezpecnost,* the StB, their elite state secret police. Not exactly the same kind of state police as you may be used to. The StB was a major player in the international espionage game. They worked terrorists as well as other groups until the overthrow of the communist government and the dissolution of Czechoslovakia in the early 1990s. When the StB was officially dissolved in 1989, Deveraux took the chance to flee the country. Probably the biggest reason for her defection was the fact that she met, and later married, a member of the British diplomatic delegation to Czechoslovakia, a Peter Deveraux."

"Wild guess," Caronti said, "Deveraux is not her maiden name."

"He was a member of British intelligence who tried to recruit her, but she wouldn't work directly against her own country. However, when the communist ideology collapsed so completely and her government fell, she couldn't stand working in support of terrorists anymore, so she defected to the West and ended up working with MI-5 when her husband wasn't allowed to operate outside of the country after he'd married her."

"So what's she doing here?" Reaper said. "And why is she going to work with us?"

"MI-5 is British counterintelligence," Straker said.

"They can operate inside the borders of the United Kingdom, and they do a pretty good job of it. While on a CT assignment in Ireland, Peter Deveraux was killed by the car bomb attacks in Omagh in 1998. Twenty-nine people were killed and two hundred and twenty wounded during that attack. Since then, his widow has made it a crusade of hers to take down the men responsible for that bombing."

A sharp knock on the door interrupted Straker's explanation. The door opened a moment later and a strikingly beautiful woman walked in. She was of medium height and wore her jet-black hair in a mid-length cut that stopped above her neckline. Her dark complexion and slight almond shape to her eyes gave her face an exotic beauty. The low heels on the shoes she wore complemented the shape of her stocking-covered legs, though they didn't look like they needed much help in that department. And the gray skirt and white sleeveless silk blouse completed an outfit that looked elegant, while still showing that the woman wearing it had a very good figure.

As the men all stood up from their seats, Deveraux moved smoothly into the room. Straker quickly introduced her to each of the men.

"This is Ted Reaper," Straker said, "the leader of this unit. Reaper, this is Margo Deveraux."

"Pleased to meet you," Deveraux said as she held out her hand.

"Admiral Straker was just telling us about you," Reaper said as he shook her hand. It was a firm grip, but not one of those where the woman tried to demonstrate she could be as strong as a man. Reaper had been impressed with what Straker said about the woman.

And she certainly looked competent enough, though he would hold off on any final judgment.

Meeting each of the men in turn, Margo then turned back to Straker.

"I can assume that you're told them why I am here?" she said.

"I was getting to the specifics of that," Straker said. "Take a seat, please, everyone, and I'll give you the intelligence we have on the situation so far.

"It was while investigating the custom inspector's death that we got our first real lead on who may have been responsible for bringing the anthrax into the country. Something must have triggered that customs agent's personal radar, or he was just being diligent in his job. Whatever the reason, he left us the biggest clue as to who may have had the anthrax. We took a very close look at his records for his last several days on the job, especially the passport numbers he had scanned."

"One of the passports was bogus?" Caronti said.

"No," Straker said, "the worst thing that was found along those lines was that someone used an expired one. The FBI ran a close check on everyone who had given a passport as their ID those two days and they found one very interesting discrepancy. The passport for a fifty-four-year-old citizen named Peter Gregg is legitimate. The only thing is that, according to Medicare records, Mr. Gregg hasn't been traveling for a while. He's a patient at the Holiday House, a long-term care facility near Chicago, where he's being treated for early-onset Alzheimer's. The guy doesn't know what century it is and can barely communicate. He has no relatives and no visitors. But somehow he recently traveled to Canada.

And he bought a late-model used car in the Chicago area within a day of returning from Canada.

"The only train that runs from Canada into Chicago by way of Port Huron starts its run from Toronto. The Royal Canadian Mounted Police had a recent unsolved murder of a Maria Curgacio in the metropolitan Toronto area. The coroner report states that she had been killed at least several days before her body was found, about the time that Gregg crossed into the United States. And she turned out to be someone with a very interesting background. That's where Margo became involved."

"When MI-5 was contacted by the Canadian authorities, they brought me into the situation," Deveraux said. "That investigation quickly brought me here. The woman who was killed was Lizabetti Cifani, an ex-Red Brigade terrorist during her younger days in Italy. Back when I was still with the StB in Czechoslovakia, the Red Brigades were just one of the terrorist organizations that received state support through my organization. With the breakup of the Brigades, she went underground, eventually hooking up with the Provisional Irish Republican Army. Specifically, she had become a member of a cell run by a Patrick Devlin. He spread his skills out to a lot of groups in Ireland and elsewhere. He is one of the most successful terrorists ever to come out of Ireland, and he's gone freelance, mercenary really, selling his skills to any terrorist group anywhere in the world."

"That can't be all that big a market," Reaper said.

"You would be surprised," Deveraux said. "Besides groups in the Middle East and North Africa, Devlin has been reported as having worked for the Russian Mafia and other major criminal groups. Anyone with the money to pay him."

"So you suspect this Devlin has been operating in Canada," Reaper said, "and now he may be in the United States."

"It certainly fits his profile," Deveraux said. "Devlin has a degree in engineering from Edinburgh, Scotland, as well as holding a second in languages. He was one of the PIRAs best weapons men, could make anything from firearms to the most sophisticated explosives, even toxins and poisons. Plus, he took training overseas in Libya and the Soviet Union in both combat skills and intelligence tradecraft.

"He fancies himself a kind of artist, a connoisseur of death. He's used all forms of weapons during his career. For one assassination in Europe, he took the target out with a crossbow. Another time, he used a disguised spray syringe of dimethlysulfoxide and nicotine to eliminate a target while they were both standing in a crowd waiting for a bus. Apparently, he had made the weapon and the toxin himself. There isn't anything he won't use. He's killed with a medieval mace, explosives, firearms, rocket launchers, poisons, and blades. And his extensive tastes don't just center around the tools he uses. He insists on the best of everything whenever he can.

"Though it hasn't been confirmed, one time he sat down in a five-star restaurant in Naples, Italy, consumed a five-course gourmet meal, even down to cigars and brandy, then left a small but very sophisticated bomb attached to the underside of the table where he had been sitting. The bomb detonated just as the police arrived, not two minutes after he had paid his bill and left. Six people were killed by the enhanced fragmentation from that device, one of them the waiter who might have been able to recognize him. The theory is that he called the police in himself. There was no particular target inside that place. It was purely an act of terror and bravado, and the best advertising he could have done to show that he was a terrorist for hire, one of the best in the world."

"So how do you know this Devlin character was the one who did the Cifani woman in Toronto?" Mackenzie asked.

"The way she was killed," Deveraux said. "She was sprayed with prussic acid, hydrogen cyanide. It used to be an assassination tool used by the KGB and some of their brother agencies in Bulgaria and elsewhere. There hasn't been a poisoning like that in Canada ever, according to the RCMP records. But Devlin loved that kind of thing, and he had been a good student of the Soviets."

"How do you know so much about this man and how he operates?" Reaper asked.

"Because he was the one who built the bomb that killed my husband," Deveraux said. "I confirmed that years ago and I've been hunting him ever since. I've been working the underground arms market to try and get a lead on him for the last several years. I've come very close a couple of times, even been in the same room with him, but he has the devil's own luck and a sense of danger that seems almost paranormal sometimes. There hasn't been a trace of him since he was seen in South Africa nearly two years ago. It's been like he dropped off the earth, retired, or was killed. And I don't accept any of those explanations.

"What I think he was doing was setting up for a major operation, something really big that would make him enough money so he could get out of this business.

He's crossed enough people over the years that he's pretty much a marked man. The PIRA wants his head for cheating them as well as taking some of their best men with him when he left. He has a small cadre of extremely loyal, and extremely competent, men.

"When Cifani was killed, her name was flagged on my computer. She was a known associate of Devlin. And her killing has his signature all over it. If he's willing to start wrapping up his network, it means he's trying to cover his trail. The only real reason for that is if he's got a major operation going down and wants to be able to disappear afterwards. That makes him even more dangerous. He's not paranoid or psychotic, but he is extremely intelligent and highly skilled. He managed to almost completely wipe out any record of his past and there are no confirmed pictures of him, not even from his university days. One real weakness of his is his addiction to the thrill of the hunt. That causes him to expose himself and that's how we'll find him."

Chapter Eleven

"This Devlin character sounds like one hell of a bad dude," Caronti said.

"That doesn't even come close to describing this man," Deveraux said. "He will kill anyone without remorse. He has a near-genius-level I.Q., but the morals of a hungry shark. Less than that even. At least a shark only kills to eat."

"But if there isn't any positive way to identify the guy," Warrick asked, "how will we spot him? Weren't there any cameras at the border crossing or customs offices?"

"The border-crossing facility at the Blue Water Bridge is in the process of being expanded," Straker said. "The office that handled the people coming in by train is a new one and not all of the cameras have been installed. We did get pictures of people going in and out of the place, but nothing of the customs desk itself. The FBI has been running biometrics scans of everyone we have a picture of from Michigan and comparing them to the Toronto airport customs pictures given to them by the RCMP. Even cutting down the pictures from Toronto to those within a week of Gregg's border crossing, that's still several thousand people. The FBI computers have only been able to come up with seven people from the Toronto Airport customs area whose facial characteristics come close to matching five of the suspects coming into the United States at Port Huron.

"The biometrics-matching system is still developing. The best of those computer matches is only seventy-three percent positive. That identification isn't good enough to stand up as evidence in court. In spite of that, the FBI is acting on the information. They're trying to tie a warm body to every one of those pictures the computer matched up. The only real problem is that almost none of the suspects has a name attached to the pictures, especially those from the Toronto Airport. We are really working from minimal information here."

"You said you've been in the same room with this Devlin guy?" Warrick said as he turned to Deveraux. "Can't you finger him for the FBI?"

"I wasn't able to pick him out with any certainty from the pictures the FBI showed me," Deveraux said. "He's been known to have had extensive plastic surgery a number of times in the past. Any one of those people could have been him. If I can watch him move, hear his voice, or look him in the eye, I'll be certain."

"What about the FBI investigation?" Mackenzie said. "They have the resources for this kind of thing and it sounds as if they have a handle on it."

"As far as the agents at the FBI are concerned," Straker said, "they are on a straightforward criminal investigation. They are treating this as if they were hunting down an international fugitive, a murderer from Canada who is taking refuge in the United States. Treating this particular quarry as just another criminal is the wrong way to go about it. They are not taking into account the skill level of a successful international terrorist and a guy who's been trained by some of the best spooks on the planet. You have to remember that this guy has been very successful in a business that doesn't accept mistakes. The FBI refuses to accept that at their highest levels. A number of intelligence agencies around the world have tried to nail this guy. Now it's our turn."

"I know we're good at what we do," Reaper said, "but what makes you think that we can get him when no one else has?"

"Several reasons," Straker said. "The most important of which is that you are the best my office can send out into the field on this kind of hunt. And you don't have to work within the same restrictions that the FBI and other law enforcement agencies have to follow. You don't have to wait for a warrant in order to act, but you've proved yourselves more than capable of showing good judgment in investigating a situation, deciding on a course of action, and carrying things through no matter how hard the going gets. And you can think out of the box—way out of the box. The federal law enforcement bureaucracy, even my own offices, have their hands tied by the law. I don't argue with that, the law is a very good thing, it keeps us from just becoming nothing more than a panicked mob. But this is a very serious situation, potentially a lethal one. I need people who can think and move like a terrorist without becoming one, and you can all do that. There may not be time to follow all of the niceties of the law, this is a war and I need warriors to fight it."

"You just want us to hunt this guy down and elimi- nate him?" Warrick said.

"I would prefer he was captured for interrogation," Straker said. "If that doesn't prove practical, I expect you to use your best judgment. We not only need to locate this Devlin character, we need to know what he has and where he intends to use it. The most important thing is to confirm whether a biological weapon exists, locate it, and secure it before it can be used."

"That's one of the problems," Caronti said. "How are we supposed to find this guy if the FBI can't? We don't even know what his target might be."

"You will have access to all of the FBI's information on the case," Straker said. "Only not directly. This of- fice will act as a cutout and feed you any intelligence we receive from the federal end. We will also pass along any intelligence you develop to them. And we have a good idea of where to start looking."

"Where?" Reaper said.

"Central Florida," Straker said. "That's where we've had one good piece of luck in trying to pick up the Gregg trail after it went cold in Chicago. Some fisher- men in Lake Wales found a burned-out car. It appeared that someone had tried to push it off the road and into a swamp to sink it, but it got hung up. They stripped it of the license and VIN plates and set fire to it. The fisher- men were scared to death it might have been holding a body from a murder or drug deal gone bad so they called in the state police."

"Excuse me," Deveraux said, "but what is a VIN plate?"

"That's a metal plate riveted to the car," Caronti said. "It's the vehicle identification number, the serial number for the car, that is put on at the factory."

"Lots of cars get stolen, mostly by kids, and they end up like this," Reaper said.

"Stolen cars taken for a joy ride by kids don't get stripped of their VIN numbers," Straker said. "They burn the cars to get rid of fingerprints or other evidence, but not someplace like where this one was found.

"The whole situation was odd enough to interest the rookie officer who was assigned to write up the case," Straker said. "He was intrigued enough to go to the trouble of digging inside the frame of that wreck and locating one of the special hidden VIN numbers, the ones most thieves don't know the locations of. When he tracked it down, the computer search set off alarm bells at the FBI. That burned-out Honda was the car that Gregg bought in Chicago. They've been concentrating their manhunt efforts in Central Florida and so far have come up with nothing much."

"That doesn't seem to be the kind of car Devlin would use," Deveraux said. "He much prefers a high-performance vehicle, not something as mundane as a Honda."

"It may be that he had to take what he could get in Chicago," Reaper said. "Or could he be keeping a low profile?"

"That's certainly a possibility," Deveraux said, "but it doesn't seem like him. Arrogance and vanity are strong characteristics of his personality. He doesn't believe anyone is smart enough to catch him, but still, he always covers his tracks very well."

"Florida," Warrick said, "what could be his target in Florida?"

"There's enough places for a flashy terrorist attack to give a guy like this the pick of what he would want," Caronti said. "Miami and Orlando are big tourist places. Even in the summer heat there are big crowds of people in open places. With the Fourth of July coming up, the crowds everywhere would just be all that much bigger."

"That's a lot of possible targets," Reaper said. "How are we going to track down the right one?"

"You aren't," Straker said. "Your job is going to be to try and locate Devlin and his people. Your edge is going to be Margo here. She's going to be working with you for this operation."

"A woman?" Warrick said. "We're a direct-action unit. A woman would just get in the way of an operation."

"I assure you," Deveraux said dryly, "I'll do my best not to hold you up."

"This isn't a suggestion," Straker said. "Our deal when I got you all out from under some heavy federal prosecution was that you would take the assignments I gave you and operate for the Department of Homeland Security. This woman is going to be the only real edge you have in finding this Devlin character. And I think you'll find that her field experience will come in handy enough. She has operated in some very hairy theaters of her own and come back to stand right here. What you and your team are going to be doing is hunting down a terrorist, very possibly one armed with a biological weapon of mass destruction. You will need every edge you can come up with."

"Lucky us," Warrick said.

————

"Well," Reaper said, "that was an interesting way to spend time at a meeting."

Having left Straker's office, the four men, accompanied by Margo Deveraux, were in the underground garage that was part of the office building. They were each holding their bags from the airport and walking along the rows of cars. Holding the keys to the vehicle Straker had given them, Reaper was looking at the cars to see which plate matched the tag on the keys.

"So," Caronti said, "what's our next move going to be?"

"Head to the safe house Straker gave us," Mackenzie said. "Silver Spring isn't that far from here. We get there and set up our computer net, contact Deckert and see about getting some of our own intelligence generated."

"Who's Deckert?" Deveraux said.

"He's our support and intelligence man," Warrick said. "Runs the base we have back home. No one you have to worry your head about."

Deveraux stopped walking and looked at Warrick. Her eyes were flashing in anger at the dismissive attitude Warrick had been giving her.

"Let's get something straight," she said, "I have been assigned to your team because Straker assured me you were the very best. That you men could go places and do things no one else he knew could. I will work with any of your people, but understand this: I am a trained intelligence professional, which none of you are. And I doubt that this Deckert individual is, either. I have tracked Devlin halfway around the globe and back again, and I have earned the right to be in on his takedown. You may not like having a woman assigned to you, but you don't have a big choice in the matter. I am qualified to operate in the field and have lived in places that would turn your hair white.

"Well, maybe not yours," Deveraux said as she pointed out Warrick's stark white hair. "But the last thing I need when I may be coming close to a target I've chased for years is a bunch of American military buckaroos acting like I'm just some weak woman who moves papers about."

"Buckaroos?" Caronti questioned.

"I'll bet the lady means cowboys," Warrick responded hotly. "And I don't like the situation no matter how good you think you are, lady. The last thing we need on a hot operation is some woman who wants the head of the target we're going after. Misjudgment on the part of someone who has a personal stake in the guy we're after can not only get you killed, it can take the rest of us down with you. Things are going to be tough enough without having to nurse an Intel weenie along on an op."

Arguing among his people was not something Reaper would normally allow. On an operation, everyone had to work together. Each member of the Four Horsemen had shed blood and sweat in the field together. On their first mission, Ted "Bear" Parnell, who had named the Four Horsemen, had died on the operation to rescue Reaper's wife and son from terrorist kidnappers. If Deveraux wanted to join their ranks, she would have to prove herself fit to do so, no matter what Straker said. Now was as good a time as any to let Warrick clear the air a bit and for Deveraux to show how she reacted in such a situation. Reaper figured that must have been part of the reason the scout-sniper had reacted the way he did, to elicit a reaction from Deveraux. Even though he was the youngest member of the team, Warrick had proven himself a cool operative under hard conditions. You couldn't let emotions overwhelm you and be a successful sniper.

Looking to the other men standing around in the underground garage, Deveraux saw nothing but mild interest in their eyes. Not even Reaper, whom Straker had told her had been a Navy SEAL and was the leader of the Four Horsemen, looked inclined to help her or stop what may be coming. She had read the files on each of these men. They were all accomplished warriors who did not easily accept someone into their ranks. That was all right; she could deal with that. And Deveraux thought she knew exactly how to get through to the ex-Marine in front of her who was making his feelings obvious to everyone.

"I tell you what, Warrick," Deveraux said, "if I can take you out right here and right now, will you accept me as one of you, for the time being at least?"

"Hey," Reaper said, "I don't want anything to get out of hand here. Everyone is going to be needed on this job."

"Don't worry," Warrick said, "I was brought up better than that. I won't fight a lady."

"That's too bad," Deveraux said, "because I'm going to fight you."

She turned to face Warrick, who, accepting the inevitable, had dropped his bag and was starting to raise his hands in a fighting stance. He was only of medium height and slender build, but Deveraux knew looks could be deceiving. He was an ex-Marine and a scout-sniper to boot. That meant the man was tough, resourceful, and wouldn't quit easily. She had to take him down quickly and cleanly. And if he was badly hurt or injured in the process, that would lessen her in the eyes of the rest of the men no matter what the outcome of the fight was.

All of that went through Deveraux's mind in an instant. As she turned to Warrick, she jumped up, snapping her feet forward one at a time in rapid succession. Her "sensible" low-heeled shoes flew off her feet toward Warrick's face.

Instinctively, Warrick raised his arms to protect his face from the flying footwear. He wouldn't have taken much damage from the shoes, but that wasn't Deveraux's plan.

As Warrick's hands went up, Deveraux dropped to the ground, her left leg folding underneath her. With her right leg outstretched, she spun on her left foot, sweeping her opponent's legs out from underneath him. As Warrick fell backward, Deveraux rolled forward, only her legs and hands touching the ground.

When Warrick hit the ground flat on his back, Deveraux was already moving through the air to land on top of his chest. With her knee on his stomach, the air left the ex-Marine's lungs with a loud "whoosh." But Deveraux wasn't finished yet. As she landed on Warrick, her arms crossed over her breasts, her hands darting inside her blouse under her armpits. What couldn't be seen by any of the men was how Deveraux was pulling special curved knives from hidden sheaths attached to her bra. They only saw her move with stunning speed. Keeping her wrists crossed, Deveraux stopped her hands, clenching the knives, inches from either side of Warrick's neck.

"Freeze!" Reaper bellowed in the same tone of voice that had terrified SEAL trainees at basic underwater demolition/SEAL training. "That's enough! Warrick, you've lost, it's over. Don't push it. Deveraux, I think you've made your point. You can put your toys away now."

For the moment, Warrick just lay there flat on his back trying to get some air into his lungs. As his eyes rolled around, he never saw the short curved blades in the hands crossed under his chin. Reaper had seen the gleam of the sharpened steel edges flash as they were drawn. There was no question that Deveraux had taken Warrick down, in a fight that lasted between ten and fifteen seconds at the most. Mackenzie and Caronti were looking at Deveraux with a new respect in their eyes as she got off of Warrick's chest. It was obvious the woman could play the game well enough for them to be satisfied—for the moment, at any rate.

With her hands held carefully open, Deveraux drew her legs underneath her and stood. Now, the short curved blades of two odd-looking knives could be seen dangling from both of her index fingers like very strange jewelry. The flat black finish of the knives stood out against the white of Deveraux's palms, the sharply curved handles pierced with a series of holes to make the wicked little tools light and easy to carry.

"I see you shop with Ernie Emerson, too," Reaper said.

As Deveraux looked at him, she moved her left hand up to her right armpit. Now, Reaper could see the plastic sheath attached to what must have been the woman's bra. The nasty little blade went back into the sheath and was seated without a sound.

"Yes, I like his La Griffe," Deveraux said as she looked at the blade in her right hand. "Mary, his wife, recommended it to me. She also suggested a good place to carry it. It works for me."

Now it could be plainly seen that a large hole in the handle, just underneath where the blade began, let the knife fit over the index finger of the hand like a ring. It was the most lethal-looking hideaway knife Caronti had ever seen.

"What's a La Griffe?" he said.

"That's what Emerson calls his Claw," Reaper said. "Okay, are we done now?"

"Looks like she may have even gotten through to this thick-headed Marine," Mackenzie said as he helped Warrick get to his feet. "He's going to be loopy for a while, but he'll be fine."

"So, anyone know a good place to eat?" Reaper said as he went back to looking for their assigned car.

"There's a great delicatessen in Silver Spring," Mackenzie said. "The Parkway Deli on Grubb Road. We have to go near there to get to the safe house, anyway."

"A deli on Grubb Road?" Reaper said. "Who would put a place to eat on a street like that?"

"Hey, they've got great corned-beef sandwiches," Mackenzie said. "Good matzo-ball soup, too."

"Maybe we should ask the lady where she might like to eat," Warrick said, a little unsteadily.

"Oh, deli food sounds good to me," Deveraux said with a bright smile. "I need to change my hose though, seems I got a run in them. Could we stop at the safe house first? My bags are already there."

"Not a problem," Reaper said.

Chapter Twelve

The safe house was a brick-walled four-bedroom ranch on a cul-de-sac road in Silver Spring, just north of Washington, D.C. One of the rooms was outfitted with high-speed Internet connections and other communications equipment, so that was immediately dubbed "the office." With a woman now part of their number, Reaper, Warrick, Mackenzie, and Caronti split the other two rooms. After years of barracks and shipboard life, sharing a room was not a major hardship.

Their meal together at the neighborhood delicatessen had been a good one. It looked to Reaper as though any friction about having a woman with them had been temporarily forgotten. Or maybe it was the demonstration of her fighting ability against Warrick. Certainly the ex-Marine was treating the intelligence expert with a lot more respect than he had shown earlier. Caronti still demonstrated a certain male viewpoint when they had stopped at the safe house to let Deveraux change clothes. He thought that legs like hers looked great in hose and they should make every effort to allow the woman a chance to get into a new pair.

A powerful desktop computer was available in the office and Deveraux wasted no time getting online after they returned from the deli. Straker had made a number of secure computer connections available to the teams, including access to restricted databases at the Justice Department, the FBI, the National Security Agency, and Homeland Security. In addition, Deveraux had her own access to files at MI-5 as well as a number of unauthorized means to enter other, even more secure locations. Though he had been becoming considerably more adept at using the Internet to gather information, Reaper was amazed at the woman's skill with the silicon and electronic wonder on the desk in front of her.

Later, everyone gathered in the living room of the house to discuss their plan of action. The place was furnished in what could politely be called "early garage sale" style. But the house had been chosen for its secure location and not its contents. The short road the house was on ended at a stream with banks that dropped over fifteen feet. There was no way anyone could easily come up them. Across the street was a huge open field surrounding a church, with no cover for several hundred yards. And anyone parking on the street to keep the house under surveillance would find themselves ticketed by local law enforcement for parking in a restricted residential zone. With any immediate questions about their security taken care of, the five occupants of the safe house turned their attention to the mission at hand.

"Does anyone have any idea how we should address

the search for this Devlin character?" Reaper said. "I am open to suggestions."

"Locating fugitives is one thing the FBI is really known for," Caronti said. "Maybe we should leave the investigation angle up to them, in spite of what Straker suggested."

"You want to tell the admiral that we're going to ignore his suggestion?" Reaper said, waiting. "I didn't think so. No, the FBI is searching for this guy, but according to the information Deveraux has downloaded, they haven't any more of an idea where he is than we do."

"Okay," Mackenzie said. "What if we stop looking for Devlin and take a different approach?"

"And that is?" Reaper said.

"The FBI is looking for Gregg," Mackenzie said, "or Devlin, or whatever he calls himself now. Since we have access to everything they find, what if we stop looking for the who and start looking for the what?"

"The what?" Reaper said. "Okay, you've lost me."

"The weapon," Mackenzie said. "Not the person, but the anthrax, the biological weapon. What would the guy need in terms of materials, location, and support to make anthrax? And especially, what might his target be?"

"The FBI has a lot of manpower looking at that end of things too," Reaper said, "along with the rest of the intelligence agencies in Washington and elsewhere."

"Probably," Mackenzie said, "but do you have a better idea?"

Silence followed.

"God," Reaper said, "you're right. But I hate bugs worse than I hate gas—and I really don't think much of nerve gas. But we have to brainstorm some ideas here.

Where do we start looking for these people? And if not the people, what would they need to make a weapon out of what they have? The alphabet-soup agencies here in Washington are going to be hitting all of the obvious places: laboratories, hospitals, colleges, and other places that work with biological materials. We have to come up with some of the odd ones, the places that wouldn't be obvious."

"So just what do you need to grow anthrax?" Caronti said, "Sheep?"

"No," Mackenzie said. "Don't worry, your girlfriends are safe."

A chuckle went around the room at that one. Even Deveraux laughed at the joke.

"Anthrax used to be known as wool sorter's disease," Mackenzie said, "especially pulmonary anthrax. The spores survive well enough in the wool of sheep and men handling the stuff could breathe them in. Actually, I'm kind of surprised that a pirate like Caronti here would even know the reference."

"Hey," Caronti said, "I'm more than a pretty face."

"Pretty face?" Warrick said, staring at his roommate.

"Enough," Reaper said, putting an end to the banter. Privately, he was glad to see the men relaxing enough with Deveraux in the room to take part in the horseplay that they were used to in times of stress. That was something Bear had always been great at. The thought of his old friend quickly brought Reaper back to the problem at hand.

"So what do you need to make anthrax?" Reaper said.

"To just grow the stuff?" Mackenzie said. "You need a viable seed culture, a reactor vessel, a heat source, nutrient solution, and time. Not a hell of a lot of sophisticated equipment, really. The Pentagon sent a bunch of college biology students out years back to see if they could make a laboratory to grow anthrax simulant and weaponize it."

"Did they?" Deveraux said.

"Took them about six months and not much in the way of money either, as I remember," Mackenzie said.

"How much time to actually grow the bacteria?" Reaper said.

"I would think a week or so to really grow a good culture," Mackenzie said. "That is, four to five days. You could have a very viable threat after less than half a day from just growing the seed stock."

"The seed stock?" Reaper said.

"That would be the larger amount you grew in, say, a test tube or petri dish," Mackenzie said, "after you inoculated it with a sample of the bacteria."

"Like a sample of the spores from a Soviet weapons lab?" Reaper said.

"Exactly like that."

"What's nutrient solution?" Caronti asked.

"Just broth, really," Mackenzie said. "Kind of a thin, sterile beef soup. Nothing more than water, beef extract, peptone, and salt."

"That doesn't sound like the jelly stuff we used in high school biology lab," Warrick said.

"It isn't," Mackenzie said. "What you're thinking of is what's called agar, kind of a gelatin made from seaweed. Nutrient solution is a liquid, a much easier way to produce this kind of bacteria in bulk."

"But what's a reactor vessel?" Deveraux said, impressed with Mackenzie's knowledge base.

"Not much more than a big jar," Mackenzie said. "Something that can maintain a controlled temperature. Industrially, it's called a fermenter."

"You mean like a beer fermenter?" Caronti said.

"Exactly like that," Mackenzie said. "Growing bacteria isn't a lot different than growing yeast. You can do it with the same equipment you use to make beer."

"You mean like in a microbrewery?" Reaper said.

"A still," Caronti said. "That won't do much good. There must be thousands of illegal bootlegging operations all over the South, let alone Florida."

"No," Mackenzie said. "A bootlegger runs a fermentation vat. But that wouldn't be good enough to grow a decent bacteria culture—not under any kind of controlled conditions, it wouldn't. And a still just isn't a part of the process. We can discount bootleggers. A microbrewery—that fits the bill nicely."

"That would also fit with Devlin's needs," Deveraux said. "And he has people in his organization very familiar with the pubs and breweries back in Ireland. That could give him an in to that kind of business. To use this kind of weapon, he would have to make a big statement, a terrorist attack that the whole world couldn't miss seeing. And one spectacular enough that they couldn't look away from it. Would a brewery—one of these microbreweries—be big enough to make what he would need?"

"Easily," Mackenzie said. "And a restaurant or kitchen could have the stuff he needed to make the nutrient solution. The peptone might be harder to find. But enough places use the stuff as a growth medium that anyone organized as well as this Devlin seems to be would have no trouble securing what he would need."

"Then that sounds like a starting point," Reaper said. "We can cut back on the size of the search by concentrating on the smaller manufacturers. Those microbreweries that have been so popular the last few years come and go all over the place. No one would even notice a new one going up, or an old one going out of business and someone still running the plant behind closed doors. Plus the little places would need only a few people to run it. That cuts way down on the number of people who would even know about the place. So we can start by looking for any microbreweries that have sold in Central Florida within, say, the last year. If we don't find any that meet our parameters, we go back another year."

"Is that the only search parameter?" Deveraux said.

"Give extra weight to any breweries with bars, especially those with kitchen facilities," Reaper said. "Brew pubs, I think they call them now."

Getting up from the couch, Deveraux headed back to the office and the computer connection there. Reaper and the rest of the men soon followed her. Within only a short time, Deveraux had entered the Bureau of Alcohol, Tobacco, Firearms, and Explosives database. They were the federal agency that would license any start-up microbrewery. After getting a list of names and places from that source, she searched out any sales sites for brewing equipment or auction sites for microbrewing equipment, cross-referencing the information with that from the BATFE.

"I have over two hundred possibles in the southeastern United States," Deveraux said. "Sixty-four in Florida alone."

"Microbrewing must be a popular business," Reaper said as he looked over Deveraux's shoulder. "So let's limit the search further. Eliminate all of the locations that were purchased by established businesses, corporations, or brand-name outlets. You can cross-check the licenses at the BATFE site against the business licenses issued over the last year in Florida. For now, just drop any that list multiple business addresses."

"Florida is a big tourist area," Deveraux said. "It would appeal to a man like Devlin. It's much easier to hide in a big crowd that changes all the time than to remain concealed in an established area. The flow of people could also help explain the number of these places in the state. Those could be some of the reasons Devlin went to that area in the first place. And if the area proved good enough, he just might still be there."

After tapping on the keys for a few moments, Deveraux looked back from the computer screen.

"That reduced the number in Florida to twenty-three places that fit the parameters," she said.

"Still too many," Reaper said. "The feds have the manpower to check out that many places, but we sure don't. Okay, limit the search further to only the businesses that are owned by limited corporations of two people or less."

More input on the computer keyboard and a short wait.

"Still twelve places that fit the bill," Deveraux said.

"How about any place that is owned outright by private citizens or a small corporation?" Mackenzie said from the doorway to the office. "You know, places that have no bank liens or mortgages on them. Bought outright with cash or something like that. Check BATFE for the name on the alcohol license and bank records."

This time, the computer input took a lot longer in order to check all of the bank records for the businesses on the list.

"That knocked the list down to only two," Deveraux said a moment later.

"Two is a number we can deal with," Reaper said. "What are the names and locations of these places?"

"There's the Beachside Ale House," Deveraux said, "a microbrewery in Miami. Wait a moment, there's a flag on this file."

She tapped on the keyboard for a moment and looked at the flat-panel display screen, her forehead wrinkled in concentration.

"No, we can take that one off the list," she said at last. "They declared bankruptcy three months ago. All of the assets of the place were sold by auction to meet their debt load. Even the empty building was sold."

"That pretty much puts them out of the running, I would think," Reaper said. "What's the name of the other place?"

"The Gaia Holistic Brewery," Deveraux said. "A new place just opened in the Orlando area. Owned by a limited partnership of two men. And the business location was paid for and started up with funds from an offshore account in the Bahamas."

"You can buy a bar with money from an offshore account?" Caronti said. "That sounds interesting."

"The Gaia Holistic Brewery?" Reaper said. "That is the weirdest name. And I'm certain I've heard of it before. I just can't think of where."

"Gaia is the Earth Mother," Warrick said. "She's the goddess for some of the New Age religions." He saw Caronti and Mackenzie looking at him strangely.

"Hey," Warrick said, "it was a girlfriend of mine from years back. She was into all of this New Age, Earth Mother stuff. She was sure she could change me over to what she considered the right way of thinking."

"And did she?" Caronti asked.

"No," Warrick said. "I'm hanging with you guys and not her, aren't I?"

"That isn't necessarily a point in your favor," Mackenzie said to his embarrassed friend.

"Well, the place fits all of our search points," Deveraux said. "That makes it a good possibility, in my book."

"Mine, too," Reaper said. "By the looks of things, not even the FBI could get a search warrant on the place. Even with the Patriot Act on their side, they couldn't get a judge to sign off on the warrant. So the only way that Gaia place was ever examined was when they got their license inspection. Probably their premises were inspected before they could get a business license, but since then, nothing. No one has been inside the place."

"No health inspection, anything like that?" Caronti said.

"Nothing on the record," Reaper replied.

As the two men were talking, Deveraux continued working on the computer.

"This is interesting," she said.

"What have you got?" Reaper said as he looked back at the computer screen.

"This Gaia place received their alcohol license more than three months ago, according to the BATFE," Deveraux said. "But they aren't open for business yet, or at least there aren't any public hours listed anywhere for them. There isn't even a phone number for the place."

"Tells me they aren't in business," Caronti said. "But someone spent a hell of a lot of money for a business front and licenses."

"Well," Deveraux said, "if they aren't running an active business, why is the power bill for that building so high?"

Deveraux leaned back from the computer screen so everyone could see the information she had pulled up. In just a few minutes, she had hacked into the power company's database and pulled up the billing record for the Gaia Brewery.

"Damn," Caronti exclaimed, "that's more than I pay to run my boathouse in Virginia Beach. And we have machine tools running in there. If they aren't open for business, they must be stacking the place full of barrels."

"Might not be barrels full of beer," Mackenzie said. "And look at who the bill was paid by. One Dr. E. Peters."

"Wouldn't a doctor be a useful person to have around if you were trying to grow a biological agent?" Warrick asked.

"Strikes me as a good idea," Reaper replied.

"So, what now?" Warrick exclaimed. "We contact the state police down in Florida and tell them what we've found?"

"If the feds haven't been able to get a warrant," Reaper said, "then the state cops won't be able to either. We don't have much of anything here to go on, not legally, at any rate. And since this whole bio-weapons threat is classified, we couldn't tell them what we suspected was in the place. If they thought it was a possible biological weapons production plant, they would go in with a Hazmat team, at the very least.

"Try and keep a hazardous materials team callout a secret from the media. They have reporters watching them practically night and day. And that sure as hell would blow the cover off of this little situation. Not exactly something that would make Straker very happy with us."

"So, we go in," Mackenzie stated matter-of-factly.

"Like the admiral said, we aren't the police," Caronti said. "We don't need no stinkin' warrant."

"Well, yeehah," Reaper said with a grin. "Back to Florida, Warrick's favorite state."

"You spent way too much time in Arizona last year," Caronti laughed. "You mean hooyah, don't you?"

"Oohrah!" Warrick said loudly, sounding off with the enthusiastic cry of the Marines.

The three men turned to Mackenzie.

"Don't look at me," he said, "we speak English in the Air Force. How about her?"

"Ummm, Yahoo?" she said, pointing at the computer screen.

The men all laughed, and Deveraux just shook her head with a smile.

Chapter Thirteen

"You're in command here," Deveraux said. "What do you want to be our first step?"

"Right now," Reaper replied, "that's the only easy answer. We get set up to conduct the rest of this operation. Right now, we're short of manpower and could use some additional materials. Caronti, you're going to fly down to Miami with Warrick and pick up our gear there. Get up to the Orlando area and set us up a base of operations. Rent a house, apartment—whatever we'll need. It's the summer now and off-season. You should be able to pick and choose a bit."

"A storage locker for the ordnance?" Warrick asked.

"Shouldn't need it," Reaper said, "but check out what's available, anyway. Warrick, I want you to do a sneak-and-peek on the area around the target. Get us some eyes-on intel. Deveraux, you're going to fly down to Orlando with me later."

"What do you want me to do?" Mackenzie said.

"I'm calling Deckert down from Michigan," Reaper said. "He can bring down some of the additional gear and ammo we'll need, so make sure I know what you want in addition to what we already have down in Florida. After he gets here, you'll drive down to Florida with him. Right now, I want more intel gathered on the area around Orlando and particularly that Gaia Brewery. Deveraux, you start hitting that on the computer. Caronti, you and Warrick hit the road as soon as you can."

Once they each had a specific part of the mission to perform, all of the members of Reaper's team went into action. Caronti and Warrick were on the road within hours of receiving their instructions from Reaper. Each person knew what was going to be necessary for the upcoming operation and went ahead to conduct his part of it. Deveraux had never worked with Reaper or his men before, but liked what she had seen at their introduction. She had been a professional in the intelligence and counterterrorism business for a long time and felt right at home working with competent people who knew their jobs. Each man could do what was needed without instructions, but they all looked to Reaper for leadership and coordination. They were a formidable force, and Straker had been right in sending men like these up against Devlin. They would make no assumptions that would underestimate the capabilities of their opponent, or the terrible weapon he had at hand.

The only real difficulty anyone had with the preparations for the operation came from Mackenzie. After making the arrangements through Straker's offices, Mackenzie had headed over to the Army Medical Center in Bethesda, Maryland. He had returned with enough syringes and serum to give everyone in the team an anthrax booster. No one was exempt from the ex-Air Force man's unrelenting needle. Deveraux was amused to watch and listen to the men's complaints about the injection—such a little thing compared to what they might be facing. When it became her turn to get the shot, her opinion came closer to matching that of the rest of the guys. Rather than face the retribution of his teammates, Mackenzie wisely saw to his own injection.

During her years with the Czech StB, and later British MI-5, Margo Deveraux had seen a lot of hard men, and quite a number of brutal men. Reaper and his team appeared as competent and skilled as the best she had ever seen among the British Special Air Service and Special Boat Service troops. None of that experience had prepared her to meet Keith Deckert, one of the men in Reaper's team that the others obviously respected, in spite of the fact that the man was in a wheelchair.

Inside of twelve hours of receiving the request from Reaper, Keith Deckert had arrived at the safe house in Silver Springs, after driving directly down from Michigan in his van. The new 2004 Chevy Express 3500 passenger van had dark tinted windows, which prevented anyone on the outside from seeing what was going on inside the vehicle. Pulling the van into the attached garage of the safe house further eliminated any possibility of outside observers seeing what was going on. The vehicle had already been modified to accept Deckert's wheelchair and had a special lift installed on the left side cargo doors. With Deckert's handicap plates, even though they were from Michigan, Reaper felt the van would easily blend in with the Florida retired community. And the van would be a perfect base to hide their surveillance activities.

When Deveraux watched Deckert move about in his wheelchair, she quickly got over any thoughts that the big man was handicapped. The big arms and chest of the man in the chair easily handled the boxes of ammunition and weapons he had brought in the back of his van. His beaming broad smile under a bushy mustache also showed his good humor when he was introduced to Deveraux.

"Finally," Deckert said, shaking hands with Deveraux after they were introduced, "we get a little class in this organization. Good-looking class, too."

"Stop trying to turn on the charm," Reaper said with a laugh.

"I don't know," Deveraux said as she put her arm around Deckert's shoulder and leaned into him. "There's something to be said about a man who knows how to compliment a lady."

Everyone in the garage laughed over that, Deckert the loudest of all.

"So what took you so long?" Mackenzie said.

"Hey, you're lucky I was at the shop when I got your message," Deckert said. "If I had been up at the island, I would still be trying to get here."

"So what did you manage to bring along?" Reaper asked.

"Just about everything you wanted," Deckert said. "I've got half a dozen M4A1 carbines with the CQBR uppers and accessories. Plus a couple of cases each of Engel Ballistic Research's 5.56mm and 9mm frangible ammo. I figured you already had the Shrike and a couple of M203's down here, so I included a case of M433 high-explosive dual-purpose rounds, as well as a couple of cases of 5.56mm linked ammo, along with some loose M855 ball. Oh, and that new DRS Technologies 3000/4000 thermal-weapon sight came in from NVEC. I figured Warrick would want his new toy, so I brought it along. Where is he, anyway?"

"Warrick and Caronti are both in Miami picking up the truck and gear we had down there," Reaper said. "We'll be hooking back up with them in a few days."

"Excuse me," Deveraux said. "Just what is a CQBR upper?"

"That's a special ten-inch-barrel upper receiver for an M4A1 carbine," Deckert said. "It makes for a very compact, light, and quick-handling weapon for close-quarters battle. There's a rail adapter system on it that lets the weapon accept accessories that make it easier and faster to use, like GG & G offset tactical flashlight mounts with M3 lights and vertical foregrips, along with carbine visible lasers. And the flat top of the M4A1 receiver lets it take the Aimpoint Comp M2 compact sight in GG & G mounting rings and Aimpoint's flip-up rear and front backup sights."

"You just had to ask him, didn't you?" Mackenzie said. "He can't get past the fact that he used to be a salesman for this stuff."

"You Americans are *so* gadget happy," Deveraux said, shaking her head.

"Hey," Deckert said with his constant humor, "when you've got it, flaunt it."

"Be nice," Reaper said. "Not only are you going to have to work with the pretty lady, she's already knocked down and beat up Warrick once already."

"Oh, I'm impressed," Deckert said. "Not everyone can best our resident jarhead. And I get to work with her? Cool."

While Reaper and Deveraux brought Deckert up to speed on the situation, Mackenzie drove the Chevy Express to the garage facilities suggested by Straker. Duplicate controls on the steering column and the floor allowed both Deckert and other members of the team to operate the van, one of the reasons Reaper had Deckert bring it down from Michigan. At the garage, technicians worked quickly to install surveillance and communications equipment.

In D.C., Deckert and Mackenzie waited to get the van back from the technicians. To use their time more efficiently, Reaper and Deveraux flew to Orlando to check in with Warrick and Caronti, who had called in that they had secured a house they could use as a base of operations in a place called Harney, north of Orlando. The two men had arrived in Miami and headed directly up to the Orlando area, stopping only long enough to pick up all of the equipment they had left in the hands of the security people at the nuclear power plant.

Once at the Orlando airport, Reaper rented a car. Deciding they needed something with a little more performance, he picked out a 2004 Mustang GT Premium convertible. The car was equipped with a 4.6-liter 300 horsepower OHV V8 engine and a five-speed manual transmission. After picking up the car and loading their bags into the trunk, Reaper and Deveraux were soon heading north to get to Harney, following the directions Caronti had phoned in to them.

"This is your idea of a nondescript car?" Deveraux said once they were on the road. "A red Mustang convertible?"

"Not at all," Reaper said as he swung the performance car through traffic easily. "Matter of fact, I think this thing makes a statement to the public. Mostly one along the lines of 'Here I am, look at me.' And it's the last thing anyone would expect to see being used in a covert investigation of anything, except maybe a race track.

"One thing I've learned is that there are times you really need speed and maneuverability. But when you actually need them, it's too late to go shopping. Those are two characteristics this car has plenty of. And red was the only color they had. What's the matter? You don't like convertibles?"

"Americans and their cars," Deveraux said.

"Yeah," Reaper said. "As Caronti would say, 'Ain't it great?' "

———

Caronti met Reaper and Deveraux at the door when they pulled up to the house.

"Hey, nice wheels," he said as he opened the door.

The house was another ranch-style home, much like the one the men had used down in Homestead. It had four bedrooms and two baths, along with a living room, family room, and kitchen. The garage for the house was detached and in the backyard. The whole yard was surrounded with a four-foot high chain-link fence.

"Nice house," Reaper said as he and Deveraux stood inside the front door. "All it needs is a dog running in the yard and a swing set for the kids."

"No kids around," Caronti said. "This is a retirement community. For the most part, it's pretty empty right now. Just about everybody is up north to avoid the summer heat."

"Where's Warrick?"

"In the shower. He should be out any minute now, I told him you had arrived. He's been spending the day and a good chunk of the night watching the target."

"Yeah," Warrick said as he came from the back of the house into the living room, still rubbing his head with a towel. He was in khaki 5.11 Academy shorts and a polo shirt with sandals on his feet. "The heat down here is only beaten by the humidity this time of year. I sucked a one-hundred-ounce Camelback dry and sweated all of it right back out."

"Camelback?" Deveraux asked.

"Kind of a backpack canteen," Warrick said. "You can drink from it through a hose without moving much, not that anyone would have noticed me."

"What do you mean?" Reaper said as he walked back to the kitchen. Rummaging through the refrigerator, he pulled out two cold bottles of Corona beer. While he was opening the bottles, everyone joined him in the kitchen and sat at the stools along one side of the counter. Reaper handed one of the beers to Deveraux.

"If that Gaia place is an active anything," Warrick said, "you can't prove it by what I've seen. It's down near Chuluo, about fifteen miles from here. Not much around it but farmers' fields and a couple of houses. I didn't have any trouble setting up a hide across the road. From there, I have a clear sight of three walls and all of the entrances.

"This place is maybe five miles from the University of Central Florida and you would think college students would be all over it. Nope, it's never open and there's only two cars that ever come to it. One's a Saab station wagon driven by a white male in his middle thirties, average height, slight build with dark thinning hair and glasses. The other vehicle is a Saturn sedan driven by a real sixties retread, looks like a lost hippie. Mid-forties, long brown hair worn in a ponytail, maybe six feet tall and thin."

"Neither of those men fits Devlin's description," Deveraux said, "even in a disguise. And they don't sound like any of the men he's worked with, either. They aren't exactly the kind of people you'd describe as slight or thin."

"I haven't run the license plate numbers," Warrick said, "but here they are."

He tossed a small open notebook on the table and slid it across to Reaper.

"Does the place look like we could do a black-bag operation on it?" Reaper said. "Break in and conduct a sneak-and-peek?"

"I don't think so," Warrick said. "That's the strange thing about it. The two sets of double doors are at the front and back toward the rear of the building on the right side. Heavy steel doors with deadbolt locks. I've watched both of these guys use several keys to open them, so they're probably double- if not triple-locked. And it looks like there's a pretty good alarm system on the place, judging by the stickers on the doors and cables leading into the building. I don't think we could break in without someone knowing we were there."

"What about just going in the front door?" Deveraux said.

Everyone just looked at her and waited.

"I mean knock on the front door and go in ourselves—disguised. Couldn't we be these liquor license inspectors or someone like that?"

"As long as we're not cops," Warrick said.

"What do you mean by that?" Reaper asked.

"That's been the only other vehicle stopping at this place," Warrick said. "In the middle of the afternoon, a sheriff's car pulled up in the parking lot and a deputy went up to the door. He banged on it and it opened up. Spent about six minutes in the place, came out, and drove off."

"That pretty much makes notifying the local law enforcement about the place a bad idea," Caronti said.

"Devlin wouldn't be above bribing locals to look the other way," Deveraux said. "He would just consider it a cost of doing business as long as they never found out what he really was doing. Then he would just kill them and run."

"You've been watching this place for how long?" Reaper said to Warrick.

"Just most of last night and part of today," Warrick said. "I went out there soon after we got here. I left setting this place up to Caronti."

"Okay," Reaper said. "Then we wait until Mackenzie and Deckert get here tomorrow. You get some food and head back out to your hide. Deveraux will run these license plates through the Department of Motor Vehicles database and see if we get a hit on them. I don't want to raid this place without more information than we have right now."

"I'm good for the night," Warrick said. "I only came in because Caronti told me you were arriving today."

"All right," Reaper said, "use your best judgment on staying out there. Is there a place we could park a van without being seen easily from the target?"

"Yes," Warrick said. "There's a side road lined with trees and brush not a hundred yards from the place.

You go down the road and pull into the trees and you have a pretty good view of the building and grounds."

"Then we'll get Deckert to set up a surveillance operation to back up yours," Reaper said. "That should tell us more."

———

Three days later, the group knew little more than they had learned from Warrick's first report. Everyone on Reaper's team took a turn watching the pub from Deckert's van. Only the same two cars showed up at the building on a daily basis. Not even the sheriff's deputy had come by again. After having watched and listened to the place for over twenty-four hours straight, none of the sophisticated closed-circuit TV equipment or parabolic microphones had picked up anything more than local traffic. The two cars were as Warrick had described them and Deveraux again said that neither of the drivers looked like Devlin or an accomplice of his. The only thing they had learned was that one of the license plates was registered to a professional medical association and the other belonged to a Bill Davis, an associate professor at the local university.

"Okay," Reaper said at an evening meeting at the house. "We have nothing much except a hunch. Something hinky is going on in that place. As a brewery, they have zip for customers. They aren't even open for business. But the power drain for that place says something is going on inside that building, and I want to know what. It could be that Devlin hired these guys to grow his bio-weapon while he's out setting up a target. Or they are the worst businessmen I have ever heard of. Either way, we need to move on this."

"We may be able to use their power consumption as a means of getting into the place," Deveraux said.

"I don't think they'll let a meter reader into the place," Warrick said. "All of the meters are outside the building by the back door."

"No, not meter readers," Deveraux said. "But how about building inspectors checking out the power? That could get us into the place through the front door while the rest of you set up for a dynamic entry at the back. Once we have both men in sight, you can come in and take the place down."

"Who's 'you'?" Reaper asked.

"Why, you and me, of course," Deveraux said with a smile.

"This sounds like a plan," Mackenzie said.

"I agree," Reaper said. "Barring anything new, we go in tomorrow afternoon."

Chapter Fourteen

The next morning, it still looked like further observation of the Gaia Brewery wouldn't come up with any more useful information than what the team already had. But just because there hadn't been any sign of additional personnel in the building did not make Reaper assume no one was there. Whatever was going on, the two individuals who came in every day acted suspiciously just in the way they moved. As far as Warrick was concerned, they acted dirty as hell. The sniper was basing his opinions on his experience from having worked for several years as a bail enforcement agent, a bounty hunter who tracked down criminals on a regular basis.

"If I was a cop," Warrick had said the night before, "all my radar would be going off on these two. I'd bet my badge that something is going on in that brewery."

The sniper went back to his hide early that morning, only this time, he wasn't simply observing. He had with him his favored EBR Wraith suppressed rifle. The 16-inch-barrel bolt-action rifle was a precision-made piece of ordnance, designed for use with a suppressor and subsonic ammunition. The SWR Wraith heavy-duty suppressor on the muzzle of the weapon reduced the sound of firing EBR 7.62mm Thumper ammunition to little more than a quiet *huff*. He would need the precise shooting ability of the weapon, along with the view the 3.5×15-power 50mm Nightforce scope gave him, to back up his teammates as they took down the building and whatever it held.

While Warrick provided precision fire support for the takedown on the brewery, Deckert would be running communications in his van. Straker's people had installed a complete radio suite in the vehicle, including an LSSC series 300 UHF satellite communications system, KG-194 encryption device, a CSD 3324E secure telephone, fax, and data system that could be hooked directly into the phone lines, and a TRIMPACK III GPS receiver. The video and digital still cameras in the van could record on either tape or disk, or their images uploaded and transmitted through the RF-3700-04CPHD digital compact-video imaging terminal.

The load of electronics in the van made surveillance a simple thing, and communications among the team members even easier. But it was a complex system, and Deckert had spent half the time during the drive down from D.C. just reading the manuals. During the long hours of surveillance, he made himself more familiar with the systems and their capabilities. He knew he could support his people without any trouble and be able to call in any support required, from local law enforcement to the U.S. military, if necessary.

While the men prepared their individual and group equipment, Deveraux was amazed to simply observe

them for a moment. It was like watching a complex
machine build itself from parts. She had worked with
some of the best special operations people in the world
during her time with counterterrorism operations in
Great Britain. But Reaper and his men were in a class
by themselves. They were such a diverse group that
only two of them, Reaper and Caronti, had even served
in the same branch of the military, with their time in
the Navy. If there was a small group of men equal or
superior to Devlin and his bunch, she was looking at
them. This was the best chance she'd had in years to
take down Devlin, to finally make him pay for killing
her husband.

Mackenzie had headed off on some errand that morning while most of the rest of the team worked at the
house. The night before, Warrick had measured out a
range going from the back doors of the house to the
inside of the garage in the fairly deep backyard, working with a tape measure and double-checking the distance. Several plastic garbage cans full of sand and
water acted as the backstop while he tested his Wraith
rifle. The soft thud of the rifle firing was so quiet you
couldn't have heard it from the front yard of the house.
Warrick measured the distance from the center of the
five-round-shot group, with all of the bullet holes over-
lapping each other, to the aiming point on his target
sheet. Then he compared the results to a ballistics table
taped to the side of the rifle's stock. The results satisfied Warrick that his weapon hadn't been damaged in
transit and he could depend on it to back up his teammates.

The same set of target cans were used the next day by
everyone in the team who was going in on the takedown.

Each man checked the zero of his Aimpoint Comp M2 sight, firing the weapon from the house and into the open door of the garage along Warrick's measured range. Inside the garage, the water in the plastic garbage cans had drained a bit and had to be replenished. But the wet sand was easily capable of absorbing the frangible bullets and the copper dust they disintegrated into on impact. The Gemtech High Activity Low Observable (HALO) suppressors on the muzzles of the weapons reduced the sound signature of firing so that it wasn't recognizable as a gunshot, even a few dozen yards away.

Even though Deveraux wasn't going to be carrying a shoulder weapon on the covert part of the takedown, Reaper wanted to make sure she was checked out on the M4A1 with the CQBR barrel assembly.

"I did work as an underground arms dealer for years," Deveraux said when Reaper handed her a weapon. Looking at the Aimpoint sight, she snapped on the power switch and adjusted the brightness of the red dot inside the lens.

"Great," Reaper said. "Then I'm certain you know which end the bullets come out of. Now please demonstrate that fact."

Slapping the thirty-round magazine into the weapon, Deveraux pulled the cocking handle back smartly, releasing the bolt and chambering the first round. Leaning forward in a slight crouch, she held the weapon down at an angle, then snapped it up to her shoulder. A controlled burst of two rounds snapped through the HALO suppressor and smacked into the target on the garbage can exactly twenty-five yards away.

Peering at the target, Deveraux saw that the small

group of black holes from her shots were well within the groups of the other men.

"Seems to be sighted in well," Deveraux said as she pulled the magazine from the weapon. Pulling back on the cocking handle again, she ejected the loaded round in the chamber of the weapon, put the safety on, and laid it on the table were the other weapons were. Bending down, she picked up the ejected round and looked at it. The dull copper-colored bullet had a cut-off appearance with a sharply pointed tip at the end of an angled cone. The rest of the projectile had the same curved sides as a regular round, except for the odd color.

"Why the specialized ammunition?" Deveraux said. "And just what is it, anyway?"

"This is EBR's special 5.56-millimeter frangible safety ammunition. It's accurate and just as deadly as a normal ball round if it hits soft tissue. Even more destructive than ball ammo if it hits bone. The bullet is a special copper alloy that shatters into dust if it hits a hard target. It can't overpenetrate a body or punch through hard materials."

"So why use it?" Deveraux asked.

"The U.S. Department of Energy likes it a lot," Reaper replied. "Especially for their security units that may have to work in a reactor area. The frangible slugs won't easily penetrate things like cooling pipes, electrical conduits, or control casings. If there're biological materials in that brewery, I want to cut down on the chances of a stray slug punching open a container of something really bad. And we have the same ammunition in 9 millimeter for our handguns, SIG P226's."

"I see," Deveraux said. "I also have a SIG 9 millimeter, but not a P226. I use a smaller P239 as a backup to my .45-caliber P245."

"Well," Reaper said, "I'm afraid you'll have to switch weapons for this operation and make your P239 your primary piece."

Reaper handed her a white box of ammunition with a green-printed label.

"Load your magazines with this," he said. "Sorry, but Engel doesn't load a frangible .45 bullet."

As Deveraux took the ammunition box from Reaper, Mackenzie came in through the front door of the house carrying a bag.

"Did you find it?" Reaper asked.

"Sure did," Mackenzie said, walking up and handing him the bag. "Only one police shop had a set, and that was because someone hadn't picked it up. I hope it fits."

"Here you are," Reaper said to Deveraux as he handed her the bag.

"And just what is this?" she said, taking the surprisingly heavy bag.

"It's a set of concealable woman's body armor," Mackenzie said. "American Body Armor and Equipment company's level IIIA. The best I could find. Reaper told me you weren't going on the operation if I couldn't find you a set, so I called around and located this. You were lucky—most of these vests are custom made. This one even has the ballistic steel shock plate shaped to fit the breast. It will stop handgun bullets up to a .44 magnum and most submachine-gun slugs."

"I thank you," Deveraux said. "And Reaper said

having this will allow me to go in on the operation, did he?"

"We all have our own R.C.V. level IIIA concealable vests for undercover work," Reaper said. "Mackenzie and Caronti will be wearing Armored Warrior tactical rigs that will stop 7.62-millimeter rifle slugs. But you and I can only get away with armor we can wear under our clothes."

Not having anything to say about the obvious protection offered by the body armor, Deveraux simply nodded and headed back to her room to dress.

"Mackenzie," Reaper said, "I need you and Caronti to prepare those breaching charges. I want you to set up for a team positive breach—absolutely, positively blow those steel doors open on the first try. Deveraux and I can watch out for ourselves on the inside if you have to go for a hot breach."

"Roger that," Mackenzie said, and he went off looking for Caronti.

———

Knowing that a hot breach meant explosives were going to be used, Deveraux was watching Mackenzie and Caronti prepare the charges. If she was going to be on the receiving end of something like that, she wanted to know exactly what was going to be used. The pile of materials the two men had gathered on the kitchen table did not lend themselves to an easy explanation. Among the coils of what looked like different types of plastic tubing were cap crimpers, rolls of duct tape, a roll of waxed paper, knives, an ammunition box with an orange sticker stating EXPLOSIVES A, and a number of large plastic IV bags full of clear liquid.

"You're going to blow a door open with saline solution?" Deveraux said with a puzzled expression on her face as she read the label on one of the bags.

"No," Mackenzie said, "they're just handy-sized bags of liquid. The real punch for these charges is a piece of Detasheet, about two ounces of explosive." He pointed to the other side of the table, where Caronti was using a knife to cut a piece of thick, gray plastic material into two square pieces.

"This stuff is the active ingredient for these charges," Caronti said, holding up the two squares. "The thing that makes it work so well is the liquid in the bags."

"The bag on the outside acts as a tamper for the charge," Mackenzie said holding up an IV bag in each hand. "The explosive is sandwiched between two bags and they're taped together." He pushed the two bags together.

"The inside bag acts as a hammer when the explosive goes off. Pretty much punches the center of the door inward, folding the whole thing in on itself. Rips the door from its hinges, and with two charges, well, it doesn't matter if the locks in the center of the two doors hold or not."

"Probably not," Caronti said with a grin.

"How do you attach the bags to the center of the doors?" Deveraux asked.

"Lots of duct tape," Caronti said. "It sticks to everything but furnace ducts."

"Actually," Mackenzie explained, "what my big friend here is trying to say is that we put a large patch of duct tape on the bags, sticky side out. We can cover the tape with waxed paper and then just peel it off when we want to attach it to the target."

"That, and we take extra rolls of tape with us," Caronti said. "The other option is to tie a loop of line to the charges and stick a wedge into the top of the door frame. Then we can hang the charges from the wedge. It depends a little on exactly what we find when we go up to the doors."

The method the men would use to get maximum effect from a minimum amount of explosives was fascinating to Deveraux. But she had her own preparations to make before they left the house on the operation. She headed back to her bedroom to ready her own equipment.

To insure that everyone knew what the plan was to take down the brewery, Reaper held a brief-back before they left for the target. Grins and jokes were gone as the men became deadly serious about what they were going to do. There was a very real possibility that they would be kicking in the door to a hornet's nest of terrorists, and they were leaving nothing to chance. Bags of equipment were laid out by the backdoor to the house. Weapons were in additional equipment bags, while a black nylon Spec-Ops-brand backpack sat next to the weapons bags. The pack had red tape on its top handle indicating that it held the explosive breaching charges.

Spread out on the kitchen table was a large sketch of the Gaia Brewery and its immediate surroundings. The sketch included a rough outline of the interior of the building, which Deveraux had located in the local city building files. Different cartridges were placed around the sketch to indicate the different members of the team.

"The two rifle rounds are Warrick in his sniper's hide and Deckert in the van," Reaper said, placing two rounds on the sketch. "Once we come up to the van, Caronti, you and Mackenzie"—he held up two shotgun shells—"get out of the cab and slip into the back. Deveraux and I will take the car north along the main road and you insert here, just before we pass the tree line on the south side of the parking lot. We can slow down enough to let you guys just roll out of the back without drawing any notice. There is damned little, if any, traffic along this road during the afternoon."

Picking up the shotgun shells, Mackenzie moved them across the sketch. "After insertion, the two of us move to where we can approach the building. There's a blind side along the back here where we can go up to the garbage Dumpster under cover from bushes and plants most of the way. Should take us a few minutes at most and put us right around the corner from the back doors."

"Then, after you two insert," Reaper said, "Deveraux and I will drive up to the front door in the truck. We can sit in the cab for a minute, looking like we're shuffling papers. Then we'll just go up and knock on the door."

"A little brazen, isn't it?" Deveraux said.

"Maybe," Reaper agreed, "but these guys can't be all that trigger happy if they're trying to run a disguised laboratory of some kind. This is a bar, so people must come up to the place occasionally, just to find out if it's open or not."

"That one sheriff's deputy did just come up and knock on the front door, according to Warrick's notes," Caronti said.

"A lady standing at the door is probably the least threatening approach we can make," Reaper said as he placed two 9mm rounds at the front of the building on the sketch. "Once we're inside, we may be able to get the drop on everyone in there. Or, we just call for the insertion to go down over the radio. Our mikes will be locked open, so Deckert in the van and everyone on the net can hear what happens. The rest of the team can still communicate over another channel."

"What's the emergency call for help?" Mackenzie said.

"Boats," Reaper said looking at Caronti. "That's probably not something that would come up in general conversation. You hear that and come busting in as fast as you can. There's also the always-popular 'execute' repeated three times depending on what we find. Deveraux, your call sign will be 'Shade.' That's reasonably non–gender-specific."

" 'Shade' it is," Deveraux said. "That sounds like one of your comic-book heros."

"Just as long as you don't think *you're* some kind of superhero," Reaper said. "There's no room for anyone like that in this small an outfit, or any outfit, for that matter."

"You don't have to worry about me," Deveraux said in an icy voice.

"If I thought I had to worry about you," Reaper said, "you wouldn't be here. Deckert in the van is going by the call sign 'Base.' Everyone got that?"

A murmur of assent went around the room.

"Remember, people," Reaper said sharply, "guns are tight on this one. Rules of engagement are open if you see a threat. But if there's something brewing inside of this place besides beer, we don't want to poke holes in just anything. Warrick is there to make sure no one gets away from this place, period. Deckert has Hazmat gear in the van with him. We also have four suits and masks in the back of the truck. Mackenzie, you and Caronti will have masks on when you go through the door. Our job is to secure the site, then we call in to Straker and give him a sitrep. He'll decide who gets called in then. If there're no questions, we have a go."

There were no questions from any of the people standing around the table. They each soberly looked at the rounds of ammunition sitting on the paper in front of them.

Chapter Fifteen

By two that afternoon, everyone was ready for the operation. Mackenzie and Caronti were riding in the back of the extended cab of the Chevy Silverado pickup truck they had used to tow the airboat only the week before. Reaper and Deveraux sat in the front seats of the truck, both wearing business attire. Devereaux looked very smart and attractive in a beige Liz Claiborne linen business suit, with a skirt that extended partway down her calves. On her feet were black shoes with medium heels. Dressed as she was, Deveraux was certain to be a distraction to the men at Gaia.

The woman might be a beautiful distraction, but Reaper was certain she could be a hell of a lot more than that. Following his recommendation, Deveraux had taken her SIG P239 as her primary weapon, carrying the pistol in a Galco concealed-carry paddle holster on her right hip. The holster was set for a forward-cant FBI draw and she had two spare eight-round magazines in a Galco leather DMC double magazine case on her belt at her left hip. The loose-fit navy blue silk blouse she wore helped disguise the fact Deveraux was wearing body armor. Recent experience in watching her with Warrick left Reaper with no doubt that the woman had several knives secreted upon her person. He just wasn't going to ask where.

For himself, Reaper was wearing the strangest assault rig he had ever worn on a hot operation. His own Level IIIA tactical RCV body armor was worn under a blue shirt with a dark red tie. At his right hip, secure on the belt holding up his charcoal trousers, was his well-worn Galco CM248 Combat Master belt holster. Into his right front pants pocket he had slipped his trusted Emerson CQC-7BW folding knife. Drawing the knife out with his thumb and two fingers would cause the patented "Wave" feature on the back of the blade to catch on the edge of the pocket, snapping the blade open as he continued the draw. The knife had served him very well for years and was with him so often it almost seemed a part of his normal clothing.

The rest of Reaper's gear was housed in a new system that he was trying out for the first time. In a 5.11 nylon-mesh concealment vest, Reaper was carrying two spare fifteen-round magazines in a nylon carrier pressed into the hook-and-pile attachment system of the vest. The magazines were in addition to the fifteen rounds in the SIG P226 in the holster on his hip. A Surefire G2 flashlight rested in a carrier attached to the vest at his left side. At the rear of the vest, on either side, he had attached the nylon holders for a pair of Peerless model 810 hinged steel handcuffs. The twelve-ounce handcuffs were the most secure models available because of the limiting movement hinge which held the two sides together. And in a pinch, the cuffs made a hell of a pair of steel knuckles, if the situation got down to hand-to-hand.

Reaper didn't expect the situation to deteriorate to where he had to fight his way out with his hands, as demonstrated by the fact that all of his combat gear was hidden under a tan suede sport coat. He expected his teammates to be able to handle any heavy combat that came up during the operation or to show such overwhelming firepower as to prevent resistance before it even started.

To call up the rest of their teammates, both Reaper and Deveraux had their Motorola Model T5420 Talk-about radios in the inside left pocket of their coats. On Reaper's belt was a second Talkabout, set to a different frequency. This radio would be locked in the transmit position to allow Deckert in the van to overhear everything that was going down in the brewery. The compact radios were more than capable of covering the area they would be operating in and had already proved their worth to Reaper on several other operations. The firepower either of the two radios could unleash was impressive, considering what the men at the other end of the line were carrying.

Strapped to his left hip, Caronti was carrying Reaper's favored Serbu Super Shorty 12-gauge pump shotgun in an SKT holster. The pistol-gripped pump-action weapon appeared to be more of a really big pistol than a shotgun. Loaded in the magazine and chamber of the shotgun were three rounds of Lockbuster breaching slugs. The ceramic and powdered metal slugs launched by the Lockbuster loads would quickly open a door by blowing off the hinges or the lock, reducing themselves to a harmless powder after passing through hard

material and thus eliminating any danger of overpen-
etration on the other side. If fired at a human target,
the Lockbuster ammunition would act as an extremely
lethal slug, smashing a person over even if they were
wearing high-level body armor.

On their right hips, Caronti and Mackenzie were
carrying SIG P226 pistols in their BlackHawk Serpa
tactical holsters. Since using them on the abortive nuclear reactor insertion, they had converted the weapons
back to firing standard ammunition. Actually, the EBR
9mm frangible-duty ammo in the magazines of the
P226s wasn't *exactly* standard ammunition, but neither
man had any reservations about the power of the composite metal hollowpoint bullets in the rounds. Along
with the magazine in the weapon, they each had forty-
five rounds of the 9mm ammunition in the magazine
inside of the P226 along with the two spare magazines
in pouches on either side of the carbon-fiber holsters.

M4A1 carbines fitted with the short CQBR uppers
were the primary weapons of both men. Large vertical
foregrips were on the mounting rails of the weapons
with visible red laser designators on the left sides of the
barrels, balanced against tactical white-light Surefire
M3 flashlights on the opposite sides.

Each of the men were well supplied for ammunition.
In their BlackHawk Omega Elite tactical assault vests
were a dozen thirty-round magazines in the six double-
magazine pouches. Each magazine was loaded with
twenty-eight rounds of EBR frangible 5.56mm ammo.
In the magazine wells of the M4A1 carbines themselves
were locked twin thirty-round magazines. Heavily taped
together with a spacer between them, the magazines
were both pointing in the same direction when locked

into the weapon. Once one magazine was empty, pulling the assembly out of the weapon and immediately reinserting it would snap a full load into place. Between the magazines in their weapons and the ones in the pockets of their vests, Caronti and Mackenzie each had nearly four hundred rounds of ammo for their carbines, and they hoped to pull off the op without firing a single round.

In the upper left side pockets of the vests were Motorola Talkabout T5420 radios along with extra sets of batteries. Stinger throat microphones and earphones let the men use the radios in hands-free mode. The carbines were attached to Chalker slings around their chests, underneath their Omega Elite vests. The muzzles of the carbines were pointing up past the left shoulders of both men, the weapons held in place with Hi-port catches on the upper shoulders of the Chalker slings.

The back of each man was also laden with equipment. Mackenzie had the Spec-Ops pack with the demolition equipment, firing devices, and breaching bag charges in it. Caronti was carrying the much more mundane but heavier breacher's pack on his back. The backpack was a skeletonized model with pockets and straps on it to secure the breacher's tools. The tools consisted of a ten-pound sledgehammer with a fiberglass handle, an insulated pair of 30-inch bolt cutters, and a 30-inch Hallagan tool that could rip off locks, rake glass out of windows, or pry open doors.

The hot summer environment didn't make carrying that much equipment very comfortable. Neither did the black long-sleeved 5.11 tactical shirts and trousers the two men were wearing along with black SWAT boots,

Hatch operators gloves, balaclavas, and Safety Tech M95 respirator masks. In the back of the Omega Elite vests were one hundred-ounce Camelback hydration systems, the bags having been filled with water and frozen overnight. The cold water was a welcome and necessary refreshment in the hot, humid, Central Florida air.

Pulling up alongside the Chevy van where Deckert was maintaining communications and surveillance watch, Reaper stopped the truck to get a last-moment report on the situation. It was also the time for Mackenzie and Caronti to move from the rear cab to the bed of the truck, where they could conceal themselves under a tarp. Stepping over to the van, Reaper opened the door to speak to Deckert, while Mackenzie and Caronti made their move.

"What's the sitrep?" Reaper asked.

"Pretty much the same as we've seen the last several days," Deckert said. "Saab Yuppie showed up about an hour ago and went in. The Hippie has been here since about one thousand hours this morning. Other than those two, nothing at all, not even much in the way of traffic. Two pickups and a beat-up station wagon since noon."

"Warrick got anything?" Reaper said. "His hide is about fifty yards closer than the van here."

"War, this is Base," Deckert said as he keyed the boom microphone on the headset he was wearing. "War, this is Base. Sitrep, over."

Listening on the headset for a moment, Deckert keyed his mike again.

"Roger that, War," Deckert said. "Will advise team. Base out."

"Same as I told you," Deckert said looking over at Reaper, "no new activity at the target. This place is just about as dead as it gets. There isn't even any activity to speak of on the police bands," Deckert waved his hand at the bank of sophisticated communications equipment. "If I listen, I can get more action from Disney World and the airport in Orlando than anything around here."

"Hopefully, that's how things will stay," Reaper said. "We're going in. Notify War."

As Reaper headed back over to his truck, Deckert was already turning back to his radios and keying his microphone. A glance told Reaper that Caronti and Mackenzie were in place in the back of the vehicle. He climbed into the driver's seat and turned to Deveraux.

"Care to visit a bar, my dear?" Reaper asked as he put the truck into gear.

The woman just turned and looked at the ex-SEAL as he drove down the road.

The one house that could be seen south along the road was beat up and abandoned. The nearest neighbor was well down the road to the north, the direction Reaper was heading. They were far enough away that even the breaching charges going off would probably just sound like thunder, if anyone noticed them. The design of the charges muted the sound of the explosion to a loud thud.

As Reaper made his turn toward the brewery, he pulled close to the side of the road and slowed. A pair of quick bounces on the truck told him that Caronti and Mackenzie had inserted for their part of the operation. He caught a quick glimpse of the two heavily laden, black-clad men as they darted into the brush next to the road.

"And now the movie," Reaper said softly.

Looking at him with an puzzled expression, Deveraux didn't comment on the obscure expression.

Only a few dozen yards farther down the road, Reaper pulled the truck into the parking lot at the Gaia Brewery. Only the Saab station wagon and the Saturn sedan were in the gravel lot, both cars parked near the northwest corner of the west-facing building. Pulling in on the south side of the door, Reaper stopped the truck and turned off the engine. At that moment, it was important to stall for a minute or two to give Caronti and Mackenzie time to get into position. Neither Warrick or Deckert had seen any sign of external cameras watching the parking lot around the building, but that didn't mean the truck wasn't under observation.

Reaching behind the seat, Reaper pulled up what looked like a black leather portfolio. Opening the brass zipper of the portfolio, he pulled out a sheaf of papers and handed them to Deveraux. Leaning forward, he pointed at the papers.

"Okay, they're in place," Reaper said as he heard two clicks as Mackenzie pressed the transmit button of his radio. "Take the portfolio, it's armored," he said as he handed the leather folder to Deveraux. "It can stop an AK-47 slug, so keep it close."

Reaching up to his ear, Reaper pulled out the earpiece of his radio and tucked it under his collar. The lack of communications was less of a danger than having someone notice a supposed city worker with an earpiece stuck in his ear like some kind of Secret

Service agent. Opening the door to the truck, Reaper stepped out onto the gravel, the dry, dusty stones crunching under his feet.

Taking the leather portfolio from Reaper, Deveraux was surprised for a moment at the weight and stiffness of it. But Reaper *had* told her that it was armor, so perhaps it shouldn't have been such a surprise. The heels of her shoes dug a bit into the gravel of the parking lot as she slid from the seat. She stopped with Reaper at the double steel doors. Trying the knob, Reaper was hardly surprised to find that they were locked. He rapped solidly, his knocks sounding out hollowly. After a moment had gone by, he knocked again, even more soundly, with the base of his clenched fist.

The pounding on the door was clearly transmitted over the radio Reaper had on his belt. That was the signal Caronti and Mackenzie had been waiting for. Caronti ran across the back of the parking lot and ducked behind the cover of the rusting steel Dumpster behind the southeast corner of the cinder-block structure. While the heavily laden Caronti moved, Mackenzie kept his weapon up and trained on the south side of the building where the rear door was. Both men had a large load of weapons and ammunition, but Mackenzie could move a bit faster since he wasn't carrying the load of breaching tools Caronti had on his back.

The thumbs-up signal from Caronti told Mackenzie that the other man was ready to cover his crossing to the building. There were brush and trees to within fifteen feet of the building, more than enough concealment for both of the men. But this final crossing of an open area was where they were at their most exposed. When the sound of Reaper's heavy knocking came over the radio, Mackenzie darted out and moved to the building in a rush.

Ducking down next to Caronti, Mackenzie turned and covered the northern end of the building. The block wall they were next to was covered with gray paint, much of it peeling away toward the bottom of the wall. There was no cover beyond that given by the Dumpster, but there were also no openings in the solid wall. Now the two men would be exposed again while they placed the breaching charges against the doors not more than six feet away around the corner. The only thing they were waiting for was for their teammates to enter the building, hopefully walking right through the front door.

If it wasn't for the cloth of the balaclava covering his face, Caronti would have had sweat pouring down his face and into his eyes. As it was, the rubber of the M95 respirator on his face felt greasy and slick from the sweat that was already on it. Biting down on the mouthpiece of the hydration adapter, Caronti took a deep pull of the cold water in the Camelback bladder on the back of his vest. The ice that had been in the bladder was mostly melted, but the only cool spot on the big man's whole body just then was where the Camelback rested against his upper spine. He didn't have time to enjoy the comfort long as the two men quickly moved to emplace the breaching charges and prepare to blow the doors.

At the front door, Reaper had other things to worry about besides the heat, though he was beginning to sweat a bit. Knocking on the front door wasn't getting much of a reaction from the inside of the building. It was coming close to the point where he would have to decide if Mackenzie and Caronti were going to conduct a hot breach and start the takedown themselves. As he knocked hard on the door one more time, a voice called out from inside the building.

"Go away," the voice said, "we're not open yet."

As Reaper was taking a deep breath, Deveraux called out in a sexy contralto voice,

"County inspector's office," Deveraux said. "Please open the door or we'll have to come back with the sheriff."

After a moment, there was the metallic rattle of a large bolt being drawn back from the door and of the lock being opened. The right-hand door opened outward a few inches and a man looked out. It was the balding individual who had driven the Saab, the one Deckert had tagged "Yuppie."

"Who is it, please?" the man said, sounding a bit strained as he looked at Reaper.

Following Deveraux's lead, Reaper smiled and stepped back, letting her move in front of the door. At all times, Deveraux was a beautiful woman. When she really turned on the sex, she positively radiated appeal. The dazzling smile she put on for Yuppie was an example of this.

"Mr. Davis?" she said in her sexiest voice. "I'm Marlene Mentor of the Seminole County Tax Assessor's office. This is Mr. Regis, one of the county engineers. Could we speak to you, please?"

The smooth, soft voice worked well in calming Yuppie down. Apparently, so did the official-looking laminated ID cards Deveraux had made the day before with her computer and some graphics programs. Both she and Reaper held up ID folders with the cards showing,

Reaper had his in his left hand, his right staying empty and free to move. The man in the doorway looked dazed for a second, then visibly came to his senses.

"I'm not Davis," Yuppie said, "He's in the back. We're quite busy trying to get ready to open, and don't really have time for anything right now."

"Oh, I am sorry about that," Deveraux said, "but I really must insist. Could we come in, please, and not talk about it here in the heat? It would be so much simpler if we could just clear up some questions now. Otherwise, we will have to come back with the authorities and run a full inspection of the premises."

"Oh, no," Yuppie said, "I don't think that will be necessary. Please do come in, but we really don't have much time."

"Oh, that's all right," Deveraux said as she stepped through the door. She stood in front of Yuppie, partially blocking his view of Reaper as he followed her inside. The trained and experienced eyes of the ex-SEAL quickly swept the room, noting the location of furnishings, doors, and the absence of any other people in the rooms.

Yuppie was standing in front of an open door leading to what looked like a small office to the right of the front entrance. To the left of where everyone was standing was an open area with a number of tables of different sizes, all of them with chairs flipped over on top of them. On the left was a long, dark wood bar with a number of glass shelves behind it. Racks were filled with glasses, but there were only a few bottles behind the bar. Some buckets and other junk littered the bar, but that was all. To the right of the bar was a swinging door with a window in it that showed the kitchen beyond it.

The wall behind the bar extended the length of the building, pierced by one other door, in addition to the one to the kitchen. That door was closed and looked to be the same kind of steel fire door as was on the outside of the building. In the open space between the far wall and the office area sat a pool table covered with a heavy plastic sheet, as well as a scattered number of tall round tables with stools placed upside down on top of them. It looked to be a completely empty bar that wasn't ready to open for a while yet.

The careful examination Reaper gave the room took only a few seconds. He noted that there wasn't anyone else in sight. But the lights were on in the kitchen, and there was the one closed door leading to the back of the building.

"Now just what is the problem, Ms.—Mentor, was it?" Yuppie said. "As you can see, we have quite a bit of work to do stocking the place and getting ready to open for business."

"Frankly, we've been keeping this place under observation for some time now," Deveraux said. "You haven't opened to the public at all. And there haven't been many deliveries to this location. But you do have your brewery license, and it's active right now. So is your business license, for that matter.

"Why you've decided not to open for business is not our concern. We don't really care. But you have been using utilities far in excess of the needs for a nonfunctioning business, especially one that doesn't have any customers and hasn't paid any sales tax. If there is some problem, if someone is stealing utilities, we need to address the situation as quickly as is practical. If you are producing product and sending it to another location for sale, that's a violation of your business license and we will have to shut you down immediately."

"There's no problem," Yuppie said. "I'm sure we can come to an equitable arrangement to satisfy—"

The steel door in the back wall opened up just then. Framed in the opening was the bearded man Deckert had named Hippie. The man was standing partly inside the back room, his right arm reaching to something on the inside of the wall next to the door. The man was nervous and appeared angry. The fact that Reaper couldn't see his right arm made the ex-SEAL tense and very alert.

"Wait a damn minute," Hippie said as he stood in the door. "Who the hell are these people?"

"County inspectors," the bald man said. "They're here to check on our utility use. They've already shown me their credentials."

"The hell they are," Hippie said, "I know everyone in the county offices and I've never seen these two. This is a rip-off!"

As Hippie ducked back into the room he had just stepped out of, he pulled his right arm back. Reaper saw the flash of brown wood, the wood used in the stock of a pump-action shotgun. Yuppie turned and stared at Reaper and Deveraux as if they had each just sprouted horns and a tail. Sweeping his right hand back under his sport coat, Reaper drew out his SIG in a practiced motion as he shouted.

"EXECUTE, EXECUTE, EXECUTE!"

Less than a half second after Reaper had his weapon out, Deveraux had her P239 in her hand. If Yuppie had been startled a moment before, he was now terrified as he looked down the barrels of two unwavering weapons, both pointed directly at his chest.

For this mission, Reaper had installed a Crimson Trace grip on his SIF P226. Squeezing the raised rubber nubs on either side of the grip caused the laser on top of the right grip panel to light up and send its beam out along the side of the weapon. The brilliant red dot had a very sobering effect on people when they noticed it on their chests. It tended to make folks who might otherwise resist decide to quickly surrender, something Reaper wanted to see happen right now. But even before Yuppie could raise his hands, the building shook with the thunder of the breaching charges detonating.

Chapter Sixteen

The thud and crash of the breaching charges caused dust to rain down on everything. In the dirty atmosphere, the laser from Reaper Crimson Trace grip sparkled and showed as a red streak through the air, a bright line that stopped in the center of Yuppie's chest. The man actually screamed in a very high-pitched, almost girlish voice. This was not someone behaving like a hardened terrorist. He seemed more like some idiot who just realized he was playing in the wrong league.

"Please don't shoot me," Yuppie babbled as he dropped to his knees. "Please, please don't shoot me. It was all his idea. He swore there wouldn't be a problem, that we were protected. Please don't kill me."

The man fell over on the floor, groveling and sobbing. Reaper pulled a pair of his Peerless handcuffs from the pouch on his 5.11 concealment vest.

"Here, cuff this clown," Reaper said as he handed the cuffs to Deveraux. "And gag him if he won't shut up."

The silence on the far side of the wall bothered Reaper more than if he had heard gunshots. If something had

gone wrong with the breach, or if there were some real
terrorists back there, they might have the drop on Mackenzie and Caronti. As Reaper headed toward the doorway, he pulled the radio out of his pocket. Before he had
a chance to key the microphone, he heard a muffled
voice on the other side of the wall call out, "Clear."

———

After Reaper and Deveraux had entered the building,
Caronti and Mackenzie moved from behind the Dumpster and around the corner. While Mackenzie stood
away from the door, he turned his back to the building
and kept watch, his M4A1 up and ready in his hands,
the barrel sweeping across the open area of the parking
lot. Stepping up to the door, Caronti turned and opened
the Spec-Ops pack on Mackenzie's back. He pulled out
one of the breaching charges and peeled the waxed
paper away from the adhesive tape. Placing the charge
firmly in the center of the door, Caronti pressed hard
on the tag-ends of the tape that stuck out all around the
charge.

With one of the charges in place, Caronti pulled the
second charge from the pack and repeated his actions
at the second door. Once both charges were solidly in
place, Caronti again turned to Mackenzie's back and
removed a pair of firing assemblies. The blasting caps
on the end of the firing lines were attached to clips that
would hold the caps firmly in place against the explosive inside the breaching charges. Uncoiling the nonel
(non-electric) shock tube they used as the firing line,
Caronti squeezed Mackenzie's shoulder to tell him that
he was moving. With Mackenzie backing up with him

and still watching the area around them, Caronti led the other man back to the corner of the building, unwinding the firing line as he want.

Once around the corner of the building. Caronti and Mackenzie could only wait for Reaper's signal. There were two sets of firing assemblies, each one connected to both charges. When Caronti pulled the ring on the igniter, a percussion primer would be fired, in turn detonating the explosive powder lining the shock tubes. The shock wave of the explosive would flash along the tubes almost instantaneously. Then the blasting caps would detonate, initiating the breaching charges and blowing open the doors. It was a very technical way of opening two steel doors, one that was guaranteed to do the job in seconds at the most.

When the "execute" call came over the radio, Caronti didn't wait to hear the command repeated. As Mackenzie squeezed his partner's shoulder to tell him he was ready, Caronti pulled the rings on the igniters. The breaching charges detonated with a heavy thud, the shock wave striking Caronti and Mackenzie only lightly, since the wave couldn't make a sharp turn around the corner of a building. As both men ran up to the gaping hole where the doors had been standing, Caronti had pulled up his M4A1 and was holding it at the ready. Charging in through the open doorway first, Mackenzie went to the right and "cut the pie," quartering the area inside the room with the muzzle of his weapon. As he did so, Caronti came in through the doorway and performed the same action on the left side.

The Surefire M3 lights firmly held by the GG & G mounts on their weapons sent streams of brilliant white light into the dust-filled air of the room. Nothing was moving in the room but the sparkling motes of dust. Hearing a soft groan, Caronti looked down almost in front of where the crumpled doors lay inside the room. The steel doors were folded in on their centers, looking as if a giant had punched them both in with a rock-hard fist. Just beyond the doors, a man lay on the floor, barely moving and making only slight sounds. A Mossberg M500 eight-shot pump-action shotgun lay on the floor beyond the man's reach. It looked like he had been struck by the steel doors when the breach went hot.

As Caronti held cover on the rest of the room, Mackenzie went over to where the man lay and pulled his shotgun farther away from him. By the looks of the blood streaming down the man's face, his nose was either broken or he had been born with a very wide and flat one. Looking up with his weapon pointed out, Mackenzie called out, "Clear!" in a loud voice.

Caronti called out, "Clear!" as he saw that his side of the room was empty of people and movement. While Mackenzie secured the injured man with plastic tie-ties, Caronti kept watch out across the open room. There were copper barrels and containers on stands around the room, lots of stainless-steel piping, and not a single sign of activity. Then there was a knock on the door at the far side of the room.

"Death," Reaper shouted out his code name. "Clear to enter?"

"Clear," said Mackenzie as he rose from the floor and went over to the door. The lock had latched the door when it had swung closed and Mackenzie had to turn the knob to open it for Reaper. He still held his weapon up and at the ready as he opened the door and stood back.

"One hostile, probably armed," Reaper said as he came into the room.

"Secured," Mackenzie said.

"That's him," Reaper said as he looked at the man on the floor. "The other prisoner says they are the only two people in the building."

"This room is clear," Mackenzie said. "But we haven't checked anything else. There's a padlock on the outside of that far door there."

Looking the way Mackenzie was pointing, Reaper could see a large steel walk-in refrigerator door dominating the wall that blocked off the northern part of the room.

"I cleared the kitchen before coming in here," Reaper said. "That room is the only one in the building that hasn't been examined. Deveraux is at the front door watching the prisoner there. Caronti, open that door."

Dropping his M4A1 to let it dangle on his Chalker sling, Caronti reached over his shoulder and pulled out the 30-inch pair of bolt cutters he had in his breacher's pack. He stepped up to the large door and looked at Mackenzie standing to his right. His partner had his weapon up and at the ready. Seeing Caronti looking at him, Mackenzie nodded to say that he was ready. A squeeze on his right shoulder told Caronti that Reaper was behind him and also ready. Placing the powerful jaws of the cutters on the shackle of the padlock, Caronti pushed the handles together, shearing through the hardened steel with ease.

Tossing the tool to the side, Caronti pulled up his M4A1 and stood to the side of the door, his left hand on the handle. At a nod from Reaper, Caronti pulled the door open and dull blue light flooded into the room.

The converted cold room was filled with row after row of plants, each one growing in a tank of liquid with plastic hoses running in all directions. Overhead on the ceiling were banks of blue white Gro-lights. It was a huge, high-tech hydroponic marijuana farm. A pot-producing facility and nothing to do with terrorists, anthrax, or anything that was of interest to Reaper or his men. They had wasted their time.

While Mackenzie saw to the treatment of the wounded man on the floor, Reaper walked back to the front of the building, absolutely disgusted with the results of several days of hard work.

"Pot," he said to Deveraux. "They aren't terrorists. They're potheads, dopers. They aren't worth our trouble, and now we have to figure out what to do with them."

"You," the man on the floor blubbered, "you mean you aren't DEA?"

"Do we look like drug enforcement agents to you?" Reaper said as he looked down at the little man.

"Well, yeah," he said, "actually, you do."

"Death, this is War," came over the speaker of the radio Reaper still held in his hand. "Company is here. Coming in from the south. That sheriff's patrol car is back."

"The alarm must have gone off from that explosion," the prisoner said. "Bill has a deputy paid to protect us. The alarm goes off in his car."

"Alarm? You have a silent alarm in the building? Shit!" Reaper said with vehemence. "This could be bad."

The patrol car came to a gravel-spewing halt as the driver stood on the brakes in the parking lot. As Reaper stood in the front door of the building, the deputy jumped out of the car and crouched down alongside the vehicle. He had the engine between himself and the building as he aimed his service weapon at the door.

"You, in the building," the deputy shouted, "come out with your hands up."

Reaper came up to the doorway after having holstered his SIG.

"Deputy," Reaper said, "we are government agents. We have taken down this drug-production facility and know the whole story. It would be in your own best interests to put that weapon down and surrender yourself."

"Let me see some identification," the deputy said.

The last thing Reaper wanted to do just then was identify himself and his men to a corrupt law enforcement officer. This guy looked to be a young kid and he would be certain to talk about what he had seen and the kind of people who had arrested him. He sounded nervous and scared, just the kind of person who could make a mistake, a lethal mistake. Reaper decided to try the hard-case approach.

"Officer," Reaper said loudly and with authority in his voice, "you absolutely do not want to fuck with me right now. Put your weapon down. This thing is over."

"You don't look like any cop I've ever seen," the deputy said. "I don't know who you are or what your game is, but you better be the one to put his hands up, and that goes for anyone else in there."

The deputy was as young as Reaper had thought. And the shake in his voice told him the man was scared.

He just might try to shoot his way out of this situation, and the last thing Reaper wanted to do was take down a police officer, no matter what the circumstances. The deputy was in a no-win situation and he had to be shown that surrender was his only real option.

"War," Reaper said quietly, "front tire, execute, execute, execute."

Across the road, Warrick heard the command and adjusted his aim accordingly. Slowly, he pulled the trigger on the Wraith. With just a few pounds of pressure, the sear tripped crisply and the weapon fired with a quiet thump. A 7.62mm 180-grain soft-nose jacketed slug exited the suppressor of the Wraith at less than the speed of sound. In front of the right knee of the deputy, there was the deep thunk sound of a bullet impact followed by the hissing of escaping air. The tire quickly went flat, as flat as the future hopes of the deputy kneeling next to it.

"The next one goes through your head," Reaper said. "There's no time to play here. Give it up and live."

The officer laid his Glock automatic on the hood of his patrol car, lowered his head, and wept.

Mackenzie came forward with the man from the back room in tow. The Hippie, as they had called him, turned out to be an assistant professor from the local university. He and his friend had set up the marijuana farm to supply the local demand. Their intention had been to open up the Gaia Brewery and distribute the pot from there. Having known the young sheriff's deputy for years, the two men had brought him into their scheme. "But it's only a little pot," the two would-be drug lords kept saying.

The sheriff's deputy was the saddest of the bunch to

Reaper and his team. The young man was finished as a law enforcement officer and would be sharing some hard time with his two partners. No one wasted any pity on any of the prisoners. The three had decided they were above a law they didn't agree with, so they would now pay the price. The only extra measure Reaper did make sure of was that the young officer wasn't physically able to do himself any harm. The prisoners were trussed up with plastic tie-tie riot handcuffs, gagged, and secured in different parts of the building. Cloth bags that had been brought to secure terrorists were placed over the prisoner's heads. There was no reason Reaper could see to allow the prisoners to get a better look at him or any member of his team.

Secured as they were, the prisoners wouldn't be able to cook up a story among themselves to explain their situation. It was suggested to the men in the strongest possible terms that they forget about just who it was who ruined their little farming enterprise. Bound as they were, the prisoners could only nod in agreement. Whoever Reaper and his people might be, the prisoners were just glad they weren't some hard-case drug lords looking to eliminate competition.

After securing the three men and policing up any specific evidence of their having been there, Reaper and his people left the area. Given that a local law enforcement officer had been involved, calling the sheriff's department was pretty much out of the question. Back in his van, Deckert was easily able to connect himself with the nearest office of the Florida State Police and inform them of just what they might find if they took a look in the Gaia Brewery, and to take note of the patrol car in the parking lot. A later report to

Straker's office would allow him to explain to local law enforcement just what might have gone down at the brewery. Or at least he could tell them as much as he wanted to.

Chapter Seventeen

Once back at the safe house, Reaper was steaming over the waste of time and resources. They had spent days on a pot bust. While Mackenzie was going over some gear in the living room, everyone else was in the kitchen with Deckert, who was cooking up some dinner. Deveraux was assisting, amazed at the LifeStand model LSC chair Deckert was using. She had never seen a wheelchair that could unfold *and* extend the seat and back, allowing the occupant to assume what was close to a standing position.

"Talk about swatting flies with a cannon," Caronti was relating with a grin. "Those idiots never knew what happened to them. By the time that clown in the back woke up from the door smacking him, he was already secured. I don't think he ever got a look at any of us."

"Well, everyone got a good look at Deveraux and myself," Reaper said. "And you can be sure their lawyers will be mentioning the unknowns who kicked in their door. We probably violated just about all of their rights in one way or another. Hell, they'll probably get off with just a slap on the wrist.

"And I really don't care right now. We can't afford to lose any more time filling out reports, explaining to the cops just who in the hell we are, or spending time in a witness box. If the contents of that back room aren't enough to convict them, screw it. We have a job to do and we damned well better get back to it."

"If we get left alone long enough," Mackenzie added as he came into the kitchen.

"What do you mean by that?" Warrick said. He was sitting cross-legged on the floor, his Wraith rifle laid out on newspapers as he carefully cleaned the weapon.

"I just saw the news on the TV," Mackenzie said as he sat at the kitchen table. "There's a story on about a drug ring being busted by an undercover government unit. Seems they nailed the owners of the place and caught a dirty cop as well. Looks like a pretty good investigation may be starting up. The local sheriff's office is denying everything, the defense lawyers are screaming setup, and the state troopers are taking the credit where they can. Must be a slow news day."

"They're probably just worried about the tourist crowds being scared off," Deckert said from the kitchen where he was chopping vegetables. "With Disney World, Universal Studios, and every other damned thing around here, tourist dollars are everything. The Fourth of July holiday is coming up, great big tourist time then."

"That's just great," Reaper said. "All we need to be is the lead story on the local news. That will make us Straker's favorite covert unit."

"No one is trying to name the 'undercover government unit' in the news," Mackenzie said. "That isn't even the main part of the story. The reports on the radio give the same story. Interviews with the local law enforcement and the state cops gives me the impression that they're more than a little pissed that someone did a hot breach and just left them the mess. Somehow, they didn't seem amused that someone was playing in their sandbox and didn't ask permission first."

"Not enough professional courtesy." Caronti grinned.

"Something like that," Mackenzie agreed.

"This kind of bull isn't going to accomplish anything," Reaper said. "All busting potheads is going to do is run us out of time before something really serious happens. So what's another way for us to go at finding our target?"

"I don't think there was anything wrong with your original premise," Deckert said from the kitchen. "If this anthrax is going to be made into a weapon, it has to be grown somewhere. Checking out the small breweries was a good idea, you just found the wrong one."

"No kidding," Reaper said. "We can go back over the lists and see if any more flags go up. There were more than twenty brew pubs in Florida. They can't all be pot farms."

"Most are just legitimate businesses," Deveraux said, "but I'll go back over the data and extend the search parameters. If Devlin has been planning this operation for as long as I suspect he has, I'll include businesses that started up a year ago, maybe more."

"That should give us something to work with," Reaper said as he leaned back in his chair at the table. "But I still think we need to approach this problem from another angle as well. Just what can we do that the government agencies aren't trying? How about going after Devlin directly?"

"There's no real way of tracing his contact or support network here in the States," Deveraux said. "The fact that he killed that woman up in Canada tells me he considers all of his previous contacts expendable. We might not know who they are, but the word is going to get out fast enough among the cells that he's eliminating his trail."

"That kind of puts a dent in his using much of the old terrorist networks," Reaper said thoughtfully. "And there're no clues that he's using any new criminal or terrorist support networks."

"If he's growing biological weapons here in the United States," Warrick said, "there's not a hell of a lot of criminal groups that would help him. They're in the business of making money, not tearing down the government."

"But there's more than enough home-grown terrorist groups that want to do just that," Caronti said. "If he hooked up with some white supremacists or militia outfits, they might be able to help him a lot."

"Those kinds of organizations just wouldn't be stable enough for Devlin to trust their support," Deveraux said. "Besides, he's in it just for the money now. They couldn't afford him."

"But al-Qaeda could," Mackenzie said. "They've had their business fronts and old funds frozen all over the world. But they've gone heavy into the dope trade. We ran into a pretty good example of that last year down in Arizona."

"Al-Qaeda has proved itself interested in this kind of weapon before," Reaper said. "They found enough evidence of that in the caves at Tora-Bora. Just because they couldn't get a bug to work for them sure as hell doesn't mean they wouldn't pay someone else to produce one."

"Sure fits the idea of Devlin using a brewery as a cover," Mackenzie said. "Al-Qaeda is sharp, but a Muslim organization probably wouldn't think of doing that."

"We're already working that angle," Reaper said. "How about trying to track Devlin by his personal habits, his tastes? The FBI hasn't tried that angle much, according to the reports Straker's office gave us."

"They didn't use that approach at all," Deveraux said. "For all of the public talk about their profiling capabilities, they're just not used much in a case like this. They called me in to talk to their profiler about Devlin, but that was about it. I didn't get the impression that they were going to use that approach much at all. They obviously considered me little more than an outsider."

"Seems we're not the only ones who slip up on professional courtesy," Caronti observed.

"We shall strive to do better." Reaper laughed. Turning to Deveraux, he continued, "What do you suggest as a starting point?"

"Well," she said, "what's the biggest city in Central Florida? The one with the largest population concentration?"

"The biggest population?" Mackenzie said. "I think that would probably be Orlando. But that's due to the tourist flow more than full-time residents."

"No," Deveraux said. "That doesn't fit with his tastes at all. He despises tourist places, considers them beneath him. He might consider Disney World as a worthy target, but he would never visit there except to gather intelligence prior to an attack. That's when he would want to disappear into the crowds."

"This is the off-season," Mackenzie said. "The number of tourists is down in the summer. But the Fourth of July is coming up, so there will be a bunch of people there then. I think it's also the fiftieth anniversary of Disneyland or something like that."

"But what are the largest cities?"

"Jacksonville and Miami are the largest cities in the state," Caronti said as he looked at a map. "Next to those, Tampa over on the Gulf Coast is the third-biggest, according to population. More than three hundred thousand people live there."

"That gives us a good concentration of people. But where would he hang out, if anywhere? What kind of place should we look for?" Reaper asked. "The best hotel?"

"That would probably be the Grand Hyatt Tampa Bay," Mackenzie said. "At least it *used* to be a four-star hotel, the only one in the area, as I remember."

"No, not a hotel," Deveraux said. "I'm certain the FBI has well covered all of those. That would be part of their normal procedure. Besides, Devlin likes to rent villas or large houses. They go well with his preferred cover of being an international playboy sort. Even that cover isn't one he always uses. He can be very self-indulgent and sure of himself to the point of arrogance. But he is never stupid."

"Indulgent and arrogant?" Reaper said. "That can be a dangerous combination, for him at least. So if he's being careful about the cover he's using and where he might be staying, how else could he indulge himself?

What are his tastes? Would he try to pick up local women? Girls?"

"No, nothing like that," Deveraux said shaking her head. "He can be an absolute monk when he's on an operation. He does have one weakness I remember, an indulgence, really. He loves to eat well. Anything from a small local spot that's famous for its cuisine to the very best restaurants. Always top-level places, no matter where he is. I'd forgotten that, I don't think even the FBI has that bit of data in their files."

"So what would be the best place to eat in the Tampa area, then?" Reaper said. "Is there some guide or something we can look up?"

"Bern's Steak House," Mackenzie said immediately. He was leaning back in his chair, his eyes closed as he turned his face towards the ceiling in reminiscence. "Some say Armani's, but that's for Italian food. I always swore by Bern's."

Everyone turned and looked at Mackenzie as he suddenly spoke up. The men were amazed that he knew so much about the Tampa area, especially the better places to stay and the best places to eat. As the physically smallest member of their team, he had never struck any of them as being a gourmand. He went on in detail about a subject he obviously enjoyed.

"Bern's has great beef," Mackenzie said, still with his eyes closed. "And they have what might be the biggest wine cellar in the United States. I know they've won awards for it. President Bush eats there when he's in town."

Leaning forward and opening his eyes, Mackenzie saw everyone looking at him.

"What?" he said. "Why the hell are you all looking at me like that? Can't a guy show a little good taste now and then? I used to eat there when I was stationed at SOCOM."

"SOCOM," Reaper said, snapping his fingers. "How the hell did we miss that one? The headquarters for the Special Operations Command is at MacDill Air Force Base. That's not six miles from the heart of downtown Tampa."

"Yeah," Mackenzie said. "Bern's is about five miles from the main gate at MacDill."

"That would be a hell of a target for a terrorist attack," Reaper said. "Especially if they have some kind of stand-off weapon. The body count might not be much, but it would be like hitting the Pentagon again."

"There's a change-of-command ceremony at SO-COM later this year, I think," Mackenzie said. "That would increase the crowd outside the building."

"That would give them a good body count," Reaper said. "When is the ceremony?"

"Not until the end of the summer at the earliest," Mackenzie said. "Two months away at least."

"That would give them time to grow and process a biological weapon," Deckert said. "Probably a pretty fair-sized one, too. They'd need a large supply to hit a military base."

"I think this Bern's place is worth a look-see," Reaper said. "One of the staff there might recognize Devlin from one of those pictures we got from the FBI. It's a long shot, but at least it's something. And we do have those photographs of the suspects from Toronto and the border crossing."

"It may not be all that long of a shot," Deveraux said

thoughtfully. "Devlin always prefers the local cuisine rather than eating the same type of food. He does have one real taste though, and that's for the best beef he can get. And what's more American than a good steak? I think this is a weakness we can really use against him."

"From what I've seen," Deckert said, "that's a dozen pictures of people who look a lot alike, at least the computers think so. I've got a camera and transmitter rig in the bag of toys Straker's people gave me. You might be able to find a spot to conceal it where it can look at people coming into the restaurant. Then we can run their faces through the biometrics program on the computer in the van. Or send them up to D.C. if you want."

"A trip to Tampa sounds pretty good to me right now," Warrick said as he got up off the floor. "I've got no heavy punch available, at least not since Matilda decided to chow down on my rifle. If that cop had been on the other side of that patrol car, I might not have been able to cover him. A fifty would go right through an engine block, no problem."

"Yeah," Caronti said, "and you would have been able to hear it from here."

"You don't get that kind of power for nothing," Warrick said. "Besides, I can come up with a suppressor for one if I needed to."

"So what do you propose?" Reaper said. "Deckert is already down here and he didn't bring a fifty with him."

"I've got that covered," Warrick said. "Serbu Firearms is over in the Tampa area. I already gave him a call yesterday and Mark has a rifle waiting for me. He's also got some ammunition and knows of a range facility where I can check out the weapon and zero my optics. The scope, ammo, and everything is there waiting for me, all I have to do is go by and pick it up. I was planning to do that while we were down in Miami after that exercise was over, anyway, to try out a new rifle. Now, I've got an even better reason to go over and pick up the weapon. He's got a serial number already picked out for me."

"Which one is that?" Mackenzie asked.

"Nine-eleven," Warrick said, smiling. "Kind of a hard number to forget in our line of work."

"That sounds like a plan, then," Reaper said. "Use your own wheels, though." Turning to Deveraux, he said, "Care to have dinner with me?"

"I think that would be lovely," she said with a dazzling smile.

"Hey," Deckert said, "I was cooking here."

"Keep some leftovers for us," Reaper said. "And get busy on the computer search. Deveraux will help you set it up."

"What do you want searched that's different from what we covered in Washington?" she asked.

"Those original parameters were pretty good ones," Reaper said, "we just missed the correct target. Go back another year at least. This operation sounds bigger and bigger each time we talk about it. One thing for certain, it wasn't a spur-of-the-moment thing. It wouldn't surprise me if this Devlin character has been planning this op for years. Put some fresh eyes on it, and we may come up with a winner. At least that's another thing we can do besides just waiting for something to happen."

Chapter Eighteen

The building was just one of many in the small industrial complex. There was nothing to distinguish it from all of the other structures, especially not in the heavy rain that was pouring down. It was a single story, steel-framed and brick-walled structure with a roll-up steel door in the back and a single steel fire door next to it. In the front was another blank gray-painted steel fire door. The glass windows on either side of the front door were darkly tinted to help keep out the sun and the interior drapes were always tightly closed. The rainwater ran down the sidewalk at the front of the building and joined the growing puddles in the blacktop parking lot.

If anyone had bothered to notice, they would have seen a small name painted on the doorway: MARS RE-SEARCH INC. The name said little and the building showed less. Since it was at the back of the complex, the doors faced out toward a swampy area just beyond the parking lot. Someone had just parked a van in front of the personnel door at the back of the building. Nothing could be seen inside of the van through its tinted windows. A faint stream of exhaust coming from the rear of the vehicle was the only sign that the engine was running. Nearby was parked a much more exciting recent model tan Chevrolet Stingray sports car. Besides the performance car, nothing out of the ordinary was around, nothing interesting could be seen. Inside the building was a different story. That action would have been of supreme interest to a large number of people.

The front office of the building was practically empty. What furnishings there were did not look to be those of a normal business office. There was an old padded chair, a cot, and a small television set placed on a folding-leg card table. A hot plate and pot sat next to the television. The contents of a small refrigerator on the floor nearby would eventually end up in the pot.

For all of the Spartan furnishings of the front office, the rooms in the back of the building were lavishly equipped. Across a spotless floor were steel racks of components. Past the racks were work tables, tool cabinets, and machine tools. A large engine lathe was sharing floor space with a big Bridgeport milling machine. A drill press was next to a work table with an assortment of hand tools, files, and a bench grinder. Cloth-covered shapes nearby suggested that there were more machines around. And along one wall was a number of different-colored steel bottles for compressed gas. Piercing a wall was a very secure steel door with cabinets on either side. The area near the roll-up back door was dominated by a stack of sandbags and a large trailer hidden underneath a heavy tarp.

As Devlin and Voorhees looked on, David Pressler concentrated on his work in the glove box. The box was a closed environment, sealed off from the outside air. The renegade technician had been using it for some of his more sensitive work developing Devlin's weapon systems. The big steel bottle of argon gas hooked up to the glove box told Devlin that the inside had an inert atmosphere, eliminating any oxygen from the interior. That was exactly what Pressler required as he used heavy rubber gloves to manipulate components within the box.

Using a pair of shaped tongs, Pressler lifted a beaker of what looked like melted pale yellow wax. He poured the thick liquid into several canisters secured to stands with laboratory clamps. When the cylinders were full, Pressler placed the beaker back onto the warm electric heater he had used to melt the material. Assembling and cleaning off the filled canisters took another few minutes, then they were passed out of the glove box through a double-door attachment that acted as a miniature air lock.

The cylinders were the size of large frozen juice cans, heavy for their size, and fitted with a threaded well on one end. The sides of the canisters were serrated, marked into separate squares by lines cut into the metal. Screwing fuse assemblies marked M206A2 into the threaded well on the end of the cylinders completed them.

"There you are," Pressler said handing the devices to Devlin. "As fresh as you can get, brand-new white phosphorus grenades. That fuse has a four- to five-second delay."

Holding the grenades in his hands, Devlin rolled them about in his palms, shaking them and hearing no rattle or slosh beyond the clinking of the loose pull ring.

"And you say these will work like the military-issue models?" Devlin said.

"Exactly like them," Pressler said. "Those are the same fuses as are used in the military models. These are just a little smaller, is all. Those square serrations are to identify them and aid the steel body in breaking up. The explosive in the fuse should throw particles of burning phosphorus twenty to twenty-five meters."

"Excellent work, as always," Devlin said "You just can't get these anymore, certainly not new ones."

"I have enough phosphorus and other materials to make several more if you wish," Pressler said.

"That would be worthwhile," Devlin said. "But for right now, I want you to show me the new rockets and warheads you've been working on."

"Do you want to see the processing facility?" Voorhees asked. "That's where the warheads are loaded and stored. To inspect it will require you to suit up in protective clothing."

"Do you have an example of a warhead out here?" Devlin said.

"Certainly," Pressler said. "I have several empties and a dummy I use to check the rockets."

"That should be sufficient," Devlin said. "Please continue."

"The only direction I have been given so far," Pressler said, "is to design and load a warhead to disseminate the powdered filler in a controlled manner. The warhead is to be carried by a rocket with a minimum range of six miles and have a controlled release point."

He walked over to one of the workbenches. Pulling its cloth over back, he revealed a large missile, more than two meters long and over fifteen centimeters in diameter. The missile had four fins at the back and a much larger set of four fins near the center of the body. Next to the missile was a pointed-nose warhead over forty centimeters long, a duplicate of the front of the missile. Pressler looked down at the dull-white painted missile with the satisfied smile of a workman who knows he has made a good product.

"The original rocket you had me turn out quickly carried a smaller warhead and was a straightforward solid-fuel design," Pressler said as he turned to face Devlin and Voorhees. "It certainly would have worked, and matched your minimum-range requirement. Since I've had six weeks to work on a new design, I've turned out a half dozen examples of this model. It's much larger that the first rocket and carries more than twice the payload in the warhead."

"It looks very familiar," Devlin said as he closely examined the missile.

"I'm certain you've seen it before," Pressler said with a smile, "or at least something very much like it, only three times bigger. This is almost exactly a two-thirds-scale copy of the American AGM-84E Harpoon missile. The plans and all of the information I needed to build this design were available either in open publications or from the Internet.

"The real heart of this missile is the engine. To increase the range and make other things simpler, I've gone with a hybrid rocket-engine design rather than solid fuel."

Devlin was a more than competent engineer himself, but this kind of specialty work required a concentration of experience he didn't have. He had worked with Pressler for years and knew he was extremely good at what he did. But the man could also be distracted by new ideas and ways of doing things. Now was not the time to experiment without a very good reason.

"I trust your judgment on that," Devlin said, "as long as you aren't letting your enthusiasm get the better of you. The solid-fuel rocket has been a proven design for some time. We need absolute dependability for this project. More than you can imagine is riding on this, besides the fact that we are all getting paid a great deal of money. Now, just what is this hybrid design, and why should we use it?"

"It's a relatively simple design that uses two energy components, much easier to get than the ammonium perchlorate and butyl rubber I used for the solid-fuel rockets. The hybrid fuel element is really nothing more than a machined piece of acrylic plastic. A chunk of Plexiglas with a hole drilled in it."

"And the other component?" Devlin asked. "I assume that's the oxidizer?"

"The system uses a gaseous oxidizer," Pressler said. "At least, it's a gas under normal atmospheric conditions. Nitrous oxide, what the Americans call laughing gas. It's available from speed shops that supply racing cars, as well as other sources."

Pressler reached underneath the bench and lifted up the parts of a huge assembly. The pieces were a shiny black fiber-wrapped tank and a black cylinder. Some brass fittings and tubing looked like they would connect the top and bottom of the two parts. In spite of the size of the parts, the way the technician handled them demonstrated their lightness.

"This is the engine assembly and the oxidizer tank," Pressler said as he laid the parts on the bench. "This is an amazingly simple design for what it does. I have a report from a high-school student who built one as a science fair project. None of the materials to make it are watched or regulated by the authorities. The equipment to make and use this engine, the igniters, valves, carbon-fiber tanks and graphite composite nozzles, I can either fabricate right here or purchase on the open market as commercial items."

"So this design is worth the trouble?" Devlin said.

"Very much so," Pressler stated emphatically. "In this configuration, the engine will supply more than eight hundred pounds of thrust for over thirty seconds. If I use a solid-fuel booster, which uses the fuel I already have on hand from the original rockets, I can modify this engine to burn for a much longer time with a lower thrust. Would you like to see a test?"

"A launch?" Devlin asked with surprise in his voice. "From here? You can't be serious."

"No, not a launch from here," Pressler said. "A test burn of an engine. The heavy rain will cover the exhaust and the noise isn't that bad. The test fixture is that sandbag emplacement in front of the door. We just roll up the door for the firing. The highway traffic just past the swamp more than drowns out the noise. The only flight testing we've done has been conducted well south of here. And it just looked like model rocketeers launching a toy. They actually have shows on the telly with people doing exactly that, launching model rockets. Some much bigger than this design."

"A demonstration will not be necessary," Devlin said as he gazed at the missile and components on the table. "I will take your word for it that this will work. And you said we can expect a longer range from this design?"

"With a three-kilogram payload in the warhead," Pressler said, "I can conservatively estimate a range of sixteen to eighteen miles, depending on the weather conditions. The large cruciform wings aid a lot in getting the extended range. All of the internal control systems are mechanical in nature. Minimum electronics, as you ordered. The fuse system for the warhead can be set to open the vents and leave them open at any time during the flight. The size of the vents can be adjusted before launch to have the payload exit nearly the entire length of the flight. Effectively, you have a small cruise missile here."

"That is exactly what I wanted," Devlin said. "You have done a magnificent job. This greatly increases the chances of success for the mission."

"If you would give me more details on that," Pressler said, "I may be better able to modify the design."

"Details would also help me in finalizing production of the agent," Voorhees said, speaking up for the first time since Devlin's inspection had begun. "The processing takes place here, but we can only grow so much material at a time."

"I agree," Devlin said. "I'll give you more details now. I prepared the launch site myself with the collapsible rail system you made. But with these new missiles, we will have to increase the size and number of the launchers. You said you had six missiles ready to go. Do they include filled warheads?"

Pressler shook his head. "Processing the raw agent takes about three days of solid work," he said. "Then just properly loading the warhead takes about a day. So far, I have three complete missiles with filled warheads attached to the rocket bodies."

"How much faster can we increase production of the raw agent?" Devlin asked, looking pointedly at Voorhees.

In her element now, the woman was not shaken by Devlin's stare.

"It takes forty-eight hours to grow a single batch of the organism," Voorhees said. "Then it's shocked with an excess of oxygen to cause it to sporulate. Forty-eight hours later we can harvest the cola-colored liquid from the fermenter and run it through the separator. In less than an hour I can reduce the three hundred and fifteen gallons of raw agent and nutrient down to a gallon or so, roughly the consistency of milk."

"So a batch takes about a week to produce," Devlin said.

"Including cleaning and recharging time for the fermenter and the rest of the equipment, yes, about a week," Voorhees agreed.

"How much agent do we get from a batch, and how many batches have you run?"

"After freeze-drying, milling, treating with bentonite antistatic agent, and running the material through a pulverizer," Voorhees said, "we're averaging between 1.25 and 1.5 kilograms of final weaponized agent per batch."

"All of that work for such a relatively small amount of agent," Devlin commented.

"You aren't taking into consideration the quality of the materials we're producing under rather crude circumstances here," Voorhees said heatedly. "That's more than a kilogram of top-quality agent, reduced to 1.5 to 3 micron particles with antistatic properties. And the final product is nearly twenty-five percent viable spores. That compares very favorably to what the United States produced at their biological warfare facilities in the 1960s."

"And just how lethal is an agent that's only twenty-five percent pure?" Devlin said.

"Considering there are hundreds of billions of spores in a single gram, and the U.S. calculated fifty-percent lethal dose is less than three thousand spores—much less actually, from more recent studies—we have more than a hundred million lethal doses per gram. And there's a thousand grams in a kilogram."

Devlin had been working with Pressler for years and accepted the details he slipped into his explanations. Voorhees was vital to the project, but she was also new to his organization and had yet to earn his indulgence.

"I assure you I know how much is in a kilogram," Devlin said quietly. "Please do not assume that you are speaking to an uneducated lackey. It would be a serious mistake."

Voorhees recognized the venom in Devlin's voice and knew she had crossed the line. There was no question that the man could be extremely dangerous, but he was the means to an end for her.

"I'm sorry," Voorhees said softly.

Devlin moved on. He had reestablished dominance and that was all that was important to him when dealing with people. "Now, how long would it take to produce the agent and load more warheads?"

"Finishing the batch that's growing now and producing another immediately, we can have enough material to fill another warhead by the end of the first week in July," Voorhees said.

Pressler nodded his head in agreement. "What's our deadline?" he asked.

"Interesting term, that—'deadline,'" Devlin said with a slight smile. "We have to have the warheads loaded and missiles in place by July twelve."

"That shouldn't be a problem," Pressler said. "Even including making more launchers, I should be able to meet that schedule. How far is the launch site?"

"About a hundred thirty miles by highway," Devlin said. "More if we have to take local streets. The trailer I asked you to modify can travel that far without problems?"

"Oh, easily," Pressler said. "We may have to cover it up for protection, though. But what is the reason that trailer will help us? I didn't think Orlando was that far away."

"It isn't," Devlin said, "and the target isn't in Orlando. We are going to aim at the shuttle launch at the Kennedy Space Center."

"The space shuttle!" Pressler exclaimed. "But, the astronauts are sealed in the cabin, even the launch control center is sealed. A biological weapon won't have any effect on the space shuttle, and these lightweight missiles won't do any real damage."

"Oh, I assure you they'll be deadly enough," Devlin said with a wide grin. "The target isn't the shuttle itself, it's the estimated quarter of a million people who will be watching the launch. This is the first space-shuttle launch since the Columbia disaster years ago. It signals America's return to space, and that makes it one of the most important space-shuttle launches ever. Tens of thousands of people will be there, every one of them a potential victim of our missiles. Even Governor

Bush and the First Lady of Florida will be among the dignitaries in attendance, but including them in our possible body count may be hoping for too much.

"What does work in our favor since the May launch delay is that NASA, in its wisdom, has dropped the restrictions along the roads and approaches for the public to view the launch site. The whole world will be watching the United States go back into space. And the news networks will be able to televise the most lethal attack ever perpetrated anywhere on the planet.

"Even if the public knows exactly what happened, the hospitals and medical support will prove woefully inadequate to deal with the influx of victims. There will be thousands, tens of thousands of people who come down with anthrax. And the clouds of agent won't stop with them. With an onshore breeze, those lethal spores will drift inland for miles, spreading out and infecting anyone who breathes them in. It will be a plague of biblical proportions."

"My God," Voorhees said, "the carnage within a week, just a few days, even, will make the World Trade Center body count look like a bad traffic accident."

"That's exactly why our principles are paying us so very well," Devlin said.

The sudden knock on the door leading outside from the garage startled the three in the big room. Will Shaughnessy, the man who had met Devlin at the door when he first arrived at the pub, walked in. He had been on watch out in the van, having brought Voorhees to the meeting.

"Devlin," Shaughnessy said. "I think there's something on the radio you should be hearing."

"There's no radio in here," Devlin said. "If it is so

important that you feel you can interrupt us, perhaps you can tell me the gist of what you heard."

"Basically," Shaughnessy said, "the police took down a pot farm well east of here. It was a pretty good-sized operation, run by a couple of Florida boys. A sheriff's deputy was indicted along with them. Some unidentified government agency conducted the operation, according to the people who were arrested, but no one knows who they are."

"How can something like that possibly affect us?" Devlin said.

"I thought you should know because of where the bust went down," Shaughnessy said. "The raid was on a new brew pub east of Orlando."

"That does make it interesting," Devlin agreed as he considered the information. "Usually, the DEA is quick to lay claim for any kind of drug bust. For that matter, it doesn't sound like any police or federal agency that I've ever heard of. They're always falling all over one another to take credit for something like this, especially if police corruption is uncovered. Only intelligence people walk away from something like this. Or others who might just be trying to send a message. I wonder if any of the boy-os from the old country are making a try at finding us?"

"What, from Ireland?" Pressler said, his voice rising from his excitement.

"Could be," Devlin said calmly. "Word came down that the Sein Fenn has been breaking things off with the active IRA. That the fighting is over and it's time to attempt a political solution. Something like what we have planned here could seriously upset that little po-tato cart."

"So what do you want to do?" Shaughnessy asked.

"Nothing much different from what I had already intended doing, but we will need some additional manpower," Devlin said. "What I want you to do as soon as you can is to contact John Mack and his boys. I want that mercenary and his men to be ready to move at a moment's notice. They are supposed to be the backup muscle for this operation and I've been paying them to sit on their hands long enough. Everyone is to be on call to move immediately. This situation is a bit more fluid than I would prefer, and a damned sight too unknown."

"And what are *we* going to do?" Voorhees protested.

"My dear," Devlin said in a smooth voice, "you are going to change into something a bit more flattering than that business smoke you have on. Something simple yet elegant, I think. You see, I am going to take you out for a fine meal tonight. After all, if someone is going to all of the trouble to find us, I don't think we should spend our time hiding under a rock. If someone is looking for us, I would like to bring them out at a location of my own choosing. Besides, it would be rude to disappoint them. Don't you agree?"

Voorhees was stunned at Devlin's invitation. She thought she had known hard and ruthless men in her life. But she was finding out just how deep the well of evil could extend in some men. And just how insane and dangerous this particular man was.

Chapter Nineteen

The sudden torrential rains that had plagued the area during the late afternoon had passed. The early evening looked like it was going to be such a perfect warm Florida night that Reaper had already put the top down on the Mustang GT for the drive to Tampa. Warrick had left several hours earlier to pick up his new rifle and give it some range time. If he was available, he would try and hook up with Reaper and Deveraux later on their "working" date that evening.

Deckert had provided Reaper with the surveillance technology: a small, weatherproof closed-circuit television camera and transmitter set about half the size of a pack of cigarettes. To increase the versatility of the system as well as record hours of video, Deckert had included a larger weatherproof box that held a receiver/transmitter system along with a power supply and DVD burner. All Reaper had to do was place the larger box within a hundred yards of the camera, and the system would record over a day's worth of video images. The transmitter could also uplink the video images in real-time to a receiver in the van. The system could be activated or shut down from the communications array Deckert had available to him.

The closed-circuit surveillance technology would be a great way to cover all of the customers who arrived at the restaurant, allowing the computer to biometrically compare them to the images from the customs facility. Before Reaper covertly installed the system, he and Deveraux were going to Bern's themselves to examine the place and interrogate some of the staff.

Following a long-established habit, Reaper drove around the neighborhood of the restaurant before stopping. Familiarizing himself with the area around a target of interest had always proven to be a good idea in the past and wasn't something he was going to forget now. South Howard Avenue, the street Bern's was on, was lined mostly with bars and other eateries. However, only a block or so off the main street, Reaper was surprised to see a much less savory neighborhood surrounding the place. He would have to point that out to Deckert, if he brought the van in close to the surveillance site.

For this evening, Reaper and Deveraux were going to conduct a soft probe of Bern's and see if it was the kind of place Devlin would patronize. If they were lucky, he might even prove to be a regular. Realistically, Reaper did not expect Devlin to regularly patronize any place. Following patterns was the best way to get caught, and he didn't think Devlin could have survived this long by being sloppy.

Pulling in to the parking lot at Bern's, Reaper by-passed the valet parking to secure his vehicle himself. Not only did that allow him to be certain where the

Mustang was if he needed to pull out quickly, it also let him walk through the parking lot, casing the area for a good location for the camera.

"You just didn't want to let the young man play with your bright red convertible," Deveraux teased. She had learned to relax around Reaper and his men, having shared enough time and danger with all of them to show her that they were indeed the consummate professionals that Straker had described.

"Must be my midlife crisis," Reaper said as he pulled a computer case from the backseat of the Mustang.

Both Reaper and Deveraux were dressed as they had been for the raid on the Gaia Brewery. Logging on to make reservations, Reaper had found dress code described as "business casual," according to their Web site. He didn't want to be underdressed for the place or stand out in a crowd. His brown suede jacket and trousers seemed to fit the bill. The only concession he had made to what was supposed to be a public evening was leaving his 5.11 concealment-mesh vest behind.

Instead of the 5.11 vest full of gear, Reaper had two spare eight-round P220 magazines each in a leather Galco High Ride magazine carrier on his belt behind his left hip. The magazines were each filled with .45 ACP Federal 230-grain Hydra-Shok hollowpoints. They matched the SIG P220 semiautomatic pistol in the Galco Combat master holster at his right hip. Not needing the special 9mm EBR Frangible ammunition, Reaper had switched from the P226 and gone back to his preferred .45 ACP SIG with the much larger and heavier projectiles. In his right-front pants pocket, Reaper had his Emerson CQC-7BW folding knife, the same one he had been carrying for years.

Except for a touch of makeup, Deveraux had also duplicated her earlier outfit. The only concession to the more social atmosphere of the evening was the addition of high-heeled shoes to her ensemble. The jacket she wore also did a good job of concealing her SIG P239. Between the pistol and the spare magazines on either side of the small of her back, Deveraux had attached a particularly unusual and vicious-looking knife.

The fixed-blade Karambit was a hook-nosed knife with the cutting edge on the inside of the blade and a hole at the far end of the grip where it could go over the operator's index finger. Such a weapon was very effective in the hands of a trained operator, and Deveraux was a very well-trained operator. The knife was one of a number of prototypes made by Ernie Emerson himself and wouldn't be on the market for months yet. She had managed to pick the weapon up from him at the same time as she had gotten the small LaGriffe blades that had impressed Warrick. The Karambit was a particularly impressive weapon that could intimidate an opponent or cut through just about anything that could be sliced by steel. She had slipped the knife on because of an impulse, the kind of impulse she had learned to trust over the years.

The pair walked up to the canopy-covered entranceway to Bern's. Keeping his eye out for a good location to conceal the camera hidden in his coat pocket, Reaper pulled open the door and waited while Deveraux entered the lobby. Following her inside, Reaper stopped for a moment and looked around at the huge foyer.

In spite of its appearance, Bern's was anything but a tourist hangout. It was unique, there was no question of that in Reaper's mind. Between the red velvet wallpaper, the tall gilt-framed mirrors, white marble, vaulted ceiling, and white brick fireplace, the interior of Bern's looked like a New Orleans bordello from at least a hundred years ago. The staff looked like they had stepped out of a Prohibition-era speakeasy, all of the women tall, blonde, and in evening dresses, while the men were in suits. The only immediate way to tell that they were employees at Bern's, rather than clientele, was by the name tags on their outfits. The maitre d' at his station inside the doorway was used to new arrivals' reactions to the decor and simply waited for a moment.

"Reservations for two," Reaper said and gave the man his name.

"Your table will be ready in a few minutes, sir," the maitre d' said after checking his list. "Would you care to take a tour of the facility? Or have a libation in the bar?"

"I think the bar for now," Reaper said looking at Deveraux, who nodded agreement.

The bar turned out to be a series of rooms to the right of the entry, the area dominated by a huge carved-wood edifice topped by a massive slab of granite. This was where the alchemist of the bottles held court. Sitting down on two high-backed cane barstools, both Reaper and Deveraux had an excellent view of the rooms to either side of them. Bending down, Reaper set his case down between the two of them. When he raised his head, they already had company.

"Anything for the lady?" the head barkeep asked, stepping up to where the pair sat.

"A martini, please," Deveraux said. "Boodles gin, very cold and very dry."

"Very well, and for the gentleman?"

"A Corona, please."

As the barkeep turned to his stock, Reaper leaned in close to Deveraux.

"So, do you think this is the kind of place Devlin would frequent?" he said in a quiet voice.

"Almost certainly," Deveraux said. "It would appeal to his sense of the theatric. And if it didn't, I could certainly get used to it. I looked the place up in a number of guides on the Internet. It serves exactly the kind of food that appeals to him, more so than any other place in Central Florida."

The barkeep placed a tall martini glass filled with a clear liquid on a napkin in front of Deveraux. The liquid was so frigid that the glass fogged almost immediately, obscuring the view of the large green olive at its bottom. Holding up an eyedropper filled with Noilly Pratt vermouth from a nearby bottle, the smiling man asked, "One drop, or two?"

In a delighted voice, Deveraux told the man she wanted but a single drop of the high-end vermouth, for an exceptionally dry martini. A moment later, he set an icy-cold Corona beer with a slice of lime in the bottle's mouth in front of Reaper, along with a tall shell glass. Crushing the lime between his fingers, Reaper stuffed it down into the bottle, then filled the glass with the pale gold beer.

Smiling, Reaper and Deveraux each took a sip of their drinks. Sighing and leaning back with her eyes closed, Deveraux visibly relaxed for a moment. Reaper just looked at the beautiful woman next to him, silently wishing they were at the restaurant for a much more peaceful reason than the one that had really brought them there. But they probably should be getting down to business.

"I suppose it would be a good idea to ask the bartender if he recognizes one of our pictures," Deveraux said, her eyes still closed. The woman leaned forward and looked at Reaper.

Startled that her words so closely matched his thoughts, Reaper continued to look at Deveraux for a second or two. Without replying, he turned and raised his glass to signal the barkeep.

Both Reaper and Deveraux had been given government credentials by Straker's office. If those weren't enough to garner cooperation, they had phone numbers they could call if they needed more local authority. Neither of them wanted to use either the documents or the numbers and thus show that they were a lot more than they seemed.

"Yes," the barkeep said as he came up to Reaper.

"Do you think you could tell us if you've seen one of these people here, sir?" Reaper said, making a snap decision to just openly ask the man what they wanted to know. Taking a set of pictures from his pocket, he laid them down on the polished granite bar top.

"Call me Kenny, please," the barkeep said as he set down the towel he had been holding. After twenty years behind the slab at Bern's, the bartender had seen a lot, and very little surprised him. He was also a shrewd judge of character and a longtime student of human nature. He liked what he saw in the two customers in front of him, though if asked, he couldn't have specifically said why.

Looking down at the pictures, he silently shuffled through them.

"They all do look quite a bit alike," he said, raising his gaze to Reaper's face.

"It is very important," Deveraux said quietly, sitting up straight in her chair.

At that moment, the maitre d' walked in to the bar and up to Reaper.

"Your table is ready," he said.

"Peter, do you recognize any of these people?" the barkeep said quietly, turning the pictures in front of him around so the other man could see them clearly.

With a slightly raised eyebrow, Peter looked at Kenny, then at Reaper and Deveraux. Deciding to go with Kenny's unvoiced suggestion of cooperation, he looked down at the pictures.

"Of course," he said almost immediately. "That's Mr. Kennedy."

"You're sure?" Deveraux asked in a questioning tone, startled at their possible luck.

"Certainly," the maitre d' said. "He and his dinner guest are at their table in Room Two at this moment."

"If it's not too much trouble," Deveraux said, "do you think we might have a table in Room Two? If there's space, of course."

Both the maitre d' and the bartender had literally met kings, princes of business, and even presidents during their time at Bern's. They both had been questioned by law enforcement, private investigators, the FBI and the Secret Service over the years. And they recognized professionals when they saw them. Besides, Mr. Kennedy had raised warning flags for the experienced maitre d'. He wasn't very surprised that people might be looking for him. But there were priorities he had to address.

"I trust that your business will not reflect badly on Bern's?" the maitre d' said firmly. "Or interrupt our other guests?"

"You can be assured of that," Reaper said.

"We would not ask if it wasn't of significant importance," Deveraux said, looking straight at the maitre d'.

"Very well then, please follow me."

Turning from the bar, the maitre d' walked out into the lobby. As they prepared to follow him, Reaper placed a fifty-dollar bill on the bar.

"I will have your drinks and change sent on to your table," Kenny said.

"Just the drinks please," Reaper said with a smile.

Room Two turned out to be a deep area with spaces between the red brick pilasters along the wall filled with photographic murals of various country scenes. Of the ten six-chaired linen-covered tables in the room, only two were occupied. A couple sat at the back of the room while a mixed foursome were on the opposite side of the room closer to the center.

Stopping at the table to the immediate left of the entrance to the dining room, the maitre d' indicated a table with a slight bow.

"Will this be satisfactory?" he asked, stepping back from the table.

"This will be fine," Reaper said. He gestured that Deveraux should sit in the chair that he had just pulled out. After she sat down, he moved to the other side of the table, set his case down on a chair nearer the wall, and sat down opposite Deveraux, with his back to the room.

Moving up, the maitre d' laid two thick leather-covered menus on the table. "Your server will be Jack," he said. "He should be with you in a moment."

"Thank you for all of your assistance," Deveraux said with a warm smile.

"Think nothing of it," the maitre d' said as he bowed slightly and left the room.

Reaper picked up his menu. He barely glanced at the twenty-seven pages of foods and descriptions. "Anything look good to you?" he asked Deveraux.

The woman had been looking over the top of her menu at the people sharing the room with them. Her eyes kept glancing at the couple at the far wall in the back. The man sitting there was Devlin. It took every ounce of control she had not to pull out her weapon and immediately shoot the bastard. It was unprofessional of her and she knew it, but right now, she wasn't certain she cared.

"Deveraux?" Reaper said softly. "You know it's considered impolite to stare. It's also a very bad idea and draws attention."

Leaning back in her chair, Deveraux laid the menu down in front of her and laughed brightly as if she had just heard one of the funniest jokes. She beamed one of her dazzling smiles and leaned in close to Reaper.

"I'm okay," she said softly, "but there's someone in the back that I would very much like you to meet."

"Oh, we'll meet," Reaper said. "That's something you can take to the bank. But not here and not now. And here's our waiter."

A pleasantly smiling middle-aged man in an impeccable black suit came up to the table and set their drinks down. His highly polished engraved brass nameplate said JACK. After Jack described the dishes of the day, Reaper and Deveraux looked over the extensive menu.

Ordering several of the outstanding steaks, they sent Jack out with their order and a warning.

"We are expecting a call," Reaper said, "and it may require us to leave at a moment's notice."

"No problem, sir," Jack replied easily. "We have a large number of doctors and other professionals who eat here regularly. I will keep your bill immediately at hand, you can pay it at any time. Would you care to order wine with dinner?"

"I heard you have a large wine cellar," Deveraux said.

"Actually, it's the largest privately held collection of wine in the world, ma'am. We have more than two hundred table wines with vintages to 1973. Our labels include fifty-five hundred reds and a thousand whites," Jack said as he handed over a wine list. It was thicker than the menu.

"You choose for both of us please," Reaper said, passing Deveraux the list and a smile.

Deveraux made a quick selection. Jack smiled, took the menus, and left.

"Relax," Reaper said very softly. "There's no way out of this room without going past us. Do you want to call Straker for backup?"

"No," Deveraux replied. "It would take too long for anyone to arrive. And there's too many possible hostages around. I never expected us to just walk in on him. That was stupid of me, and this man does not allow for you to make mistakes. We need to wait until he moves on his own into a more open area. We have to find out where he's growing the weapon—that's the most important thing.

"I recognize him in spite of the changes he's made, but he hasn't seen me in years. The last time he saw me, I was a redhead, and I don't think he looked much past my chest. I doubt very much he will recognize me.

"The woman he's sitting with is quite a looker. I wonder if she's local talent. Did you leave the recorder for the closed-circuit camera on back in the car?"

Reaper just nodded his head slightly.

"Then slip me that camera from your pocket, if you would, please."

Reaper palmed the tiny camera package and its transmitter in his big hand and then placed his hand, palm down, on the table. Smiling, Deveraux placed her hand over his and the pass went smoothly, unnoticeable by anyone more than a few feet away.

"Does this whole thing strike you as far too easy?" Reaper said with a smile. "Finding this clown on our first real try?"

"You have to be lucky sometime," Deveraux said. "But that doesn't mean we should be foolish. This only looks easy because I know his tastes; no one else does, except for the people who work with him. You've only been chasing him a few days. I've been after him for years. Still, there's no reason to let our guard down, even for a moment—not with someone this dangerous."

———

"Have I ever told you my theory about the people of the world?" Devlin said to Voorhees, who was sitting at the opposite side of the table with her back to the room.

"I have no idea what you mean," Voorhees said.

"The idea is that there are only six hundred people in the world," Devlin continued. "The rest are merely an optical illusion put here by God to confuse us. Eventually, everyone will meet everyone else."

"You can't be serious," Voorhees said, stumped by what Devlin was leading up to.

"It is the only explanation for how someone that I haven't seen for nearly ten years could just walk through the door of the restaurant where I happen to be eating. Please don't turn around, dear—that would give us away."

Startled at what Devlin had said, Voorhees had to stop herself from turning in her seat.

"Just who is it?"

"A lady from my past," Devlin said as he leaned back in his seat, obviously enjoying himself. "She has been steadfastly chasing me since before the change of the millennium. Blames me for her husband being at the wrong place at the wrong time. Poor man was blown to shreds. I'm certain she wants to spend some time with me, discussing philosophy intimately. Though I believe her idea of an intimate relationship in this case would involve a soundproof room and a selection of medieval torture devices, preferably red-hot ones."

"So, what are we to do?" Voorhees asked breathlessly.

"Why, finish this delicious meal, of course," Devlin said as if it was the only thing in the world they could do. "The rest will come to me as needed."

Chapter Twenty

The Number Two dining room at Bern's was a quiet area of clinking tableware striking against china. Conversations were low and quiet, the sound level peaking occasionally with a burst of laughter from the group in the center of the room. That pair of couples was enjoying a pleasant evening in each other's company. They took no notice at all at the high level of stress centered on the couples at each of the opposite ends of the long room. If they could have recognized the tension in the ether around them, they would have run screaming from the place rather than having a second bottle of wine.

For the next hour, Devlin made a show of obviously enjoying his meal. Voorhees just picked at her food, in spite of quiet admonishments from the other side of the table. She ate mechanically when warned by Devlin not to draw attention, that the waiter might wonder what was wrong with her meal. Her immediate concern was not with the apparently deranged individual sitting across from her. It was centered much more on the success of the upcoming operation. It was very hard to see such a possible risk to her years of planning and sacrifice, something Devlin couldn't possibly understand.

What Voorhees didn't know—couldn't know—was that a great deal of Devlin's viciously outrageous behavior was an act, a camouflage. The man was supremely intelligent and constantly balanced all possibilities against the known facts of a situation. Making people uncomfortable was a simple and easy way of keeping them off balance. The sudden appearance of someone from his past was unexpected and threw his balance off, not a situation Devlin easily accepted. Things could have a simple explanation; coincidences did happen. But that was anything but the safe way to plan, especially now that Devlin suspected he knew who the "unknown government agents" were who had been mentioned in the news broadcasts earlier that day.

Reaper tried to concentrate on the excellent medium-rare fourteen-ounce Delmonico steak in front of him, or at least look like that was what he was doing. Not only was the meal very well prepared and served, dealing with it helped him ignore the itching feeling on his back, the one that screamed to him to turn around and face the threat. He knew that it was much better for him to watch the door and allow Deveraux to occasionally glance around the room, particularly toward the couple in the back, but that didn't help the itching much. She had seen Devlin before and could recognize him, and Reaper trusted her judgment.

Even under the stress she felt right now, Deveraux knew the value of eating. In her experience, there could be a serious break between meals, so you fueled up when you could, especially when the possibility of a long chase coming to an end soon was a very real one.

The woman ate and kept up some nonsensical small talk. Reaper smiled, nodded, chewed and swallowed, not really paying attention to whatever it was they talked about.

The only real action Deveraux had seen at Devlin's table was when the man had made a cell phone call a half hour earlier. There was nothing that showed in his face or reactions to say the call was anything but a harmless one—but what Deveraux had learned in the years of chasing her quarry was that nothing Devlin ever did was simple or innocent. His every action could have several meanings, usually ones that held the worst consequences for those around him.

The evening had worn on, the attentive staff refreshing the coffee that just about everyone in the room was enjoying. Reaper had already paid the bill after signaling Jack. He and Deveraux appeared to be little more than an attractive professional couple relaxing over coffee at the end of their day.

———

The soft chime of a cell phone could just be heard above the noise of the restaurant. Making an apparently fumbling move toward his coat pocket, Devlin pulled out his phone as the third ring sounded, and the device went silent. Glancing at the glowing blue screen of the cell phone for a moment, Devlin smiled slightly to himself as he slipped it back into his pocket. Then he returned his attention to Voorhees.

"And now the game's afoot, my dear," he said in a low voice. "We shall finish our excellent beverage and move on shortly. I would appreciate it very much if you would not even glance at the couple sitting at the table next to the doorway. Particularly do not glare at the woman, no matter how much you may wish to. I am certain that we will be seeing them again in the near future. Perhaps you can satisfy your curiosity at that point.

"Do not rush. Remember, appearances can be everything. Be calm and we shall walk out together. Nothing will happen here, of that I am certain. If they were prepared to take action now, things would have already taken place. No, we shall be able to choose the time and place of our next meeting, be assured of that. Now let us take our leave before those other couples remove themselves. They can act as our cover."

———

As she saw Devlin and his lady starting to get up from their table, Deveraux leaned forward, smiling brightly, and touched Reaper arm.

"Time to go," she said softly, laughing a little as if sharing a private joke.

Setting down his coffee cup, Reaper touched his lips with his napkin as Devlin and Voorhees walked by. All he could see was that the blonde was holding on to Devlin's arm and leaning into him. He hadn't seen her face but knew that Deveraux was taking a surreptitious picture of the couple with the compact camera she had hidden in her napkin. There was a manual

ON/OFF button on top of the camera case just for such uses. She had already gathered a number of shots of Devlin sitting at the far end of the room and as he approached. Now it was the woman who interested her. The lady was working a little too hard to snuggle up to Devlin. And she was too careful about not looking around the room. Her identity could be an interesting one.

Picking up his case from the seat next to him, Reaper stood up as soon as Devlin had passed from sight. Deveraux was already up and moving out the doorway, trying not to appear rushed but not wasting any time in following Devlin. The camera she now had in her pocket hadn't been set up to cover the front of the building. They had no way of knowing what vehicle Devlin would use if they lost sight of him.

"Please do come back when you are off duty some time," the maitre d' said, holding open the front door. As they walked past, Deveraux smiled at the man.

"I look forward to the opportunity," she said sincerely.

In the parking lot, Deveraux stood at the entrance to the awning while Reaper headed for the Mustang. She would watch the exit from the parking lot while Reaper picked up the car and looked for Devlin. Tossing his case into the rather small backseat of the open Mustang convertible, Reaper could see Devlin holding the door of a silver Chevrolet Corvette convertible. The wedge-shaped model was one of the newest, a 2005, if Reaper wasn't mistaken, and could give the Mustang GT a serious run along the roadways.

"What in the hell is it with bad guys and Corvettes?"

Reaper asked himself out loud as he climbed into the Mustang. He had begun his new career with Homeland Security several years earlier by chasing a bad guy across the back roads of Michigan. Only then, he had been driving Deckert's considerably modified Checker Cab. The cab's engine could practically power a WWII fighter plane. He hoped the Mustang would prove as good in this pursuit.

The red sports car certainly sounded good as Reaper fired up the big engine and headed over to where Deveraux was standing. As he pulled up, Reaper leaned way over and pulled the door handle on the passenger side.

The situation could be rapidly changing, but not so much that he couldn't appreciate the well-shaped length of nylon-encased leg that Deveraux showed as she slipped into the Mustang. Leaning forward, Reaper kissed the woman on the cheek as he wrapped his right arm around her shoulders.

"Silver Corvette," he said softly into her ear. "Give them a second to get ahead of us."

With a girlish giggle, Deveraux leaned into Reaper and rubbed her hand along his leg. Moving along the other side of the parking lot, the silver Corvette passed in front of the Mustang and made a right turn onto South Howard.

"Is he heading for the expressway?" Deveraux said as Reaper followed the Corvette at a safe distance.

Even in the darkness between street lights, the Corvette's distinctive taillights made it relatively easy to follow. Reaper held back a reasonable distance, trying to balance the need for caution against the possibility that the Corvette could suddenly turn and disappear. The fact that the Mustang sounded like the muscle car it was as the exhaust echoed off the surrounding buildings also forced him to maintain a sedate pace, matching the speed limit exactly.

"He can't be heading for the crosstown expressway," Reaper said. "It's a toll road, according to the map, and there isn't any way to get on it for miles. Besides, he's about to pass under it."

It was a nerve-wracking mile of travel, with Reaper trying to hold back in the very light traffic and keep the Corvette well in sight. Then Devlin's car stopped at a red light with the left-hand turn signal flashing.

"Well, that's convenient for us," Reaper muttered, "he's turning west on Kennedy."

"Does it strike you as odd that he would use his turn signal?" Deveraux asked in a puzzled tone of voice.

"He might just be trying to avoid a police car," Reaper answered. "That 'Vette practically comes with a set of preprinted traffic tickets in the glove compartment."

"Like this car does?" Deveraux teased. "You had to pick a red one."

"Torch red, if you please," Reaper said, grinning. "And it was the only color they had."

As the light changed and the Corvette completed its turn, Reaper sped up to make the interchange on the same light. The Mustang engine growled as he went into the turn, controlling his speed and turning radius carefully so as to not squeal his tires and draw the attention of the driver in front of them. Kennedy Boulevard had a higher speed limit then South Howard. There was also a much greater flow of traffic, though it was still relatively light for the weekday evening.

"There they are," Deveraux said sharply, "two hundred meters, right lane."

"On them," Reaper replied.

The conversation in the car stopped as Reaper paid close attention to the traffic in front of him. Both he and Deveraux knew exactly how important not losing Devlin was. The Corvette was driving well within the limits of the traffic flow. If Devlin knew he was being followed, he showed no sign of it.

After another mile and a quarter, the turn signal of the Corvette went on again.

"He's making a right onto the Mabry Highway," Reaper said as he once again sped up. He had reduced the distance between the two cars to less than a few hundred feet but still wanted to get to the intersection quickly. Traffic was light enough that he could weave among the slower cars and get to the turn quickly.

"He's heading north," Deveraux said as she looked at the map from the glove compartment. "I'll bet he's heading to I-275."

"It would be the fastest way out of town," Reaper agreed.

Not another word was spoken as they followed the Corvette north and onto the cloverleaf that fed into northbound I-275. Now the Corvette sped up considerably, going nearly ten miles an hour over the speed limit as the miles rolled past. Reaper fell back slightly, and then accelerated to keep pace.

"Where in the hell is this guy going?" Reaper said finally as the lights of Tampa started to fall away behind them. They had traveled over five miles on the expressway and were coming up to the last intersection before I-75, which was more than six miles away.

As they passed the entrance ramp, neither occupant of the Mustang noticed the three heavy black civilian Hummer vehicles coming onto the expressway and falling in behind them.

Remembering that Warrick was going to be in the Tampa area, Reaper decided to see if he was close enough to provide backup. Reaching into his pocket, he pulled out his cell phone and flipped it open. Pressing one of the speed-dial numbers, he held the phone up to his ear and waited for an answer.

"War, this is Death," Reaper said as Warrick answered the call. "We are heading northbound on I-275 approaching the I-75 intersection. We should be there within about five miles. How soon can you rendezvous with us?" He paused, listening. "Roger that. Death out."

As Reaper closed the phone and slipped it into his pocket, he looked into the rear-view mirror.

"When can Warrick reach us?" Deveraux asked.

"In about ten minutes," Reaper said as he continued to keep one eye on the mirror. "He was heading west on I-4 back to Orlando, but hadn't gotten to the I-75 intersection yet. It's not very far, maybe fifteen miles from here, but he may not get here fast enough."

"What?" Deveraux said as she turned away from watching the Corvette's taillights.

"We're being followed," Reaper said. "Those Hummers behind us have been closing in and they're now covering all lanes of the highway."

Turning in her seat and looking back the way they had come, the woman could see the big powerful Hummers coming closer in the darkness.

"Can you lose them?" she said turning to Reaper.

"No place to go," Reaper said through clenched teeth. His mind racing, the ex-SEAL came up with a possible option, or at least a trick that might help them.

"Here," he said to Deveraux after pulling something from his pocket. He handed her a tiny Gerber mini-task light, a flashlight no larger than a thumb. "See if you can reach the upper part of the brake pedal. You should feel a switch there, pull the wires out of it."

Not completely understanding, Deveraux took the light and bent over in the cramped confines of the Mustang. The car, with its center console and bucket seats, had been built for comfort and speed, not for the convenience of someone trying to modify the system while the vehicle was moving.

As Deveraux tried to reach the switch Reaper had described, two of the Hummers moved to the center lane and were starting to come abreast of the speeding sports car. The Mustang had acceleration and handling ability superior to that of the Hummers, but if Reaper allowed the big vehicles to box him in, they would loose that advantage. The heavy, powerful Hummers could easily shove the Mustang off the road or put it into a lethal spin.

"Hang on," he said as he pushed the accelerator to the floor.

The roar of the big engine blasted out as Reaper gave the Mustang all the gas it could take. The blast of wind past the open roof of the convertible made hearing difficult at best. The noise of the engine now made shouting the only way to be heard.

Deveraux grunted as she was shoved back against Reaper's right leg. She was still trying to reach the

brake pedal and disconnect the switch as Reaper forced
the sports car to speed ahead.

In the distance, the lights of the Corvette grew smaller
as it also accelerated to outrun the pack of vehicles coming up from the rear. It now was obvious that Devlin had
been leading Reaper and Deveraux into a trap, and the
jaws of that trap were starting to close.

Chapter Twenty-one

"I've got it!" Deveraux said, her voice muffled from her face practically being buried in Reaper's leg. Reaper could barely hear the woman.

"Yank them out!" Reaper shouted. "Then get your seat belt back on. This is going to get rough."

Though the Mustang had acceleration, the Hummers also had power. The big vehicles were again growing larger in the rear-view mirror.

"What the hell have they got in those things," Reaper wondered aloud, "rocket engines? We should be leaving them in our dust."

The Hummers were heavy, but they had been tricked-out with huge turbo-charged engines and drive trains. They didn't have the acceleration of the sports car, but they had power to spare. As they drew closer to the speeding Mustang, Reaper could see small flashes of light coming from the open side windows.

"Bloody hell," Deveraux cursed. "They're shooting at us."

"Here," Reaper said, pulling his SIG P220 from his

hip holster and putting it into Deveraux's lap, "nail them as they go past."

"Go past?" Deveraux wondered as she picked up the big handgun in her left hand. While she spoke, she drew out the P239 she had at her own belt with her right hand.

As the Hummers closed up from the back, Reaper watched them with one eye as he also looked out across the road ahead. The multilane divided highway was straight at that point, with paved shoulders. Suddenly, a cracking sound rang out and a star-shaped hole appeared in the windshield.

"Brace yourself and be ready to shoot," Reaper shouted.

"Ready!"

Reaper practically stood up on the clutch and the brake pedal, mashing them both into the floor.

The tires on the Mustang smoked as the sports car shuddered. The antilock brakes helped keep the car from sliding out of control, but as it slowed, Reaper suddenly pulled it over onto the right shoulder. The wires Deveraux had pulled were connected to the brake light switch. Without that circuit working, the pursuing Hummers had no warning that Reaper was putting on the brakes until the screeching came from his tires.

Without time to properly respond, the Hummers flew past the Mustang as it came to a smoking stop. They weren't ready to react, but Deveraux was. When the Hummer in the far right lane drew even with them on the left, she started shooting.

The thundering booms of the guns were lost in the screaming of tires and roar of engines as the Hummers zoomed past. Slugs slammed into the side of the closest vehicle, doing nothing more than scarring the black paint. Then a face in an open window appeared—a black gaping mouth and white blob of a face—which quickly disappeared into a red mist. One of the Federal Hydra-Shok slugs from Reaper's P220 had sped through the window and directly into the shouting mouth of the driver.

The Hummer slipped to the side, across the shoulder, and into the soft grass of the median strip. Flipping over on its side, the big vehicle skidded along the ground. Gasoline from a ruptured fuel line sprayed across the grass. The stink of the fuel filled the air along with the stench of burning rubber and hot metal. It was a small miracle that nothing ignited.

"Take the wheel!" Reaper shouted. Without waiting for an answer, he popped his seat belt open and rolled over into the backseat.

Without questioning him, Deveraux released her own seat belt and stuck the empty pistols, their slides locked back, into the center console. Clambering into the driver's seat, she secured herself in place and then turned to Reaper.

"Go!" he shouted as he pulled a case up from where it had been stashed under the front seat. The case had been in the Mustang since Reaper had put it there that afternoon. He hadn't expected to need its contents at all that evening, but right now he was very glad he had the heavy container in his hands.

The two remaining Hummers had gone into reverse and were backing up to the Mustang, their tires smoking on the concrete roadway. As the big vehicles came closer, Deveraux put the Mustang in gear and released the clutch. Deveraux jinked the sports car from one side of the road to another, searching for an opening between the approaching Hummers. In the back seat, Reaper was trying to brace himself against Deveraux's wild maneuvers while he opened the case.

Within the container were the components for a Shrike light machine gun, including an M4 lower receiver group. A new addition to the weapon system was an M203A1 40mm grenade launcher mounted underneath the handguard to the belt-fed Shrike.

He pulled the parts from the case and snapped them together with skill and efficiency. Long practice had made the ex-SEAL more than competent with weapons, and the Shrike was no exception. The Four Horsemen had been using it ever since Caronti had brought one of the prototypes up to Michigan several years earlier. Now all of the time spent practicing assembling and disassembling the weapon was proving its value.

As Deveraux moved to the right, one of the Hummers slipped over to try to block her. The two vehicles were only yards apart when the woman twisted the wheel, turning the Mustang enough so that it could just slip between the two black killers on the road.

Rounds fired from the right side Hummer slapped into the side of the Mustang as Deveraux passed it and floored the gas. As she slipped through the gears, the Mustang took off down the road leaving the Hummers well behind them. The Corvette was no longer anywhere in sight, but Reaper thought he knew of another source of information as to just where Devlin might have gone.

Stuffing into his pocket one of the gold-tipped 40mm M433 high-explosive grenades from the case, Reaper grabbed up a plastic box holding two hundred rounds of belted 5.56mm ammunition. Snapping the box into place underneath the M4 receiver, Reaper pulled the end of the ammunition belt out and laid in into the feed tray. Slamming down the feed cover of the Shrike and pulling back the cocking handle on the left side of the weapon charged it.

The last thing he did before facing the approaching Hummers was twist the knob on the side of the sight that activated the Aimpoint M2 comp mounted to the Picatinny rail on top of the Shrike's feed cover. Kneeling on the backseat of the Mustang, Reaper stuck his head up into the slipstream of air roaring past the open vehicle. Ignoring the incoming rounds from the two approaching Hummers, Reaper shouldered the Shrike and pulled the trigger.

The machine gun roared and brass poured out of the ejection port along with the separated metallic belt links. The slipstream snatched at the brass as it came out of the gun, pulling it away to bounce unnoticed along the concrete. Steel-cored M855 projectiles zipped from the short barrel of the Shrike at over 2,600 feet per second. Astounded, Reaper watched the slugs slam into the Hummers with no effect. Only paint chips and sparks flew as the dozens of projectiles slammed into and bounced off the hood and bodywork of the two vehicles.

"Damn it," Reaper cursed, "they're armored!"

Hoping to buy some time, Reaper triggered off one long hammering burst, heating the barrel of the Shrike and pouring bullets from the muzzle. The wind blew away most of the powder smoke.

In spite of the wind, there was still enough of the sickly sweet stench from the burning powder swirling around his head to cause Reaper's eyes to water heavily. He ignored the smoke, leaned into the weapon and kept firing.

The nearly solid stream of bullets slammed into the target Reaper was aiming for. The armored windows of the Hummers might resist penetration from the light 5.56mm slugs, in spite of their steel penetrators. But the glass could crack and craze, which is exactly what it did.

Thick white stars appeared across the windshield of the closest Hummer. The driver was being blinded by the damaged glass, unable to see much of what was in front of him. The gunners with their own M4 carbines and AK-47 rifles on either side of the Hummer couldn't even stick their weapons out the open side windows for fear that the hail of bullets would strip the guns away, along with their hands.

With the bolt slamming shut on an empty chamber, Reaper lowered the searing-hot Shrike. Leaning hard against the backseat, he pressed the barrel release and jacked the M203A1 grenade launcher open for loading. The one round of 40mm Reaper had pulled from the case had a blunt, rounded nose, anodized bright gold. It was a 40mm M433 high-explosive dual-purpose round. The little 40mm grenade at the front of the round would not only explode and send fragments flying through the air, the blast of the shaped charged would punch through at least two inches of steel. Reaper doubted very much that the Hummers were armored that well.

The case that held the rest of his ammunition, including more 40mm grenades, had fallen from the rear seat during all of the motion as Deveraux tried to make the Mustang a hard target for the Hummer gunmen to hit. Reaper had one round he could be sure of. Once again, he got up, braced himself, and fired at the approaching Hummers.

The "bloop" of the M203A1 was lost in the roar of the wind and engine noise. But the blossoming orange-red flower of the explosion against the square black grill of the Hummer thundered out with authority. The nearly blind driver of the vehicle never saw Reaper fire the grenade launcher that killed him.

The nose of the heavy Hummer was punched down by the explosion, driven into the roadbed. Appearing to move almost in slow motion, the rear of the blasted Hummer rose up into the air as the vehicle started to flip over. Slamming down into the concrete, the top of the Hummer was crushed.

Now it was the other Hummer's turn to fall back and twist from side to side, trying to throw off Reaper's aim. But the case of ammunition had spilled onto the floor and the few 40mm grenades that had been in it had rolled underneath the seats, out of reach of the desperate Reaper's scrabbling hand.

With no more fire coming from the Mustang, the Hummer started to speed up. Coming forward with a vengeance, the heavy black transport full of gunmen started to close with the Mustang. Even though it wouldn't stop the approaching armored Hummer, Reaper grabbed up another 200-round ammunition box from the floor and started to reload the Shrike. Then Deveraux yelled something unintelligible from the driver's seat.

As Reaper looked up and ahead of the Mustang, he saw a pickup truck come from the opposite direction on the highway. It bounced and slammed across the median strip. Whoever was in that truck wanted to get into the side of the road where the Mustang was in the worst possible way.

As the speeding sports car raced past the now stopped pickup truck, Reaper recognized the other vehicle. It was Warrick! And by the look of things, he was getting something big out from the behind the driver's seat.

Slowing down wouldn't help the situation, no matter what kind of surprise Warrick had in mind, so Deveraux kept the gas pedal pushed to the floorboards. Warrick flew out of the driver's side door, pulling a long object along with him.

The Hummer ignored the pickup as Warrick laid across its hood. He snuggled in to the shoulder stock of the big rifle. Settling the glowing red crosshairs of the Horus scope on the back of the Hummer as it came up behind the Mustang, he squeezed the trigger of the massive rifle.

The Serbu BFG 50 automatic made a thundering roar, and a nearly four-inch-long piece of hot brass was ejected from the right side of the weapon and bounced off the windshield of the truck. Out of the muzzle of the rifle came a slug over two-inches long, ripping through the air and leaving a bright red trace behind it. The red trace streaked up to the speeding Hummer and merged with the back end of it. The composition inside of the M20 armor piercing incendiary-tracer projectile splashed across the inside of the Hummer, spreading acrid smoke inside the vehicle.

For the driver of the Hummer, that was enough. The wheels of the heavy vehicle smoked again, and the driver slowed and pulled the Hummer off the road. The lights of the beaten Hummer faded as they bounced across the open grassland at the side of the highway. Warrick didn't need the other nine rounds of M20 API-T ammunition remaining in the magazine of his new rifle.

———

With the last of the Hummers gone and Devlin long out of sight, Deveraux pulled the Mustang over to the side of the highway. The only thing that had turned out well so far was the fact that they were both alive, and that there was practically no traffic on the highway. At least innocent bystanders hadn't been caught in the crossfire.

Sliding down into the backseat, still holding the smoking hot Shrike away from contact with anything, Reaper took a deep breath and blew it out. Turning in her seat, Deveraux looked back at Reaper.

"I don't think we're going to be getting the damage deposit back on this car," she said. "Bullets probably aren't covered as road hazards."

With a wide smile, Reaper looked at the woman who had just driven the Mustang through some of the worst traffic problems he had ever seen.

"Now I know why I haven't been busy on the dating scene," he said, grinning. "This modern nightlife is too rough for me." Then his expression turned serious. "You'd better start backing up to where we left Warrick. We have to get back to that Hummer and check it out before the cops show up. Thinking about that, I want us to be long gone before they get here, and the clock's ticking. I'm sure somebody's called this in by now."

"We can just cut across the median strip and head back to the Hummer first," Deveraux said. "You can call Warrick on the cell phone and have him meet us there, can't you?"

"I would if I could still think that fast," Reaper admitted after a moment. "Must be the wind scrambled my brains."

As Reaper was juggling the hot machine gun while trying to pull out his cell phone, Deveraux put the Mustang back into gear and drove up to an emergency crossover she could see just a few hundred feet ahead. Turning around on that gravel roadbed would be a lot better than risking getting the low-slung sports car hung up in a soft spot on the grassy median. Warrick's truck may have been able to bust through that stuff, but the Mustang was built for speed and power, not terrain.

Deveraux drove the Mustang back along the southbound lanes at a much more sedate pace than they had used while heading north. Getting in contact with Warrick over his cell phone, Reaper told him what the immediate plan of action was, and thanked him for his timely and precise intervention.

It seemed almost amazing to look at things now, but the Mustang had traveled not much over a mile from where the first Hummer had been taken out. Stopping to check out the flipped vehicle, Reaper noticed the stench of gasoline in the air.

"Stay back and keep the car ready," he told Deveraux. "If this thing pops, there's no use in both of us getting burned."

It only took a quick look after pulling open the door for Reaper to recognize that there were three dead bodies in the Hummer. It was obvious what had killed the driver: the huge gaping wound in what was left of his head was a graphic example of the efficiency of the .45-caliber hollowpoint. The two passengers had been smashed about by the rolling of the Hummer. Arms were bent unnaturally in places where there were no joints, and the heads of living people couldn't be tilted at these angles.

Reaper made a quick but thorough search of the bodies and the interior of the vehicle. Everything he took, which was disappointingly little, went into his coat pockets. Even the contents of the door pockets and glove compartment were stripped out. Taking a moment, Reaper looked closely at the two M4 carbines and the single MP5A3 submachine gun that were strewn about the Hummer. What he found didn't surprise him and he left the weapons where they were. A few rounds of the spent brass went into Reaper's pockets along with all of the other material he had found.

The lights of approaching emergency vehicles were starting to flash beyond the horizon as Reaper turned back to the Mustang. This time, he reclaimed the driver's seat and headed back in the direction that would eventually take them to Orlando. Warrick was already well on his way to the same destination.

"I don't know why you don't like the dating scene," Deveraux said as they passed a number of police cars screaming along in the opposite direction. "You sure know how to show a lady an interesting time, that's for sure."

Reaper's laughter was lost in the wind streaming past the open convertible.

Chapter Twenty-two

"So what do we have here?" Deckert asked as he set a pot of coffee and cups on the kitchen table, and joined the rest of the team who were already sitting there the next morning.

"Not a whole helluva lot," Caronti answered as he tossed a pack of cigarettes back onto the table.

"Mostly just pocket litter, and not much of that," Reaper admitted. "Whoever was running that crew, they made sure there was nothing in the way of identification on anyone. All they had on them were cigarettes, matches, some cash, coins, and Florida driver's licenses with bogus addresses. They match up with the DMV database, so they cost a buck or two to put together as phony IDs. Even the weapons had their serial numbers cut out. Not drilled or ground out—the metal was milled away. Not even the FBI can raise a serial number when the metal is missing entirely."

"Professional job, too," Warrick said as he picked up one of the pieces of fired brass on the table. Turning it over, he looked at the headstamp on the bottom of the case, the letters and numbers stamped around the primer. He read the information out loud.

"WCC 02, that's the Winchester cartridge company, 2002. This is pretty fresh military-issue ammo. Nothing special about it at all, you can get this stuff on the open market all over the place."

"And you lost this Devlin character and his lady?" Deckert asked as he leaned back in his chair.

"He was gone before the first bullets started to fly," Deveraux said. "There's not much question that he set up that ambush specifically for us."

"Probably made us from the start," Reaper commented with disgust as he sipped at his coffee. "He drew me right into that trap like he was reeling in a fish. We didn't get a damned thing."

"Oh, I wouldn't say that at all," Deveraux said. "Losing him was bad. I wanted him in custody more than anyone else here, but those pictures I took of him and his date last night told us quite a bit."

"What's that?" Mackenzie asked.

"Her identity," Deveraux said simply. "I ran her pictures through the MI-5 and Interpol data bases and came up with an identification. She turned out to be someone very significant to Devlin's operation.

"Her given name is Christina Voorhees," Deveraux read from the computer printout she held. "Of course, that doesn't tell us anything about whatever alias or identity papers she may be using now. The record they had on her at MI-5 proved more than interesting. A deep background check shows she was born in Rhodesia and spent her youth there. Then she obtained her South African citizenship not long after Rhodesia became Zimbabwe.

"According to her dossier, she positively hates the United States and blames it for what happened to Rhodesia. When the government turned over and it became Zimbabwe, Robert Mugabe became the first president, then just another dictator. He squeezed the white farmers from their land holdings, either seizing them outright to give to his supporters or ignoring the farmers' pleas when squatters took over and began murdering them. That's how her family lost the farm they'd had for five generations. Her mother, father, and two older siblings were hacked to death by machete-wielding squatters.

"The politicians and public here in the United States were quick to condemn the whites in Africa back when Rhodesia was still a country, no matter how long they had lived there. Atrocities and criminal actions against whites were ignored; they certainly didn't get any sympathy in the world press. When Rhodesia became Zimbabwe and Mugabe first went into office, the United States government was quick to point out how the country could now move ahead in the world. The politicians here quickly forgot their part in putting that bloodthirsty dictator into power. Her family's farm was just one of hundreds of white-owned properties seized by Mugabe's thugs. She was studying in South Africa when all of this happened and wasn't allowed to re-enter Zimbabwe even to claim her family's bodies.

"This woman is tough. She was pushing herself to become a doctor of medicine, concentrating in research, before all this happened in her life. After her family was killed, she was approached to work with a black-ops unit buried in the South African Defense Force. Their 'Project Coast' developed biological weapons and assassination tools. They had some very nasty materials to work with, like Ebola, the Marburg virus, Rift Valley fever, and anthrax. Voorhees proved a brilliant researcher and an asset to the program. But the change in the South African government drove her from that country. Now there isn't much question that she's hooked up with Devlin and his project. That is a very dangerous combination."

"Dangerous combination?" Caronti exclaimed. "This babe hooking up with this Devlin character sounds like the worst thing that could happen."

"Just about," Deveraux agreed, "and we know that they have had a sample of the Soviet anthrax 836 strain inside the United States for over two months now. That gives Devlin the ability and the material to make a devastating biological weapon. All he needs is the means to grow it, and the means to deliver it."

"So just how can this stuff be delivered as a weapon?" Warrick asked.

"Depends on how he makes it," Mackenzie said. "It's normally grown in bulk as a liquid. Then it's concentrated into a slurry. That's not even very hard. It's the processing afterward that's very hard. The best weaponized form of an agent like this is as a dry powder. Making it into an effective powder is also the hardest thing to do, but it sounds like this Voorhees woman is capable of that."

"More than capable," Deveraux agreed. "Factions in South Africa actually used biological agents in the field in Rhodesia during the fighting there. There's no reason to think that Voorhees didn't learn everything that the South Africans could do, and then added her own research to that."

"So we're back to trying to locate the weapons factory," Reaper said. "That still sounds like our best bet."

"Yeah, but where do we look?" Caronti said. "That pub turned out to be a waste of our time."

"Right," Reaper agreed, "*that* pub was the wrong one. That doesn't mean the idea is wrong; we just haven't found the right place yet."

"You went through a lot of those small breweries in the D.C. databases didn't you?" Deckert asked as he played with one of the cigarette packs.

"Yes, microbreweries and places that both brew and serve on the same premises—brew pubs," Deveraux responded. "We found more than two hundred that had been started or changed ownership within the last year, sixty-four in Florida alone."

"Any of them have this name?" Deckert asked as he tossed a book of matches across the table. He had pulled the matches from inside the cellophane wrapper of the cigarette pack.

"The Freedom Pub and Brewery," Deveraux read from the cover of the matches. "I'm not sure, but it does sound familiar. I'll check it out."

As Deveraux got up and headed back to where she had left her laptop computer, the rest of the team sat at the table, drinking their coffee and poking at the materials that lay in front of them. It was only a few minutes before Deveraux came back into the room. She looked a little flushed with excitement as she held up the matchbook.

"They're on the list!" Deveraux exclaimed. "The Freedom Pub and Brewery opened to the public some six months ago—and it's near Tampa, not much more than an hour's drive from here. I have their address and listed hours from the BATFE data base. The only reason we didn't go anywhere with that place originally is that a Miami-based corporation owns it. But all of the financing came out of a bank in the Cayman Islands."

"Isn't that where a bunch of the old drug lords used to launder their money?" Warrick said.

"More than just drug lords," Deveraux agreed. "A number of terrorist organizations have run their financing through those banks to purchase weapons. It wouldn't be a big step to use an account there to set up a dummy corporation here in the States, one you could use to buy a pub."

"And it's obvious that Devlin has been planning his operation for a long time," Reaper said. "So having a pub that's been open for a while would fit. And it would give him time and a place to set up his weapons factory. I would say this place is definitely a hit."

"I agree," Deveraux said, "but we'll have to move fast to check the place out. Since that one Hummer got away from us last night, Devlin has to know that we got away. He'll pack up and move his operation as quickly as he can. That's always been his way."

"Then we move on this Freedom place now," Reaper said. "Mackenzie, you, Caronti, and Warrick are going to have to go in on point for this one. Devlin made Deveraux last night at the restaurant and he got a good look at me as well. Since this place is an open pub, you'll just go in as customers and keep an eye on the place. Deckert, you coordinate surveillance from the van. We'll decide our next move after we've scoped the place out."

———

The Freedom Pub and Brewery was on the east side of Tampa, near the I-75 and I-4 interchange. The convenient yet quiet location had given the place an excellent customer flow, which had contributed greatly to its commercial success and growing popularity. At the same time, that location meant that the pub also had easy access to a number of escape routes.

To make sure that they would be able to cover the place completely, Reaper had everyone on his team involved in the stakeout of the pub. Depending on what the others spotted inside the place, he didn't intend for either himself or Deveraux to actually go inside the building. He also wasn't planning on a repeat of the action from the night before. Feeling undergunned when facing armored vehicles was not an experience Reaper cared to have ever again. Every vehicle now had a weapon in it that carried an M203A1 40mm grenade launcher. And loaded in the chamber of each launcher was an M433 high-explosive dual-purpose round.

Lying on the backseat of the Mustang was the Shrike, still mounted on the M4 receiver. Under the barrel of the machine gun was the same 40mm launcher that had proved its worth the night before. Another full two-hundred-round belt box was clipped underneath the receiver of the weapon, the belt already fed into the feed tray of the Shrike. All Reaper had to do was look up at the taped-over bullet hole in the windshield of the Mustang to realize just how close they had come to being put out of operation, permanently, the night before. He would not allow such a mistake to be made again.

———

Inside the pub, someone else was reflecting on mistakes, both recent ones and life-long errors. Shaughnessy had started out fighting for his ideal of a free Ireland. Along the way, those lofty goals had become corrupted until he was fighting just because that was the only thing he knew. Following Devlin had finally come about because he thought that he had found a man who still had a vision that Shaughnessy himself could follow, since he couldn't see his own anymore. Devlin's view of the world was little more than using it as a means to make himself, and the men who followed him, rich.

Wealth just didn't hold the same appeal for Shaughnessy as it once had. Anyway, money would only be good as a means of escape if Devlin's big operation succeeded. It probably wouldn't be able to buy much in the way of comfort after that, just the ability to run.

The only thing that did hold appeal for Shaughnessy was the major part he'd had to play in the big plan. That was for him to set up, and get running, the pub that would provide the site for the production of a horrible weapon.

Shaughnessy had found out that he liked dealing with the public. He enjoyed pulling the taps and serving a noisy, boisterous crowd. The smell and sound of the place had evoked memories of his boyhood back in Ireland. It was easy for him to see how his father had enjoyed such a life in the old country. Maybe it was fitting that fighting against the troubles that had taken that life, and his father, away from him was now the very thing that was pushing him toward it.

———

"Leviathan," Reaper called out over the radio, "this is Death, do you have anything to report?"

Caronti had stepped out of the front door of the Freedom Pub, making a show of stretching a bit and looking around as if waiting for someone. The pub was in the parking lot of a long strip mall, sitting out on one end, separated from the other buildings by several dozen yards of blacktop. On the far side and back of the pub was a grove of low trees and scrub. The other stores in the strip mall had proven helpful to Reaper and his team. Their vehicles had blended in with the rest of the parking-lot traffic coming and going at random times during the day.

"Leviathan here," Caronti said quietly, as if he were thinking out loud. The tiny microphone of the headset picked up his voice clearly enough. The system made it look as if he was just wearing a hands-free cellular phone, and an observer would have had to look closely to have seen even that. "This is a nice place, and the beer's pretty good, too. Other than that, there isn't much else to say. There's no sign of anyone matching the descriptions you gave us of Devlin or Voorhees. It doesn't look like there's anything going on out of the ordinary, either. It's getting late and the customers are thinning out a bit."

"Roger that," Reaper said. "Will advise. Death out."

Turing his radio mike off, Reaper leaned back in his seat. In the Mustang with him was Deveraux. She and the rest of the team had heard the conversation over their own radios.

"So, what do you want to try?" she said as she looked over at Reaper. "Everyone except Deckert and the two of us has been in the place, and they haven't seen anyone or anything suspicious."

"We can't just keep spending time here," Reaper said. "While we're looking at this place, Devlin could be halfway across the country. I think the two of us need to do an eyes-on examination of this place and either hit it or write it off. If Devlin and Voorhees are in there, they're probably in disguise. If we walk in, we could instigate a reaction of some kind, at least. If they aren't in there and it's a dry hole, then at least we can move on to something else."

"I agree," Deveraux said after considering Reaper's words for a moment, "but what if they *are* in there and they spot us first?"

"By what Caronti said, the possibility of that sounds pretty slim, though that still leaves a chance. Our best bet is to go in with everyone and try and stack the deck in our favor. Warrick and Mackenzie can filter in first and take up a position on one side of the room. We can go in a few minutes later and head for the opposite side of the room. Caronti is already at the bar, so that dispersion should give us a crossfire in just about any direction.

"Deckert can stay in the van where he's already parked and maintain outside watch. That spot lets him see both doors of the building without standing out too much. If Devlin sees us and bolts, we'll know. If he decides to make a stand and fight, all the backup we have will already be in there with us. Right now, there are few customers and we'll be in a constrained area.

Might give us the best chance we have of shutting this thing down right now, one way or the other."

"If he fights, though, he'll probably try to take hostages," Deveraux said thoughtfully. "Hiding behind the innocent is nothing for him."

"Then we'll just have to not give him the time to do that," Reaper said bluntly. "We have the firepower at hand to dominate the situation as Caronti described it. All of us have our sidearms and Caronti has my Super-Shorty under his jacket. Believe me, that little twelve-gauge has a serious psychological effect on anyone who has to look down the wrong end of it. And Deckert is available to call in support from the local PDs or Mac-Dill, if the shit really hits the fan."

There weren't any worthwhile arguments Deveraux could think of to throw at Reaper's logic—at least, not any that would have any real effect on the situation they were facing. Reaper knew his own abilities and those of his men better than anyone; his plan sounded like a good one.

"Anything will beat having to sit out here in the car most of the evening," Deveraux said. "I think I could use a pint about now."

"First round's on me," Reaper laughed. Getting back on the communications net, he informed the others of his plan. Mackenzie and Warrick said that they would go in together and Deckert acknowledged that he would keep watch.

"I'll be just about in the center of the long side of the bar," Caronti said, speaking softly. "There're two empty tables to the left of the door as you come in. And there's a bunch of empty booths along the right-hand wall. They face the long side of the bar."

Once Caronti had walked back into the pub, Warrick and Mackenzie got out of their truck and headed for the building. They had each been there once earlier in the day and would simply look like two friends who had come back for a drink. At least that was how they were going to play it.

"In position," came over the radio a few minutes later. "Second table, left side of the door."

"And now, da movie," Reaper said, quoting a line from a bad TV movie host. Deveraux just looked at him with a puzzled expression on her face before she got out of the car. The walk to the pub was a short one, but it felt like the one of the longest marches she had ever been on. This could be nothing, or it could be the end of a multi-year chase for the man who was responsible for her husband's death. The woman remained quiet as they walked up to the pub and Reaper pulled the door open.

Directly in front of the pair was a long row of ten booths running along the wall and looking like they extended to near the back of the building. To the left of the door were the two tables Caronti had described, Warrick and Mackenzie sitting nearly in the opposite corner. The waitstaff looked to consist of one woman in her mid-twenties and a slightly older male bartender. Outside of those two and Reaper's people there were only three customers in the bar. Moving to a booth and sitting down, Reaper and Deveraux could look over each other's shoulders at the rest of the room. If the smell of bleach and yeast were any indication, the back room was where the brewery was. The lights were out back there and the entire area was covered in darkness.

Sitting quietly, Reaper and Deveraux looked over a menu of the brews the place had on hand. The waitress came over to them and they both ordered what looked like straightforward ale. Nothing seemed amiss and there was no sign of anything out of the ordinary. It was just a little after six in the evening, and Reaper was willing to wait and simply observe awhile.

Besides, he thought after the waitress brought two frosty mugs and set them down on the table, *the ale is pretty good.*

———

Inside the office just to the side of the kitchen door, Shaughnessy looked though the one-way glass that made up the back of one of the wall decorations. He recognized the man and the woman sitting in Booth Four as being the pair from the restaurant. Devlin had gone to some pains to describe the people exactly, especially the woman. They weren't hard to notice, though they did make an effort to appear to be a couple out having a drink. Their eyes were the only thing that gave them away at all, as they looked around a lot more intently than anyone visiting a new bar usually did. Just as the large biker-style man in the denim jacket and dark glasses sitting at the bar did, and the two men at Table One. He reached under the desk and pressed a button that lit up a signal at the bar. In a few minutes, Henry the bartender came into the office, and Shaughnessy gave him some instructions that startled the man.

———

Reaper had seen just about enough of what was going on inside the pub as he finished his drink. Before he could say a word, the bartender called out, "Sorry folks, but we're closing early tonight. Last call, please."

There was a little grumbling from a man who looked like a regular sitting at the bar near Caronti. But no one ordered another drink. Deciding that there were too many other people in the place, and the setup just didn't feel right, Reaper got up from the booth.

"Okay, dear," he said to Deveraux, "time to call it a night. I think we should just head back out to the car, don't you?"

Every member of the team caught that Reaper was calling off any action as they heard his comments over the radio headsets.

Deveraux just smiled and said, "Yes, dear," as she got up from the booth.

After paying the bill, Reaper led the way to the door, where the waitress was standing.

"Sorry for the early night folks," the woman said. "Please come again."

"Thanks, we intend to," Reaper said as he and Deveraux left the pub.

"Okay, look sharp, everyone," Reaper announced over the net as he and Deveraux returned to the Mustang. "This is something out of the ordinary, from the way the staff is acting. There's someone in there we didn't see who's calling the shots. That bartender didn't look happy after he came back out from the kitchen. Hold your positions and we'll just wait them out for a while."

After receiving acknowledgements from everyone on the net, Reaper settled in to watch the pub again. There was no conversation in the vehicles or over the net as everyone just watched the situation unfold. It was after nine o'clock when the waitress and the bartender left. Neither person looked very happy about something, and they spoke to each other for a moment before heading to their own cars. There were still some lights on in the place—the glow could be seen through the glass-fronted door. Finally, the last light went out.

"Head's up, there's movement at the back door," Deckert said over the net.

"I see him," Reaper replied as he watched a single man walk to a car at the side of the parking area. As the man reached the car, he stopped and looked back at the building. Before anyone could react, he did something so unexpected that the team just stared in shock for an instant.

The man bent forward, spread his legs, and leaned on the hood of his car in the classic frisk position. He reached back under his sports coat and pulled something from behind his back. As he tossed what everyone could now see was a gun to the grass behind his car, the man went back to leaning on the hood.

"Boss?" Warrick started to say over the net. "Just what in the hell is . . . ?"

"I've got him," Reaper said, firing up the Mustang.

Slowly driving over to where the man leaned against the hood of the car, Reaper stopped the Mustang and shut the engine off. The man leaning on the car hood didn't move and didn't say a word.

As Reaper got out of the car and pulled his P220 from his belt holster, the man lifted his head and spoke, "Took you long enough to decide whether to come over or not," he said. "My name is William Shaughnessy, and I would like to surrender. I have some information to trade for a deal."

Chapter Twenty-three

William Shaughnessy quickly proved to be a gold mine of information about Devlin and his operation. Outside of Deveraux, none of Reaper's team were trained intelligence specialists with knowledge of how to conduct deep interrogations of prisoners. So, while Deveraux was conducting a field interview with Shaughnessy, Reaper got in contact with Admiral Straker back in Washington. If the admiral was upset about being awakened late at night, he didn't show any sign of it as he listened intently to what Reaper had to say. As soon as Reaper had hung up, it was Straker's turn to get on the phone and interrupt the sleep of a lot of other people.

Within an hour of Reaper's call, a crew from the intelligence desk at SOCOM was on their way to the Freedom Pub to take charge of the prisoner and continue his interrogation. A specialized hazardous materials team was also coming to seal off the pub and deal with what Reaper and his people found there. The Four Horsemen wouldn't normally be working with outside people, but this situation was a special one, even for them. Contact was kept to a minimum, but the intelligence kept flowing.

Everyone concerned knew that Shaughnessy's change of heart had been a phenomenal stroke of luck. Such things happened, but they could never be expected. There was no way anyone was going to waste the opportunity to possibly capture Devlin before he could put his final plans into effect.

From the information Shaughnessy had given Deveraux, the main production facility for Devlin's anthrax culture was hidden in the cold room of the pub. In spite of the man's assurance that there was no one else in the building, Reaper and his people were taking no chances.

Having brought in the M4A1 carbines they had in their vehicles, the team carefully swept the entire pub. As one person entered a room, he was covered by two of his partners. The cold room at the back of the pub was the final location they had to clear. While being covered by Warrick, Caronti went up to the large refrigerator door, Reaper close in behind him. There was no way they could be sure that the room beyond was empty. There could be nothing, or Devlin and his people could be on the other side. So far, everything Shaughnessy had told them had proved out, but that didn't mean enough to Reaper or his men. They had lived this long by minimizing risk and always being as careful as they could.

Having taken up a spare M4A1 rather than his Shrike light machine gun, Reaper shouldered his weapon. The signal squeeze on his shoulder told him that Mackenzie was ready to come in behind him as they went through the door. Passing the squeeze signal on to Caronti, Reaper braced himself for the entry.

Hauling back on the handle, Caronti pulled the big door open as fast as he could, backing up to get out of the entry team's way. Reaper darted into the room, moving to the left, keeping a foot away from the wall and sweeping his side of the room with the muzzle of his weapon. At almost the same instant, Mackenzie was doing the same thing on the other side of the room.

"Clear!" Reaper shouted.

"Clear!" came the same shout from Mackenzie.

The only things to come under the muzzles of the two men's weapons were the kegs and boxes of beer bottles you would expect to find in such a room. There was no movement, no sign of others anywhere to be seen. In spite of their long training and experience, both Reaper and Mackenzie could feel their hearts beating faster as the adrenalin that had poured into their systems prepared them to fight for their lives if necessary. That training kept them moving, searching the room, and looking behind any cover. Now it was time to let Shaughnessy show them the hidden entrance inside the cold room.

With Shaughnessy's hands secured in front of him with plastic riot cuffs, Deveraux brought him into the room. She remained behind the man, her SIG P239 held in tight against her right hip to prevent it from being grabbed, the muzzle of the pistol centered on the prisoner's back. Warrick and Caronti remained outside the cold room to keep watch on the rest of the building.

"The door is behind that rack of kegs there," Shaughnessy said as he pointed to the far wall of the cold room.

"There's an electronic interlock on the door, we have to close the outer door before the inner wall unlocks. When the door closes, the lights have to go out before you can turn them back on again. It's another safety interlock."

"Go ahead," Reaper said, "but no sudden moves."

As both Reaper and Mackenzie clicked on the M3 flashlights mounted on their M4A1s, Shaughnessy pulled the big refrigerator door shut and the room was plunged into darkness. The two brilliant white beams of the M3 lights kept tracking Shaughnessy as he went over to the light switch and the room was once more illuminated from the ceiling fixtures. Going over to the keg rack, Shaughnessy rolled it back out of the way and popped open the steel wall panel. Then he pulled open the hidden door built into the wall.

The alcove beyond was empty except for the Tychem suits hanging from the walls. One glance at the protective equipment and the decontamination showers inside the closetlike room was enough to convince Reaper that they had found what they had been searching for.

"They didn't even bother turning out the lights," Shaughnessy muttered as he was pulled aside by Deveraux.

The white room on the far side of the tiny room was glowing with light. The laboratory equipment, stainless steel fixtures, and strange machinery were enough to convince Reaper that this wasn't another pot farm.

"They used the bleach to decontaminate the suits every time someone exited the room," Shaughnessy said. "That's why the place stinks of it so much. The same bleach solution is used to sanitize the brewery equipment, so the smell never stood out that much. I always hated it, though."

The likes and dislikes of the terrorist were of no concern to Reaper. But he filed away the bit of information even as he made a decision regarding what they had just found. There were no people inside of the room and it was too well lit and open, in spite of the machinery in it, for anyone to hide in it. And by the looks of things, Reaper did not want to send any of his people in there.

"Okay," he said, "this is more than we can handle right now. We're securing the area and leaving this to the experts."

There was no argument from the rest of his crew.

———

While they waited for the intelligence people to take Shaughnessy away, Deveraux had continued her interrogation of the man. He had no idea what Devlin's primary target was. His end of the mission had been to keep the pub operating and move the materials around as necessary. Devlin hadn't trusted anyone with the whole plan, only the parts of it that they each were directly involved in. But what Shaughnessy could tell Deveraux was the location of the processing facility where he had left Devlin and the rest of his people that morning. That was the information that Reaper and the team had to consider after they turned both Shaughnessy and the pub over to the people from MacDill and SOCOM. They had left the pub and were standing around the open doors of Deckert's van.

"They've have a twelve-hour head start on us," Reaper said. "Straker has left it up to us to decide what we do next. We can go and take down this processing plant and check out Shaughnessy's story, or we can turn it over to Homeland Security and let them bring in the feds."

"Everything Shaughnessy has said so far has proven true," Deveraux said. "He had decided to surrender to us earlier this evening, even paid off his people tonight and told them the pub would be closing. I think he's being honest in his decision to cooperate."

"It sure would be a shame not to carry this mission all the way to the end," Mackenzie said.

"We've always seen it through in the past," Warrick agreed.

"Sounds like we're all in agreement," Reaper said, "we continue on and take down Devlin and the rest of his crew, starting with this processing plant."

There was no disagreement from anyone. Reaper went over to speak to the people from SOCOM about his intentions. He wanted to get his people out of the area before the crowds really started to gather.

"Do you want to wait for our quick-reaction force to come in from MacDill?" asked Major Krolin, the officer in charge of the Hazmat team.

"No," Reaper said, "we need to move fast and keep this as quiet as we can. There's no question now that we have a major terrorist with a WMD in the area. My team and I can evaluate the situation quietly and call you in if we have to."

"My orders are to follow your directions, sir," Kronin said. "My people will be on call as you need us."

"Hopefully, all you'll have to do is secure the area," Reaper said.

The processing plant was inside of Building 512 on Beakman, an industrial area just north of the I-4 and US 301 cloverleaves. The address was less than three miles from the Freedom Pub, close enough for convenience while still far enough away to help insulate the two locations from each other. Once on Beakman, Reaper had no trouble locating the correct building. The industrial park had an index map at the entrance the road, which circled around the area. Shaughnessy had told them Devlin had named the front company for the place "Mars Research Inc," and it was listed in plain sight on the map. The relatively small, isolated building looked simple, innocuous, and altogether dangerous to Reaper's trained eye.

The place was at the back end of the industrial complex, with enough open area around it to make a surreptitious approach difficult. The swampy area behind the building would make coming up to it from that direction very difficult for laden men, and all of Reaper's people were carrying a very full load.

In the back of Deckert's van were footlockers and equipment bags filled with all of their equipment from the Orlando house. For this operation, they were not going in dressed in civilian clothes. Instead, Reaper and his team had geared up, changing to 5.11 tactical pants and shirts along with black SWAT boots. Over their Armored Warrior tactical rigs, everyone had on a BlackHawk Omega Elite tactical vest with a full load of a dozen magazines of ammunition. SIG P226 pistols were in the BlackHawk Serpa holsters at each person's right thigh, and their M4A1 carbines had the CQBR short barrel assemblies mounted in place with their M3 Surefire lights, laser designators, and Gemtech HALO sound supressors on the muzzles. Each weapon was loaded with EBR frangible 5.56mm ammunition, chambered and ready to go.

Enough time had passed to give Devlin every opportunity to leave his processing plant and move on to

another location. But that wasn't the safe way to plan.
Reaper and his team would take down the building as
if the terrorists were in place and ready for them. The
only thing they would try to avoid was a hot breach.

The materials they found in the hidden room of the
pub had confirmed that Devlin had a very dangerous
weapon. Just how much of the biological agent he had,
and what he had packed the brew in, Shaughnessy hadn't
known. What he had told Deveraux was that weekly
trips had been made to the Beakman address to deliver
the output of the hidden laboratory. Reaper wanted to
avoid a firefight if possible, and the best way to do that if
anyone was in the building was to hit them with sudden,
overwhelming firepower. That was the rule in the SEAL
Teams and it would work now. Reaper was going to depend on the frangible ammunition, along with the skills
of each of his people, to keep any biological device inside the place intact and relatively safe.

Parking his van where he could view the entire front
of the building, Deckert would maintain communications and secure that means of escape. He had the Shrike
light machine gun at hand, a two-hundred-round belt
box locked in place and loaded, and a M433 HEDP grenade loaded in the M203A1 underneath the barrel. The
wheelchair might prevent him from being able to move
quickly over the ground, but there was nothing wrong
with his shooting ability. He would seal off the front of
the building for as long as Reaper needed him to.

Instead of providing precision cover fire, Warrick
was going to penetrate the building along with the rest
of the team. Deveraux was going to perform rear-guard
action at the door, covering the rest of the men's backs
as they went into the structure. No lights were seen

shining from anywhere in the structure. Shaughnessy had said there was a single man, Devlin's weapons expert, who stayed at the site around the clock, but there was no sign of anyone now. The big roll-up garage door at the back of the place could explain why no vehicles were parked outside. The only way Reaper and his team could confirm that the building had been abandoned was to enter it and see for themselves.

Long practice was what allowed the team to set up for the takedown as quickly as they had. As a fellow professional, Deveraux had blended in with the group well enough to pull her own weight. Now was the time for coordinated action as everyone lined up in what was called a "train." The squeeze signal was passed along from the back of the train to the front, from Deveraux to Warrick, Mackenzie, Reaper, and finally Caronti, acting as the breacher. Caronti drew his ten-pound sledgehammer from his breacher's pack. At Reaper's signal, he swung it hard, directly onto the door lock.

No booby trap detonated as the door swung open violently. There was just the rapid movement of the train going through the door as Caronti stepped out of the way. He would now back up Deveraux, becoming the rear guard for the operation. Dropping his sledgehammer and pulling up his M4A1 dangling from his Chalker sling, Caronti took up a position on the outside of the building, beside the now-open door.

Voice communications were going to be difficult. Reaper had decided against everyone wearing the Tyvek protective suits they had available. The bulky plastic-like material could get hung up in the tight confines of a rapidly moving takedown. And they could get in the way during a firefight. But everyone was wearing a

Safety Tech M95 respirator mask to protect them from inhaling the deadly anthrax they suspected was in the building.

Looking through the large shatterproof plastic lenses of her M95 mask, Deveraux watched Caronti smash open the door and Reaper dart into the building. Right behind him was Mackenzie, followed by Warrick and then herself. She didn't have time to note the greasy feel of the Halo-butyl-rubber mask on her face, the chemically clean smell of the air coming through the M95 filtration cartridge, or the sound of everyone's breathing through the mask, which resembled a bad Darth Vader impression. There wasn't time to think, only to perform her part of the takedown.

Once inside the door, Deveraux could hear Reaper and the others calling out, "Clear," as they moved through the building. On the left side of the doorway, she stood with her back near the wall, facing into the room. The only real light was from the Surefire M3 flashlights attached by the GG & G offset mounts to the rails on the CQBR barrels. The men moved quickly through the structure, passing by racks of equipment and machine tools as they cleared the building.

All that Reaper found of interest in the front office was a steel wastebasket filled with the black ashes of burned papers. Only a few of the papers hadn't burned completely, and Reaper stuck what looked like the corner of a page into his pocket.

The rest of the furnishings in the room told the story that someone had been living there, but the tossed-about nature of the place said they had left in a hurry. There was no one in the building, nothing but machinery and materials. Picking up the wastebasket, Reaper turned and headed back to the rear area.

"Boss," Mackenzie said as Reaper came into the room, "we've got cabinets of protective gear here. And a steel door that smells of bleach."

It was a heavy steel fire door with a Medico lock cylinder on a Yale deadbolt. This thing was not going to open easily, and Reaper did not want to conduct an explosive breach. Setting down the wastebasket, he looked into the cabinets and saw the colored Tyvek suits they contained. When he broke the seal on his mask by sticking his finger under the edge of the rubber, Reaper could smell the stench of bleach in the air, proof enough to him that they had found Devlin's processing facility. Inside the roll-up garage door were tire tracks on the concrete floor, but no real clue as to what had made them.

There was something wrong with the place, but Reaper couldn't put his finger on it. They had only been inside the building for a couple of minutes, and the ex-SEAL couldn't shake the felling that he was missing something.

He walked past the racks of steel gas bottles along one wall, looking at what were familiar labels to him, green bottles of oxygen, orange tanks of argon, brown nitrous oxide tanks, and the short, squat acetylene tanks used in gas welding.

"Reaper," Warrick called from the center of the room, "here's something interesting."

The ex-Marine was standing next to a bench with a large object covered with a tarp. He was holding a couple of items Reaper couldn't make out.

"I have no idea what these plastic cylinders are," Warrick said as Reaper came over. He was holding a clear chunk of plastic, solid except for what looked like a quarter-inch hole down through the center of it. "But these things are composite rocket exhaust nozzles, that I'm sure of. And these steel cylinders could be rocket bodies, big ones."

Holding up the other object in his hand, Reaper could see that it looked like a double funnel shape cut into a black material.

"Okay," Reaper said. "What the hell is this under the tarp?"

"I don't know," Warrick answered, "I haven't looked yet."

Reaper flipped back the edge of the tarp. Sitting on the table was a huge box with a glass front. Underneath the glass were two wide holes with rubber sleeves in them. The inside of the box was dark, with only a small red glow near the bottom of it. All that could be seen were some bulky shapes inside of it and wires leading to some conduits that ran along the ceiling.

Turning his M4 toward the box, Reaper shined the light attached to it into the box. What he saw made his blood run cold.

There was a large container in the box, a squat metal cylinder surrounded by smaller glass jars filled with what looked like yellow sticks of wax in water. But at the back of the big metal cylinder was a paper-covered chunk Reaper had seen many times during his military career. It was an M5A1 block of C4 plastic explosive surrounded by steel bolts. There were multiple leads from a small electronic device leading into the block. Looking very closely, Reaper could see that the ruddy glow and movement came from a set of red numerals on the front of the electronic device. It was a countdown booby-trap timer—and it was close to reaching zero.

"Run!" Reaper bellowed. "Booby trap! Get the hell out of here now!"

The final gift left behind by Devlin was a charge of explosives attached to the last container of anthrax slurry. The jars were filled with the leftover white phosphorus and the bolts would add to the fragmentation of the explosion.

The delay timer had activated when the back door was opened. A 180-second delay gave whoever came in the door three minutes to enter the room and drop their guard before the blast destroyed all evidence of Devlin's activities. And the contamination from the anthrax would make sure that it was a long time before anyone would be able to examine the rubble closely.

All of Reaper's people were in the big room except for Caronti. As he headed for the door, Mackenzie grabbed up the wastebasket Reaper had set down. The act was almost instinctive, the urge to gather all possible intelligence before abandoning a place, even in the face of danger. Warrick just held on to the objects in his hands as he ran for the exit. As the last one through the door, Reaper grabbed what was left of the lock and pulled it shut behind him. Even the damaged door would be able to help hold the contamination inside the steel-framed brick structure. As he ran away from the doorway, everyone headed for the swamp only a few dozen feet away across the blacktop. As Reaper dove into the muck, the timer ran out behind him.

The blast thundered out, blasting the anthrax slurry all over the inside of the structure. The bolts attached to the explosive block were thrown around at the velocity of rifle bullets. Several of the bolts smashed into the steel gas bottles along the wall, puncturing them and causing the contents to jet out and add to the conflagration. A huge fireball from the ignited gases rushed through the room, consuming everything in front of it.

The tinted glass windows in the front office disintegrated and threw shards out across the parking area. In his van, Deckert was rocked by the blast wave but was almost miraculously left untouched by any of the flying glass. He was stunned but unhurt.

Under the swamp water, Reaper's team had been protected from the worst effects of the explosion, but had still been tossed about by the blast. Coughing and hacking from the water that had flooded their respirator masks, everyone stood up in the knee-deep water and heavy black muck. They were dirty, stinking, and completely soaked, but everyone was alive and unharmed.

As he pulled off his respirator, Warrick sputtered and spit mud. "God, I am starting to hate Florida. I don't care if they are protected. One fucking croc comes up right now and I'm going to blow it away."

Chapter Twenty-four

"We got bupkus," Caronti said as he came into the kitchen the next morning. Reaper and the rest of his team had spent a long night making sure that the Hazmat team from MacDill Air Force Base had the situation under control at the industrial site where the biological weapons factory had been blown up. The only thing that had really helped keep the incident under wraps was the fact that it was the week of the Fourth of July and most people were either recovering from the extended holiday weekend or had left on vacation.

The media had been told that the explosion was the result of an illegal fireworks factory that had been using hazardous chemicals and storing them improperly. The possibility of unexploded ordnance being on the site was enough to help explain why the military was there, and to keep the questions of the reporters to a minimum, since the investigation was ongoing. All local law enforcement knew was that the feds had listed the incident as being under their jurisdiction, due to possible stolen military materials being involved.

Having spent a long time dealing with the situation the night before, Reaper was in a foul mood.

"At least we're certain Devlin will never use that place again," he growled as he sat at the table with a cup of coffee. "Now, if we can just figure out where the son-ofabitch is going, that would be a big help."

"I've got a fair idea where the target is," Deveraux said as she came into the room closely followed by Mackenzie. "It wasn't until Mac here told me something that we figured it out. We use a different system in Britain."

"System?" Reaper said in a puzzled voice. "What system? And what do you mean you have an idea where the target is?"

"Our mailing system," Mackenzie said as he walked into the kitchen and poured himself a cup of coffee. "More exactly, our zip-code system."

"That fragment of paper you stuck in your pocket from the wastebasket was a piece of unburned computer printout. It wasn't too badly damaged after being dunked in that swamp. The rest of the material in the wastebasket didn't tell us anything," Deveraux said as she laid a document protector on the table. Between the plastic sheets was the bit of paper Reaper had saved from the night before, practically the only hard piece of uncontaminated intelligence they had collected before the blast at the facility tore the place apart.

"I thought we had figured that one out last night," Caronti said as he picked up the document protector.

"We did," Deveraux said, "only I hadn't known the significance of the five numbers that could still be read on it. The rest looked like the outer edge of what could have been a map. It wasn't until Mackenzie looked at it that we could make any sense at all of what the code was, it's not the kind I'm used to using."

"Four numbers really," Mackenzie said as he sat down at the table. "We had to extrapolate the first digit. Only part of it could be read."

"So just what in the hell is it?" Reaper said in an exasperated tone.

"32920," Mackenzie stated simply. "The zip code for Cape Canaveral."

"Specifically," Deveraux joined in, "it's the printout of a detailed weather report taken from a Web site that covers that area of Florida. We found the site a few minutes ago. The location of the zip code corresponds to where it's found on our printout page."

"Cape Canaveral?" Reaper wondered as he quickly considered the possibilities. "Damn, he's trying for the space shuttle! That's got to be it. They're scheduled to launch, what, next Wednesday?"

"My thoughts exactly," Mackenzie agreed. "But I don't think he's trying for the space shuttle itself."

"No," Reaper agreed, "that wouldn't be a very good target for a biological weapon."

"But the crowds watching a launch would sure as hell be," Caronti added. "The news said that they're expecting a quarter of a million people to be lining the shores to watch the launch. Most of them are probably there already, camping and waiting for the launch."

"And all of the news groups will already be on site to film the shuttle launch," Deveraux said. "It would be one of the most publicized terrorist attacks ever, possibly even more so than when the towers came down on 9-11. People wouldn't start dying right away, it would take several days for the anthrax to really take hold.

But when that happened, the whole world would find out, and the films would already have been taken of the attack. That would be something that would appeal to Devlin, and it would be an attack that he could sell to the highest bidder."

"There are more than a few groups in the world that would pay big bucks to have the United States attacked during such a huge media event," Caronti said.

"Very true," Deveraux agreed, "but there are only a few terrorist organizations that could afford the kind of money that Devlin would charge for such an event. His attack would make history."

"One outfit immediately comes to mind," Reaper said. "Al-Qaeda. They've got the money to pay for such a thing. But how could Devlin believe he could possibly get away with such an attack? He has to know that the U.S. would hunt him to the ends of the earth."

"You can be certain he has an escape route planned out," Deveraux said. "Most likely several of them. Getting away is practically his trademark. As far as tracking him down would go, he has to have that covered as well. It's not like finding one man is all that easy. Bin Laden has pretty well proved that."

"But how can he expect to attack such a huge target?" Mackenzie wondered out loud. "An aircraft? Maybe a small crop duster? That wouldn't work, there's an Air Force base right there next to the launch facility. They enforce an aircraft exclusion zone that extends for forty miles."

"A rocket," Warrick said from the other side of the doorway. "A ballistic rocket attack, that's what he'd use. Probably more than one, and big, powerful ones at that."

The ex-Marine walked into the kitchen from the back room they had been using for an office. In his hand, he was holding the plastic cylinder that he had picked up during the raid the night before.

"I've been talking to my friends on the NFA list," Warrick said.

"The what?" Mackenzie asked.

"NFA list," Warrick explained, "it's a professional association of insiders in the worldwide arms industry. It's made up of designers, manufacturers, international arms dealers, experts in the military and civilian ordnance business, law enforcement, the military, even politicians. Everything from nuclear scientists to writers make up its ranks. It's kind of a secret group."

"And what, you're a member of this secret cabal?" Mackenzie said sarcastically. "They let you join?"

"More like an illuminati with guns than a cabal," Warrick laughed. "And yes, as a matter of fact I am a member. You can't ask them to let you in, you have to be invited. Personally, I think it's a hell of a resource, and this bit of intel here just about proves that." He set the plastic down on the table in front of everyone. "Real experts can make it look easy. I'm sure the folks in D.C. could have come up with what this is, but probably not as quickly. It took the 'listers all of about twenty minutes to identify this chunk of plastic and tell me what it can do. Especially when combined with some of the other materials I saw last night."

"So just what is it?" Caronti asked.

"Rocket fuel," Warrick said simply. "No kidding, there's a kind of rocket engine that uses plastic chunks with a hole in them like this one. The plastic cylinders act as the fuel and an oxidizer is added to it from a tank, probably one of the ones that were along that wall."

"I saw oxygen, acetylene, and nitrous-oxide tanks," Reaper said. "Which one would they use?"

"Probably the nitrous oxide," Warrick said as he sat down at the table. "At least that was the consensus of the members I contacted. Oxygen would work, but the nitrous would be better. From the size of the tubing I saw as well as the dimensions of the nozzle I found, the guys told me what the probable thrust of the rocket would be, and they made a pretty good guess at its maximum range."

"So what do your experts think we may be facing?" Reaper asked.

"Any number of rockets, from one to a dozen," Warrick said. "Each one could have a range of as much as twenty miles depending on its finished size, payload weight, and design."

"Jesus wept," Caronti said. "And they made these things at that factory we hit last night?"

"Probably," Warrick said. "They certainly had the materials and tools at hand to do the job."

"By the looks of that booby trap," Mackenzie said, "they had the skills as well."

"We have to get this information to Straker," Reaper said. "He may have to get the shuttle launch delayed."

"Based on what? A scrap of paper and the educated guesses of a bunch of anonymous experts?" Mackenzie said. "That's not much to base an order on. Not when it will delay the first shuttle launch in over two years. This is a hell of a lot more than just another shuttle launch. It's going to be the proof that America can return to space. If anything goes wrong, the shuttle fleet will probably be grounded permanently. That will kill the space station and put a real crimp in our surveillance satellites. Some of those birds haven't been replaced or maintained for years. We're already going to lose the Hubble Space Telescope. I've heard talk among my old Air Force buddies that one reason for this launch is to maintain one of the secret birds that's keeping an eye out for nuclear materials in the Middle East. Losing something like that could cost us a city down the line."

"If this launch is so important—" Warrick began.

"It is," Mackenzie said with certainty.

"—Then there's also going to be a hell of a lot of important people watching the event. They're going to be targets, too. How are we going to convince them not to come without telling them enough about the attack to start a panic about a possible anthrax attack?"

"You'd better hope it is enough to convince somebody," Reaper said. "We don't know where Devlin went or what he has with him. Right now, this is the best guess we have, and it feels like a good one."

Chapter Twenty-five

It was only a few days after they had arrived at the launch site in Cape Canaveral that Devlin had stopped appearing happy about the situation. In the center of the bay area behind the roll-up garage doors were the launching rails of the rockets on their fully adjustable stand. Everett Maypole, Devlin's man at the site, had been working hard to first construct and set up the launching rail system, and then to extend it to accept more rockets. The long, white-painted rockets looked exactly like their namesake, the Harpoon missile, as they lay along the rails, their lethal warheads pointing toward the roll-up doors.

For the last several days, all of the men had been living in the rather stark quarters that Maypole had set up in the offices at the front of the building. The rooms had little more than sleeping cots and a few steel chairs and folding tables. An electric hot plate, microwave, and small refrigerator in one of the rooms made up the kitchen. The only real amenity in the place was that one of the offices had a bathroom that offered a shower.

A combination television set and radio was the only source of news beyond the radios in the vehicles.

The launch platform for the rockets had been prepared with care. The plastic strip curtain that covered the inside of the roll-up doorway was rigged to drop away when the mechanical counter on the launcher came close to zero. A second backup timer was set to blow the curtain free of the doorway if it didn't drop. The rocket ignition system was hardwired into both mechanical and electronic timers. Multiple redundancy insured that the rockets would launch after Devlin and his men had driven south to safety.

The rails of the launcher had been very carefully aligned to give the most efficient flight path for the rockets. They would spread out and cover nearly half the total area of the north end of Merritt Island. The onshore breeze from the Atlantic to the east would help spread the streaming clouds of anthrax spores, carrying the lethal agent far inland and spreading it over dozens of square miles. The crowds lining the roads and beaches to watch the shuttle launch had been estimated on the news to number more than a quarter million.

It was all very good for Devlin's plan. It was only the almost last-minute delay of the launch of the shuttle Discovery that had completely disrupted his carefully laid out plot.

"A fuel sensor?" Devlin raged. "A damned fuel sensor stopped this launch at nearly three hours to zero? Damn these Americans and their pussyfooting around. There's four of the blasted things on the fuel tank, they should just lift off and be damned."

"They are just being exceptionally careful," Pressler

said. "It's the fact that this launch is so important to the American space program that makes it such a valuable target. If something goes wrong, the space program will soon be little more than a few museums and some old rockets. This action is nothing particularly unusual, though. These kinds of delays have happened on a regular basis for almost every shuttle launch and even the normal rocket liftoffs. Besides, the news is saying that they could have liftoff by Saturday."

"Fine, leave the rockets in place for the time being in case they restart the countdown," Devlin ordered. "If they delay to Saturday, we can break down the launcher and conceal the rockets again later today. Setting up Friday will be soon enough. If anyone comes about, there won't be anything for them to see."

"Couldn't we just arm the system and launch now?" Maypole suggested. "The crowds will still be there, they can't possibly disperse for hours yet. Some are setting up picnics and barbecues for dinner, from the pictures on the news channels."

Devlin looked at the man thoughtfully, considering his suggestion. Thousands of lives depended on his decision. Finally, he shook his head.

"No, not after all of my planning. We need the shuttle launch itself to help cover the flight of our rockets. Everyone would be watching Discovery lift off and few would even notice our rockets. The smoke and noise of the shuttle going up would also help hide our launch. No one in the crowds would think they had been exposed to anything for days, any cough or symptoms they felt could be blamed on the smoke from the shuttle boosters. They wouldn't seek out medical attention until it was too late and the hospitals were flooded with victims.

"This will be the greatest biological attack in history. The whole world will know of it and quake with fear when they see the all-powerful United States brought to her knees. Twelve kilograms of weapons-grade anthrax, released from a line source covering miles of land. The clouds would be driven by the onshore winds deeper into the country, creating even more victims. We will be able to ask any price, and receive it, for a weapon that does so much damage."

The rest of the people in the room just looked at their leader. The man was almost raving, but it was fascinating to listen to him. It must have been a little like this for the German people when they heard Hitler give his speeches. As for John Mack, the leader of the mercenaries Devlin had hired for additional manpower, it was the idea of a huge payoff that held his attention. And Mack was nursing a growing hatred for the people who had killed his men on the highway outside of Tampa. Following Devlin, no matter how much a growing lunatic he could be, would give Mack the best chance of seeing someone pay for the deaths of his men.

"No, I am not risking all of that by launching too early," Devlin continued his speech. "We will wait out the delay, no matter how long or irritating it is. At the worst, the launch window extends to the end of the month. NASA wants to see this bird lift off the pad as badly as we do. So we shall sit. The final payoff will be worth it for all of us.

"And everyone stays in the building! I don't want so much as a cigarette butt found outside to indicate anyone is here except the caretaker. The locals already have accepted Maypole in that role and he will be the only one to leave for supplies. Is that absolutely clear to everyone?"

A murmur of agreement went through the small crowd of men standing in the bay. Voorhees simply looked on with ill-concealed disgust at the situation. She, too, was disappointed to have come so close to her goal of revenge on the United States for her family's destruction only to have had it delayed once again. But she would maintain her own counsel for the time being and not rage about the situation as Devlin was doing.

———

"I'll be damned, they stopped the countdown."

Caronti was the first one in the room to speak out loud the thing they all were thinking as they watched the TV screen. Reaper's team had moved their base of operations from Orlando to a rented condominium apartment in Rockledge, a town across the river from the southern end of Merritt Island. There was no question in anyone's mind that the countdown clock was stopped and the launch scrubbed because of what they had discovered only a few days earlier.

It was an urgent series of phone calls and computer communications with Straker's office at Homeland Security that had started the ball rolling. While decisions were being made in Washington, Reaper abandoned the rental house in Central Florida in order to come to the Space Coast area and follow their leads there. Now they were in a position to quickly respond to possible developments in the area.

While still maintaining the secrecy surrounding the

official existence of Reaper and his men, Straker had immediately delivered to the FBI the information and intelligence they had uncovered in the Tampa area. He was astonished when the premier federal law enforcement agency all but dismissed the evidence he placed in front of them. The secret weapons-manufacturing plant and laboratory had been destroyed and military Hazmat teams had secured the biological materials. With Devlin's apparent base of operations destroyed, the FBI considered the situation now just a manhunt.

As far as the FBI was concerned, the evidence that had been gathered from both the pub site and the destroyed plant was tainted to the point of uselessness in a criminal court of law. Even the intelligence community was dismissing the value of some of the information, since the people at the Special Operations Command had refused to turn over Shaughnessy until their own interrogations were completed. He was a military prisoner, in the opinion of the SOCOM authorities at Mac-Dill Air Force Base in Tampa.

Because of the situation surrounding the surrendered terrorist, the rest of the federal agencies weren't taking the results of Reaper's work seriously. The whole thing was just another example of the age-old turf war between the military, the intelligence community, and law enforcement.

It was their ability to operate above all of the petty political maneuvering in Washington that helped make Reaper and his Horsemen so valuable to Straker and his office. The information that the Horsemen had gathered at a high risk to themselves was far too vital to allow it to be buried as a minor addendum to a federal investigation. The ex-SEAL admiral had long operated as a man of direct action, he knew when it was time to ignore the personal risks and just get the mission done.

By calling in personal favors and browbeating others into cooperation, Straker had obtained a private meeting with the president of the United States to directly present his case. Through his reputation backed up by the intelligence and materials uncovered in Tampa, he had convinced the president of the mission's importance. It was the president who had personally ordered NASA to postpone the shuttle launch for the time being. Straker had gained time—incredibly valuable time—that Reaper could use to stop Devlin and his plot.

There was no question that someone in Florida had an operational biological WMD. Not even the most egotistical and oblivious of the authorities in the FBI could ignore the anthrax uncovered by the Horsemen. But the FBI was still treating the situation as if it was the work of a crazed individual or criminal group, not the carefully considered and detailed plans of a professional terrorist.

Everyone with Reaper knew differently and did not underestimate Devlin and his abilities. He was anything but crazed. If the FBI kept treating the professional terrorist as if he were just another incarnation of the Amerithrax killer from several years earlier, only the Four Horsemen would have any real chance of stopping the man. And stopping him meant preventing another major terrorist attack on United States soil, one that could have a body count that would make 9-11 look like a practice run.

As everyone else was still watching the television and speaking quietly among themselves, Reaper came back into the room. He heard each of them voicing their opinion about what they had just seen happen at the Kennedy Space Center.

"Okay, folks, I just got the word from D.C. Admiral Straker did it—he convinced the president to order that the launch be put on hold. But the delay is limited and flexible. NASA is still going to try to set up for another launch before the July window expires and they're pushing him to let them go ahead. We've got some time, but I don't know for sure how much. So we have to find Devlin quickly and put his countdown on permanent hold.

"Admiral Straker has put his reputation and career on the line because of our say-so. We have to prove that his trust isn't misplaced. Through the Department of Homeland Security, the resources of the U.S. government are pretty much at our disposal. We can call for just about anything we want that could help us take Devlin down, short of a nuclear strike. To do that, we have to find him first. I am open to suggestions, people. This is just about as important as things can get."

For several moments, everyone sat or stood around the room silently, contemplating what Reaper had just told them. The situation for Deveraux had gone beyond being one of personal retribution for Devlin's involvement with the death of her husband. Now he could be responsible for the death of thousands, and that was an atrocity she could help prevent.

"One thing we should ask is, What gives us the edge over all the other agencies that will be working on this problem?" she said to everyone in the room.

"For one thing," Mackenzie said out loud, "there isn't a question in any of our minds that this is a very real threat. It goes way beyond threat level red. The action this guy is planning is the kind of thing that starts wars, really big ones. It seems to me that the FBI doesn't take this quite as seriously as we do. At least they haven't acted as if they believe the thing could go down as we've laid it out for them."

"Screw the FBI," Caronti growled. "We know just how real this situation is."

"Well," Warrick said thoughtfully, "one thing we're pretty sure of is just what kind of delivery system he's going to use for the attack. If he did decide to change to a different kind of delivery system for the anthrax, say a crop duster or a small boat and sprayer, most of what he did in that manufacturing plant of his would have been a waste of time."

"Wasting time is not something Devlin does very often," Deveraux said with conviction in her voice. "No, he wouldn't change things for a number of reasons. First off, the kind of attack that would use a plane or boat would mean that he would have to trust a confederate to actually deliver the attack. He would never do such a thing himself. Anyone flying a plane or piloting a boat to deliver anthrax would be on a suicide mission. They would never survive the attack. And it would be too slow a method. He would want the attack to happen swiftly and decisively. Besides, he would never trust anyone but himself for the last stage of such an important mission. He likes to pull the trigger. That's a weakness of his."

"That kind of attack has already been considered by NASA," Mackenzie said. "They have measures in place to deal with threats like that to prevent attacks on the shuttle itself. The Federal Aviation Administration sets up a temporary forty-mile no-fly zone around the shuttle launch site. And Air Force F-16s enforce it. You have all of the local airports closed and even commercial flights as far away as Orlando are affected."

"An attack from a small boat is guarded against, too," Caronti said. "At least one coming from the Atlantic side of the space center. The Coast Guard patrols the offshore waters to keep out any incursions from small boats. Mostly they're trying to prevent a boat from being used to launch an attack against the shuttle with a missile or something like that. But they also clear away the water traffic in case something goes wrong during a launch and crap starts falling from the sky. Then there's the Navy rescue boats that are out there on the water in case of an emergency."

"Okay, but what about the inland waters?" Reaper asked. "The Indian and Banana rivers. Does the Coast Guard cut off water traffic on them, too?"

"Nope, those stay pretty much open. The local water cops patrol them, but that's just to control the traffic. There's a hell of a lot of pleasure boats and small craft out there watching the launch from the water."

"So Devlin could launch his attack from a small boat? Say a thirty- or thirty-five-foot commercial fishing boat?

"I don't think so," Warrick said firmly. "It wouldn't be a stable enough launch platform, even if it was moving, not for a simple ballistic rocket, anyway. He didn't have the materials at that plant to build any kind of missile guidance system. There wasn't anything that I saw that could have been built and put into a small missile. His rockets are going to be fin-stabilized ballistic weapons that will be aimed at launch. And they're probably going to be on very low-flying trajectories at that. A boat would just rock and roll too much to trust it for a multiple launch system, the rocket could just plow right into the water. No, he would need a stable platform, a land-based one."

"That's something different we can run with," Reaper suggested. "Let's look at this problem from the point of view of the weapon being used. You said your NFA list experts had estimated the maximum range of this kind of rocket, didn't they?"

"Up to twenty miles," Warrick said, "but it's been a couple of days since I asked about it. Some of the people may have a better idea of the range now that they've had time to think about it. I'll go online and check with them now."

"Remember," Reaper warned, "this is a very confidential situation. Saying too much could still start a public panic."

"Hey, what goes on the list, stays on the list. We've discussed confidential material often enough to know what the rules are. If you mention anything in public that came up on the list, you get thrown out of the group. And that's the nicest thing that happens to you."

"Fine. That takes care of checking up on the weapon," Reaper said after Warrick had headed to the room where they had set up the computers and high-speed lines. "Now, what about the launch site? That's the real question. Could we do another computer search? Find every likely location for a concealed launch site that fits the parameters, one within twenty miles of the Space Center?"

"You mean like industrial buildings, storage areas, vacant houses, lots, things like that?" Deveraux asked.

"More like rentals and new businesses along those lines. That's what's worked for Devlin so far. There's no reason to think he hasn't prepared this stage of the plan the same way."

"But that could mean dozens of locations—possibly hundreds."

"We've been told we have all kinds of resources at our disposal. I think it's about time we used some of them to cut down on the numbers if there are too many probable contacts."

"What if we watched to see if any of the possible sites accessed the Internet?" Caronti asked. "We figured out that the shuttle was the target because of that weather report you tracked down. They should need the same kind of report for the launch day. You can't fire a rocket without knowing which way the winds is going to be blowing. If Devlin hasn't changed his method of doing things, there wouldn't be any reason for him to change his source of basic information, either. As far as they know, all of their printouts were burned."

"That's right," Mackenzie said. "To use a biological aerosol, you would have to have up-to-the-minute weather information. The Internet would be one of the best places to get that."

"So we should trace the computer access to the weather sites on the Internet from all of the suspected targets?" Reaper said. "That would be a job. But the one that looked up the information the announced day of the launch would have a good chance of being the one we're looking for. Especially if they check up and confirm the information from the same site multiple times as the actual launch time comes up."

"That would be cutting things close," Caronti said. "We would have to react very quickly to last-minute intelligence. Not a very comfortable margin for safety."

"No, it isn't," Reaper agreed, "but it's not anything we haven't had to do more than once before. That kind of quick action is something a small unit like ours can do a lot better than anyone else can. Plus, we can keep things a hell of a lot quieter than a bigger unit moving in would."

"Following that much computer activity would be very difficult," Deveraux said as she shook her head. "We don't have the facilities to process that much information. Even just watching the site where that burned printout came from would be just about impossible, with what we have available. Then there are the additional problems of tapping the land lines for dial-up access and the wireless systems, and cell phone would have to be added to the mix. Who has the ability to track all of that, track the activity of the Internet and all of the possible lines of communication, and still do it in a timely manner?"

"The NSA does," Deckert said, speaking for the first time. "The intelligence community already follows cell phone calls, tracking wireless computer transmissions isn't all that much more work for them. The National Security Agency can already track any kind of electronic communications on the planet, just about. And they can watch the Internet, they already do. We would just have to ask them to put our watched site on their list.

"For this emergency, I'll bet Homeland Security could get us any kind of wiretap we wanted on every place we come up with. It's not like we're looking for legal evidence for an arrest or anything. The supercomputers at the NSA base in Maryland could keep track of everything we wanted without even trying hard."

"That sounds like a plan," Reaper said, "or at least a direction to move in. Deckert, you work with Deveraux and set up the parameters for the computer search. I'm going to get back on the horn to Washington and bring Straker up to speed on our plans. He may be able to give us a backdoor to access what you want at the NSA."

Chapter Twenty-six

"We've got a hit!" Deveraux shouted from her seat at the computer. "A rock-solid hit!"

Deveraux had been maintaining a daily watch on the connection that had been set up between her computer and the great super-computers at the NSA headquarters in Fort Meade, Maryland. The computer search of available records had resulted in forty-seven possible launch sites that would fit Devlin's needs. These sites had been located all along the Space Coast area, from Titusville in the north to Cocoa Beach in the south. Everything from rented garages, boatyards, factories, manufacturing facilities, and office buildings had been selected and examined by Reaper and his team.

Only a handful of those sites had proven viable, but that still made nearly a dozen places that had to be watched. Deckert's suggestion to use the facilities at the National Security Agency had been what saved the plan. Now that idea was paying off.

Only one of the places on the list had accessed a watched weather-reporting site on the Internet. The location was at a small combination manufacturing facility and office building located in Cape Canaveral, one of the optimum locations according to the search profile Deckert and Deveraux had put together. Like the other locations on their list, the building had been examined by some of Reaper's people. No activity at all had been seen in the building, but a note had been made regarding the place's almost ideal location. Now, not only had the site gone on-line to call up the weather report the day before, it had just done so again for the second time that morning. And this was the day of the shuttle launch, according to the NASA announcements.

"Where's Reaper?" Deveraux asked as she went into the kitchen area.

"In the backyard working out before it gets hot again," Caronti said as he sat at the table with a cup of coffee. "It's nice out there this early in the morning."

"You might want to finish that coffee," Deveraux said, heading to the outside door. "It looks like we have a solid lead on Devlin's launch site."

In the postage-stamp-size backyard, Reaper was completing his morning workout routine. During their search for Devlin, working out in the yard had become a daily ritual for him. Instead of going to a well-equipped gymnasium as was his preference, he remained at the condominium, refusing to leave the area even for the time he would have needed to exercise. The situation for days now had been tense and fluid; at any moment they could have located Devlin and had to move into action immediately. Refusing to be separated from his people at such a critical time but needing the exercise to blow off steam as well as keep his abilities up, Reaper had been conducting an extensive series of calisthenics for an hour or more every morning.

Standing at the edge of the yard for a moment, Deveraux watched Reaper complete a series of pushups with his feet raised up on a chair. The muscles in his arms and back stretched and bulged as he pushed his body up and down in a smooth motion, sweat gleaming on his skin even in the relatively cool early-morning air.

This was a man Deveraux had come to admire over the weeks she had been working with him. The respect Reaper's men held for him was obvious, and she had come to learn that was a respect based on ability, leadership, and trustworthiness. If there was a man she had to work with on such an important operation, she was glad that it was Reaper. He wasn't hard to look at, either. At that moment, Deveraux was enjoying the fact that she was delivering good news, in spite of the serious possible consequences it held for both of them.

Standing up, Reaper picked up a towel he had draped over the back of a chair and wiped himself off with it. One look at Deveraux standing nearby, and he knew what the news was.

"A hit?"

"Absolutely. The same place that went online last night."

"Then we have a go," Reaper said firmly. "The liftoff for the shuttle is only a couple of hours away. If this place isn't it, then we've run out of time. Has there been any report from Deckert or Warrick?"

The night before, the same location had accessed the Internet through a wireless connection. That had been enough to put the team on high alert. To establish surveillance on the location, Warrick and Deckert had gone to Cape Canaveral soon after the computer activity had been detected. They had kept the building under watch, spelling each other for the entire night.

"Not since they established their observation post last night," Deveraux said. "I haven't spoken to either of them this morning, and Deckert hasn't sent any messages."

Rubbing the towel against the back of his head, Reaper looked at his watch and considered the situation.

"It's twelve miles from here to Canaveral. It'll take us about twenty minutes to get there, with the traffic and everything. Tell Mackenzie and Caronti to get ready. I want us out of here in five minutes or less. Gear packed, low profile. Our Federal IDs will get us past the police checkpoints, but I don't want any bored reporters seeing us and trying to make a fast news story.

"Send the intelligence on to Straker; he can decide who to give it to in Washington. As far as anyone else goes, we have to keep this dead quiet. That location is in the middle of a populated area. It isn't as isolated as the other two were. If Devlin and his crew suspect they've been spotted, they could just launch immediately or threaten to detonate a warhead. It's not like he's shown any reluctance to use that anthrax of his. We have to take them down quickly and completely. Local law enforcement would only get in the way at this point; we can call them in after everything is over."

The team had cleaned, checked, and rechecked its assault gear and weapons over the last several days. They'd already packed body armor, vests, ammunition, boots and clothes on board their vehicles in the parking lot of the condominium complex. Reaper had already stowed the rigs for both himself and Deveraux in the trunk of the new Mustang he had leased.

The tape covering the damaged widow of the previous one was something Reaper had figured would just draw more attention to the car, and tag it for Devlin if he spotted the bright red vehicle in the area. The Mustang GT had already proven its value to Reaper, so he had picked up another one. The only real difference between the two cars was that the new Mustang was white. Mackenzie had immediately made his usual wry comment.

"A white Mustang," Mackenzie had said. "You sure that's what you want, a white Mustang?"

"It's a good car," Reaper shot back at his friend. "Damn, first Deveraux complains that she thinks a red one stands out too much and now you comment on a white one. So what do you think is wrong with it?"

"Nothing, nothing at all," Mackenzie said with a deadpan face. "I just thought the idea of Death riding a pale horse is a little overdone. Don't you?"

The rest of the team had laughed while Reaper just stared at the man.

The time for joking ended as the team headed out to where Warrick and Deckert were watching. While Reaper had dressed, Deveraux contacted the pair and gave them a report of the situation. Warrick had established a sniper's hide inside one of the uncompleted condominium buildings. So far that morning, no one from the construction crews had shown up yet.

"It's like there's some kind of holiday today," Deckert had reported over the radio. "There's no one here, no movement at all. I think everyone is out watching the shuttle launch."

Reaper was glad to hear it when Deveraux told him the news. No people on the street meant that there would be fewer chances of any civilians coming into the area at the wrong time. They would have to slip up to the building silently and take it down fast and hard, something Reaper had no question that his people could do. But more than anything else, they had to locate the rockets and secure them before moving on Devlin and his people.

One big problem with the upcoming launch was that the traffic had become much worse than Reaper expected. It was more than an hour before they crossed into Canaveral and cleared the checkpoints. This time the police were just waving cars and trucks past, directing and controlling traffic more than checking out individual vehicles and their occupants. No one in Reaper's crew, either the Mustang or the pickup truck, even had to show their IDs to the officers. Driving past the street where the suspected launch site was located, Reaper and Deveraux made the turn toward where the condominiums were under construction. No one else was on the side streets, and the buildings to either side were closed up and dark. Behind the Mustang Reaper was driving were Caronti and Mackenzie in their pickup truck.

Past the construction site was a crowded area of trailers, open Dumpsters, and other materials stacked along the wide pier that stuck out into the Banana River. Among this cover was Deckert's van, parked where he had a good view of the back and side of the target building. Carefully leaving their vehicles in concealment from the target building, Reaper, Deveraux, Caronti, and Mackenzie crossed over to the van. They climbed in through the driver's side rear door, unseen by anyone across the street.

"Took you long enough," Deckert said as they all settled into the van.

"Traffic," Mackenzie quipped.

"Give us a sitrep," Reaper said.

"Not much at all to report," Deckert said as he picked up his binoculars and looked at the building across the street. "There has been no visible activity at all. I've driven in front of the place several times during the night and there were no lights shining in any of the windows. Warrick has switched over to his thermal sight and hasn't seen any sign of a guard or other security posted on the place. The only movement at all was last night at 1835 hours, when one guy left the front of the place and came back forty-five minutes later with a couple of grocery bags under his arms. That was it. Since then, nothing at all has moved."

"So there's at least one tango inside the building."

"Just the one guy is all we've seen. He looks like a caretaker more than a terrorist."

"According to the program, this is the only location that tripped the computer watch at the NSA," Deveraux said. "It has to be the place."

"Is Warrick on the radio net?" Reaper asked.

"He checked in about fifteen minutes ago," Deckert said. "He's up on the third floor of the fifth unit over in a concealed position, right across the street from that big roll-up door in the side of the building. He can see across the entire roof of the place from where he is."

Taking the microphone Decker indicated, Reaper pressed the button on the side and heard the speaker crackle.

"War, this is Death."

"Death, this is War."

"Give me a sitrep."

"No activity to report," Warrick said. "But I have spotted something interesting."

"What is it?"

"Do you see the small colored ribbons next to the fence posts across the street?"

Picking up Deckert's binoculars, Reaper focused them on the fence line surrounding the sides and back of the building. Sure enough, across from the roll-up door were a number of different colored ribbons next to several of the posts holding up the steel-link fence. The small bits of color looked almost like scraps of plastic bags that had become stuck on the sharp ends of the fence wires.

"Roger that," Reaper said into the mike, "I see them."

"Well, those ribbons are duplicated on this side of the street. I'll bet if you were inside that big roll-up door and looking through a sight, they would line up for you—just like the aiming stakes you use when you set up a mortar."

That was a significant point. The innocuous ribbons could give someone a known aiming point to use when setting up a large weapon. The two ribbons would be set up along a carefully surveyed line, laid out with the help of a sensitive compass. Then all you would have to do is line up the ribbons with each other through a set of crosshairs. When the markers were aligned one on top of the other, an indirect-fire weapon such as a rocket launcher would be aimed in a known direction. Adjusting things from there would be fast and easy, all you would need is a map and a scale on the weapon sight. It was just the way Reaper would have done it.

"Okay, that's enough to convince me. We're going to take down that building."

"But what about the warheads?" Deveraux said. "Is there anything we can do to neutralize them?"

"I have an idea," Mackenzie said as he reached for the microphone. "War, this is Famine," he said as he keyed the mike.

"Famine, this is War, go ahead."

"Can you tell how much water is in that tank on the roof?"

"Wait one," Warrick said and the radio went silent.

In his hide, Warrick swung his big Serbu Firearms BFG-50 Auto up and in line with the roof of the building across the street. On top of the receiver of the rifle was mounted a DRS thermal weapon sight. The TWS 3000/4000 sight could detect heat and showed it as different intensities of light on a gray scale. Variations in temperature showed up on the screen inside the sight as lighter or darker areas. The water in the tank hadn't warmed up much in the early morning light yet and was at a different temperature from the metal surrounding it. The level of the water would show as a dark shadow against the lighter (warmer) metal at the top of the tank.

"It's about three-quarters full," Warrick reported back over the radio.

"Roger that, War. Famine out."

"What was that all about?" Reaper asked.

"That water tank is a backup gravity feed system for the fire-control sprinkler inside that building," Mackenzie said. "If you set off the system, it would spray its contents all over the inside of that warehouse and the offices at the other end. If we filled that tank up with bleach, that could control any anthrax spills inside the place."

"And just where are we going to get that much bleach?" Caronti asked.

"Right over there," Deckert said, pointing off to the construction area.

"That's right," Mackenzie agreed.

Deckert was pointing at one of the small buildings that held supplies for the condos. Inside the metal hut were bags and plastic tubs of chemicals along with several brown cardboard drums with metal tops held in place with clamps. Most of the materials were for the swimming pool nearby when it was finally finished and filled.

"Those cardboard drums hold powdered chlorine," Mackenzie explained. "One drum dumped into the hatch on top of that tank would make a hell of a concentrated bleach solution. You were supposed to have been a great climber, Reaper. Think you can hump one of those drums up to the top of that building?"

"Damn," Reaper swore, "those are what, fifty-pound drums?"

"More like hundred pounders by the look of them," Mackenzie said. "Didn't you ever take care of a pool?"

"In the Teams we usually swam in the ocean," Reaper said, "not just in swimming pools like in the Air Force. But strip off the tools and strap one to Caronti's breacher's pack frame and yes, I think I can get it up there. There's a telephone pole at the far side of the building, isn't there?"

"Yes," Deckert replied. "It's nearly up against the wall

on the south side of the building. Near the front by the offices, about a foot from the wall. It extends up past the roof."

"Then I can use that as a ladder," Reaper said. "That'll make the climb a lot easier—faster, too. Caronti, you and Mackenzie can set up to breach the front door after I dump the chlorine in the tank. I want us ready to move as soon as that crap is in place. We're running out of time. The shuttle countdown has less than an hour to go."

"Not a problem," Caronti said, "I've got a spare pair of bolt cutters you can take with you. The small gates in the fence all have padlocks securing them. We saw them when we checked the place out a few days ago. I seriously doubt anyone has taken them off since then."

"I'll go with you," Deveraux said firmly to Reaper. As he turned to face her, she continued, "I can cover your climb from the ground. Don't argue. You'll be carrying far too much weight to handle a weapon and defend yourself effectively during the climb."

There didn't seem to be any argument Reaper could put forward against Deveraux's logic. The woman was right, no matter how much he didn't like it. Mackenzie would be operating as Caronti's shooting partner. Warrick was performing his sniper's duties and Deckert would run the communications. There was no one else to partner with him and nothing to do but agree with Deveraux and get on with the mission.

Chapter Twenty-Seven

The last two weeks of enforced waiting combined with the close proximity of too many people had strained Devlin's group almost to the breaking point. No one had been able to leave the building; not even Devlin had broken his rule. The only one who could go outside was Maypole, who was already known in the neighborhood. Even the mercenaries on Devlin's team who smoked hadn't been able to leave the building, and no one wanted them smoking inside, especially not with all of the weapons and rockets that were there. The smokers had to satisfy their nicotine cravings by climbing up the stairs in the main garage bay and sitting on the landing below the open roof hatch to smoke. Looking down to where the rockets would be launched from, they had enough ventilation to clear the smoke away safely.

Everyone was so on edge that the final announcement that the shuttle would be lifting off came as almost a letdown. The idea that a simple sensor, one of many in a redundant system, could ground such an expensive undertaking seemed ridiculous. It was just possible that Devlin's planned attack, and the possible destruction of a big part of the U.S. space program, could turn out to be a blessing to the economy of the United States.

That was the thought that amused Devlin as he gathered everyone together in the main office for a final briefing and review of the firing schedule. In spite of their irritation at repeating everything once again, Devlin wanted to be certain that they hadn't forgotten any of their critical timing or tasks.

"And at T minus ninety minutes, you do what?" Devlin asked Pressler.

"I perform a final check of the rockets," Pressler responded mechanically. "Go over the checklist, top off the nitrous oxide tanks, confirm the setting and running of the timer and firing circuits, both mechanical and electrical. And trace the cutaway lines for the curtain."

"And then nothing until T minus thirty minutes?"

"My men and I run a check on the living quarters and make certain all traces of our presence here are removed," Mack said. "Either flushed down the toilet or packed into garbage bags."

"Don't forget to run bleach through the drains of all the sinks and the shower," Voorhees reminded him. "That will destroy any possible traces of anyone's DNA that might have been caught up in the traps. The toilets too."

"If we have to worry about the FBI collecting DNA samples and analyzing them for comparison to us," Mack sneered, "it's already too late. We'll be their prisoners."

"All the more reason to leave no trace of any evidence behind," Voorhees snapped back. "If they can't prove we were here, they can't charge us. And don't let your men forget to pack up all of the trash."

"You don't have to worry about my men," Mack almost shouted. "We know how to do our jobs. Everything is already cleared out and packed in the van. There's only a final inspection to perform, anyway."

"That's excellent," Devlin said in a soothing tone of voice. "Then all we have to do after that is wait and listen to the radio for the countdown to reach T minus ten minutes. At that point, the doors can be opened and the vehicles leave the building. Mack, you and I will hold back and arm the final systems at T minus five minutes. Then we will leave and join the others outside. Maypole will take the panel truck, you and your men will be in the Suburban, and the lovely Voorhees and myself will be in the Corvette. We should be at least a mile away before the rockets fire."

"Are you certain about the final timing?" Mack asked. "Once we leave here, there won't be enough time for us to turn back and shut down in case of another scrubbed launch."

"NASA is more than dependable on this matter," Devlin said confidently. "They have published the schedule all over the Internet. The launch sequence enters its terminal count at T minus nine minutes. At that point, the internal computers and power supplies on board the shuttle take over. The launch is almost a certainty after that. It would take a major malfunction to stop the countdown at that stage. And you can be sure that Mission Control is not going to let that happen. There are more than two hundred thousand people here in person to watch the United States return to space. Even the First Lady is in the VIP area along with Governor Jeb Bush. Millions more will be watching everything live on the telly all around the world. NASA will not want to disappoint them, and neither will we."

———

The morning hadn't really started to heat up yet but Reaper was sweating hard, as if he had just completed an ass-kicking workout. The only problem was, his workout wasn't over yet. Besides the load of boots, clothing, armor, assault vest, gloves, ammunition, and weapons he was carrying, he had a backpack laden with a seventy-five-pound drum of powdered chlorine. At least it hadn't been a hundred-pound drum, he thought wryly.

Having reached the fence line on the opposite side of the target from where their partners were, Reaper and Deveraux were crouched down behind an electrical junction box. In spite of the need to catch his breath for a moment, Reaper hated the feeling of exposure as they hid behind the steel box. It was broad daylight, and not half a mile away on the Banana River, pleasure boats were floating along as their occupants watched for the shuttle liftoff. Anyone who drove by would have seen the two next to the box and neither of them looked like electrical workers.

"Okay, give me the cutters," Reaper told Deveraux. "I'll go up and cut the lock on the gate while you cover me from here. If things look good, I'll head on in."

Taking the thirty-inch set of bolt cutters, Reaper took another breath and darted to the fence. The padlock on the gate was a good one, but the shackle never stood a chance when a strong ex-Navy SEAL applied a set of hardened steel jaws to it. The gate swung open and Reaper trotted to the building only a few yards away. When Reaper reached the cover of the wall next to the telephone pole, Deveraux got up and ran, stopping only long enough to close the gate behind her.

Reaper glared at the woman who had followed him into the yard against his instructions.

Looking back at Reaper, Deveraux shrugged as if to say, *What, you wanted me to stay back there and watch?*

There wasn't time to bitch about anything. Reaper looked up at the telephone pole and saw something that made him smile and forget the weight for a moment. Climbing stakes stuck out on either side of the pole, starting just a few feet off the ground and continuing up to the cross tree, well above the edge of the roof. The climb had suddenly gotten a lot easier.

But still Reaper had to lift each foot and place it on the stake above it, shoving hard with his legs and pulling with his arms. He was carrying more than his own weight in gear and material. Only his almost-religious attention to physical fitness made the climb possible. Finally, he reached a point where he was just below the edge of the roof.

"War," he said quietly, "Death in position."

The microphone on his headset picked up his near whisper and transmitted it. Only a second passed before an answer came back.

"Death, War. The way is clear."

As he hugged the pole, Reaper pulled his M4 CQBT carbine up and held it in his right hand like a big pistol. The Chalker sling attached to the weapon helped stabilize it as he slowly lifted himself to a point where he could peek out across the roof.

There was nothing Reaper could see on the roof but sheet steel, tar sealant, and seagull droppings. The brown pelican standing on the edge of the roof at the river side of the building suggested that no one was up there with it. If there was a guard, Reaper couldn't see any sign of him, and Warrick would have already warned him, in any case.

Reaching over with his weapon, Reaper laid his right arm on the rooftop. Letting go of the climbing stake with his other hand, he grabbed the edge of the roof and levered himself up on his arms. He refused to allow himself to think about the three-story drop to the blacktop below as his arms shook with the strain. Pulling up one leg, he swung it over the edge of the roof and forced himself up.

Taking a second to breathe, Reaper oriented himself while he knelt down on the warm sheet metal. There was an open hatch near the center of the roof, but no one showed their head and there wasn't any noise coming from inside the building. The silver water tank was only a short distance away. He quickly made his way over to the tank in a low crouch, moving as quietly as he could. Once in position, he dropped his M4 and allowed it to hang at the end of his Chalker sling while he tried to take off the heavy pack frame without dropping it on the roof. Finally, he just knelt down and leaned backward, resting the heavy drum of chemicals on the dirty sheet metal. Getting free of the drum was easy then.

Standing, Reaper could see that a simple clamp held

the hatch on top of the water tank in place. Spinning the handle, the hatch raised up easily. The smell of wet, moist air hit him in the face, which was a hell of a lot better than the suddenly sharp chemical smell of the bleach as he pulled off the lid of the drum. The stink got worse, making his eyes water, as Reaper pulled the drum up and dumped its contents into the water.

Shaking his head to get the sting out of his eyes, Reaper lowered the drum to the rooftop. Quickly stepping away from the open tank, Reaper desperately tried to keep from sneezing as the toxic dust got into his nose. He went though a long, painful couple of moments until the urge passed. His eyes no longer watering, Reaper picked up his M4 and turned to the open hatch.

"The package has been delivered," he said softly. "I repeat, the package has been delivered."

A series of "Rogers" came out of his earpiece as his teammates acknowledged the situation.

———

Having stubbed out his cigarette, Eduardo Rodriguez, one of Devlin's mercenaries under John Mack, got up to close the roof hatch and head back down to the Suburban. He was tired of being in the building and hoped that the payoff from Mack would be worth it. A soft noise from out on the roof caused him to freeze. Silently, he ducked down near the wall and looked up at the opening, waiting patiently. He had more than enough experience to know if he had heard something or not, and he wasn't going to stick his head up right away to check it out. That was how people lost their heads, and he wanted his to remain just where it was.

Down on the floor, Mack was walking up to the roll-up
doors to raise them and send the vehicles out.

———

A sudden loud mechanical noise rose up from the open
roof hatch in front of Reaper. It sounded like the doors
were being opened inside the building. Carefully
crawling up to the hatch, he lifted his head enough to
look down inside the large room below him. The big
garage door had opened, he could see the light from
the open door falling through what looked like long
hanging slats with gaps between them. There was the
sound of engines starting and Reaper leaned farther
over to try and see what was inside. Suddenly, a hand
came up from the open hatch and grabbed him, pulling him forward and off balance.

Rather than just fall uncontrollably, Reaper suddenly
moved with the force that was pulling at him. He had
been discovered and now he had to take back control of
the situation. He fell into the open hatchway. As he
dropped, he smelled the stinking breath of a smoker as
the other man's hands tried to get a grip on Reaper's
equipment or harness.

Before he hit the platform at the top of the stairs,
Reaper grabbed at the man who had pulled on him,
twisting his body and rolling the man over. Both figures
tumbled down the steep steel stairway, rolling over and
over as they fell. The same armor and gear that had
caused him to lose his balance now protected Reaper
from the sharp edges and corners of the steps as they
fell. Reaper heard rubber tires screeching on concrete as
someone pealed out below.

The two men impacted on the landing at the bottom

of the top flight of stairs with Reaper on top, smashing his attacker against the steel grid of the platform. He needn't have bothered: The angle of the man's head indicated a broken neck, and the large crease in the side of his skull told how the impact with a steel corner had finished the mercenary's tobacco cravings forever. But the situation Reaper had literally fallen into was not one he had planned for.

The sudden stuttering of a suppressed weapon rang out from somewhere outside of the building. The burst was a long, hammering one that ended in another squeal of tires. As he grabbed for the M4 dangling from his Chalker sling, Reaper looked down the second flight of stairs and into the muzzle of another M4, this one in the unwavering hands of a man who looked like he knew exactly how to pull the trigger.

As Reaper froze, the sound of two more suppressed weapons opening fire came from outside. This time the sound came from the opposite direction as the first. There was a pair of sharp cracks followed by a heavy metallic crunch.

"Shit," the man in front of Reaper cursed. "You get down here, and drop that weapon right now."

"I can't," Reaper said as he slowly got to his feet, "it's strapped on by a sling."

"Then just walk down here slowly and keep those hands away from your body. If I didn't need a hostage, you'd be dead. Maypole! Get the hell over here, you useless git, and cover this guy. I'll bet this is our friend from that wild ride in Tampa. I want to be sure he feels right at home for as long as he's living with us."

As the other man came over, Reaper looked at the big launcher sitting in the middle of the floor. There were four white-painted rockets, each approximately eight feet long and more than six inches in diameter. Something about the rockets made them look very familiar to Reaper. Then he knew. The X-shaped wings in the center of the body, the four tail fins. These rockets were modeled after the Navy's Harpoon missiles, which Reaper had seen many times during his military career.

"Nasty looking, aren't they?" the man covering Reaper said. "And this is about as close as you're going to get to them. They launch in just a few minutes, only you won't be alive to see them go."

Chapter Twenty-eight

Kneeling down at a front corner of the building, Deveraux had been scanning the front doors of the office building as well as the south-facing wall. She knew that Mackenzie and Caronti were going to be hitting the north-facing wall any moment now, and that Deckert was covering the back wall, which faced the river. But with Reaper up on the roof, Deveraux felt she should try and cover as many exits to the building as she could from a single position.

The sudden noise of the big steel door rolling up startled her.

"I have movement at the south wall," she whispered. "The big door is opening up."

"The same thing is happening on the north wall," Warrick's voice stated as it came over her earpiece.

"Reaper is up on the roof."

"Not anymore, he just dove into the building, for some reason."

Before Deveraux could make another comment, a tan Corvette with white racing stripes came out through the open garage door. The woman driving the car wasn't very good at handling a high-performance vehicle. She stepped on the gas too hard and squealed the tires as she started to move. The convertible top of the vehicle was down, and even as far away as Deveraux was, she recognized the driver's flowing hair. It was Voorhees, the same woman who had been with Devlin at the restaurant in Tampa. And she turned her head and saw Deveraux standing at the edge of the parking lot.

Snapping the M4 up to her shoulder, Deveraux aimed at the sports car as it turned and accelerated toward her. The Gemtech HALO suppressor on the muzzle of the CQBR barrel reduced the normal roar of the short, nasty weapon to a stuttering series of pops and hisses. As she had seen Reaper do in the rear window of the Mustang, Deveraux aimed at the low sloping hood and windshield of the Corvette.

The EBR frangible 5.56mm ammunition the M4 was loaded with could normally go right through the thin construction of the Corvette. But the streamlined design of the car made it impossible for the alloy projectiles to strike the surface, any surface, of the sports car head on. The slugs skipped across the hood of the car and spanged off the windshield. Holding the trigger back, Deveraux hammered the entire magazine into the oncoming vehicle, with no apparent effect.

But the splashing projectiles did distract Voorhees. She ducked and swerved, almost at the last moment. The bullets terrified her. Instead of smashing into Deveraux head-on, she struck the woman a glancing blow with the right front bumper of the car. Rather than being thrown through the air or crushed under the wheels, Deveraux crashed violently into the hood of the car, rolled to the side, and fell off onto the blacktop.

Unable to stop in time, the Corvette struck the chain-link fence close behind where Deveraux had been crouching at the corner of the building. Stunned, Deveraux lay faceup on the ground, looking up into the sky. Her weapon rested across her chest, still attached to her Chalker sling. Her right arm was twisted down behind the small of her back and the SIG P226 pistol in the Serpa holster at her hip was useless, the grip shattered and jammed into the firing mechanism. Her physical conditioning and muscles had prevented Deveraux from being severely injured by the impact, but she was badly stunned.

Screaming her rage, Voorhees pushed the door of the trapped Corvette open and turned to where Deveraux lay on the ground. Attacking the supine woman, Voorhees was almost foaming at the mouth, her face twisted and ugly as she shouted incoherently in a language Deveraux didn't recognize. As she grabbed the M4 and pulled it away Voorhees actually lifted Deveraux from the ground, freeing her arm and forcing her stunned body into action.

Almost of its own volition, Deveraux's right hand grasped the handle of the Emerson fixed-blade Karambit, her index finger slipping through the hole in the handle. Closing her fist on the handle in the classic "ice pick" grip, Deveraux pulled the wickedly curved, razor-sharp blade from the fitted kydex sheath.

As Voorhees was still trying to pull the M4 far enough away from Deveraux's chest to be able to turn the weapon around and use it, Deveraux struck back.

Sweeping her hand around in a hard curve, Deveraux slashed from right to left across Voorhee's torso. The curved blade of the Karambit was sharp on the inside, and that acted to pull the soft tissue of the abdomen into the cutting surface. The edge bit deeply, the skin gaping open. Blood, severed intestines, and other organs poured from the huge wound.

Voorhees' head tilted back spontaneously, her mouth open in a silent scream as the shock of the injury overwhelmed her system. There was no pain in the eyes that turned upward. The wound was too massive for the brain to register it. Automatically, Deveraux flipped her right hand over and pulled her arm back in a return slash. This time the target of the wicked blade was the woman's exposed throat. The edge of the knife bit into the left side of the neck and sliced deeply, severing the jugular vein and the carotid artery before passing through the esophagus and then the arteries and veins on the opposite side.

Voorhees' heart continued to beat for a few seconds before she fell backward, blood spurting into the air from her throat. Her head lolling, barely held on by what remained of her neck, Voorhees collapsed to the ground, dead.

The bloody knife still in her hand, Deveraux shuddered as reality set in. But she had people depending on her, and she forced herself to stand. The stench of blood and human waste made her gag as she wiped the mess from her weapon. Choking back the contents of her stomach as it tried to escape, Deveraux removed the empty magazine from her weapon and slipped the loaded twin that was attached to it back into the receiver. A sharp blow of her hand released the bolt stop and the weapon was loaded with a metallic sliding scrap and clack. Voorhees had died struggling for an empty weapon.

———

On the other side of the building, Caronti and Mackenzie had a much less dramatic time with the Suburban that sped out of the door to the building and turned toward them on the street. Both men snapped up their M4s and pulled the triggers. The impact of their slugs caused even less damage than Deveraux's. The heavy SUV was fully armored and the frangible 5.56mm projectiles did little more than scar up the paint. But up in his sniper's hide, Warrick had a considerably heavier-caliber weapon than 5.56mm.

Even though he was firing Israeli IMI match ball ammunition, it was .50-caliber. Each projectile was twice the size of an entire 5.56mm round. The weapon he was using was a new semi-automatic .50-caliber rifle with a full ten-round magazine seated in place. Even through the SWR compact Omega X50 suppressor, the sound of the big fifty firing was impressive, though fortunately not deafening. The slugs snapped through the air as they broke the sound barrier. They smashed into the armored window of the SUV and passed through the heavy glass and plastic to pierce the bodies of the occupants. One of those hit was the mercenary at the wheel.

Fifty-caliber bullets don't make slight wounds, especially not when they enter the chest of a target. The Suburban continued rolling for a distance with a dead man at the wheel until it crunched into a telephone pole. The big vehicle stopped with the engine still running and the pole tilted about 30 degrees from the impact.

━━━━

Even though the big door to the back of the building was open, Warrick still couldn't see inside the place with his naked eyes. Over the radio, he could hear that Reaper was in trouble, but there was nothing he could do to affect the situation if he couldn't see anything. There was a curtain of some kind across the door, a barrier made up of opaque plastic strips moving in the breeze.

The thermal sight on the BFG-50 Auto allowed Warrick to see through the plastic curtain, but not very well. The insulating characteristics of the plastic and the movement of the strips combined to blur the images he could see. Quickly flipping through the controls on the DRS TWS 3000/4000 sight didn't help the situation. All Warrick could make out was the hazy outlines of two human figures. He was certain that Reaper was one of them.

"Death, this is War," Warrick said into his radio. "Death, this is War. I have two targets, I repeat two targets inside the building. If you want me to take one out, raise your hands high and surrender. I say again, raise your hands high and surrender. Trust me, boss."

Over his earpiece, Reaper could hear Warrick clearly. He couldn't make an aggressive move, or say anything. The man in front of him was holding his weapon in steady hands, the muzzle pointed directly at Reaper's head. One wrong word or action and all of the body armor in the world wouldn't be able to keep him alive, not with a bullet through his brain.

"I surrender," Reaper said, slowly raising his arms up

over his head. His weapon dangled from the Chalker sling on his chest. It was as useless to him as if it was outside the building. He would never be able to reach it.

"Surrender?" Mack laughed. "You surrender . . . ?"

A half-inch hole suddenly appeared in the plastic behind Reaper. A beam of light shone through the hole, dust sparkling in it as the motes settled toward the floor.

The long curtain didn't even shake. The 649-grain full metal jacketed slug made a loud crack as it smashed through the M4 carbine in John Mack's hands, into his chest, and out his back, making hash of his heart and lungs. He never had a chance to finish his sentence. Mack died with a wide-eyed look of astonishment on his face. Striking the floor and deforming against the hard concrete, the bent slug had ricocheted into the wall with a piercing whistle.

Maypole was out of the way and to the side, still pointing his weapon at the ex-SEAL. Taking advantage of the other man's astonishment, Reaper swung hard to his left, his left arm lowered with the forearm held vertically and braced for impact. The arm swept the barrel of the man's weapon aside. With his right hand up, the fingers folded and the thumb held in tight, Reaper thrust upward with the base of his palm in the other man's face. Reaper drove his palm-strike with all of the power in his considerable shoulder and arm muscles, his arm bones and wrist in line for stiffness.

Bone and cartilage crunched under the onslaught of the heel of Reaper's hand. Blood spurted from the crushed nose, but the other man never felt it. The killing blow had broken the nasal and lachrymal bones to fragments and driven the razor-sharp shards deep into the brain behind them. Dead almost instantly, Maypole fell limply to the floor.

Devlin had frozen in the partly open doorway leading to the back of the building as the sound of the shot rang through the structure. The back room had been somewhat sound-deadened by the previous owners, so Devlin hadn't heard the action in the main bay or out in the street, but he recognized the sound of a ricochet close by, and with a glance, took in the scene.

The situation was a bust. His people were dead or captured, the operation was over, and it was time for him to go. This rapid series of thoughts went through the terrorist's head as he instantly decided on a course of action. Mack lay on the floor in a growing pool of blood, his weapon smashed and a huge hole in his chest.

A snap sounded above Reaper's head. The mechanical timer had reached the end of its countdown and the plastic curtain had dropped free of the ceiling. The plastic lay heaped in a large pile.

Light streamed into the building. In the center of the room, the rockets gleamed in the sudden light, their noses pointing out the doorway and into the cloudy sky. Their deadly contents waited in the warheads of the weapons for their upcoming release. It was T minus two minutes and counting to the liftoff of the shuttle Discovery.

Looking past the man he had just killed, Reaper recognized Devlin just as the other man ducked into the back room and slammed the door. The terrorist could be doing anything from running away to getting ready to set off another weapon. There was no way to tell what he was planning, and not a chance that Reaper would give him the time to decide what to do.

"War, this is Death," Reaper said out loud.

"Death, this is War," came back over the earpiece.

"Take out the rockets," Reaper ordered. "Don't worry about me, just do not let these rockets fire for any reason, no matter what! Is that understood?"

"Understood, Death. They will not fly."

Trusting his man, Reaper stepped over to the door through which Devlin had just disappeared. Pausing for a moment, Reaper ducked down and quickly crossed to the other side of the doorway. Stopping and pulling up his M4 with his left hand on the pistol grip, he reached back with his right hand for the doorknob. Touching the knob with his outstretched hand, he slowly turned it. The latch clicked as it opened.

Holes suddenly began appearing in the door as the sound of gunfire rang out from inside the room. Bullets streamed through the door, several of the slugs passing dangerously close to the anthrax-filled warheads of the rockets. Inside the room, Devlin had emptied the magazine of his MP5K submachine gun in one long, ripping burst. He waved the muzzle of the weapon about, sending the thirty 9mm rounds in the magazine across the door and through the wall. Tossing aside the smoking-hot, empty weapon, Devlin ran toward the back of the room.

———

In his firing position across the street, Warrick could now plainly see the rockets lying on their launch rails. No one was in his line of fire. Through the thermal sight, the leftover warmth of the nitrous bottles being filled made part of the rockets glow with light. The heat had been generated by the gas being compressed inside the bottles. Because of his sources, Warrick knew exactly how the system worked and how to safely disable it without damaging the warheads.

Settling the BFG-50 Auto tighter against his shoulder, Warrick took careful aim and squeezed the trigger. The suppressor threaded to the muzzle and extending back over the barrel reduced the sound of firing, but it did nothing to mitigate the fierce recoil of the very powerful weapon.

Even as the heavy kick of the weapon drove him back, Warrick fought to force the weapon back into line for the next vital shot. As the empty cartridge case ejected from the rifle bounced off the concrete floor, Warrick aimed the gas-operated weapon for his next shot.

Reaper heard the big .50-caliber bullets smash into the rockets in front of him in a steady rhythm. He stepped away from the wall while fragments of the rockets sprayed across the room. Reaper kicked backward with all of his weight and strength. The door swung open wildly, smashing back against the wall.

Reaper turned and was inside the room instantly, darting to the side and the cover of the shadows. Moving along the wall, the muzzle of his weapon up and tracking for any targets, Reaper "cut the pie," making certain there was no one in front of him before moving to the next area.

From behind an open metal Dumpster in the far corner, filled with what looked like wood scrap and fiberglass, Reaper saw two objects fly through the air to land and bounce across the floor. Even as his brain tried to identify the cross-hatched cylinders, his reflexes were sending him back to the doorway. His mind screamed, *Grenades!* and Reaper dove through the door, hitting the concrete on the other side and rolling away.

With a sharp bang, the white phosphorus grenades exploded into brilliant white-orange flowers. Streaming trails of thick white smoke followed the particles of burning phosphorus, which had ignited on contact with the air. The particles spread throughout the room, sticking to whatever they contacted and continuing to burn. Anything flammable, wood, paper, or fiberglass, was quickly engulfed in flames. Nothing could survive in the searing inferno the room had become. By rolling to the side, Reaper managed to avoid several phosphorus fragments that followed him through the door.

Looking back over his shoulder, he could see the glow of fires burning inside the smoke-filled back room. The phosphorus smoke was very thick and hot, intended to be used by the military to generate a rapid smoke screen. A stink of ozone accompanied the burning phosphorus, as well as something else—a sharp acrid odor Reaper knew but couldn't place. Then it came to him: plastic. He was smelling burning or hot cut plastic. Looking up toward the rockets on their launching rails, Reaper feared the worst.

With the first glance, Reaper knew Warrick had followed his orders. The rear section of each rocket was twisted and torn, ripped open by the power of the fifty. The engines were destroyed. The odor he smelled in addition to the ozone was from the burning igniters among the plastic fragments. The rockets had tried to launch; the firing sequence had already started when the precise

.50-caliber slugs from Warrick's weapon had torn the engines apart. It had been that close—a matter of seconds.

Pushing through the plastic curtain on the south wall of the building was a horrible apparition straight out of a horror movie or nightmare. It was Deveraux. The beautiful woman was completely covered in blood, tissue, and filth. She smelled like a cross between a slaughterhouse and an open sewer. She was limping on an injured leg, but her weapon was up and ready to fire.

As Reaper stared, Deveraux could see the fear in his eyes.

"It's okay, she said, "it isn't mine."

Coming in through the north door were Caronti and Mackenzie. As they walked into the building with their weapons at the ready, the heat from the fires finally set off the overhead sprinkler system. The reek of chlorine filled the area, overpowering the stench of the phosphorus and plastic. The decontaminating shower would prevent the anthrax in the warheads from spreading, even if they opened. The Four Horsemen could leave the building and wait for the Hazmat teams to come in and take over.

In the background, steadily climbing into the sky on a pillar of smoke and flame, the shuttle Discovery roared into space.

EPILOGUE

After a very long day speaking to federal, state, and local law enforcement, some of them very irate at an "outsider" operating in their territory, Reaper was ready to call it a night. Taking Deveraux out to another dinner, this one uninterrupted by anything, sounded like a great idea. Especially since her worst injury was nothing more than a twisted ankle. But there was one more conversation that he had to finish first. Admiral Straker was on the other end of the phone with something important to say.

"The president wants to meet you and your team at a private ceremony in the White House," Straker said. "He wants to thank you for your actions on behalf of a grateful nation and give you his personal thanks for most likely saving the First Lady and the Governor of Florida. I believe the man feels he owes you one. Not a bad position to be in for an ex-Navy chief, eh, Reaper?"

"All I'd like to know is that Devlin is dead and in

hell. And if he isn't, that the president can give me a couple of minutes alone with him, preferably on a small raft in shark-infested waters off Gitmo."

"No body was ever found?"

"Not a trace of one. And he couldn't have been burned up in the fire, it wasn't hot enough and didn't burn very long. No, he used those white phosphorus grenades to cover his tracks."

"Pretty ballsy to detonate those things while you're still in the room. Phosphorus is a hell of a nasty weapon."

"Never said he was a coward, or crazy. The Hazmat team did say they found a covered thirty-inch drain behind the Dumpster in that back room. The drain was an illegal one and they traced it out to the Banana River."

"We'll find him. You can count on that, we know what he looks like now. Is there anything else you want?"

"Yes, hair dye."

"Hair dye? What in the hell for?"

"We couldn't clean up for hours after the assault. The bleach from those sprinklers turned all of our hair blond. Mackenzie is particularly hard to look at."

The phone hung up with a click, but not before Reaper heard the sound of the Admiral's booming laughter.

———

At the customs desk in Charles deGaulle Airport in France, the tall man with the short-cropped blond hair stood by as the inspector checked through the carry-on bag with the name "Daniel Shae" on it.

"And what are these cigars in the glass tubes for, monsieur?"

"Oh, personal use is all," Devlin said with a smile, "just personal use."